SADDLING THE DRAGON

He bridged the distance between them in less than a heartbeat. Suddenly, he stood close by gazing down at her with eyes that flashed with summer lightning, then darkened into silver flame.

Tilting her face up slightly, Gabriel brushed his mouth across her own, not quickly or harshly, but gently lingering, as though he already knew she had never truly been kissed before.

Their breaths mingled. And Serenity could taste him on her tongue as her lips parted to yield to his gentle assault. It was pleasant. Sweet. Compelling. Something swept through her like a sun-warmed breeze on a summer day.

Their bodies did not touch, except for his hand that remained at the back of her neck, his thumb against her cheek just in front of her delicate ear. Only their mouths . . .

Then, Gabriel moved away.

There was something unfathomable in his expression. "Be careful, my Serenity," he murmured softly as he gazed down at her with silvery eyes. "When you saddle a dragon and hope to ride—the dragon may take you where *he* wants to go."

GABRIEL'S FIRE

GLORIA PEDERSEN

LEISURE BOOKS   NEW YORK CITY

To my children,
Brett, Tawni, and Neil,
with love now and forever.

A LEISURE BOOK®

January 2000

Published by

Dorchester Publishing Co., Inc.
276 Fifth Avenue
New York, NY 10001

ISBN 0-8439-4669-5

The name "Leisure Books" and the stylized "L" with design are trademarks of Dorchester Publishing Co., Inc.

Printed in the United States of America.

But how could I forget thee? Through what power,
Even for the least division of an hour . . .
                              —William Wordsworth

Prologue

Charleston, South Carolina 1812

Entering his hotel room and closing the door behind him, Gabriel Harrowe was unaware of the woman who watched him from the shadows.

The room was dark except for the moonlight that streamed in through the open window. For a moment, he stood letting his eyes grow accustomed to the scant light; then, crossing to the window, he gazed down at the city below him.

Wild and dark, his harshly handsome features were unreadable, though a muscle tensed slightly along his firm jaw and his silver gray eyes were like shards of ice. He had left the dinner party at the Beaumarchais estate early—shortly after Charles Beaumarchais announced his daughter Veronique's betrothal—and had walked for some time before returning to his hotel room.

I was a fool! he mused blackly, his anger barely held in check. *I should have known Veronique would do exactly as her father dictated—even wed whatever man her father chose.*

As a gentle breeze wafted in to ruffle his night-dark hair, Gabriel continued to stare down at the lights of Charleston. An arresting study in silver and black, he stood silhouetted in the moonlight, his arrogant brow, his slightly hawklike nose, his firm, sensuous mouth and strong jaw etched in silver light, the hollows of his face and cheeks defined in black. His face appeared at once handsome yet unyielding.

Several months before, Gabriel had returned to the Carolinas intending to take up his place at Marihaven, one of the most beautiful plantations in the French Santee. Marihaven had once belonged to his grandfather. Now, it was his. The mansion at Marihaven, which had been gutted by fire during the War for Independence, had since been restored. Everything awaited him. Yet, the decision to finally settle down and take up his rightful heritage had not come easily to Gabriel, nor had it come quickly.

After his schooling in England, Gabriel had become involved in one dangerous thing after another, some of which he would just as soon forget. Then he had come home briefly, only to turn back around and join the young United States Navy. Ambitious, he had worked his way up through the ranks and had fought in the Barbary War. Later, he had left the navy to command a vessel of his own, the *Firefly,* a scarlet-masted beauty built for speed.

Everyone said he was indeed his father's son. During the war, his father, Nicholas Harrowe, had been an adventurer as well. Yet, his father had given up his reckless ways after he wed Gabriel's beautiful, fair-haired mother, Elissa. Theirs had been a love beyond compare.

Gabriel had hoped to find that kind of love as well. For a time, he had thought perhaps he and Veronique . . .

Suddenly, Gabriel's long, lean body tensed as he became aware of something he had not noticed when he first entered the room. A hint of roses. A haunting scent. Unmistakable. Before he could turn around, he felt delicate hands glide up the length of his spine. *Veronique!*

Pivoting slowly, Gabriel stood with his back toward the window.

Veronique remained hidden in the shadows.

"Gabriel," she said, her voice softly seductive. "Hold me."

Frowning darkly, his mouth hard and bitter, Gabriel replied, "You shouldn't be here." Then he added tersely, "Or do you consider your betrothal to the senator only a minor inconvenience?"

"Please, Gabriel," she cajoled. "Don't be angry with me."

He could not see Veronique as she stood in the darkness. Still, he knew only too well how enchantingly beautiful she was, with her pale gold hair and innocent green eyes. Any man would find her difficult to resist. But he was determined not to play her games. Not now. Not ever again. He just wanted to be rid of her.

Intending to push her toward the door, Gabriel reached out to grab Veronique. The moment he did so, Gabriel knew he had made a mistake. A big mistake. Veronique was naked!

As she pushed up against him, Gabriel's strong hands grazed her satin flesh. *Damn,* he thought helplessly. He could feel the soft, warm curves of her body and the touch of her silky, unbound hair as it brushed against his cheek.

Fighting his body's response to her, Gabriel did not move. Sweat beaded his brow as he felt Veronique move to unfasten his fine linen shirt and kiss the hollow near the base of his throat, then push aside the fabric as she trailed feather-light kisses down his bared chest. He groaned softly.

Raising herself up on tiptoe, Veronique tangled her delicate fingers in the dark hair at the back of his head as she sought to bring his mouth down to hers. Despite himself, slowly, slowly, he bent his head. Her small pink tongue brushed the hard line of his mouth, teasing, parting, until she could nibble at his lower lip. Then, after a moment, she pressed her open mouth to his and he could taste her intoxicating sweetness. He was drowning in sensation, and something in the back of his mind made him wonder at what point he would no longer be able to resist her.

Damning himself for his weakness, Gabriel trembled as he felt her hands slide down his chest and move lower. Much lower. Unconsciously, he held his breath. Then he gained control once more.

Forcing himself, Gabriel pushed her roughly away. "You might as well go home, Veronique," he stated acidly. "It's over."

Veronique was not about to give up so easily. "It doesn't have to be, Gabriel. We can still be together. My marriage will not interfere. I only agreed to that to please my father." Then, twisting her body closer, her warm breasts pressing provocatively against his chest, she added, "You never expected me to be your wife."

A bitter chuckle escaped Gabriel. His wife? The irony of it was that he had actually considered it. Such vows obviously meant nothing to Veronique.

"Get your clothes on," he ordered with cold finality. He could not see her face in the darkness, but his own was grim. "I am not taking what you have to offer, Veronique."

"You don't mean that," she purred.

"Oh, don't I?" he countered. His voice was deceptively low, though he was fast losing control. "If you know what is good for you, Veronique, you will get your clothes on and get out of here, now."

For a moment, there was a stunned silence.

"Don't tease," she murmured petulantly. "I hate it when you act this way."

"Now!" he repeated.

Veronique's breath escaped in a slow hiss. Rejection was foreign to her. She did not know how to deal with it. Every man she had ever known had fawned over her. Wanted her . . .

Stepping back, Veronique replied haughtily, "How dare you treat me this way?" Her voice was starting to rise as her temper flared. "It is I who should reject you. You are detestable. You mean nothing to me. Oh, you are handsome, in a barbaric sort of way. Dangerous. I found that fascinating for a time. But I felt nothing for you. You are cold. Ruthless. You will never love . . ."

"Love?" Gabriel interjected angrily. "Is that what we speak of now, Veronique? It seems we are both incapable of such an

12

Gabriel's Fire

emotion. At least you have taught me that." Then he added coldly, "I want nothing more to do with you, Veronique."

"You . . . loathsome . . . ".

"Get out," he spat, then waited. He could hear Veronique moving about in the darkness, but he could not see her. Was she dressing?

Without warning, Veronique sprang at him. Unprepared, Gabriel had no time to fend off the small knife she held in her hand. He felt the vicious slash of the cold steel seemingly from out of nowhere. With a savage force, it tore from his temple and down across his cheek. The weapon had probably come from the table near the bed. *My own knife!* he thought with shock.

For a long moment he just stood there.

Laughing almost hysterically, Veronique backed away. "Now see if you can forget me," she cried. "There will never be a day you are not reminded of me. Never! I'll forget you. But you will never forget me. I'll be there each time you look in the mirror."

Stunned, Gabriel did not immediately feel the pain. That would come later. A muscle tightening in his lean jaw, his body's reaction predatory, with an effort he resisted the impulse to strike Veronique. Reaching up, he felt his slashed face, and his hand came away wet and sticky. With a cold fury, he held himself in check. He had to be rid of Veronique before he wrung her beautiful neck.

Reaching out for her, Gabriel pulled Veronique hard against the wall of his chest. His mouth came down to kiss her viciously and long, ravishing her mouth, until he felt her melt against him and knew that she responded. This was what she had wanted all along, and he knew it. What she had been waiting for. Veronique was just jaded enough to enjoy even more having him take her after such savagery. When her breath came in small gasps, he moved away to scoop her into his arms. He could feel the heat of her naked body, her smooth, flawless skin beneath his grasp, but he did not move toward the bed.

13

Instead, Gabriel headed toward the door and jerked it open with Veronique still in his arms. Suddenly terrified, Veronique began to kick and struggle when she realized what he intended. Gabriel grasped her more firmly as she fought for him to release her.

His hard gray eyes as dark as the smoke from hell, Gabriel carried her out into the hallway. His face was starting to throb painfully and he could feel blood trickling down his neck. Even Veronique's kicking and pleading would not stop him.

Her arms and legs flailing, Veronique screamed as Gabriel headed for the stairs. Hotel-room doors flew open as guests heard the commotion in the hall. Openmouthed, they stared as Gabriel started down the stairs with the naked, furious woman in his arms. Below, the people remaining in the large, richly appointed lobby gazed upward.

Reaching the bottom of the stairs, Gabriel strode to the center of the lobby, Veronique still in his arms. Unceremoniously, he dumped her in the middle of the floor.

Letting out a shriek as she landed, Veronique sprawled on the unyielding surface. There was no doubt she would be ruined. Everyone would know. There would be a scandal. It would be the talk of Charleston. Just as he would have to live with the scar Veronique had given him, Veronique would also have to live with this. He could almost feel sorry for her. Almost . . .

Leaving Veronique on the floor surrounded by a rapidly growing crowd of people, complete with gaping looks and shocked whispers, Gabriel strode out of the hotel. He did not look back. It felt good to be out in the cool night air.

A bitter smile gracing his handsome face, now marred by the ugly slash, Gabriel once more thought of the disastrous mistake he had made by ever caring for Veronique in the first place. It had been a bitter lesson. From now on, he intended to be wary where women were concerned. Had he not learned? There could be a whole lot of trouble lurking behind a pair of innocent eyes. . . .

Chapter One

Serenity Penn hastened along the moors that separated Mill Hill from the south shore of Nantucket Island. Her rangy wolfhound was by her side. Over her wealth of flame-colored hair, she wore a wisp of a bonnet that allowed stray tendrils to escape, tormenting her eyes. She brushed them away with a delicate hand. A chill wind whipped at her long skirts.

Slim and graceful, Serenity possessed a look of vibrant good health. Her features were beguiling, with dark brows arched above sooty lashes and remarkable eyes, high cheekbones, a straight nose, and a full, rose-kissed mouth.

Overhead, angry clouds roiled and tossed. A storm was threatening, and soon it would be dark. She must find Joshua quickly. . . .

Serenity could not help worrying about her younger brother. Though at eighteen years of age he stood a full head taller than she, Joshua had nearly drowned at the age of two, and it had left him with the mind of a small child. He would not realize the danger.

Earlier, two vessels had been sighted from Mill Hill. Serenity, as well as many of the other islanders, had gone to see them. The first of the ships to appear was a remarkable vessel, with raked-back scarlet sails and a lean hull. The vessel was obviously built for speed. Her sleek lines, the American flag at her masthead, the thin line of gun ports along her sides, easily identified her as an American privateer, and she had a second vessel in tow.

15

Some distance behind, a British frigate was in pursuit of the privateer and her prize, but as the windmills on the hill had ceased turning it had become a slow-moving chase. Now, the wind had come up, and with the storm fast approaching, the vessels had moved closer and were beginning to fire upon each other. She could hear the resounding booms of their guns in the distance. No doubt Joshua had gone down to the shore to take out the boat, hoping to get a closer view.

It was beginning to rain. Stopping to catch her breath, Serenity's gaze searched the distance for any sign of Joshua. Her eyes were a dark blue, or so she had been told. She had never seen them clearly for herself, since Quakers were discouraged from owning mirrors. Yet, even so, she was quite certain of their distinctive hue.

One time, her father had told Serenity that her eyes were as blue as the patches in her grandma's quilt, and Serenity had never forgotten his words. Though the Quakers did not approve of frivolous things that served no purpose other than to adorn, her paternal grandmother had somehow managed to acquire a piece of deep blue velvet and dispersed the tiny blocks of color among the more serviceable browns. Serenity had always believed the result was quite lovely.

In truth, Serenity thought she must be much like her grandma, for she too harbored a love for certain things that were not readily accepted in the Quaker way of life—a flower for her father's grave, a forbidden book of beautiful poems.

More, Serenity had been schooled on the mainland and did not use the familiar language of the Quakers. And then there was her scandalous penchant for taking off her slippers and hiking up her skirts to walk barefoot in the sand. Even the slight dimple at one corner of her mouth, which appeared each time she smiled, seemed to warn of a wayward nature. "Be cautious, Serenity," her mother had often admonished her from the time she was small. "Lest the devil see thy smile and sweep thee away to sit at his footstool."

Serenity's mother and father were both gone now. Her

mother had died when she was twelve, and her father had passed away a year ago, leaving only Joshua and herself to mourn them.

She and Joshua still lived in the small house her father had built within sight and smell of the ocean, and though she sometimes longed for something more, in her own way she was content. She loved the island and all its natural beauty. There was something almost magical in the white sands and the tang of the sea and honeysuckle, blue water in the sunshine, fish-hawks flying, water lilies in a quiet pond, salt winds and a gray Maushope mist, and sandy roads that trailed like ribbons of moonlight over purple moors.

For a time, Serenity had thought she would wed and have a family of her own. After returning from her schooling on the mainland, David Ramsdell had asked her to be his bride. They had been friends since their childhood. But the day for her wedding had never arrived. Serenity had waited for David three long years while he sailed around the Horn aboard a whaler, only to learn that the man she had intended to marry had been swept overboard not a month after he had left. Of course, after a suitable time, other young Quaker gentlemen had come to call—eager to win her favor—yet none of them had been David, and eventually, one by one, she had turned them all away.

Now, at twenty-eight, Serenity was already what most would call a thorn-back, or spinster. Still, she had accepted what could not be changed. If she must live her life alone, then she was prepared to do so. Out of necessity, the women of Nantucket had learned to be strong and independent. The island's major industry was whaling, and the men on the island left their women alone for years at a time.

Finally catching sight of a small open boat that was battling its way to shore in the growing swells, Serenity breathed a sigh of relief. Picking up her long skirts, she dashed forward. Her wolfhound, Biscuit, raced along by her side. When she had reached the shoreline, she unhesitatingly waded into the water.

Drawing near to where she stood, Joshua hopped over the side of the boat, and the two of them dragged it up onto the shore.

"I was worried, Joshua," she scolded.

Joshua gave her an innocent grin. Rake-thin, he was dark-eyed and possessed sensitive, boyish features. "The ships were firing cannons," he stated blandly, as though she had merely come to watch.

Serenity nodded. She could never be angry with him.

For a moment, her blue gaze turned in the direction of the vessels. She frowned slightly. She could see the privateer's scarlet sails and sleek lines. It would be a shame to have it destroyed by the British vessel, not to mention the men who were aboard. The war was difficult on Serenity and all of the Quakers of the island. Nantucket lay thirty miles out to sea, off the tip of the Massachusetts coast, exposed, isolated, out of sight of the nearest land. In wartime, it was defenseless. The mainland was unable to protect it, and the British had block-aded the American seacoast. Consequently, the Quakers, who saw it as a violation of their religious principles to take part in the fight, had been forced to make an agreement with the British. They must remain neutral, and that neutrality included not going to the aid of any American privateers.

More rain was beginning to fall. Telling herself that there was nothing she could do except offer up a prayer for the men's safety, Serenity turned to Joshua once more. "Come. We must hurry home before the storm grows worse."

Joshua tilted his head back and gazed up at the angry clouds for a moment, as though he had not heard. Sticking out his tongue, he tried to catch some raindrops on it. Then, looking back down, he gave her a delighted grin. "Rain," he said.

"Yes, Joshua. Rain," she repeated, holding out her hand to hurry him along. "We will get wet. We have to . . . "

At that precise moment the storm began in earnest, and a sudden deluge spilled from the heavens before she could finish.

Laughing delightedly, Joshua grasped hold of Serenity's prof-fered hand. Starting to run, he dragged her along behind him.

"Come on, Biscuit," Joshua called back over his shoulder to the rangy wolfhound. "We'll race . . . "

A loud banging on the door awoke Serenity with a start. She sat up in confusion. Who could it be at such a late hour? Outside, the rain beat against the window although it was still the middle of the night.

Struggling into her heavy robe, Serenity made her way to the front sitting room. Her long fiery hair fell in disarray about her slender shoulders, the ends of it curling slightly, and a faint dusting of rose graced her high cheekbones.

A fire still glowed in the oversized fireplace, and a low growl told her the dog had taken his place by her side. "Hush, Biscuit," she cautioned the wolfhound softly. But, though she had said the words, Serenity was glad for the animal's presence. The dog had been a stray of indeterminate origin—its huge wiry-haired appearance reminiscent of the wolf dogs of Ireland that had died out around the turn of the century. It had appeared out of nowhere at her door on the day after her father's death. Somehow it had seemed an act of providence at the time. Since then, the dog had been her constant companion in the small house near the coast.

Securing a lantern, Serenity went to the door. Drawing it open, she saw two men looming in the stormy darkness, their faces and forms obscured by the pouring rain.

Trembling slightly, Serenity held the lantern higher. Her eyes were drawn to the man who stood the farthest back. His shoulders were burdened by yet another man, whose head hung down limply. The man appeared injured or unconscious.

The man nearest to Serenity drew his rain-soaked hat from his head and clutched it in his hand. "Sorry to bother you, ma'am," he said politely, as though it were a common occurrence to appear at a door in the middle of the night, in the midst of a storm. "My name is Thomas Brady. An' this here is Kane."

The moment he spoke, Serenity realized Thomas Brady was young. Perhaps as young as Joshua. She only hoped Joshua would not awaken until after the men had gone.

"Our cap'n has been hurt bad," young Brady continued. "An' our ship's surgeon is dead. Me an' Kane here are tryin' to find him some help. He'll likely be dead 'fore mornin' if we don't, ma'am. Will you help us?"

Serenity gazed at the men in dismay. What was she to do? It was obvious the men were from the scarlet-masted privateer that she and Joshua had seen late that afternoon. Yet, she was forbidden to help them. It could endanger the entire island.

"Please, ma'am," the young man continued once again, "he's losin' blood fast. Can we bring him in?"

Serenity's troubled thoughts warred within her. Was it wrong to help them, or more wrong to turn them away?

Squaring her slender shoulders, Serenity ignored her anguished emotions. She had no choice. "I'm sorry. The British will not allow us to aid Americans."

"But, ma'am, we can't take him farther," Brady said desperately. "He has to have help now. Don't you see? You're our only hope."

Oh, what was she to do? How could she turn them away? Still, if the British soldiers on the island were ever to find out . . .

An eternity seemed to pass. Then, with a resigned sigh, Serenity nodded and murmured softly, "Bring your captain inside. I will see what I can do."

But the men drew back as the dog let out a low growl and moved to block their path.

Seeing their plight, Serenity placed a quieting hand on the wolfhound's coarse back. "Stay, Biscuit," she ordered softly. Then she pivoted toward the men once more. "Please forgive my dog. He does not take well to strangers."

Eyeing the animal suspiciously, the men followed her inside.

Serenity led them to the small front bedchamber. It had been her father's room. Since his death the year before, everything had been kept exactly as it was. Now Serenity cringed slightly as the two men lay their injured captain upon her father's bed.

"He has a shoulder wound, ma'am," Brady explained. "But

Kane dug the musket ball out. An' there's a deep gash on his right leg that's bleedin' bad."

Serenity had noticed the care with which the two men had placed their captain on the bed. It was obvious there was more than loyalty involved.

Turning, the man called Kane shot her a hard glance, his eyes the most compelling she had ever seen. Strange, wary eyes. Serenity could see the doubt written in his searching gaze. Did the man believe she was incapable of seeing to his captain? Or did he believe instead that leaving his friend with her was tantamount to delivering him into enemy hands?

A troubled frown creasing her delicate brow, Serenity's blue gaze swept back to the injured man as she inquired softly, "What is his name?"

"Name is Captain Harrowe, ma'am," the younger man replied. "Captain Gabriel Harrowe."

For a moment more, Serenity studied the injured man. With his long legs stretched out across the bed, he appeared to be tall. Perhaps in his early thirties, his hair was black and far too shaggy, and he wore a short, dark beard that emphasized the harsh lines of his pale, drawn face.

She noted with dismay his sodden, blood-soaked clothing as he lay on the clean linen bedclothes. Had she made a dreadful mistake by agreeing to help him? What if there was nothing at all she could do?

Brushing a long, silky strand of hair from her cheek, Serenity glanced up to find Kane's eyes on her once again. Now there was no accusation in his gaze, though there was something else. His slow perusal made Serenity feel as though he was seeing her anew.

A faint blush staining her cheeks, Serenity was painfully reminded of her state of undress, her unbound tresses falling loose to swirl softly about her shoulders. Why had she not thought to fasten them before going to the door? Though Brady seemed not to have noticed, it was apparent that the man called Kane most certainly had. What was it that she had seen reflected in his eyes? And why had there been a hint of a smile on his face as he gazed first at his injured captain and then back at her?

Serenity hid her surprise as Biscuit left his place by her side to go over to Kane and thrust his nose into the palm of one of the man's hands. She had never seen the dog be so friendly to a stranger before.

For a moment, Kane glanced down at the animal and gave the dog a pat, then he wheeled about and started for the door. "We have to go," he said softly. "It's time we got back to the ship."

Brady started to follow him, but as he reached the door he turned back once more. "Thanks for seein' to him, ma'am. Our cap'n is a good man. He'll come out o' this fightin'. You'll see." An instant later, they were gone.

At midmorning the following day, Serenity was once more by Gabriel's bedside. She had left him only long enough to slip into a dress and don her white bonnet, then take care of feeding the chickens and gathering the eggs, before hurriedly returning to his side. There was a hole in the roof of the shed that needed mending before the next storm, and she should have baked bread to take to an elderly neighbor. But those chores would simply have to wait until a later time.

Dipping a cloth in cool water, Serenity bathed the man's fevered brow. She had done everything she could, but would it be enough? Life was sacred. Even the life of the stranger who had been brought to her door. Now it was difficult to think of the man as a stranger, when by necessity she had seen to his needs more intimately than she had to any other's.

His shoulder wound was clean though deep, but the gash in his thigh had needed stitching. Serenity had done her best. Still, as the hours had slipped away, his fever had risen steadily and his breathing had become more labored. Would her best be good enough to save him?

The injured man moved restlessly on the bed.

Stroking his forehead with the cool, damp cloth, Serenity could not help wondering about him. His name was Gabriel. She liked the sound of it. It was a good, biblical name, the name of one of the angels. But what kind of a man was he? It was obvious he was no stranger to violence. Barely hidden beneath his short dark beard, a vicious scar ran from his temple and down across his cheekbone. Unconsciously, she traced a delicate finger across its length, then quickly drew it away. How had it come to be there?

Yet, even with the scar, Serenity was forced to admit that his face did not appear unpleasant. Still, appearances told nothing of the man inside. He might well be named for an angel, but it was possible that once he was awake he might favor more the devil.

Indeed, his scarred visage reminded her of something she'd read of long ago during her schooling on the mainland. He was like a dragon—dangerous, ageless, powerful.

The soft knock on the door had gone unheard and Serenity was not aware that Joshua was even in the room until he suddenly appeared at her side. "Serenity?" he said hesitantly as he stood gazing at her with curious dark eyes.

"Joshua . . ." she returned in surprise. How could she explain to Joshua about the strange man in their father's bed?

Joshua gave her a lopsided grin, then he replied, "I came to read." It had been difficult for Joshua to learn to read even a few simple words, but with Serenity's patience and careful tutoring, it was an accomplishment of which he was very proud.

She had forgotten about their lesson.

Sighing wearily, Serenity straightened her slim back as she explained, "I am sorry, Joshua, but our reading lesson will have to wait. I must take care of this sick man today."

Crestfallen, Joshua frowned at the man in the bed. "What is his name?" he asked slowly, stubbing the toe of one boot deliberately against the bedpost like a petulant child.

Gazing once more at the fevered man as he tossed restlessly upon the bed, Serenity replied softly, "Gabriel." She hoped

23

Joshua would not ask anything more. "Perhaps we could read tomorrow, Joshua. Later, I will make a special treat. An apple pudding . . . "

His spirits lifting noticeably, Joshua beamed at her. "Tomorrow, we will read," he said happily. Then, he swiftly pivoted and raced out the bedchamber door.

After Joshua had gone, Serenity heaved a weary sigh and sat back down on the chair. Others would surely learn of the stranger in her father's bed. But Gabriel was far too ill to be turned over to the British authorities, yet how could she explain his presence otherwise?

Moistening his mouth with a clean cloth dipped in fresh water, Serenity was startled to see Gabriel's dark lashes raise for a brief moment. His eyes were gray, yet they appeared almost silver as they met hers. Then, once more, his eyelids closed, and for the first time since he had come to be there he seemed to rest more easily.

Involuntarily, Serenity's hand reached to brush a lock of dark hair from his forehead. "Oh, Gabriel," she murmured softly. "I hope, one day, neither of us will regret the day you were brought to my door."

As her eyes darkened to a blue as deep as the velvet patches on her grandma's quilt, Serenity was overcome by weariness. She rested her head on the bed near his side, choosing to forget for the moment that the man named Gabriel Harrowe was a threat to them all.

Chapter Two

Obed Ramsdell peered down his long nose at her. "Thou art making a dreadful mistake, Serenity," he said, speaking in the familiar language of the Quakers. "There is no way to shelter the man without deceit, and that deceit most certainly will draw others into it. Now is the time to turn him over to the British authorities, before it is too late."

Obed Ramsdell had been the father of her fiancé who had been lost at sea, and Obed still showed concern for her, even though she and David had never actually wed. Serenity knew why he had come. Undoubtedly, someone had found out about Gabriel, and Obed had been delegated to see to the matter.

Gazing at Obed's stern face as he stood there in his broad-brimmed hat, swallowtailed coat, and high, straight collar, Serenity replied patiently, "I am sorry, Friend Obed. But I feel I have no choice. It would be unforgivable to turn Captain Harrowe over to the British as yet. He still drifts in and out of fever, and his wounds are not yet healed. How could he survive if the British took him prisoner?"

Obed's features softened slightly. "Then, what explanation can there be for the man's presence?" he asked. "It is no secret he is here. This is a small island. The British will know something is amiss and question people. We have only recently reached an agreement of neutrality with them. Who knows how the British might retaliate? There is risk to us all."

A slight frown creasing her brow, Serenity thought the matter over carefully for a moment. What should she do? It was not right to endanger the entire island. Still, as she thought of

Gabriel lying wounded and helpless in the next room, it seemed far worse to consider turning him over to the British in his present condition.

"Captain Harrowe is a man," Obed declared firmly. "Granted, for the moment, he is much too ill to present a danger. But what kind of man is he? If he recovers, he may not be so docile. It is in thine own best interest, Serenity, not to harbor him."

Sighing softly, Serenity turned away from Obed and walked over to the place where Biscuit lay sleeping near the fireplace hearth. How could she dispute Obed's sound logic? Everything he said was true.

Pivoting slowly back toward him, Serenity leveled her delicate chin with determination. "I have to do what I think is right," she replied softly. "Until he is fully recovered, I refuse to turn Captain Harrowe over to the British. Please understand . . . "

Seeing there was no way to dissuade her, Obed nodded his head and started for the door. Serenity followed. However, an unexpected knock stopped them both before they could reach it. For a brief moment, Serenity's gaze met Obed's as they exchanged glances, and she could see the concern written there. Then Obed stepped back and waited.

Drawing the door aside, Serenity hid her wary expression. Her guest was one she would not have chosen to see. It was Lieutenant Evan Lancaster, a British officer, and this was not the first time the man had appeared at her door. He had come quite frequently.

Lieutenant Lancaster was nearing thirty, with slightly wavy brown hair and a well-trimmed mustache. He was tall and slender, and Serenity had once thought that the British young women must find him quite appealing. Yet, Serenity had discouraged his efforts at anything more than a polite friendship.

Smiling at her, Lieutenant Lancaster slowly perused her face, then pointedly let his admiring gaze slide down her slim neck. He took in her softly rounded breasts as she stood there in her plum gown and white apron, then move back up again before making any effort to speak. "Good day, Miss Penn," he said, as he removed his hat. "May I come in?"

"Yes. Of course," Serenity murmured. As the lieutenant stepped inside, she caught Obed's guarded look. It was obvious he, too, was concerned by the lieutenant's unexpected visit. "Lieutenant Lancaster," she continued, hoping he had not come about Gabriel, "Obed Ramsdell has also come to pay a call."

Lieutenant Lancaster nodded his head curtly in Obed's direction. "We've already met," he said. The lieutenant's eyes seemed to scan the simple room, the oversized fireplace, and austere furnishings, then stop to rest upon the closed door to the bedchamber. "I've heard you have another guest, as well, Miss Penn. Is that true?"

Carefully hiding a look of surprise and distress, Serenity allowed her own gaze to drift to the bedchamber door just as Lieutenant Lancaster's had done. What was she to do? How could she explain Gabriel's presence? Somehow she must protect them all.

Turning toward the British lieutenant, Serenity gave him a faint smile as her blue eyes met his gaze. "Yes," she said evenly. "My fiancé has returned. But, unfortunately, in his absence he contracted a fever. Until he recovers, he is staying here under my care."

His hard eyes sweeping back to Obed Ramsdell, Lieutenant Lancaster seemed to seek confirmation. "And is that why you are here, Mr. Ramsdell? To visit her fiancé?"

Obed cleared his throat and gazed steadily back at the lieutenant. "The man Serenity was planning to wed has been gone for several years," he replied. It was not exactly a lie, nor was it precisely the truth.

"May I see the man? Pardon me, your fiancé, Miss Penn?" The lieutenant's piercing eyes seemed to gauge her reaction.

"Of course, Lieutenant Lancaster," Serenity replied quickly. She could certainly not deny him. That would only make the man all the more suspicious. "But it would not be wise to draw too near. They say the fever is very contagious."

Crossing over to the door, Serenity opened it carefully, hoping not to disturb Gabriel into thrashing about and revealing his bandaged shoulder. The British lieutenant came over to stand beside her. For a moment, Serenity was frightened that the lieutenant would go all of the way inside the room to get a better view.

Gabriel slept restlessly, his dark hair damp against the linen-covered pillow, sweat beading his brow, a flush upon his skin. There was no mistaking the fact that he suffered from a fever, just as she had said.

Lieutenant Lancaster drew back, satisfied. "Will you wed soon?" he inquired, a frown creasing his brow. "I should like to be there."

Serenity hid her shock. Was this some test the lieutenant had devised to make certain she was telling the truth? It was unheard of for a British officer to attend a Quaker wedding.

Taking a deep breath, Serenity met his eyes squarely. "As soon as my fiancé has recovered, our names will be proposed at the Monthly Meeting of the Society of Friends." Inwardly, she cringed at yet another lie. The lie would be just one more thing she must repent, and her list was steadily growing.

Obed Ramsdell's silence gave credibility to the statement.

Lieutenant Lancaster started for the door. Pausing, he took Serenity's unwilling hand in his own for a moment. "Please accept my congratulations, Miss Penn," he murmured. Then he strode briskly out the door without a backward glance.

After the British officer had left, Serenity pivoted around to meet Obed's disapproving gaze. Still, whatever he was thinking, Obed said not a word as he, too, stalked out the door.

It was evening. Serenity sat by Gabriel's bedside once again, while the lantern light cast strange shadows of monsters and goblins upon the walls and the corners were left in shadowy darkness. The only sound was that of Gabriel's breathing and an occasional whimper from Biscuit as he rested on the hard floor near her feet.

Several times throughout the day, Gabriel had roused slightly, and Serenity had tried unsuccessfully to give him a sip of broth. Even as she did so, however, she tried to thrust from her mind the thought that her concern for his welfare might well prove contradictory in the end. Once he'd recovered, she would have no other choice than to turn him over to the British, and what would happen then? What if the British were to order him hanged?

Serenity tried to concentrate on the book she held in her hand. It was a book of poems. A forbidden book of poems. The poems were by William Wordsworth, and Serenity had always found the words quite lovely. They conjured up marvelous pictures in her mind, and she hoped the Quakers would change their stance in regard to poetry one day. In the meantime, the book had become one of Serenity's treasures, although she must wrestle with her conscience each time she picked it up to read from it. Still, tonight, she felt in need of its soothing diversion. At least it kept her from considering Gabriel's ultimate fate.

Serenity was not aware that Gabriel was awake, or that he watched her, until he startled her by saying, "What is your name?"

For a moment, she did not respond. She had seen to his physical needs, perhaps even saved his life, yet this was the first time Serenity had actually heard him speak, and it had taken her aback. Peering cautiously at him over her book, she replied, "My name is Serenity." Was that her voice, sounding so foreign and strained?

"Read to me, Serenity," he said, his voice low though distinct.

Serenity hesitated. Perhaps he would go back to sleep.

"Read to me, Serenity," he repeated, his voice stronger and more resonant now. "I'd enjoy hearing the sound of your voice."

Slowly, Serenity turned in her book until she found the first page of a poem. It was one of Wordsworth's loveliest.

She could tell he was waiting.

Softly, she began, " 'There was a time when meadow, grove, and stream . . . ' "

Was he listening? Though Gabriel had turned his face away, somehow she knew that he was. She could see his chiseled profile and a dark lock of hair that had fallen onto his forehead.

Relaxing slightly, Serenity continued to read, " 'The Rainbow comes and goes, And lovely is the Rose . . . ' "

Gabriel's silver eyes had closed shortly after Serenity had begun, but she was fully aware that he did not sleep. Lilting and gentle, her soft voice was almost musical in the quiet room as she continued, " 'Waters on a starry night . . . Are beautiful and fair . . . ' "

Several days had passed since the moment when Gabriel had first spoken to her. Yet, in the brief time since, Serenity had come to look forward to their conversations. It was pleasant talking to him. Although he revealed little of a personal nature about himself, it was clear that Gabriel was well educated and had been many places and seen numerous things. She delighted in hearing him tell about the Carolinas, which was where he had been raised, and about Europe. In turn, she continued to read poetry to him each night, although at times she suspected he cared not a whit for poetry, but merely liked to have her near.

With each passing day, it was becoming more and more difficult to think of turning Gabriel over to the British. He no longer seemed a stranger. Even now, as she moved about the bedchamber tidying up the room and she could feel Gabriel's eyes upon her, Serenity felt guilty when she thought of what she must do.

"You have the bluest eyes I have ever seen," Gabriel remarked, breaking into her reverie and completely disarming her as she started to dust a table near the bed.

Glancing up to meet his silvery gaze, Serenity could not help smiling. She did not know what had prompted his comment, yet any mention of the blue of her eyes brought fond memories of her grandma's quilt.

Setting aside the linen cloth with which she had been dusting the table, Serenity explained, "My father always told me that my eyes were as blue as the patches on my grandma's quilt."

"Ah, you have not seen them yourself, then?" he inquired. "You have never looked into a mirror?"

Serenity busied herself around the bed, straightening the bedcovers before she replied, "No. Possessing a mirror is a vanity. A reflection in a glass does not prove worth or show what is in your heart."

For some strange reason, this seemed to please him. There was a touch of amusement in his silvery eyes and a hint of a smile about his mouth. "I should like to see your grandma's quilt," Gabriel said. Then, he added, "It must be very beautiful."

Serenity threw him a quizzical glance. Surely he did not mean it. Somehow the thought of him wanting to see her grandma's quilt seemed so out of character for the rugged man lying in the bed. . . .

She laughed. Light, bubbling laughter. She could not help herself.

Watching his reaction, Serenity saw his mouth crinkle at the corners. She could tell he wanted to laugh too, yet somehow he could not let himself. Did he come from such a serious world?

When her laughter had died away, though it still teased at the corners of her mouth and sparkled in her eyes, Serenity countered with mock seriousness, "I've never had a man ask to see my grandma's quilt before."

"Never?"

"Never," she replied.

He seemed in no hurry to end their conversation. "Do you make it a habit of taking in every stranger who is brought to your door?"

"It would have been impossible for me to turn anyone away who was so badly injured. I merely did what I had to do."

31

"I will bet as a child," he observed candidly, "you mended broken wings on birds as well."

"Sometimes," she murmured. "Sometimes I did my best to save other things. When I was eight, my father took me with him to a neighbor's to buy a lamb. By the time we arrived, the man had already sold most of his lambs and he only had two remaining. One was a strong and healthy lamb, while the other lamb was small and sickly. I begged my father to buy the sickly lamb." She smiled as she remembered, and the dimple showed at the side of her mouth. "You must think that strange."

"And did your father buy the lamb you wanted?"

"He wanted to. He tried to. But the neighbor refused to sell the lamb to my father. The neighbor said he could not take such advantage of him, since the sickly lamb would never last out the winter. He had even quit feeding the lamb so it would die more quickly. I pleaded with my father to take it anyway. I could not leave the lamb to die. When the neighbor saw that I was not about to change my mind, he offered to give the lamb to my father. But my father took out his money and insisted on paying the same price he would have for the healthy lamb. He told the man that the lamb's worth was in the eye of the beholder. My father was a wonderful man."

"And did the lamb live, after all?"

She shook her head. "It died during the winter, just as the neighbor had said it would. But I didn't care. For as long as I had the lamb I loved it and took care of it. It had value to me."

Concluding her story, Serenity took a step closer to the bed and leaned over Gabriel to straighten his pillow.

Reaching out one slender arm, without warning Serenity felt the soft fullness of her breasts brush against his hard chest for a moment. At the contact, there was an unaccustomed flutter in the pit of her stomach. Perhaps Gabriel had not noticed. Glancing down into his harshly handsome face, mere inches from her own, her eyes widened in embarrassment and her cheeks flamed as she realized that he had noticed it indeed. Quickly, she started to draw away.

Gently grasping her arm, Gabriel held her there. His eyes were no longer filled with laughter. His face was serious. For a moment, the atmosphere was charged between them. Then, slowly, he released her.

Quickly stepping away from the bed, Serenity kept her eyes averted as she drew a deep breath and smoothed her white apron over her simple gown, trying to regain her composure. The unexpected contact had left her feeling alarmed and shaken. Although she had touched him daily in caring for him, Gabriel had never touched her before. It made things different somehow. Still, when she glanced back over at him, there was not the slightest indication that anything had occurred. His chiseled features appeared implacable. Closed. Shuttered.

Serenity was suddenly uncertain. Was she wrong? Had she merely imagined that something had changed between them?

Chapter Three

The hour was late, yet Gabriel lay gazing up at the ceiling unable to sleep, his thoughts dark and brooding.

Damn Kane for leaving me here, he thought for the hundredth time. Despite himself, he could think of nothing else but Serenity.

Serenity. The name suited her. There was a calm assurance about her that he could almost feel. He had been watching her for days—the way she moved, her special grace, her quiet efficiency—since the moment he had first realized where he was and had managed to make some sense of the situation.

How Kane must have laughed when he left him here, knowing she was a Quaker. No doubt Kane would believe he would lie here day after day, gazing at the exquisite creature whose innocence was almost palpable, and slowly lose his mind.

And Kane was right. . . .

She wore some kind of a bonnet that was as white as sea foam and as fragile as a daisy, and her hair was fiery copper, a rich, vibrant color that accentuated her creamy skin. Her eyes were the color of sapphires and her features were elegant. And her body was perfection as well, with high, firm breasts, a tiny waist, and softly curved hips. He wondered what it would be like to have her warm and yielding beneath him. . . .

Just let me get well and get out of here, Gabriel told himself fiercely. With any luck, Kane would be back for him in a few days. In the meantime, he must try to get his strength back and force himself to keep his mind off the woman.

Sitting up in bed, Gabriel dangled his feet over the edge. He felt a wave of nausea sweep over him when he tried to stand.

Serenity had left him a shirt and a pair of pants on a chair near the bed. They had been her father's. Sweat beading his forehead, he reached for the pants and slowly drew them on, but the effort cost him a great deal and he decided not to bother with the shirt.

Despite himself, his thoughts returned to Serenity. He had become a part of her routine. Each day Joshua would come to read, and Serenity would patiently listen. Each night, after Joshua had gone to bed, Serenity would read to Gabriel, her voice sweet and musical. He had never really cared for poetry before, but she made it seem like magic.

Each time she bent over him, to fix his pillow or to smooth the bedcovers, he wondered what it would be like to press his mouth to the soft underside of her delicate chin, just where her throat began. . . .

Determinedly, he tried to take a few steps. His breathing was labored. *Take it slow,* he told himself.

He took several more steps. His wounds and the fever had left him weaker than he supposed. He felt their effects as he made it across the room.

Stopping for a moment, he leaned his back against the wall. He needed to rest. His shoulder and leg were starting to throb.

The lantern light was turned low. He could not see the chair in which Serenity usually sat, but he knew it was there. Perhaps he could grasp hold of it and use it to make it back to the bed.

Taking one step and then another, his legs felt heavy. Leaden. Just a few more . . .

Unable to sleep, Serenity sat in her bedchamber, mending the pair of breeches that Gabriel had been wearing when first he was brought to her door. His shirt had been beyond repair, but with a little work his pants could easily be salvaged. All they would need was some stitching.

She had already prepared for bed. Her silky hair hung loose, draping softly about her shoulders and down her back. She had not donned her robe, but wore only a white nightgown with long sleeves that clung to her breasts and the curves of her body. Frowning slightly, she bent to her task, trying not to think of the man who slept in the next room. He filled too many of her thoughts already.

The moment she heard the crash, Serenity dropped her mending and instantly was on her feet. Dashing to the door, she raced to Gabriel's bedchamber.

Rushing into the room, Serenity ran over to kneel by his side. He lay on the floor, his head awkwardly angled, his legs and arms twisted and splayed. "Gabriel . . . " Serenity said anxiously as she leaned over him. "Are you all right?" She shook his shoulder, trying to rouse him. "Oh, please, Gabriel, speak to me. . . . "

Gabriel opened his eyes and gave her a wry grin.

Suddenly, her concern made her angry. It burst forth in an unexpected tirade. "Whatever were you thinking of?" she demanded impatiently. "Your wounds are not yet healed. It was foolish to get out of bed. Do you not *know* any better?"

This time, Gabriel really did grin. "Apparently not," he answered ruefully.

Gabriel was enthralled by the way she leaned over him, her dusky hair falling forward to brush against his bare chest. He liked her nearness even under these circumstances.

"Then we must get you back to bed. And quickly . . . "

With an effort, Gabriel pushed himself up to a sitting position, but he found it impossible to stifle a low groan.

Serenity was suddenly anxious once again. "Oh, Gabriel," she murmured, her eyes looking suspiciously cloudy. "Let me help. . . . "

He had not meant to upset her, but he could not deny the satisfaction of having her so close. "I can get back to the bed," he stated. "On my own . . . "

Managing to make it to his feet, Gabriel had to grasp her for support. His hands felt her smooth skin through the thin fabric of her gown. He waited for a moment.

Trying to take a step, he faltered, and this time his hand accidentally brushed against one soft breast. She was like a Dresden doll, small but perfectly formed. He took a deep breath. He was not certain which was worse, trying to get back to the bed or the fact that he wanted Serenity with him in it.

Steeling himself, his eyes stormy gray and his lean jaw taut, Gabriel took several more steps and finally reached the side of the bed.

Serenity turned away as he divested himself of her father's pants. When he had finished and was once more resting in the bed, his back propped up against the pillows, his lower half discreetly hidden by the bedcovers, Gabriel said, "You can turn back around now, Serenity."

Gazing at her in amusement as she slowly pivoted to face him, Gabriel slanted her a wicked grin. "I see no need for you to have turned away," he drawled, a hint of mockery in his voice. He was deliberately baiting her, wanting to see what her reaction would be. "You've seen me in considerably less than the pants. It seems I have no secrets where you are concerned."

Quickly dropping her gaze, Serenity found a sudden fascination with a spot on the floor somewhere near her bare feet.

Then, glancing back up at him, her blue eyes sought his. A hint of a smile touched her face as she replied with complete innocence, "You have a fine body. . . . "

Gabriel muttered an imprecation under his breath. What was she doing to him? His silvery gaze swept over her as she stood in the lantern light, her body clearly outlined through the thin fabric of her nightgown. He was painfully aware that she had a fine body too.

Just let her leave while he was still able to use some common sense. If she did not . . .

When he was silent for a long time, Serenity spoke again. "Will you be all right now, Gabriel?" She seemed nervous. "I should return to my bedchamber."

"Yes," he stated flatly, a muscle tightening in his jaw.

Despite his answer, Serenity did not leave. Instead, she drew nearer to the bed. Placing a delicate hand upon his arm, she seemed uncertain. "Please don't try to get out of bed again. You are much too weak. . . . "

Weak? He *was* weak, that was for certain. But not in the way Serenity meant. He had never had to wrestle with his conscience over a woman before, and he was not convinced he would win the battle. In the past, he had always lived for the moment, taking what he wanted without any thought of the consequences. Now, with Serenity, everything was suddenly different.

Without another word, Serenity spun away and slipped quietly from the room. Drawing in a ragged breath, he watched her go. He told himself he should feel relieved. Still, despite all logic to the contrary, there was only an aching sense of emptiness after she was gone.

Serenity opened the door and allowed Lieutenant Lancaster to step inside. It was evening, a strange time of day for the young British officer to be calling. Nearly two weeks had passed since his previous visit.

Standing near her side, the dog let out a low growl.

37

Glancing down at the wolfhound, Lieutenant Lancaster said, "There is no need for your dog, Miss Penn. You are quite safe with me."

His shrewd eyes resting intently upon her face, Lieutenant Lancaster extended his hand and took Serenity's for a moment. She trembled slightly at the contact. She was not comfortable having him touch her. Biscuit growled once again, much more loudly this time.

The lieutenant quickly drew his hand away. "Perhaps you should put your dog in another room. Then we could speak more freely."

Though Serenity wished she could refuse, she had no desire to offend the British officer. Perhaps he would get to the purpose of his visit more quickly if she did as he requested. "Come, Biscuit," Serenity commanded softly, leading the animal away.

After she had put the wolfhound inside her bedchamber and quickly shut the door, Serenity returned to Lieutenant Lancaster.

"Miss Penn," the British officer began. Then he corrected himself. "Serenity . . . " His tone was decidedly intimate as he moved closer to her. "We have no need for such formality between the two of us. I should like to call you Serenity. Would you call me Evan? It would please me very much."

Serenity did not reply. Her mind was on Gabriel, sleeping in the next room. She hoped he would not awaken and decide to leave the bedchamber.

Sighing softly, Serenity kept her eyes from straying to the door behind which Gabriel slept as she replied. "Lieutenant Lancaster, may I ask the purpose of this visit?" She refused to call him by his given name, regardless of his pointed request.

"May we sit down, Serenity?" the lieutenant asked, taking her hand once again and drawing her over to the simple settee. He waited until she was seated beside him before he continued. "I have come to discuss a matter of grave importance with you."

His voice sounded friendly, disarming, and the words were

innocuous enough. But Serenity sensed something odd in his manner.

Lieutenant Lancaster smiled patiently at Serenity. "I have been to see you on numerous occasions, Serenity. Certainly you must realize I have sought to know you better." He kept his voice low. "I was quite distressed to learn that your fiancé had returned. I wanted you to know I understand."

For a moment, the lieutenant's hand moved to rest caressingly upon her shoulder. Then, with a sigh, he drew it away. "We both know there was an American privateer near the south shore, shortly before your . . . fiancé . . . returned. It was a scarlet-masted vessel. A distinctive and admirable ship. It did not slip away from the British patrol vessel until well into the night, and then only under cover of the storm and leaving its prize behind." He paused for a moment, as though he expected some reply.

What was the lieutenant implying? Had he learned the truth about Gabriel?

Folding her hands primly in her lap, Serenity stiffened her spine before she replied. "I fail to see how an American vessel can have anything to do with either me or my fiancé, Lieutenant Lancaster."

The officer's hand came up to grasp her chin gently but firmly, making it impossible for her to escape his gaze. His face drew closer to hers. "I think we both know what it means, Serenity. I have a certain fondness for you. I mean only to protect you. Allow me to look after your welfare. That is all I ask. Trust me. You have no reason to be afraid of me." As though to emphasize his words, he smiled briefly and removed his hand from her chin.

For a long moment the British officer's eyes searched her face, then he continued. "All I want is your company, Serenity. Your friendship. My home is in England. A man grows lonely when he is far from his home."

"Please, Lieutenant Lancaster," Serenity interjected, "it is late and I am weary. Perhaps some other time." If the man had some undeniable evidence that Gabriel had been aboard the American privateer, surely he would have acted upon it before this.

Rising slowly to his feet, Lieutenant Lancaster drew her up to stand facing him, as he murmured, "You will consider what I have said. Won't you, Serenity?"

"I am not precisely certain what it is that I am to think over, lieutenant," she replied innocently, taking a step backward. "But I shall give our conversation careful thought, I assure you."

Once he had gone, Serenity stood gazing at the door through which he had just disappeared, worrying her lower lip with her fine white teeth.

It had been nearly two weeks since the night Gabriel was first brought to her door, and in that time his recovery had been rapid.

From the beginning, Serenity had told herself that when he had recovered she would turn him over to the British authorities; the entire island was in danger so long as she protected him. Yet, tonight, when Lieutenant Lancaster had come, she had suddenly realized that she could never do as she had intended. She could never turn Gabriel over to the British.

Tormented by confusing emotions, a slight frown creasing her delicate brow, Serenity sighed softly, then slowly pivoted around. She was not expecting to see Gabriel. She had assumed he was still sleeping. Yet as she glanced up, there he stood lounging in the bedchamber doorway, gazing directly at her, his silver eyes hooded like those of a hawk.

With his uninjured shoulder he leaned against the doorframe, his long legs nonchalantly crossed. He appeared to have been standing there for some time. His chest was bare, the white bandage on his wounded shoulder stark against his tanned skin.

She had disapproved at first when he had asked her for a straight-edged razor to shave his short beard away. But tonight, in the firelight, she found the effect quite appealing, and the scar across his cheek only added to his harsh good looks.

Gabriel was very handsome, Serenity concluded as she gazed at him. Slightly ruthless-looking perhaps, but handsome nonetheless. Still, he frightened her just a little. She had to admit that too. Whatever there was about him as he stood gazing at her, it had not been there before. There was something new about his mouth—a slight curl to his upper lip—that made him appear almost dangerous.

Continuing to survey her as he leaned against the doorframe, Gabriel demanded softly, "Why didn't you tell your Lieutenant Lancaster the truth about me?"

"You were listening?" she countered, ignoring the fact that he had referred to the lieutenant as being hers. It was more a statement than a question.

Gabriel nodded, his silver eyes pinning her down as one would a butterfly. A long moment passed, and he left the doorway to move toward her.

"Yes, Serenity, I listened," Gabriel said simply, coming over to take her hands in his, turning them palms upward and cradling them in his own, his thumbs resting in the center on the slight indentation. "The matter concerns me, as well you know," he continued, as he stroked her delicate palms with his thumbs, massaging them in tiny circles, around and around. "You hold my fate in these two small hands."

Gazing up at his handsome face, Serenity wanted to draw her hands away. There was a certain intimacy in his touch, as her two hands lay within his own and he traced circular patterns upon their inner side. Involuntarily, her slender fingers curled around his thumbs to stop their sensuous movement. Then, glancing down, she realized what she had done and quickly pulled her hands away.

Gabriel stiffened slightly. "Why didn't you turn me over to the British authorities just now when you had the chance? That is what you intended to do from the start, isn't it?"

41

Gloria Pedersen

Serenity felt mesmerized by him, the way he spoke, his harshly handsome face, his long, lean body standing so close to hers. She gazed directly into his stormy eyes, knowing his accusation had at one time been true. "You were not fully recovered. I could not . . . "

The expression on Gabriel's face did not change. He seemed not at all surprised. "Ah, I see," he murmured. "Then, that is still your intention, Serenity? You're just waiting until I am well enough to survive aboard a prison vessel, or perhaps walk to the gallows on my own?"

Suddenly she felt trapped. She offered no reply. How could she tell him the truth, that just that evening when Lieutenant Lancaster had arrived she had realized she could never turn him over to the British authorities? If he knew, Gabriel might misunderstand.

It seemed he bridged the distance between them in less than a heartbeat. Suddenly, he stood close by, gazing down at her with eyes that flashed with summer lightning, then darkened into silver flames.

His strong, capable fingers toyed with the ties of her bonnet, as Gabriel unfastened the dainty strands. Slipping it from her hair, he reached over to drop the flimsy article softly on the table near the lamp, watching the bonnet for a moment as it made its descent. Then his eyes returned to hers once more.

Standing mere inches from him, Serenity could hear his quickened breathing. Gabriel reached one hand toward her, resting his thumb gently against her rose-dusted cheek, while his long fingers curled around the nape of her neck just where wisps of her hair always managed to escape. It seemed she could not breathe. She waited, wondering.

Tilting her face up slightly, Gabriel brushed his mouth across her own, not quickly or harshly, but gently lingering, as though he already knew she had never truly been kissed before.

Their breaths mingled. Serenity could taste him on her tongue as her lips parted to yield to his gentle assault. It was pleasant. Sweet. Compelling. Something swept through her like a sun-warmed breeze on a summer day.

Their bodies did not touch, except for the hand that remained at the back of her neck, his thumb against her cheek just in front of her delicate ear. Only their mouths . . .

Then Gabriel moved away.

There was something unfathomable in his expression. "Be careful, my Serenity," he murmured softly as he gazed down at her with silvery eyes. "When you saddle a dragon and hope to ride—the dragon may take you where *he* wants to go."

Chapter Four

They walked the white sands of Nantucket all morning, watching the gulls and seahawks soar and swoop above the clear blue ocean, the tang of sea mist in the air. Then they moved inland, Joshua and Biscuit running ahead while Serenity and Gabriel followed behind.

Gabriel had recovered from his wounds and grew stronger each day. Serenity knew he would soon have to leave. Since the night when she had avoided telling him the truth—that she could never turn him over to the British—there had been no more mention of it. Neither had there been any mention of the kiss they had shared.

Up ahead, Joshua and Biscuit stopped near a pond.

Indicating that she too wished to rest for a moment, Serenity and Gabriel found a place to sit a short distance away. "How is it that I am the first to grow weary? Do you never tire, Gabriel?"

"Oh, I tire," he responded with a twinkle in his silver-gray eyes. "I simply refuse to admit it."

Serenity glanced over at him and smiled. "Why must men always persist in hiding the way they feel?"

Stretching his long legs out before him, Gabriel leaned back against a stump and proceeded to get more comfortable. "It's our male pride. We hate to admit we're not invincible. It might shatter too many illusions," he joked. "Now, tell me about Maushope's smoke."

Gabriel had taken more than an idle interest in learning about Nantucket during the past few days. He seemed to want to learn everything he could, and she had obliged. Undoubtedly, it was a way for him to keep his mind off other things. Without being told, Serenity knew he watched the horizon day and night for the return of his scarlet-masted vessel and his men.

"It is said that Nantucket was discovered by a giant named Maushope," Serenity began, drawing her knees up beneath her. "The legend goes that Maushope lived on Cape Cod. One day, an enormous bird swooped over the Sound in search of food and snatched away an Indian babe. The Red Men's arrows could not stop the bird. And Maushope was so angry that he jumped into the sea and waded after it."

Serenity paused, smoothing her plum gown and dusting some white sand from its lower edge. She could feel Gabriel's smoky gray eyes on her as she did so, and a hint of color rose to her cheeks. He made her feel unsettled. What was it he was thinking?

Nervously, she went on. "Maushope did not look where he was going and continued on until he reached Nantucket. The Indians did not know of the island. Once he was there, Maushope staggered up the beach and through the woods to a lonesome pine. And there, seated out on a limb, was the dreadful bird, picking at the little papoose's bones.

"Poor Maushope," Serenity continued, trying to sound properly mournful. "He was so overcome that he filled his pipe with poke—since he had no tobacco. And he shook his fist and bellowed, and the tears ran down both sides of his big red nose, while the fumes from his pipe blew all the way back to Cape Cod."

Suddenly, Serenity gave Gabriel a smile that showed the dimple at the side of her mouth. "Now, whenever there is fog," she finished with a twinkle in her eyes, "everyone says, 'Here comes Maushope's smoke.' "

Gabriel's silvery gaze held hers for a moment, a hint of a grin teasing at his hard mouth. "Quite a fanciful story, for a people who thrive on plainness," he observed candidly. Then, taking a dark russet tendril of hair from her cheek and twirling it around one finger, he seemed to ponder something else. "How is it you were never wed?" he asked, before he released it.

"I nearly was, once. I was betrothed to David Ramsdell, Obed Ramsdell's son. We had known each other since we were children. He was a fine young man. But he was swept overboard while sailing on a whaler."

"And afterward? Surely there were other suitors?"

A dusting of rose sprang to her cheeks. "There were others who came to call. But I chose to turn them away. I had no desire to be wed, and I did not mean to mislead them."

"Then, you are content here on Nantucket?"

Her blue eyes darting away from his for an instant, Serenity gazed into the distance at a well-remembered spot. "I am content," she murmured. "The island is like a patchwork in itself. It is made up of bits and pieces of my life. Wherever I go I am surrounded by memories. Even in this place. Here is where my fiancé David asked me to wed. Over there," she said, indicating the small knoll she had been gazing at a moment before, "is the Friends Burying Ground, where my father is laid to rest."

Turning slightly, Gabriel peered at the place to which her hand had motioned; then his gaze swept back to her once more. "No markers," he stated, showing no surprise. "I take it the Friends would find that unseemly?"

Serenity smiled. "You are learning our ways quickly, Gabriel." She started to stand up, and he moved to help her. "Once there was a woman who planted a rose upon her husband's grave, and later she was sent from the Meeting in disgrace."

"Harsh treatment, for so small a crime," Gabriel observed dryly.

They stood facing each other. His strong hands still cupped her elbows, as they had when he helped her up. He seemed reluctant to release her. "Do you ever long for something more, Serenity? Have you never yearned for a ball gown? Music? To dance the night away?"

She started to draw away from him. Her eyes could not meet his. "Once, I dreamed of a ball gown. When I was much younger, of course, and attended school on the mainland. I had seen a gown in a store window that was of blue velvet—almost the same shade as the patches on my grandma's quilt. I dreamed. . . . But I have no need of ball gowns. It is not our way."

Gabriel tilted her chin up gently, so she would meet his gaze.

The sunlight danced on Gabriel's dark hair, the harsh lines of his face gentle. He seemed to study her. She was afraid. Afraid of herself, and afraid of him. Afraid he would kiss her again, just as he had the night when Lieutenant Lancaster had come. Only this time it would be without pretense, in the clear light of day, when she could no longer tell herself that it was only the night's magic that compelled him.

Momentarily, she felt his warm mouth on hers, touching, parting. But Biscuit's sharp bark and a shout from Joshua caused them to quickly draw apart.

Biscuit arrived first, with Joshua not far behind. They were both dripping wet and Joshua held a limp water lily in his hand, his dark eyes filled with innocent delight.

"For Serenity," Joshua said, holding out the lily.

The circumstances of the previous moment were instantly forgotten as Serenity admired the flower. Water dripped from the stem and dampened the sleeve of her gown. "It is beautiful, Joshua. The most beautiful flower I have ever seen." Then, noticing her brother's bare feet, she reminded gently, "And where are your shoes? Did you leave them by the pond?"

Joshua ignored her questions. Reaching in his pocket, he drew out a smooth black rock with a white ring all of the way around it. "For Gabriel," he said, placing the rock carefully in Gabriel's hand. Then, quickly pivoting around, Joshua darted away, back toward the pond.

Once Joshua had gone and they were left alone again, Serenity found it difficult to face Gabriel. She did not want to talk about what had happened before Joshua's intrusion. Instead, she smiled as though the matter were forgotten. "Joshua likes you, Gabriel."

Cradling the small black rock in one hand, Gabriel's dark brows furrowed in thought as he watched Joshua and Biscuit run back toward the pond. "Do you care for every stray and misfit you find, Serenity?" he questioned softly, as though he had not heard.

"Strays and misfits? I don't understand."

"Joshua. The dog. Me. Here on this island, we are all strays and misfits of sorts," Gabriel said, his stormy eyes swallowing her. Then, he added thoughtfully, "You are too trusting. You never question. You care for others without giving any thought to the consequences to yourself."

"You speak in riddles, Gabriel."

Gabriel turned toward her. "You are sheltered here. You cannot always control another's actions. You take care of Joshua. You tell him what to do. But what happens if one day Joshua does not behave precisely as you expect him to? Are you prepared for that, Serenity?"

"Joshua is my brother," Serenity replied firmly. "I shall always protect him in any way I can."

Yet, even as Joshua and Biscuit joined them a few moments later and they started for home, Serenity was left disturbed by what Gabriel had said. What did he mean? Was Gabriel really speaking about Joshua, or was Gabriel warning her about himself?

Obed Ramsdell stood at the door, his shrewd gaze on the man who stood before him. "It is well Serenity is out, Captain Harrowe. I have come to see thee, and I think we should speak alone. It is time we discuss a matter of grave importance."

Gabriel stepped aside and allowed the older man to enter. Once he had offered Obed a chair, which the man curtly declined, Gabriel waited for him to speak.

"As thee most certainly knows, it is a breach of the island's neutrality to aid anyone from the continent," Obed explained. "The British have named their terms, and we have formally agreed."

Obed paused for a moment, clearing his throat, then drew himself up to his full height before he continued, "Our vessels were not safe to leave the harbor without harassment. Our whaling industry was suffering so long as the British controlled the seacoast and we did not declare our neutrality. Now, things are much better. We can travel to the mainland to obtain wood to use for heating our homes in winter. Our shipping is safe." He cleared his throat again. "We are a people who abhor violence. We ask only to abide in peace. Surely, thou must realize the risk in our aiding an American, Captain Harrowe."

Gabriel had met Obed Ramsdell before, when the man had come to visit Serenity. Gabriel had no reason to believe that the man was not well intentioned, and it was obvious he cared for Serenity. Still, Gabriel was not certain what Obed was getting at.

"I have appreciated all Serenity has done to aid and protect me while I recovered," Gabriel said. "I also acknowledge the fact that you were kind enough not to turn me over to the British yourself. You have my gratitude, Mr. Ramsdell."

Obed clasped his hands behind his back and began to pace as he replied, "It is not thy gratitude that I am concerned with, Captain Harrowe." He stopped in his pacing. "Serenity is a good woman, much like a daughter to me. Yet, she created a deception in order to protect thee, and I was asked to participate in that deception. I know thou had no knowledge of this in the beginning. But this deception may well prove the undoing of the entire island if the British learn of it. And I must call upon thy conscience, and thy regard for Serenity, to aid in our dilemma."

A muscle tensing in his strong jaw, his brow furrowed, Gabriel gazed back at Obed with a distinct lack of patience. What was it the man wanted?

Obed's face was grave. "Serenity told Lieutenant Lancaster that thee were her fiancé, Captain Harrowe."

Gabriel hid his shock. "There must be some mistake. . . . "

"If thou leaves here," Obed interrupted, "without wedding Serenity, she will be left in grave danger. She could be imprisoned in a British jail. There is also the fate of the island, should the lieutenant discover that others had knowledge of her deliberate deception and kept it secret. I need not tell thee of the abuse Serenity might suffer at British hands. All because she aided thee."

For a moment, Gabriel did not know what to say. Then, cold fury took over. Obviously, Serenity had more woman's wiles than he had ever imagined. She had seen her chance to gain a husband and she had taken it. Obed's words about Serenity's sacrifice meant nothing. An innocent or not, it was clear Serenity had trapped him in an impossible situation. He had been left with no choice but to wed her.

"I appreciate your visit, Mr. Ramsdell," Gabriel replied, a muscle twitching along his jaw, his eyes like shards of ice. "I can assure you that I will see to the matter. Immediately."

Serenity arrived home shortly after dark. She had spent the afternoon with a neighbor, Anna Hussey, who had taken ill and needed help with her young children. Serenity liked spending time with Anna's children. It was doubtful she would have babes of her own, and she delighted in holding them and playing with them as often as she could. As a result, she had completely forgotten the hour.

Gabriel was waiting for her when she stepped inside the door. There was something in his manner that warned her all was not well. "I am sorry I did not return more quickly, Gabriel," she said, her blue eyes searching his ruggedly handsome face. "I was delayed at Anna Hussey's. She was ill . . ."

"There is no need to explain," Gabriel interjected, his manner cool and reserved. "At least, not in regard to where you have been."

Serenity felt suddenly uneasy. Why was Gabriel looking at her in such a strange manner? Nervously, she started to turn away.

Quickly grasping Serenity by her slim upper arms, Gabriel forced her back around to face him and held her there. "Obed Ramsdell came to see me today, Serenity. Do you know what we talked about?"

Lifting her delicate chin, she looked him squarely in the eyes. "Should I know?" she countered softly.

Gabriel did not release her arms. He stood gazing down at her. "It seems, my Serenity, that you have neglected to tell me a very important fact. How is it I was not informed of our impending marriage? Even the British believe I am your fiancé."

Serenity took a deep breath. For a moment, it seemed her heart had stopped. She had hoped Gabriel would never find out, that he would be gone before this day would ever come. Now, his anger was obvious.

Gabriel's harsh face was mere inches from her own. "I did not mean for you to find out," she murmured helplessly. "There was no need. You will be leaving soon. It is none of your concern."

For a moment, a flash of silver fire lit his eyes, and a muscle tensed along his strong jaw. "Ah, that is where you are wrong," he ground out fiercely. "The matter concerns me a great deal, Serenity. The British have left me alone here because of your little deception. Now, if I leave, they will know it was just that. What did you think would happen then? Or is this all some kind of a game? Did you think I would be noble enough to wed you, if only to assure your safety?"

Jerking from the hold he had on her arms, Serenity pivoted away, refusing to face the glaring accusation in his eyes. How could this have happened? She had taken him in. She had saved his life. Protected him. Now, he was acting as though she had done something unforgivable. How could he think she had deliberately set out to trap him into marriage, when she had no desire to wed him at all?

Taking a deep breath, Serenity spun back around to face him. There was a touch of defiance in the tilt of her chin. "There is no need to fear, Gabriel," she said irritably. "I have no desire to wed you."

Gabriel looked as though he might explode. "Not wed me?" he shot back incredulously. "Not wed me?" he repeated again as he moved toward her, his silver eyes blazing.

"No," Serenity replied firmly.

Reaching for her, Gabriel pulled Serenity roughly into the circle of his strong arms, his long, lean body grinding forcefully into her own as she sought to escape. "It seems you do not understand," he said, a touch of menace in his voice. "You have no choice but to wed me. Neither of us has any choice. You have already seen to that. Either it's your neck or mine. And, trust me, I have no desire to end up in the hands of the British."

Her cheeks were dusted with color, her discomfort at being held so intimately adding to her already strained emotions. "Let me go. You cannot force me to wed you."

"You think not?" he responded.

"I think not," she replied, brushing up against him accidentally as she tried to put more distance between his hard body and hers.

Unexpectedly, Gabriel released her. There was something in his expression that she could not quite define. A muscle twitched in his cheek as he shot back, "I owe you my life, Serenity. You do not deserve a British prison for your efforts, no matter how repulsive the idea of wedding me might seem." Then, he added, "And, if that is not enough to persuade you, then bear in mind your actions may well affect the welfare of the entire island. There are others to be considered. The war is not over yet. And it would take very little for Nantucket to lose its neutrality. Do you choose to be responsible for that?"

Gabriel's words stung her. He was right. Why had she not turned him over to the British at the first opportunity?

Gabriel awaited her answer.

Worrying her soft lower lip with her teeth, Serenity knew she must be reasonable. If Gabriel was indeed willing to wed her, then she would be foolish not to agree. Obviously, it was what Obed Ramsdell had thought was for the best or he would not have spoken to Gabriel in the first place. It seemed little enough sacrifice to protect the island's safety. She could not ask others to suffer for what she had done.

Her back stiff, her head held high, Serenity said with cool dignity, "Are you free to wed me, Gabriel?"

It was apparent by the expression on Gabriel's face that that was not what he had expected her to say. Rant, perhaps. Rave, maybe. Or out-and-out refuse. But not inquire as to his availability for marriage.

His mouth grew hard once more. Women were not to be trusted. "If you were hoping I am not, Serenity," he retorted icily, "rest assured I am quite available."

A slight frown creasing her delicately arched brow, Serenity was not finished. "And once you have wed me? What then?"

Gabriel's features were unfathomable.

Suddenly, Serenity wheeled away, not wishing to hear his reply. Whatever it was he said would make no difference. She had gotten herself into this, and it was much too late to turn back now.

Chapter Five

The Quaker meetinghouse was bleak. One thin coat of whitewash covered the walls and pews, giving it a meager lonely appearance, while the single barren room was divided by a six-foot high partition that effectively separated the men from the women. Little boys sat with their fathers, while little girls sat with their mothers. In front, there was a raised platform where the church elders sat, called the Facing Bench.

In winter the meetinghouse was cold and damp, while in summer it was hot and dry and smelled of dust because the windows were kept closed. Today, it was neither hot nor cold, but still many of the men in their beaver hats perspired, wiping their faces nervously with their handkerchiefs, and the women in their gray or plum bonnets fidgeted uncomfortably beneath the scrutiny of the British officer who had entered it a short time before. Lieutenant Evan Lancaster stood near one door in full uniform, waiting, his manner stiff and formal, a slight frown creasing his brow, his impatience evident in the tap of one boot against the hardwood floor.

The meeting began with the mandatory questions, while the brothers and sisters sat with bowed heads. *Dost thou love thy brothers as becomes a follower of Christ? Hast thou proper regard for the plainness of thy dress and bearing? Dost thou abstain from the use of intoxicating liquor as a beverage? Art thou acting according to thy conscience in all things?*

Serenity barely heard the words. The day for her wedding to Gabriel had come far too quickly, thanks to Obed Ramsdell's forceful expedience. "It is better to have done, Serenity," Obed had told her shortly after her confrontation with Gabriel. "Do what is right, and the good Lord will bless thee." But even as Obed had said the words, Serenity doubted with all sincerity that the Lord was about to bless a union that seemed such a travesty of His sacred purpose.

Dressed in a gown of pale mauve and a bonnet of the same hue, her fiery hair peeking out in wispy tendrils about her face, drawing attention to her blue eyes and the heightened color of her cheeks, Serenity came forward to join Gabriel at the front of the room.

Standing before her, dressed in a black swallowtailed coat, his crisp white shirt emphasizing the tan of his harshly chiseled face, Gabriel could almost have passed for one of the younger of the church elders. Only the mark of violence across his cheek gave him away. Still, Serenity could not help noting how handsome he looked as he took her hands in his, his grasp firm yet gentle, and she trembled slightly at his touch.

Both she and Gabriel had been well versed in what they must say. It was amazingly simple to bind one's life to another's within the Quaker faith. A Quaker wedding did not require any pledges of obedience. Instead, the couple needed only to hold hands before God and all of those assembled and agree to love and cherish. She and Gabriel would, also, be expected to use the familiar language of the Quakers, thee and thou, as was proper for the solemnity of the occasion. They had both agreed.

There was a hushed silence. Everyone waited.

His eyes as gray and unfathomable as the cool dawn mists, Gabriel began calmly and evenly, "I take thee, Serenity, as my wife. And pledge my love and devotion."

It sounded as though Gabriel had truly meant the words. But Serenity knew differently. She wanted to cry out that Gabriel spoke a lie, yet she knew that she would endanger too many people if she did.

With a slight shudder, Serenity murmured softly in reply, "I pledge to love and cherish thee, Gabriel, as my husband. Forevermore."

It was over so quickly that there was no time for regrets. And, shortly thereafter, Lieutenant Lancaster slipped from the room, while the brothers and sisters lapsed into a silence that continued for more than an hour.

Despite herself, Serenity was aware of no one else in the room but Gabriel. They had both taken their seats after their vows, but she could still feel the possessive way he had held her hands and she found it difficult to breath. She had wed a tall, dark-haired stranger whom she really knew not at all.

Silently, she prayed that the meeting would go on and on. She could not bear the awkwardness of the situation once it was over. Surely Gabriel would not expect to share her bed. . . .

No, Serenity told herself firmly. Theirs was a union of necessity nothing more.

The night had closed in. Haloed by mist, a crescent-shaped moon glowed overhead, while stars twinkled like the rarest of diamonds.

Restlessly, Gabriel stood gazing up at the bejeweled night sky, his dark hair ruffled by a soft breeze. He was reluctant to go back inside the house. He had avoided speaking to Serenity since they had returned home from the meeting; there was nothing more for him to say. If it were possible, he would leave Nantucket tonight without ever seeing her again.

The fact of the marriage did not bother him. In truth, he had given up thinking he would ever wed at all. Love was an illusion meant only for fools. He wanted no part of it. And marriage for any other reason was simply an alliance. Why not use it to repay a debt? At least that seemed as noble a cause as any other.

Gabriel's dark brows drew together as he stopped to consider what he had done to Serenity. She had deserved more than to be forced into this sham of a marriage. She deserved to one day have a real home and children. She had merely wed him to ensure the safety of the island, sacrificing her own happiness in the process, and had he never come to Nantucket, she would not have been forced into it.

He could not allow himself to feel too much for her. He and Serenity were husband and wife in name alone. They came from two different worlds, and there was no future for the two of them together. Now that they were wed, they would each go their separate ways. Serenity had her life, and he had . . .

A grim set to his mouth, Gabriel turned and slowly walked toward the house. He was weary. With any luck, Serenity would already be asleep. . . .

Noiselessly, he stepped inside the whitewashed cottage and walked across the room. No lanterns were lit and the fire had died down to embers. Before the fireplace, Biscuit lay sleeping.

Starting for his bedchamber, Gabriel glanced over at Serenity's room. He could see the door was slightly ajar, and a lantern glowed from within. Hesitating for a moment, he wondered if Serenity was still awake. He did not want to disturb her. Yet, his own guilt at not having spoken to her earlier, after they had come home from the meeting, made him go over to the door.

Serenity stood with her back toward him, a delicate porcelain statue in a shallow copper tub, water glistening on her back and slim buttocks. Her flame-colored hair was loose, rivulets of water streaming from the ends.

Squeezing a cloth above her shoulders, she drew it down her slender arms and to her wrists. For a moment, his breath caught in his throat as he stood gazing at her. She was incredibly lovely. Serene. Virginal. Yet she was not a child. The heat in his loins told him she was every bit a woman. A desirable woman.

Letting his breath out slowly, Gabriel started to turn away. He had no right to watch her, even if he had made her his wife that very day. No right at all. Then, as though she had sensed he was there, Serenity slowly pivoted around.

Once, years before, Gabriel had seen a tree split by lightning not fifty feet from him. It had crackled and then exploded, shaking the ground where he stood, leaving the air charged and his heart pounding. Now, he knew that feeling again as her startled blue eyes met his.

Serenity made no effort to shield herself, but simply stood there, ankle deep in the copper tub, the cloth in her hand poised above one rose-tipped breast. Waiting. Despite himself, he wondered what it would be like to take the cloth and draw it over her satin skin, to caress her every curve and hollow, to awaken the sleeping beauty within the exquisite form. Would ice become fire?

He took a step closer to her. He could see the moisture that clung to her dark lashes, making them spiky and thick, and the droplets of water shining on her high cheekbones. For a brief moment, she ran her tongue across her soft pink mouth, and he felt a sudden ache to taste her sweetness.

56

Forcing himself, Gabriel took a deep breath and closed his eyes, trying to thrust the vision of her from his mind. When he gazed at her again, despite himself he found he had moved another step closer.

The muscles in his long, lean body were taut, and his mouth was hard. *Serenity, I want you so badly I can hardly breathe,* he thought to himself, thankful she could not read them.

Gracefully, as though he was not even there, Serenity dipped low to wet the cloth in the water once more, then stood again to stroke it across her silky skin. It was that which stopped him.

Already he had begun to know her so well. No matter how many times Serenity might die inside to have him watch her, he knew she would never deny him. She had been raised to do what she thought was right, and he was her husband. She would refuse him nothing. He was free to take her right then and there, if he so chose. A husband's privilege. Yet she would do it out of a sense of duty, because that was what was expected of her.

Though he had never prided himself particularly on his scruples, he still had no desire to take her to his bed, knowing the only reason she would come to him was out of obligation. *Better Veronique,* he told himself caustically. At least Veronique had wanted what he could give her—even if she did possess the morals of a stray cat.

An unfathomable expression on his harshly handsome face, his gray eyes suddenly hard and impersonal, Gabriel started to turn away and leave the room. But as he reached the doorway he paused, his brooding gaze sweeping back to her once more.

"Good night, Serenity," he murmured almost regretfully. Then, a moment later, he closed the door.

Serenity could not stop thinking of Gabriel. She was fascinated by his strong hands, the dark lock of hair that fell onto his tanned forehead, his silver eyes that always managed to shield his thoughts, the hint of a smile that sometimes played around his mouth.

Why had he turned away from her on their wedding night? He had every right to expect to come to her bed, even if there had been no choice in their marriage. She would not deny him. Yet he had walked away. Had he found her lacking in some way?

It was true she'd almost been a spinster. Perhaps he had known many other women—younger, beautiful women—and she suffered by comparison. Was that it? It was prideful for her even to care. Yet, to know that Gabriel did not want her, that he found her unattractive . . .

Three days had passed since that night, and still he had kept his distance. During that time, Serenity had found herself wondering, repeatedly, what it would have been like had he decided to remain. She knew such thoughts were most certainly sinful, or improper at the very least. A good Quaker woman would only consider it her duty to please her husband. She would never . . .

As she gathered the morning eggs, Serenity could not stop thinking about it, and her blue eyes kept straying to where Gabriel worked nearby, repairing the door to the shed. Watching the play of muscles across his strong back, his dark head glistening in the sunshine, she thought that he was remarkably beautiful.

Glancing up, Gabriel stopped what he was doing when he saw her standing there.

"Serenity . . . ?" Gabriel said, coming over to where she stood. He had finished mending the door, and sweat glistened on his skin. He ran the long fingers of one hand through his dark hair and shook his head slightly. "I plan to repair the roof, while I'm still here. One more heavy rain and you might get wet inside the house, as well as out."

He gave her a grin that made a little ache begin inside.

"You are very thoughtful, Gabriel," she said, dropping her eyes so he would not see how the idea of having him leave affected her. It was true; she no longer wanted him to go. Still, she could not deny that she had known it was the way it would one day be.

"Joshua can help with the chores," he continued. "But there are a few things I wanted to take care of myself."

Serenity glanced up to find his gaze intent upon her. She could feel the warm color rise to her cheeks. "When do you plan to leave, Gabriel? Will you take a whaler?"

The matter of turning him over to the British had been settled when they were wed. There was no longer any reason for them not to discuss it openly. Gabriel gazed off into the distance at the coastline before he replied. "My men will be back for me before long, Serenity. I expect the *Firefly* to return at any time."

"Oh, I see," she replied simply, as though the matter held little importance. When he said nothing more, she turned to go.

With the basket of eggs in one arm, Serenity started toward the house, but just at that moment Biscuit came bounding across the yard, chasing after a wildly clucking hen. Making a quick turn around her skirts, the dog sped on past, nearly knocking Serenity down in his haste. Trying to regain her composure, Serenity failed to see the coil of rope that lay on the ground near her feet. As she became entangled, one ankle twisted beneath her and she lost her balance.

With a cry, Serenity landed on the ground in a splatter of eggs. More startled than hurt, she pushed herself up to a sitting position. She was smudged with dirt. Her bonnet was askew. Eggs dripped from her hair, her face, her hands, and smeared the front of her apron and mauve gown. If Gabriel had found her unattractive before, he would most certainly find her much worse than that now.

"Serenity . . . " Gabriel said, rushing to her side. "Are you hurt?"

Tears glistened in Serenity's blue eyes. She knew that she must look hopelessly ridiculous. If Gabriel dared to laugh . . .

He loomed above her. The corners of his hard mouth twitched. His silver eyes twinkled. As though he could not help himself, he slowly began to grin. Then, for the first time since they had met, Gabriel laughed.

There was one whole intact egg near Serenity's right hand. One perfect egg. It was the only one that had been spared. Her temper flaring, she reached for the egg, and before she could reason what she was doing, she sent it sailing through the air directly at Gabriel.

With a smack, the egg struck Gabriel just above the center of his forehead. And cracked open. For a brief moment there was a surprised look on his face. Then, slowly, slowly, the shell and its contents spread downward.

Aghast at what she had done, Serenity could not take her eyes from Gabriel. There was utter and complete silence.

"Gabriel . . ." she murmured helplessly, as she watched him wipe the egg from his eyes with the back of his hand.

"Was that a show of temper, Serenity?" he asked with total innocence, though his eyes had begun to twinkle once more. Then he laughed again. Deep, rumbling laughter.

She was angry and humiliated. Why had he this power to make her lose her temper? No one had ever affected her this way before.

Pushing herself up, she tried to get to her feet, but her left ankle would not support her. "Oh . . ." she said as she sunk back down to the ground in total frustration.

Tears started once more in her eyes. How could she ever face him again? She had behaved abominably. And here she sat . . .

Leaning down, Gabriel scooped her up into his strong arms and cradled her against his hard chest.

Serenity did not try to resist him. It was disturbingly pleasant being in his arms. She was in no hurry for him to release her.

Aware of his warmth and his musky scent, Serenity gazed cautiously up at him. There was eggshell in his hair and his face was smeared with yolk. But, though there was still a suspicious twinkle in his eyes, the laughter was all gone. In its place, there was something else. A surprising gentleness.

Holding her protectively in his arms, his silvery gaze resting on her own egg-smeared face, Gabriel said evenly, "I think it would be wise to get you back in the house before Obed or one of the Friends decides to call. Somehow I think they would not understand, Serenity, why you were throwing eggs at your new husband."

Chapter Six

Clad in her prim white nightgown, Serenity sat in her bedchamber brushing her hair in long, deliberate strokes, a slight frown creasing her brow. There was confusion in her eyes.

After she had learned of her fiancé's death, Serenity had become convinced that she would never wed. And she'd had no regrets. Her life was full. Well-ordered. Serenely content. Then Gabriel had been brought to her door, and her world was suddenly turned upside down.

Since the moment he had first intruded on her life, he had wreaked havoc with her emotions. She had planned to turn him over to the British, and then she had changed her mind. She had refused to wed him, and then she had found herself giving in and doing precisely that. And this morning, she had lost her temper completely and even resorted to throwing an egg at him.

What was happening to her? One moment she was angry with him, and the next . . .

Even now, she could still feel the rush of warmth that spread to her cheeks each time his silvery gaze met hers, the feeling of butterfly wings in her stomach whenever they touched. She remembered his kiss, warm and compelling, the night he had warned her of the dragon. *The dragon may take you where he wants to go.* And that day near the pond, when they had walked with Joshua, the restless stirring deep within, like a tender flame . . .

Why did Gabriel have this effect upon her? It was all so new. So troubling. She had never felt this way before.

Sighing softly, Serenity set her hairbrush aside and smoothed the silky hair from her cheek. It was late and she was weary, yet she had no desire to seek her bed. It would be impossible to sleep. She could not put thoughts of Gabriel from her mind.

Gabriel stood near the fireplace, his eyes on the flickering flames. He had let Biscuit in the house when the dog scratched at the door, and had added some more wood to the fire. Now he stood in the quiet room wrestling with his own dark thoughts. It was easy to see that he would get no more sleep tonight than he had the night before. He could not stop thinking of Serenity. Each night he spent the hours tossing and turning as he waited for the dawn.

He had never known anyone quite like her. Enchanting temptress. Innocent child. And he was undeniably attracted to them both.

A hint of a smile graced his hard mouth for a moment as he remembered the way she had looked that very morning after she had thrown the egg at him. It was obvious she had been as surprised by her own reaction as he was. She would never know how difficult it had been for him, at that particular moment, not to sweep her into his arms and claim that sweet mouth of hers, to feel the warmth of her in his arms.

Since the night when he had watched her bathe, he had vowed to keep his distance. He had told himself that it was because he did not want Serenity to come to him out of a sense of obligation. Yet, there was more to it than that.

Despite the weeks the two of them had spent together on the island, Serenity did not truly know him. In the past, he would have taken what he wanted without a second thought. There had been many women before Veronique. Veronique was not the first; she was simply the most memorable. And he had never regreted walking away from any of them.

He had been known as an adventurer, a black sheep, the rake-hell son of Nicholas Harrowe. His parents had despaired of him ever settling down. He had always been too restless for commitments. His younger brother Brandon possessed all the quiet discipline in the family. It was Brandon who should have inherited Marihaven. Brandon who was the better son. Brandon who should have lived.

Now, with Serenity, his past had come back to haunt him. Perhaps it was because she was a Quaker, or simply because she was Serenity, but he refused to hurt her. And he knew that if he intruded on her life any more than he already had, he most certainly would. Everything he represented was wrong for her. He had no choice but to stay away from her. Still, despite all reason to the contrary, it had been impossible for him to stop wanting her. . . .

"Gabriel?" Serenity murmured, breaking the stillness of the room as he stood gazing into the fire.

Pivoting slowly, Gabriel kept his face carefully devoid of any emotion, though he was well aware that her silken hair fell loose about her slender shoulders and she was already dressed for bed.

"Serenity . . . " he said. "Was there something you needed?"

Her eyes were incredibly blue.

Silently, Serenity moved toward him.

His jaw tensed slightly. "Is your ankle bothering you?"

"No," she responded softly. "It is much better. But I could not sleep." She paused for a moment. "You could not sleep either, Gabriel?"

His shirt hanging open to the waist, Gabriel stood with his feet braced apart. His expression was carefully shuttered. "No," he replied tersely, not wishing to elaborate.

Taking several steps in his direction, Serenity stopped not an arm's length away, her face tilted slightly upward, her eyes resting on his unyielding face.

Once again, Gabriel was struck by how very beautiful she

63

was. Her enchanting features were carefully sculpted, her cheekbones high, her mouth full, the curve of her delicate chin clearly defined, her body slim and graceful.

For a moment, they both stood there gazing at each other. Then Serenity moved still closer, until her body was mere inches from his own.

Her blue-velvet gaze was unusually bright and searching. "I was cold," she whispered. "I wanted to be near the fire. . . . "

Gabriel drew in a deep breath. She was standing much too close. He could see the slim column of her throat and the rise and fall of her softly rounded breasts, their tips jutting impudently against the fabric of her gown.

Despite himself, Gabriel could not help thinking that if he were to lean down, his mouth would touch her own. And then . . .

He remembered his vow to keep his distance.

"Don't you know that fire can burn, Serenity?" he asked, his low voice like a whispered caress. Gently, he reached out one hand to stroke her dusky hair as though he soothed a child.

She did not move away.

"But do you not know as well, Gabriel," she murmured softly in reply, "that even the drab moth is often drawn to the flame?"

A hint of surprise crossed his handsome features. A drab moth? Was that what she believed? She could not have been more wrong.

"My Serenity," he countered softly. "Be assured, you are no drab moth, if that is what you were thinking."

He could not help himself. Bending, he gently kissed her forehead. "You are the most beautiful woman I have ever seen." He kissed the tip of her nose. "Your beauty comes from within . . . "

I had better stop now, he told himself firmly. A moment more and it would be too late.

He brushed a kiss across her soft pink mouth.

She sighed softly and leaned the slender curves of her body

against him. "Teach me what it is to burn with fire," she whispered. "Teach me, Gabriel . . . "

In that moment, Gabriel knew he was truly lost. Utterly and completely.

His handsome face intent, his arm slipped around her small waist and he drew her up hard against his chest. He could feel her satin skin through the thin fabric of her gown.

Her body pressed to his, Serenity gazed up at him with shadowy blue eyes sparked by silver flames. Her breathing was shallow. Quick.

"Serenity . . . " he murmured. He could not think rationally. His own breath was harsh and labored. With fevered urgency, his mouth claimed the warmth of hers. Parting beneath his own, he discovered its honeyed interior. Its pagan sweetness. Then, suddenly it was over.

Without warning, Biscuit had let out a low, ominous growl.

Gabriel jerked away. With predatory grace, he wheeled about, expecting some form of danger, his eyes like cold gray steel.

Hackles up, Biscuit stood not two feet away. The wolfhound's head was lowered, his eyes rolled back, his mouth curled to reveal his long, jagged teeth. Snarling, the animal did not back away.

With a start, Gabriel realized that the dog was growling at him.

Gabriel did not know whether to laugh or to utter a vile curse. It was obvious the dog had sensed that his mistress was in some kind of danger. Maybe the wolfhound thought he was holding Serenity against her will, or perhaps the animal was simply a good judge of character.

Gabriel turned to Serenity. Her cheeks were dusted with color, her mouth slightly swollen, her eyes far too bright. It did not matter the reason, the moment was shattered. Wheeling about, she darted from the room before he could stop her.

Starting after her, Gabriel thought better of it and halted, letting his heartbeat slow, the heat in his loins fade away. Was it not better this way? He would be leaving soon. He had no right to claim Serenity when he had every intention of walking away.

Still, he threw a black glance in the dog's direction. The hackles remained raised on the wolfhound's back, and a low growl continued to rumble from his shaggy form.

"It looks like you win," he observed dryly to the dog. Then, turning away, he strode out the door and into the night.

Breathlessly, Serenity awaited Gabriel in his darkened bed-chamber. She had run away from him before. She had not meant to. But she had been frightened by her own emotions, the way he made her feel. She would not run from him again.

Soon, Gabriel's vessel would arrive, and he would go away. She would never see him again. It was not in her power to change that. Yet, for tonight, for this one night only, she wanted his touch, his fevered kisses. To know what it was to truly be his wife. . . .

Gabriel entered the room so soundlessly that for a moment Serenity was not even aware he was there. Silently, she watched as he crossed over to the window. His tall, lean frame was sil-houetted in the misty moonlight. Her heart hammering painfully, she took a step toward him.

"Gabriel . . . " she said softly.

In the scant light, Serenity saw him wheel about, and for an instant the suddenness of it frightened her. She drew in a quick breath. Was he angry with her for being there? She could not bear his anger.

Steeling herself, Serenity drew closer to him. She could not see his expression in the darkness. She wished she could. It might have made this moment easier for her.

He remained as immobile as a statue. It seemed he was determined to make this even more difficult for her, if that was possible.

"Gabriel . . . " she began once again. She could not see his eyes, only the curve of his harshly handsome face and the dark lock of hair that perpetually fell onto his forehead. Still, she was totally aware of him, and the dangerously masculine quality that was his.

A chill sweeping through her, she trembled slightly. He was so near and yet so far. For a moment, she wondered if she had made a dreadful mistake. What should she say to him?

Serenity drew in a deep breath. "Touch me, Gabriel," she murmured softly. "Lay your hands on my body."

For a long moment more, he stood there. Then he came toward her. She stood perfectly still. When he was near enough to touch her, his fingertips trailed up the length of her arms and to her throat. As they curved around her slender neck, his thumbs tilted her chin upward so that he could place a kiss on her parted lips.

With utter gentleness, his mouth grazed her own, its moist heat teasing at hers. Something curled within her belly as he did so. It felt pleasant. Then he stepped back.

He seemed to hold himself away from her, as though he were testing whether he should go on.

Sensing his indecision, she moved forward to lean up and place a hasty kiss upon his hard mouth. It was a child's kiss. Innocent. Passionless. Trusting. Then she quickly drew away again.

"Oh, Serenity . . ." he said, his voice almost a pained whisper.

"Touch me," she repeated.

With one deft movement, his hands released her gown at the shoulders, and it fell like a whisper about her slender ankles. She could feel the shock of the cool air on her breasts; then she felt the warmth of his hands as they brushed against them. Almost reverently, he caressed her body with gentle strokes that made her flesh tingle. It felt wonderful and frightening at the same time. Brushing her hair back from her neck, slowly he placed small kisses along the curve of one side, and then along the other.

His arms moved to encircle her waist, and he pulled her to him, his mouth once again finding hers. This time, he kissed her in a way she had never been kissed before. It was a deep, penetrating kiss. One that held great promise, and spoke of something almost primitive. It took her breath away.

Unconsciously, Serenity arched her back toward him, seeking to get much closer. She could feel the roughness of his clothing, the length of his body next to hers. Something deep inside her made her feel incomplete, as though she had been created precisely for him and could not be whole without him in some fathomless way. She whimpered softly.

Scooping her up in his arms, Gabriel carried her to the bed. It took several moments more for him to join her there, and when he did so she could feel that his flesh was bare as well. Lying beside her, he gently began to explore her mysteries, his finger-tips discovering, his mouth following soon after. It was sweetly intoxicating, and a fire began to burn inside her.

She wanted to know him as well. Could she make him feel the same way? Her small hands tangled in the back of his dark hair and brushed over his hard-muscled chest. She liked the tex-ture of him beneath her fingertips, his sweat-dampened skin. With unpracticed skill, her hands slid down his sides. And lower. He drew in a sharp breath.

Fiercely, Gabriel drew Serenity to him and kissed her. This time he was more demanding, less restrained. Moving down-ward, his mouth found the tips of her breasts and trailed kisses across her stomach. His hands became more intimate. It made her feel uncertain. Something was building deep inside her, like waves whipped by a fierce summer storm. It was building and building until she felt as though she might shatter into a thou-sand tiny pieces. She wanted to escape, yet she was compelled to stay. Her heart beat rapidly.

Shifting slightly, Gabriel moved between her thighs. "I will try to be gentle," he murmured in a thick voice.

"Be gentle, if you so choose," she replied, her hand tangling once more in the dark hair at the back of his head as she pulled him down to brush a brief kiss across his lips. "But, Gabriel . . . oh, Gabriel," she entreated, with a little catch in her breath, "please be quick. . . ."

Anna Hussey was sick once more. Serenity suspected it was from too many children, too much work, and a husband who rarely came home, but she was still happy to help Anna in any way she could. She had gone over to the Husseys' shortly after breakfast to help with the children.

Gabriel had been gone when she awoke. Serenity was not certain whether it was because of what had happened between them, or if he had simply left to watch for his vessel. Yet she was almost glad she did not have to face him.

It had been wanton of her to approach Gabriel. Now, in the clear light of day, she could not believe she had actually done so. What must he think of her? Though it was not morally wrong and he was her husband, her cheeks flamed at the abandoned way she had behaved and the memory of what had followed.

Still, as the rest of the day wore on, Serenity yearned to see Gabriel. Was he angry? Theirs was to be a marriage in name alone. Had she lost his trust? Would he forgive her?

Late in the afternoon, Serenity started for home at a brisk pace. Biscuit was by her side. Before she could reach there, Serenity was halted by Joshua as he tried to catch up with her.

"Serenity! Serenity!" he called out as he ran after her. "It's here. The ship is here. Gabriel's ship. Come see . . . "

Shocked, Serenity stopped precisely where she was. Gabriel's vessel? The *Firefly*? She was not even aware Joshua knew which one it was. Surely it could not be.

"Joshua, are you certain it is Gabriel's vessel?" she asked, hoping desperately that he had made a mistake. "Tell me what it looks like."

Joshua looked suddenly proud and important at being able to answer a question for Serenity. "It's fast like the wind," he said, using his hand to demonstrate. "With sails the color of . . . " He searched for the word, then added triumphantly, " . . . fire."

Joshua knows! Serenity thought in despair. It *was* Gabriel's vessel. The *Firefly* had returned!

Whirling about, she started to race toward home as fast as she could, her skirts whipping about her knees. Was Gabriel gone? Had he returned to his vessel already, without even a farewell?

Chapter Seven

Accompanied by two British soldiers with muskets in hand, Lieutenant Evan Lancaster approached Serenity's small frame house. Dressed in his bright red British uniform, his wavy brown hair and well-trimmed mustache glinting in the sunlight, the lieutenant was an impressive figure. Yet, the hard scowl on his face belied any hope that this was purely a social call, and his step was brisk with determination.

He would count himself many times the fool if what he suspected was true. The scarlet-masted vessel had returned, and he doubted it was a mere coincidence. Obviously, the ship had come for Gabriel Harrowe.

He should have been much firmer with Serenity in the beginning. But his attraction to the exquisitely beautiful Quaker had affected his better judgment. If he could now prove that she had willingly given her protection to a man from an American vessel, she would never enjoy such leniency again.

For a moment, a grin flitted across the lieutenant's face as he considered that possibility. Perhaps the situation was not so unfortunate after all. It might even work to his advantage. He had never wished to wed the innocent fiery-haired beauty, but merely to gain her affections for a time. Now, if his guess proved correct and she was already wed to an American privateer—a man soon to be captured and sent to a British prison—Serenity would have no alternative but to accept his attentions. Without any commitments or complaints.

Just ahead, Lieutenant Lancaster could see Joshua standing before Serenity's house, scuffing one square-toed shoe in the sandy earth.

Ordering his men to wait at a distance, Lieutenant Lancaster chose to approach Joshua alone. The youth lacked intelligence, but he might prove useful in some way. If handled properly, Joshua might tell him if the pirate was still about, and he and his men could then take the man by surprise.

As the lieutenant approached, Joshua glanced up with a troubled expression on his face.

"Joshua," the lieutenant said, once he had reached him, "what say you? Is Madame Harrowe at home?"

Joshua continued to scuff his toe in the earth. "Can't go in," he replied. "Serenity's sad."

The lieutenant frowned slightly. What was this? "Sad, you say, Joshua? How is that? Why is she sad?"

Joshua's dark eyes avoided his, as though he knew a secret he was not about to tell. "Don't know," he said evasively.

Immediately suspicious, Lieutenant Lancaster drew closer to Joshua, his manner threatening. "It is a sin to withhold the truth, Joshua. You know that, don't you? That is your Quaker faith." His gaze held Joshua in his place. "Now, tell me precisely. Why is Serenity sad?"

Joshua looked upset. He bit at his lower lip.

At the young man's continued resistance, the lieutenant prompted him irritably once more, "It is a *sin,* Joshua."

"The ship came," Joshua replied hesitantly. "Gabriel's ship. He didn't say good-bye." Joshua shook his dark head remorsefully. "It made Serenity feel bad. Gabriel shouldn't have done that."

"Are you talking about the ship with scarlet sails, Joshua?"

Joshua slowly nodded his head.

Lieutenant Lancaster looked pleased. He might have missed capturing the American, but things had still worked out as he had planned. Now Serenity was at his mercy. And Joshua had given him the means by which he would ensure her cooperation.

A sly look on his face, the lieutenant ordered, "Go down to the shore and see if the vessel is still there, Joshua. Serenity has no need of you now. I shall see to her welfare. And, mind you,

71

Gloria Pedersen

don't say a word to anyone. You understand me? If you care for Serenity, you must keep it our secret. Understand?"

Pivoting around smartly, the lieutenant went back to his men.

Without explanation, he curtly dismissed the soldiers and sent them away. If the American was already gone, there was no further need for them. He could easily handle Serenity by himself.

The dying rays of the sun filtered softly through the windows to scatter patches of light and shadow about the room.

Her blue eyes cautious, Serenity stood facing Lieutenant Lancaster in the front sitting room. It was obvious he had come with a purpose, but she had no idea what it could be. She had banished Biscuit to the bedchamber at the lieutenant's request, and the dog whined and scratched anxiously at the door. "Lieutenant Lancaster," she began, not wanting to prolong his visit a moment longer than was necessary, "please tell me why you have come."

"Don't you know why, Serenity?" he asked, a smile curving the line of his mouth just below his mustache. "Ah, I think you do."

"I have no knowledge of what you imply," she stated, now uneasily aware of the way he was watching her. It was not in her nature to be frightened or easily intimidated. Yet, this time . . .

A self-satisfied gleam was in the lieutenant's eyes as he replied complacently, "Where is your new husband, Serenity?" Then, he continued, as though he already knew. "It seems he is not about. Surely, he has not grown weary of wedded life already?"

Serenity felt distinctly uneasy. The lieutenant's questions were far too pointed. Had he seen the *Firefly* and guessed at Gabriel's leaving? She drew a deep breath and leveled her delicate chin. It was best to stand her ground, no matter what the lieutenant had already discovered.

Aware that Biscuit continued to growl and scratch at the door, Serenity glanced in that direction, then back at the lieutenant, sorry now that she had not kept the dog by her side.

"I have no need to question my husband's whereabouts, Lieutenant Lancaster," she countered primly. "Now, if you will excuse me? The hour is growing late."

"Much later than you think, my dear. And I have no intention of leaving. Not just yet. In fact, I intend to see a great deal of you from now on," he said, giving her a broad smile. "Would you care to ask me why?"

"Please, lieutenant. I have no time for games. . . . "

"This is no game," the lieutenant interrupted, his voice suddenly harsh and humorless. "Joshua has confirmed all of my earlier suspicions about your erstwhile husband. And since you have already proven that you would protect another before you would protect yourself, I should warn you that Joshua will be the one to suffer for aiding in this little scheme if you find yourself unable to cooperate. You do care about Joshua, don't you, my pet? If you wish to protect him, you shall look to me exclusively for your companionship in the future. And that future shall begin right now."

Serenity drew back from the lieutenant in horrified silence. Despite her sheltered life, she was well aware of what he was implying. The very idea was vile. Unthinkable. Moreover a sin. She was wed to Gabriel in the eyes of God, whether or not they lived as man and wife in the future.

Without waiting for any reply, Lieutenant Lancaster crossed the room in two long strides and grasped Serenity's arm, pulling her to him.

Without any preliminaries, his mouth came down on hers, hard and hurtful. Then, as she tried to twist away, one of his hands came up to grasp her by the chin, his fingers digging into the soft flesh around her mouth and forcing it open so that his tongue could thrust inside.

With revulsion, Serenity managed to jerk away from him. She tried to will herself not to fight. It was not their way. But his touch made her feel soiled. Abused.

One hand grasping her cap, the British officer jerked it from her head, releasing her fiery hair and sending it cascading down around her shoulders. Then, roughly, he forced her back against the wall, his hard body mere inches from her own.

Once again, Biscuit barked and jumped frantically at the door.

Standing there helplessly, Serenity knew the lieutenant intended to violate her. His face was flushed, and there was a glazed look in his eyes. He had spoken of her cooperation, but she knew her answer did not matter. She was certain he would force himself upon her without a moment's hesitation.

The lieutenant grasped the front of Serenity's gown.

Helpless tears started in Serenity's eyes. She shuddered as the pinning of her gown gave way. A moment later, his hand rent the fabric of her chemise, then closed over the softness of one breast as his mouth sought hers once more.

Unable to endure his assault a moment longer, she screamed.

Unexpectedly, Joshua burst through the door. Throwing himself at the lieutenant, Joshua attacked the man with a sudden fury.

Helplessly, Serenity gazed on. Because of her, Joshua had resorted to violence—and it would only make matters worse. He was no match for the lieutenant, a trained British officer.

With horror, Serenity watched as the lieutenant knocked Joshua to the floor, then began striking him repeatedly with his fists, one blow following another. Joshua cried out in pain, putting up his hands to try to protect his bloodied face.

Rushing to where they grappled on the floor, Serenity sought desperately to stop the lieutenant from hurting Joshua. Releasing his hold on the youth, the lieutenant came to his feet and wheeled about, striking Serenity viciously and knocking her backward.

Instantly, Joshua scrambled to his feet as well. With an angry roar, he shoved the lieutenant away from Serenity with all his might. Caught off balance, the lieutenant went crashing down. His head struck the edge of the stone fireplace as he fell.

Lieutenant Lancaster lay there, his face ashen, while Joshua

74

sank back down to the floor and huddled with his arms about his knees.

"Joshua, are you all right?" she asked anxiously as she knelt by his side.

There were tears in his eyes and blood ran from his nose. Holding him close like the child he was, she stroked his dark head while he sniffed loudly. "It is all right, Joshua. You need not be afraid."

Joshua's chin quivered as he gazed up at her. "He hurt me and he hurt you, Serenity."

"I know Joshua," she murmured softly, glancing at the man who lay on the floor. "He should not have hurt us."

Lieutenant Lancaster did not move. He lay in a strange position.

Disengaging herself from Joshua, Serenity gave her brother a reassuring smile, then turned and crawled on her hands and knees to where the lieutenant was sprawled. Was he badly injured? She reached out a hand to touch him. He still did not move. Then Serenity saw it: A trickle of blood ran from the back of his head. With shock, she realized the lieutenant was dead.

With her dark hair loose and her gown in disarray, Serenity's thoughts were troubled as she knelt on the floor beside the lieutenant. Silently, she offered up a contrite prayer. It was a violent act that had ended his life, and she could not help feeling responsible. She had always been taught to turn the other cheek. To shun violence. Now, in resisting the lieutenant, she had been responsible for his death. How could she live with her conscience over such a matter, regardless of the circumstances?

She had but one choice, and that was to turn herself over to the British authorities and take full responsibility. It was her only chance for retribution. For eternal forgiveness. Still, if she did so, there would be questions. The authorities would learn of Joshua's involvement as well. They would discover that it was he who had shoved the lieutenant. And what if they charged him with murder? Joshua could never survive in prison.

Rising to her feet, Serenity went to Joshua and helped him up. Somehow she had to protect him. "Come, Joshua. And quickly. You must help me hide Lieutenant Lancaster. We must take him as far from here as possible."

Sniffing again, Joshua gave her a doubtful look. "You want me to hide the body, Serenity?"

"Yes, Joshua. It would not be well if the British found him here!" She deliberately avoided telling her brother that the lieutenant was dead. It was better if he did not know.

Her mind raced over what she must do. It was nearly dark. They had to act quickly. Was the *Firefly* still in the harbor? Could they reach her before she sailed? It would be dangerous, yet she could think of no other way to protect Joshua. Before long, the authorities would find the lieutenant's body. And they must be far away before that happened.

If only it was not Gabriel's vessel. How could she ask him for help? Gabriel had already turned his back on her, leaving without even a farewell.

Giving Joshua a reassuring hug, Serenity added, "Do not be afraid, Joshua. I shall take care of everything. I promise . . . "

The moon left puddles of light on the still, dark water, while the rhythmic lapping of oars from the skiff barely broke the silence.

There were three of them in the boat—Serenity, Joshua, and Biscuit. Under cover of darkness, they had slipped down along the coast and waited until the night mists had started to close in. Then they had taken the skiff and begun to make their way to the *Firefly* as she lay in the harbor.

They moved cautiously and quietly, not wishing to be sighted by any of the men aboard the vessel. Once aboard, they would hide until the *Firefly* was out on the open sea.

Serenity had left everything behind, save one bundle that contained a few articles of clothing and her grandma's quilt.

The quilt was the only vestige of her past that Serenity had allowed herself. She knew they would never be able to return to Nantucket, and she could not bear to leave the quilt behind. Once they had reached the mainland, Serenity was determined to seek work to provide for both herself and Joshua, perhaps in teaching or minding a store. She knew they could survive on their own.

Joshua did not fully understand that they were leaving the island forever. It seemed merely an exciting adventure to him. Serenity was dreading the moment when her brother finally realized the truth—that they were leaving their home and all they knew behind forever. She and Joshua had only each other now. Still, she was convinced that would be enough.

The *Firefly* rose suddenly out of the mists before them, the current chirping around her anchor chain and bow, her raked masts barely discernible as they lifted into the sky. Because of her long, low design, her bulwarks were near enough to the water so that Serenity was certain she and Joshua could easily climb aboard from the boat. Yet, admittedly, getting Biscuit aboard might well prove a bit more difficult.

Silently, Serenity watched as Joshua scaled up the side of the vessel. He knew what he was to do. First, he was to make certain no one was about. Then he would hoist Biscuit aboard with the aid of a rope she would fasten to a canvas sling cradling the dog's midsection. Lastly, Serenity would follow. It seemed a simple plan. She only hoped they would not be caught while trying to put it into action.

As she waited anxiously, one other thing concerned Serenity as well: Gabriel. A slight frown creasing her brow, she worried her lower lip as she thought of facing him. Would he be angry with her for stowing away aboard his vessel? Undoubtedly, he had thought never to see her again. And she had thought never to see him. But neither of them had been left with any choice in the matter.

As soon as he was aboard, Joshua dropped the end of the rope back down to her. Quickly wrapping the sling around Biscuit's stomach, then fastening the rope to it, Serenity crooned softly in the animal's ear. "Hush, Biscuit. Hush. Make no sound." She knew her words were of little use, but she could only hope the wolfhound would sense the importance of keeping silent. If they could just bide this one night, without being discovered . . .

Serenity held her breath as Joshua started to hoist up the dog. Though Biscuit made not a whimper, it seemed an eternity as she watched the animal slowly ascend the side of the vessel. After what seemed an agonizing wait, she sighed in relief as she realized that the animal was finally aboard.

A few moments later, Joshua dropped the end of the rope back down to her again. Twisting the rope securely about her waist, Serenity grasped her bundle in her arms and waited for Joshua to lift her as well.

Everything was going precisely as she had planned. Soon they would all be safely aboard. Then they could hide in the hold until they were out to sea. As she was hoisted up the side of the vessel, Serenity closed her eyes for a moment, thinking of Gabriel once again. Why was it she had the feeling they were escaping the wrath of one storm, only to face another?

Chapter Eight

The hold of the *Firefly* was dark and dank and extremely disagreeable. It was a miracle they had gotten there in the first place without discovery, yet once they were there Serenity had found it even harder to remain.

Serenity was certain there were rats in every corner, rats with gleaming eyes and sharp teeth, and, undoubtedly every other manner of horror and pestilence lurking in the darkness. Only her firm conviction that what she was doing was the right thing forced her to remain.

The night passed. Then, by the activity they could hear above them on deck, Serenity knew it was day. It was only a matter of time until they were discovered—and she was beginning to dread that most of all.

Only two nights before she had gone to Gabriel, lain in his arms, let him make love to her. Then he had callously left without a word of farewell. Now, despite what had happened, she must plead for his help.

"Blimey, m' maties! An' what've we here?" a rasping voice said a short time later, as Joshua was dragged roughly to his feet by the scruff of his neck, while Serenity crouched nearby. "Looks like a wet-eared young bloke an' a bit o' skirt. All stowed away nice and tidy. Just waitin' for ol' Donovan to come along."

Serenity shuddered as the man gave her a toothless grin, one brawny arm locked around the hapless Joshua's neck as he struggled to be free.

The man continued to leer at Serenity in the dim light from the opening of the hold, as he observed, "A might scrawny for m' tastes. Flamin' tits and arses, an' I'm in m' glory. But I reckon the lass has good teeth. That's in 'er favor." He gave her another toothless grin.

Biscuit began to growl ominously.

Rising quickly to her feet and placing a hand on the wolfhound's back, Serenity quieted the animal. It would not do to have Biscuit attack one of the ship's hands. It would only make matters worse.

Quelling her fear, Serenity leveled her delicate chin and managed to say politely, "Good day, sir. We are Quakers. If you would kindly take us to see your captain, we would be greatly in your debt."

The moment she had started to speak, the man had gazed at her in startled surprise. "Damn my eyes! You two be blinkin' Quakers?" he asked, as though the very idea proved almost ludicrous.

"We are Quakers from the island of Nantucket," she informed him politely. "Now, if you will please take us to see your captain?"

Taken aback, slowly the man released his hold on Joshua's neck. He shook his head and gave her a hard scowl. "The cap'n won't like this none, that's for sure. The devil's whiskers! He might even heave the lot o' you overboard. An' it'd serve you right, you stowin' away on 'is vessel." He paused for a moment, giving them both a hard, measuring look, as though searching for a way to remedy the situation. Then he added, "I s'pose the lad could earn his keep, though. We're short a hand, an' he looks able. But I can tell you right now, missie, the cap'n ain't got no use for a woman who won't warm his bed. An' there'd be no other reason to keep you 'round."

The man's crude assessment of his captain's reaction to her presence did nothing to boost Serenity's confidence. It had never occurred to her that Gabriel might be far different aboard his vessel than he'd appeared on the island. Perhaps she had never really known him at all. And it would do no good to remind Gabriel that she was his wife. Theirs had never been a marriage in the true sense of the word. Her only hope was to appeal to Gabriel in Joshua's behalf. He could not turn his back on them once he knew what had happened. And as soon as they reached the mainland he would never have to see them again. She and Joshua would manage on their own.

Still, Serenity was dreading the coming confrontation with Gabriel as Donovan assisted them from the hold. Surprisingly, the huge man was almost gentle despite his bluster, even giving Joshua a hand with Biscuit. However, once they reached the deck, Donovan quickly regained his former gruffness and briskly ordered them to wait for him there while he went to seek his captain.

Serenity trembled slightly as the crew started to gather round. Still, not wishing to alarm Joshua, she gave him a reassuring smile.

"See here, cap'n," Donovan explained, as he led the way

back to them a few moments later, "a couple o' stowaways.
Quakers, they be. What d'you want me to do with 'em? Toss
'em overboard, or use 'em for fish bait?"

Tired and disheveled, Serenity stood clutching the bundle
containing her grandma's quilt. Her cap was crooked, fiery tendrils of silky hair escaping from its outer edge, and there was a
smudge of dirt on her cheek. Still, she held her head proudly
and leveled her delicate chin as Gabriel strode toward her.

An almost imperceptible look of surprise crossed Gabriel's
features the moment his eyes met hers. Then, almost immediately, his expression faded to a hard, unfathomable scowl, and
a muscle tightened along his jaw. Here aboard his vessel, he
appeared taller somehow, more overpowering, more a
stranger.

"What say ye, Cap'n?" Donovan prompted again. "What
d'you want me to do with 'em?"

A second man strode forward to take his place by Gabriel's
side. Serenity recognized him. It was Kane, the man who had
left Gabriel at her door on the island when he was injured.

A flicker of surprise lit Kane's eyes as he recognized her.
Then he turned and exchanged a glance with Gabriel.

"Should we get rid of 'em, Cap'n Harrowe?" Donovan
asked once more. "Set 'em adrift in a jolly boat? They hail
from Nantucket."

A frown creasing one dark brow, Gabriel remained silent.

"We're less than a day off the island, captain," Kane
observed without emotion. "It's not too late to turn back."

Once more, a muscle tensed along Gabriel's strong jaw.
Serenity was aware of the brooding way he was looking at her.
It was obvious he was not in the least pleased to see her.

Sensing the charged atmosphere, Biscuit growled softly and
moved closer to Serenity's side.

Gabriel's steel-gray gaze rested briefly on the animal, then
swept over Joshua. For an instant, Gabriel's eyes softened as he
inclined his head in acknowledgment. After which, he shot a
glance at Kane and ordered, "Give the boy some work, Kane.

And make certain it's something he can handle." Then, regaining his hard edge once more, his attention returned to Serenity. His words were not meant for her, however. "Take the lady to my cabin, Donovan. And see to it that she remains there for the time being. I'll deal with her later."

"Aye, aye, Cap'n. An' what about this mangy brute? You want me to take 'im to your cabin too, sir?"

For a moment, Gabriel's eyes caught and held hers. She dared not ask it of him, but she prayed Gabriel would not put Biscuit back down in the hold.

Witnessing the silent exchange between the two of them, Kane did not wait for his captain to reply. "Of course, Donovan," Kane interjected smoothly. "Take the dog too." Then, throwing Gabriel a wry glance, he added, "It appears our captain has taken a fancy to all kinds of pets—since his stay on the island."

Serenity awaited Gabriel in his cabin, her nervousness and dread growing increasingly by the moment. Still clutching her bundle, she sat perched on the edge of a chair, worrying at her lower lip with her fine white teeth.

Gazing about her, Serenity sighed softly. The oak-paneled cabin was sparsely furnished. The wide built-in captain's bed; a sturdy desk covered with books, maps, and a worn-looking sextant; a small table with an edge to keep the tableware from slipping off in rough weather; a chest for clothing. It told little of the man who claimed it as his own; she had no sense of Gabriel here.

As she sat there, she tried not to think of her home on Nantucket. If she were there, it would be time to gather the eggs. Then Joshua would come in and they would read. Perhaps in the afternoon she would visit Anna Hussey and her children. Now all of that was gone, and she knew that she would miss it terribly. But there was no going back.

Glancing up with a start, Serenity saw Gabriel looming in the doorway as the door was pushed aside. Then, slowly, he closed the door behind him and stood facing her from the center of the room.

"Would you care to tell me the meaning of this, Serenity?" Gabriel began, a frown creasing his brow, his manner cool and aloof.

Serenity drew a deep breath. It was unsettling to be alone with him. "I am sorry to trouble you, Gabriel. But I must ask for your aid." Pausing, her wary gaze searched his. "Joshua and I found it necessary to leave Nantucket. We boarded a skiff to reach your vessel, then climbed aboard and hid in the hold. I knew it was only a matter of time until you found us. But I hoped by the time you did, we would be far enough from the island that you would not make us return."

Something flickered across Gabriel's harshly handsome face. Was it irritation or concern?

"I know it is much to ask, Gabriel. But if you would see us safely to the mainland, we would trouble you no further. And we should be no bother. I promise you."

His look was incredulous. "No bother . . . "

"No bother," she replied hastily. "We will work to earn our keep. It will be only for a short time."

For a moment, Gabriel gazed in the direction of the ceiling, as though he could not believe what he was hearing. Then his eyes swept to her once again. She silently prayed that there would be no need to tell him anything more.

Turning his back to her, Gabriel took several long strides, then abruptly wheeled back around. "Exactly why is it that you cannot return to the island, Serenity?" he asked bluntly. "I have yet to hear the reason. Or do you expect me to believe you are acting merely on a whim? I am no fool, Serenity, though it is obvious you take me for one."

Serenity found it painful to meet his gaze. How could she explain to him the terrible thing that had happened to Lieutenant Lancaster? He was not there. He could not know . . .

"Serenity . . . " he demanded once more.

It would appear she had no choice. Still, she did not want to involve Joshua in the telling any more than was absolutely necessary. It was better if she took the entire blame for the lieutenant's death; it was justly hers to begin with anyway.

Steeling herself, she replied simply, "Lieutenant Lancaster is dead. And I am responsible." She waited for him to make some reply, but when none was forthcoming she continued. "I would have turned myself over to the British authorities without delay, but Joshua was there at the time. I could not risk having the British arrest him as well. I had to protect him."

Momentarily, he appeared stunned. "Are you telling me that you killed the lieutenant, Serenity? I find that hard to believe."

Slowly, Serenity nodded her head. "Yes," she affirmed in a voice barely above a whisper. "I know what you must think of me, Gabriel. But I cannot deny I am responsible for Lancaster's death." She did not go on. She could not bring herself to tell Gabriel about the lieutenant's unwelcome advances and the man's brutal treatment of Joshua. It would seem only to justify the taking of the man's life, for which she was certain there was no justification.

Casting her eyes downward, Serenity clutched her bundle more securely to her. Gabriel's silence told her that he believed her.

"Will you help us, Gabriel? Please . . . "

A light wind ruffling his night-dark hair, Gabriel stood on the quarterdeck, his lean body tense, a troubled expression on his chiseled features. His mind was on Serenity.

"Would you care to tell me about her, Gabriel?" Kane asked matter-of-factly, approaching him from behind. For some time, a strong friendship had existed between the two men, and when they were alone Kane used Gabriel's given name rather than calling him "Captain."

Not bothering to turn around, Gabriel continued to gaze straight ahead. "There's nothing to tell," was his curt reply.

Kane was nearly as tall as Gabriel, with penetrating eyes that appeared sometimes brown, sometimes green. Ruggedly handsome, he sported a touch of gray in his brown hair and a short beard.

"How long have we sailed together?" Kane asked patiently. "Five years now? Six? Since you took me off that blasted British hellship and saved me from being cut to ribbons by a cat-o-nine? They called me a deserter, but you blew them out of the water and took me aboard the *Firefly*. You know I'll never forget that. And I'd stand by you, right or wrong."

"You care to tell me what you're getting at, Kane?"

"In these past five years I've gotten to know you, my friend. True, there are a few things I missed out on—like how you got that scar on your cheek. But, for the most part, I've been there beside you. Now, devil take it, I feel I don't understand you at all. Would you care to explain just what's going on between you and the lady?"

Gabriel leveled his gaze on Kane. He was in no mood to discuss Serenity with Kane, friend or not, yet he could see no way around it.

"You were the one who left me on that damnable island," Gabriel reminded him irritably. "Her name is Serenity. I could tell you recognized her the moment you saw her on deck today."

The wind was starting to come up. Kane braced himself against it. A slight grin touched his mouth as he replied, "Yes, I remembered. She's not an easy woman to forget. I'll admit that." He paused for a moment, his eyes resting on Gabriel's face. "I almost felt sorry for you at the time, leaving you there with her. She's beautiful. And a Quaker. I figured you would go crazy wanting to bed her. But you're a man of principles. I never doubted you could handle it. And once you were off the island, I thought that would end it. I've never known you to linger over a pretty skirt for long."

Gabriel frowned darkly. "For what it's worth, when I left the island I didn't expect, nor did I want to see her again. I felt it was best that way."

"If that's the truth, then turn back for Nantucket," Kane countered hastily. "It's the logical thing to do. It would only be two days out of the *Firefly*'s way. The lady is not some common doxy you'd tumble for a fortnight, then leave at the nearest port. Not to mention the fact that there's a war on and she's in danger so long as she remains aboard this vessel."

Gabriel had meant what he said when he told Kane he'd thought it was best if he never saw Serenity again. Yet, now that he knew what had happened to the lieutenant, he could not return her to Nantucket.

"I have no intention of turning back," Gabriel countered, aware that the subject was rapidly becoming a matter of contention between the two of them.

Kane looked stunned. "Damnation, man! And would you care to tell me why not?"

A muscle twitched along Gabriel's strong jaw. He could not tell anyone about the British officer's death, not even Kane. Serenity was definitely in need of protection. Besides, there were still too many unanswered questions. Something about the whole situation was not right. Serenity had been deliberately evasive when she told him about what had happened, and he had not missed the anguished look on her beautiful face and in her blue eyes. If he thought the lieutenant had hurt her in some way, he would have gladly killed the man himself.

"Serenity won't be going back to Nantucket," he said with finality.

"Then you refuse to give the Quaker up? Have you lost all decency? You intend to use her and then discard her without a second thought?"

Gabriel's silvery gaze swept back toward the water, and a muscle twitched beneath his scarred cheek as he replied, "Not exactly . . . "

"What is it, then?" Kane asked bluntly, refusing to let it go.

Gabriel's response was equally blunt. "She's my wife. . . . "

Witnessing Kane's look of total astonishment, Gabriel

added, "And if you do not choose to answer a number of very pointed questions for the crew, I would suggest you not mention that fact—since I intend to be bunking with you for the time being."

Chapter Nine

Slipping through the cabin door with Biscuit close behind her, Serenity ascended the stairway to the deck. It was a brisk morning. The wind was up; the deck was wet and slippery. Walking gingerly, she fought to keep her balance. Wisps of red silky hair were torn from beneath her cap, tormenting her eyes, while her skirts whipped about her legs, making it difficult to walk. Biscuit followed along dutifully, not leaving her side.

Suddenly, the dog growled and halted in his tracks, his hackles up, and Serenity came face-to-face with the largest, most unpleasant-looking man she had ever seen.

Moving between her and the towering man, Biscuit growled again, this time louder and more viciously.

Serenity stood there uncertainly, at a loss for what to do.

As if from out of nowhere, Gabriel appeared. "Back away slowly, Valentine," he ordered softly. "The dog won't bother you so long as you don't get too close to her. Just back away slowly."

"Aye. Aye, Cap'n Harrowe," the ship's hand replied, obviously willing to do just that.

Surprisingly, the man did not seem so fearsome after he had spoken. In fact, Serenity was almost sorry they had not met more favorably; it was wrong to judge a man by his appearance.

Once the ship's hand had made his hasty retreat, Gabriel

wheeled about to face her. He looked tired, and something about him made him appear much harsher here aboard his vessel. His eyes appeared as cold as steel, and the scar on his cheek was more pronounced.

"Serenity," he demanded, "what are you doing out on deck?"

Despite herself, Serenity smiled. She felt a strange delight at seeing him again, even though she knew perfectly well he did not share her feelings. "Biscuit was growing restless inside the cabin. He needed his morning walk, and I assumed you were busy. I did not wish to bother you, Gabriel."

Though his gray eyes softened ever so slightly, his manner was still restrained. Heaving a sigh, he said, "Serenity, aboard this vessel, you can't move about as you would on Nantucket. You must use caution; these men are not like the Friends. You need to have someone with you at all times if you choose to leave the cabin."

"But I have Biscuit," she countered rationally, as though he had failed to see the obvious.

Gabriel threw a brief glance in the dog's direction and shrugged his broad shoulders slightly. "Yes. You have Biscuit," he concluded softly. "And at this point I suppose it is just as well. However, I still think it's advisable for you to be accompanied while out on deck. I'll see to it that Kane is with you from now on—whenever I am not available."

Though it was evident that the ship had been through many battles, the *Firefly* was a remarkable vessel, clean and well cared for. Still, Serenity found it was not as easy to stroll about as she had thought. When the open deck was wet, it was hazardous, and she had to watch her step. She quickly began to realize why it was so often said that one had to get one's sea legs.

Gabriel was uncomfortably silent while they walked, and his only move to touch her was when she slipped once on the deck and he quickly reached out to steady her. Not that she was hoping for anything more. No. Not at all. Their marriage and that wonderful night of passion were definitely in the past. Still, it was almost a relief when he took her belowdeck to the cabin once more, for more reasons than one. It was difficult being in his presence when he chose to act as though they were strangers.

As they stepped inside the cabin, Serenity was greeted by a simple meal of hot biscuits and thick slices of cheese that had been prepared and left on the table. It reminded Serenity that she had not as yet had breakfast, and she was decidedly hungry. Glancing over at Gabriel, she waited to see if he planned to eat with her.

"You are staying?" she asked without preliminaries.

For a moment, Gabriel seemed to hesitate; then a muscle tensed along his jaw. "I need to get back to my men," he stated tersely.

Suddenly, Serenity was filled with questions.

"Gabriel," she said, leveling her delicate chin, "I have need to talk to you. I must speak of the future. You now know of Lieutenant Lancaster's death. What is your decision? Will you take us to the mainland, or do you intend to return us to Nantucket?"

The mention of the lieutenant drew a dark frown from Gabriel, but he offered no reply.

"If you will just leave us on the mainland . . . "

There was a flicker of something in Gabriel's silver-gray eyes.

"I wish not to be a burden," she continued soberly. "I am your wife in name alone. You have no obligation to me. I asked for your aid only for Joshua's sake."

Gabriel's face suddenly became hard and implacable. Abruptly, he responded, "Serenity, there is a war going on and the British still blockade the coastline. Considering the circumstances, I have no intention of returning you to Nantucket. But neither will it be an easy matter to leave you on the mainland. For the time being, you have no choice but to remain aboard the *Firefly*." Then, after pausing for a moment, he ground out curtly, "And rest assured, I am well-reminded of our relationship . . . "

Serenity gazed at him in dismay as he wheeled about and

Gloria Pedersen

strode out of the cabin. It was obvious that she had made him
angry. But why? She had meant only to find out his intentions.
Had it been the mention of their ill-begotten marriage? Well, he
need not fear; she would never bring the subject up again. That
was one error she also wished desperately to forget.

With his long legs braced apart, Gabriel stood on the deck of
his vessel, frowning darkly at the man who stood before him.
"Would you care to explain the meaning of this, Kane? Since
when did every man aboard this vessel take leave of his senses?
Or should I ask? I have no doubt it has something to do with
Serenity."

Kane threw him a rare grin. "You've noticed, then?"

"How could I have failed to?" Gabriel retorted irritably.
"When I chose not to return Serenity to Nantucket, I never
imagined the entire crew would become addled because of it. In
all my time at sea, I've never seen so many shirts in need of
mending, nor minor injuries that needed a woman's attention,
nor stomachaches and the like, as I have in the two weeks since
she's been on board. They're wearing a path to her cabin door,
like a pack of panting schoolboys."

"You know how to put a stop to it, Gabriel. It's simple. Tell
them she's your wife. Warm her bed. That'd put a stop to it.
Maybe then every man-jack aboard would stop tryin' to ruffle
her skirts."

Gabriel shot him a challenging glance. "She's a Quaker. That
should be enough—"

"To keep them away?" Kane countered. "Hardly. She's a lady.
That's a wonder to men like them. They're a bit in awe of her.
Most of them haven't been around a woman who didn't come
with a price. Still, if anything, you should be relieved," he continued, his hazel eyes touched by a hint of amusement. "The
Quaker's in no danger from them; they think she's a saint. The
first man to lay a hand on her would have six other men on his
back in a thrice. If things were any different, you could have

90

found yourself fighting off the entire crew over her. Single-handedly. Would that have been any better?"

"Including you?" Gabriel asked bluntly, his steely gaze pinning Kane to the spot where he stood.

Kane hesitated for a moment. "She's your wife, Gabriel. Though at the moment I'd be hard pressed to understand why. An act of conscience? Repayment for her saving your life? I'm not blind. You've been edgy as a mountain cat since she's been on board. One would suspect your own emotions are not quite as intact as you'd have everyone believe where the lady is concerned."

With several small steps, Serenity marked the confines of the cabin, then she stopped and pivoted slowly around. A short time before, Joshua had come to take Biscuit for his evening walk. Then, shortly thereafter, another visitor had arrived.

"You have been most kind to me, Kane," Serenity said softly, her delicate face turned upward to meet the man's compelling gaze. "But you need not apologize for your captain."

Kane appeared dissatisfied with her reply. "He could have returned you to Nantucket. . . ."

Serenity sighed. She could not explain to the first mate why Gabriel had not done so. Yet, she had come to realize the magnitude of the situation in which she had placed Gabriel. He could not reveal the details of Lieutenant Lancaster's death to anyone, and his silence regarding her continued presence aboard the ship made him suspect in the eyes of his crew. It was no secret that every man aboard expected their captain to break down her door at any moment and take her upon his pallet. They saw her as the helpless victim, waiting upon their captain's slightest whim, when all the while Gabriel was merely protecting her from her own folly.

"Kane, your regard is greatly appreciated," she said lightly. "But I need not fear the captain. His harshness is to be understood."

A doubtful expression crossed Kane's features. "Still, should you ever need anything . . . "

"And just what might she need, my friend?" a strong voice interjected as the door was swung wide and Gabriel stepped inside. His dark brows were drawn together in a frown, and his sensual lips were tight. For a moment, he stood there glowering at the two of them.

"Nothing, Captain. Nothing at all," Kane replied. He started to make a hasty retreat.

As the other man left the cabin, Gabriel remarked pointedly, "I'll see you on deck, Kane." Then, briefly, a muscle tightening along his jaw, Gabriel continued, "Did I interrupt something?"

Serenity did not like his manner. She had only seen Gabriel behave this way one other time—the night when he'd told her they would wed and she had disagreed. This time, she would not tolerate his show of temper.

There was a flash of fire in her blue eyes. "You need not take your ire out on Kane, when it is clearly me with whom you are angry."

"Did I say I was angry?"

"You leave little doubt."

"Have I need to be, Serenity?" he asked. "The entire British Navy could not have done more to disrupt my vessel than you have done with your two small hands in the short time you have been on board. One would think that gives me the right to be a little angry."

Serenity frowned. "I fail to see . . . "

Lithe and dangerous, he stood there gazing down at her. "Do you?" he inquired. His long, lean body seemed to dominate the room.

She had vowed never to lose her temper with him again, but his manner was insufferable. If he had not been brought to her door, she would never have found herself aboard his vessel in the first place. As if that were not enough, it did not help matters that suddenly she was reminded in vivid detail of the night she had spent in his arms. And she was appallingly certain he was thinking of the same thing. Hot color rose to her cheeks.

Pivoting quickly around, she refused to let him see how he was unnerving her.

But he did not leave, and she could feel the charged atmosphere between them. Without speaking, he moved to stand behind her and his strong arms encompassed her small waist, drawing her backward against him. Slowly and sensuously, with her back pressed to him, his hands massaged her stomach in enticing circles, then moved up along her rib cage, taking her breath away.

Slipping upward, the palms of his hands cupped her breasts gently but firmly. They tingled, and a treacherous warmth began to spread through her. He had no right . . . Yet he did. He had every right.

He kissed the side of her neck, just below her ear. She tilted her head slightly to give him free access, feeling the heat of his mouth. It was a sweet torture, reminding her of so much that she had vowed to forget.

She could feel his hard contours through the thin fabric of her gown. His strength. His heat. His fingertips brushed the tips of her breasts, teasing. Tantalizing. She leaned against him.

"Please stop . . . " she murmured helplessly. "Please . . . "

Turning her in his arms, he did not release her. She saw his eyes were like silver, shot through with lightning. A dark lock of hair had once more fallen onto his forehead. His mouth was mere inches from her own. She already knew what it would feel like to have his mouth claim hers. To have his body . . . She had gone to him innocently the first time. Now she was innocent no longer.

Abruptly, there was a sharp rap on the cabin door. Instantly alert, Gabriel wheeled away from her, his composure again intact.

At his command, Kane swung the door open. "Sorry, Captain," he said, his concerned gaze flickering briefly over Serenity's disheveled state. He hesitated. "I thought you'd want to know. A vessel has been sighted."

Gabriel's body tensed. "Where away, Kane?"

"Directly astern, sir."

"What flag does she fly?" Gabriel shot back.

"No flag," Kane replied.

"Don't leave this cabin, Serenity," Gabriel ordered tersely, his steely gaze making her aware that he would brook no argument. Then, in less than a heartbeat, he and his first mate were gone.

Still shaken, Serenity sat down numbly on the bed. Her emotions were in a turmoil, but it was not due to the sighting of any strange ship. What did it mean? Gabriel's anger; the way he had held her; was this some kind of game for which she had not learned the rules?

Chapter Ten

The vessel, an armed frigate, had not shown its colors until it had nearly been too late. The cannons had been primed. But the ship had turned out merely to be another American privateer, hailing from Virginia, and the two had parted company as the darkness of the night closed in. Still, for Gabriel, it had been a sobering experience.

He could hardly engage in any kind of a battle with Serenity on board. He knew that now. Meanwhile, his men, with the heat of the thwarted confrontation still hot in their veins, were all the more desirous of seeking out and taking the next British vessel that came into sight. The only solution was to get Serenity quickly to the mainland. But where? How could he break through the British blockade to set Serenity ashore?

Knocking softly on the door to the cabin, Gabriel hesitated for a moment. It was late. If Serenity was already asleep, he did not want to disturb her. Yet, if she was still awake, she should be told that there was no longer anything to fear. Gently, he pushed the door open.

The lantern was still lit. Biscuit raised his head for a moment, then whimpered and lay back down.

Clad in a white nightgown, Serenity lay upon the bed. Her copper hair was spread about her on the pillow. Long and silky, it lay like a shadow about her enchanting face, now made almost angelic by slumber. Her grandma's quilt was drawn up to just below the gentle swell of her breasts. He could see them rise and fall with her quiet breathing.

Suddenly, he felt the weariness that had become such a part of him. He wondered what it would be like to lie in bed with her again, to feel her warmth beside him. He had not forgotten what it had been like before, though he'd denied it from the first moment he had known she was aboard.

It was not going to be an easy matter resisting Serenity until he could see her safely from his hands. Still, that was what he had to do. She came from another, gentler world. One in which he had no wish to intrude. If anything, he deserved someone more like Veronique. Someone who had no illusions about what they were getting, and undoubtedly would give back the same.

Serenity stirred. "Gabriel . . ." she murmured.

He moved closer to the bed. His long, lean body cried out to hold her. "Go back to sleep. There is no more danger. The ship was only another American privateer."

Her dark lashes fluttered for a moment, then her incredible blue velvet eyes opened wide. She stretched her arms above her head, and a hint of a smile touched her soft pink mouth. "I am sorry I made you angry, Gabriel. With so much anger in the world, it is wrong for us to cause each other pain as well."

"It was nothing," he replied, no longer certain why he had been angry with her in the first place. It was not Serenity's fault if all his men were behaving like complete imbeciles over her. She had not asked for it.

Turning, he went over to put out the lamp and leave her to sleep.

"I have been meaning to thank you, Gabriel. Joshua has been extremely happy since he has been on board the *Firefly*. It had always been his dream to one day be a ship's hand, as his father was before him. He would never have had the opportunity. You have been most kind to look after him. . . ."

His strong hands poised by the lamp, Gabriel glanced back over at her and replied, "Joshua has been no problem." Serenity had raised herself up. For a moment, his eyes rested on the smooth curve of her neck, then followed it to the hollow at the base of her throat. Not too long ago, he had traced kisses along that very path. "I have reached a decision, Serenity. I plan to see both you and Joshua to the mainland as quickly as possible. You're not safe so long as you remain aboard my vessel. There is always the chance we might have to confront the British." Then, as though that was all he had come to say, he put out the lamp and started for the door. "Good night," he said softly.

With the slightest movement, Serenity was suddenly there beside him. He could feel her presence in the darkness, her slender body close to his. A warning voice sounded inside him.

Placing a delicate hand on his arm, Serenity detained him. "It was most kind of you to have come," she murmured in barely more than a whisper.

Gabriel hesitated. Unbidden, the memory of her warmth came back to haunt him once again. It would be so easy . . .

A muscle tightened along his jaw and he quickly stepped away from her. "Damn!" he cursed softly under his breath, knowing he was a fool for wanting there to be anything more between them. He shook his head. Then, wheeling about, he strode out the door and did not stop until he had reached the deck, where the cool night mists engulfed him.

* * *

Would she ever understand Gabriel? Would she? When he was being his kindest, it seemed she understood him less than when he was full of anger.

Since the night he had come to her cabin, Gabriel had scarcely spoken a word to her, and except for the knowledge that he intended to leave her on the mainland as soon as possible, she had no idea of what he might be thinking. Yet, she could see no reason for him to avoid her.

Although she'd vowed to stop thinking of him, there was little else for her to do. She had tried to keep busy since coming aboard the *Firefly*; idleness was a luxury she had never enjoyed. Still, aside from mending occasional shirts for the crewmen or tending to minor wounds, she had nothing else to fill her days.

It was this lack of something to do that finally prompted Serenity into cajoling Kane into giving her a more thorough tour of the vessel, complete with an inspection of the cannons. However, had she'd known at the time that it would meet with such disastrous results only a short while later, she might have thought better of it.

The brass cannon went off with a resounding boom, knocking Serenity backward with its tremendous force. Stunned, she landed rather ignominiously on her derriere, momentarily deafened by the blast. She should never have encouraged Donovan and Brady to take their demonstration quite so far; the two men had unintentionally set the cannon off while Kane had been distracted elsewhere.

Although there was no major damage done, Serenity continued to sit there as Kane rushed to her side. "It is my ankle," Serenity explained, wincing at the pain. She did not care to explain that her posterior hurt as well, and that there was still a ringing in her ears. Kane appeared distressed enough as it was. "I turned it once before, not long ago," she said, remembering vividly the day she had thrown the egg at Gabriel. "It was still weak. But otherwise I am fine."

Her face smudged with soot, Serenity smiled brightly up at the man who had come to be her friend since she had been aboard the vessel. "If you will but give me a hand, Kane, perhaps it would be well if I returned to the cabin, before the others come to investigate."

Kane frowned. "Are you certain you're all right, Quaker? I was wrong to have left you alone for even a moment with these clumsy oafs."

"It was merely an accident," she countered. "Please. Do not let it trouble you."

Kneeling down beside her, Kane scooped her into his strong arms. "We'll get you back to the cabin, then we'll take a look at your ankle," he said, lifting her up. "And rest assured there'll be no more demonstrations of cannon while you're aboard this vessel. It's fortunate the captain wasn't here, or every man involved would feel the sting of the lash before this day was out."

With that, Kane strode purposefully toward the deck with Serenity cradled in his arms. However, their progress was halted scant moments later when they came face-to-face with the very man they both had been silently hoping to avoid. Gabriel!

Serenity gasped. There was a look of hot anger on Gabriel's face that was instantly masked by a far too casual demeanor.

"Would you care to explain the meaning of this, Kane?"

Grimacing slightly, Kane stood helplessly with her in his arms. "Would it do any good, Captain?"

"No. At this point, I would think not. But you might try . . ."

"It was my fault," Serenity volunteered, anxious to shield Kane and the others from what she knew would undoubtedly be a most unpleasant confrontation.

"How is that?" he countered dryly, his icy stare making a touch of bright color rise to her cheeks.

As the crew gazed on, Gabriel and Kane stood awkwardly facing each other, Serenity still cradled against Kane's chest.

Without a word, Kane reached out and thrust Serenity toward Gabriel, dropping her unceremoniously into his arms. Although taken by surprise, Gabriel's strong arms caught and held her. For a moment, Serenity was afraid to look up. Then, despite the seriousness of the situation, she could also see the humor, and a smile teased at the corners of her mouth.

"That will be all, Kane," Gabriel snapped. Then, turning on his heels, Gabriel strode purposefully in the direction of the cabin with her still in his arms. Once inside, he kicked the door shut behind him. Striding over to the bed, he set her down.

Laughing silently, she gazed up at him. "The only thing missing was the basket of eggs . . ."

Gabriel did not reply. He was looking at her in a way that made her breathless. It was fiery and intense. Leaning down, his mouth touched hers. It felt achingly wonderful and left her shaky inside. Would he stay? She was utterly shameless to want him so. Yet . . .

He drew away. His hand brushed back the silky hair from her cheek, then he gently ran a fingertip caressingly along her rosy lips.

"You are so very beautiful," he said, his eyes a deep silvery gray. "Even with soot on your face . . ." Then he was gone.

Kane had been forced to suppress a grin when he'd seen the smudge of soot upon the captain's cheek. He remembered well the soot from the cannon that had been on Serenity's face only a short time before. It was obvious his friend was having a difficult time keeping his distance from the woman, despite his strong determination to do so.

Kane had to admit that he too had fallen under Serenity's spell since she had been on board. But the beautiful Quaker was his captain's bride. And if that was not enough to make him keep a tight rein on his emotions, Kane had also witnessed the way Gabriel and Serenity looked at each other whenever they thought no one else was aware. The way Kane saw it, if the two of them were not in love already, they were the next best thing to it.

Admittedly, there was a time when Kane had thought Gabriel

incapable of ever loving at all. Kane knew about the death of Gabriel's brother, Brandon, and how Gabriel had always held himself personally responsible. Somehow his bitterness over the whole affair had colored Gabriel's existence, leaving his friend with a desire to keep a barrier between himself and anyone who tried to get too close. Obviously, Gabriel was determined not to make any exception where Serenity was concerned. However, Kane had no doubt that his friend would be an incredible fool if he let her get away. . . .

"Captain," Kane said, briskly approaching him on the deck.

The crimson sky was turning to dusk. Lost in thought, Gabriel was watching its dying rays, a frown creasing his dark brow. He wheeled about. "Kane . . . " he said.

"I think you should take a look at her," Kane responded hastily.

"What are you talking about?"

"The Quaker," Kane shot back. "Her ankle has started to swell. I think it could be broken."

"Broken?" Gabriel asked. "How well did you examine it?"

Kane hesitated. "Not too well, Captain. I was afraid of hurting her and figured you wouldn't want anyone else touching her."

Gabriel looked torn. "I'll see to her," he said. "It seems we'll have no peace so long as Serenity is aboard. The sooner we set her ashore, the better."

Kane kept his expression innocent. "That might be true, my friend. But on the other hand, I have a feeling the days might be damned long after she's gone. . . . "

Kane grinned to himself as Gabriel strode away. Everything was working exactly as he had anticipated. He had already sent Joshua to take the dog for a walk and told the boy not to return until he told him to. Now, he would just have to sit back and see what happened. With any luck, Gabriel and Serenity would do the rest.

* * *

There was a soft knock on the cabin door; then Gabriel stepped inside. His face was grim.

Serenity was seated on the bed. She had not been expecting him and was already dressed for bed, brushing her flame-colored hair in long, sweeping strokes. Her ankle, though tender, had not prevented her from getting around.

"Gabriel . . . "

He came toward her. "I came to have a look at your ankle."

"Oh," she replied. "That is most kind of you, but my ankle is quite all right. You need not trouble yourself."

"It is no trouble," he countered, his manner brisk. He knelt beside the bed. "Which one is it?"

She set her brush aside and smiled sweetly. "This one. The same one that I injured on Nantucket."

Gently, his long fingers checked her slender joint. As his head bent toward it, Serenity had to resist the impulse to brush the errant lock of dark hair from his forehead, merely to touch him. She was enjoying his concern, though she guiltily reminded herself that there was no need for it at all.

"Why did you leave without any farewell?" she asked bravely.

"When?"

"On Nantucket."

Gabriel glanced up at her. His eyes were suddenly sparked with a silver flame. "I thought it would be better that way."

"Better for me? Or for you?"

She saw the familiar tensing along his jaw. His hand lingered on her leg just above the ankle. He did not reply.

"Were you angered because I came to you?" she asked. "Did you not find me pleasing?"

He started to rise as though he meant to leave. She slipped from the bed and moved to stop him. His ruggedly handsome face loomed above her, and their bodies were close enough to touch. He was the most compellingly masculine man she'd ever known. Still, she was not afraid.

Gloria Pedersen

"If I promise to try very hard to please you, will you stay?"

Suddenly, she was inside his embrace, and the gentle probing of his tongue seared her mouth. She felt its tender touch. Curling her arms around his neck, she tangled her fingers in his thick dark hair.

As if in reply, Gabriel's hands slipped up the side of her slender body, drawing her still closer. Then he lifted her slightly to arch her toward him. She could feel the hard contours of his body through her nightdress and was aware of his musky scent. She caught her breath.

His own breathing quickening, Gabriel murmured, "I don't think we should be doing this. . . . "

"Why?" she whispered, grazing the curve of his neck with soft kisses. "Why? I want to know what it is to have you make love to me again."

With a groan, Gabriel pressed her down on the bed. Poised above her, he tasted her rose-tipped breasts through the thin fabric of her nightdress, leaving the material taut and damp. His tongue teased a circle around the small buds, until she felt a strange, erotic languor sweep over her. Then, moving downward, his questing mouth kissed each curve and hollow through the fabric of her gown.

The way he made her feel was so sweetly intoxicating that she wanted to put all else from her mind. But, no; she had promised him that this time she would please him. He would not regret . . .

Rolling to one side, she traced patterns around his earlobe with her small pink tongue. Then, moving to nibble at his lower lip, her delicate hands slipped downward to part his shirt. Her silky hair fell forward as she bent to kiss his strong bare chest.

With insistent hands, she removed his shirt, then moved to his breeches. She could feel him tremble as she set out on a quest of her own. Gabriel's body was so strong, so well-formed. She felt his passion flare beneath her touch, and sweat dampened his smooth flesh.

The first time they had come together she had been unaware of her own feminine powers; *he* had been in command. Now, it was strangely exhilarating to know the way she could make him feel as well.

Growing impatient, Gabriel started to push her back on the bed. With one swift movement, he urgently pulled her beneath him and arched her head back to trail tiny feverish kisses down her neck. The heat from their bodies left her nightdress damp and tangled about her hips, her long legs exposed. Gently sliding it up, he moved between her thighs. His face was drawn; his hard body was poised above hers.

"No," she whispered, not yet content to have him claim her. "This time, I promised to please you. . . ."

For a moment, his silvery gaze traveled over her face. Then, in a pained whisper, he murmured, "Rest assured, sweet Serenity, you have pleased me quite enough already. If I am to have any regrets of this night, it will not be because of you. . . ."

Chapter Eleven

"It will soon be dark, Quaker," Kane said. "Are you ready?"

"Yes," Serenity replied in a small voice, glancing at the bundle containing her grandma's quilt and her few belongings that sat waiting on the bed.

"We plan to slip through the blockade under cover of darkness. Tonight clouds will cover the moon. With any luck the British won't spot us. But you'll need to put out your lantern, Captain's orders. There can't be the slightest light visible aboard when we go through the blockade."

Turning, Serenity did not want Kane to see the sudden look of anguish that crossed her face. Now that the time had come, she was finding it more difficult than she had imagined to leave the vessel, never to see Gabriel again. It had been destined to end this way, even from the beginning. She knew that. Yet, despite everything, only the night before when Gabriel had held her . . .

"There is no need to be afraid, Quaker."

Her troubled eyes moist with unshed tears, Serenity turned back around. "Was he so anxious to be rid of me, Kane? You must tell me."

"No," Kane replied, knowing precisely whom she meant, his manner oddly gentle. "I think not. But he has no other choice, Quaker. You can't remain aboard the ship. You'll be safer on the mainland. What he feels—or doesn't feel—makes no difference."

"Will I ever see him again?"

Kane heaved a weary sigh. "I couldn't say. The captain is not an easy man to understand. There are times even I'm not certain what he's thinking." Wheeling about, the man started for the door. "The captain has given me orders to see you and Joshua to shore. I'll be back for you when the time comes, Quaker. Be ready. We'll have to move quickly. There won't be much time."

Serenity numbly watched Kane go. The man had always been kind to her since she had been aboard the *Firefly,* and she was not sorry he would be the one taking her to shore. Still, she had hoped that Gabriel . . .

The wait in the darkness was plagued with worry. Her legs curled beneath her on the bed, Serenity tried to rest, but she could not help contemplating the future. What would it be like to live on the mainland? She had never been there before except as a student, and then she'd boarded with a distant cousin. How would she and Joshua survive?

She was uncertain how much time had passed when the door was jerked open. Through the darkness, she could see a tall, masculine form looming in the space.

For a moment he just stood there. "Serenity . . . "

It was not Kane. It was Gabriel.

"I'm here," she said, rising from the bed.

"Are you ready?"

"Yes," she replied tersely.

Stepping forward through the darkness, Gabriel gently grasped her slender shoulders. "Kane will see you to shore," he explained heavily. "I have a contact on the mainland. His name is Reynolds. He was my commanding officer when I served in the Navy. He'll look after you and take you on to Washington. I'll have word sent on ahead. When you reach there, Reynolds will take you to the home of someone who'll be expecting you. You and Joshua will be safe."

"It was not necessary, Gabriel. You need not trouble yourself. Joshua and I . . . " She paused to draw a deep breath. "We can manage."

He drew her closer. "Don't make this more difficult, Serenity . . . " Surprisingly, he bent to kiss her.

She did not resist. The kiss was warm and compelling, yet there was something bittersweet in its finality. She knew it was farewell.

Finally releasing her, he murmured, "Come. There's little time . . . "

Even as she followed him, Serenity ached inside. Her emotions were in turmoil. Suddenly, it seemed unbearable that she would never see him again. She wanted to stop him. To throw herself into his arms. If only everything could be different . . .

Bathed in the scant light of the moon, Serenity, Joshua, and Biscuit were lowered into a small waiting boat. Then, with Kane and Joshua manning the oars, they started for shore. Serenity refused to look back at the ghostly shape of the *Firefly* as they got farther and farther away. It hurt to know she was leaving Gabriel behind as well.

Once they had reached the shore, Kane admonished them to stay there while he went in search of the man called Reynolds. Huddled together, they waited. An interminable length of time seemed to pass. Then, finally, Kane and another man appeared out of the darkness, along with a horsedrawn carriage.

After hasty introductions, Reynolds held a lantern high while

Kane prepared to climb back into the boat once more. Dawn would soon be etching the sky, and the *Firefly* would be in grave danger if the vessel did not slip back through the blockade before it was light.

Nodding at Joshua and giving Biscuit a final pat, Kane turned to Serenity. "Good-bye and good luck, Quaker," he said.

Impulsively, Serenity moved forward to give Kane a hug. "I want to thank you, Kane. For everything."

There was something almost tender in the way he gazed at her. "If ever you should need anything, Serenity . . . "

"I shall be all right," she murmured. "Take care of the *Firefly*. And I shall miss you all."

Kane seemed to hesitate. "He's a fool . . . " Kane said, just loudly enough so that only she would hear.

There was no need for Kane to explain exactly whom he meant. But, as she watched him climb into the boat and saw it slip away from shore, one word repeated itself over and over in her mind, bringing a disturbing ache to her heart. *Gabriel* . . .

The journey to Washington was a pleasant one, and after a brief stay at the Reynolds estate, they'd been on their way.

Admittedly, John Reynolds was an impressive man. Just on the verge of being elderly, with a slight paunch and sideburns that blossomed about his round cheeks, he was well versed in everything—the history of the land, all of the flora and fauna—and he was only too pleased to point out everything noteworthy along the way. Serenity found the man completely fascinating. In a deep, rumbling voice, he entertained as well as informed.

"Of course, L'Enfant was never to complete his great plan," Reynolds explained as they discussed the beginnings of Washington, the capitol of the young nation. "You see my dear Serenity the poor man was booted for various reasons. Andrew Ellicott took over, assisted, it would seem, by a talented and often overlooked free Negro by the name of Benjamin Banneker. But L'Enfant and his dream of a Federal city were at the start of it all."

Clad in her cap and simple gown, Serenity smiled. "The city sounds delightful, sir. I am eager to see it."

"Well," he said proudly and cleared his throat. "I hope I have described it adequately, since it is to be your new home. Captain Harrowe has bid me send a message on ahead so the Fairadays will be expecting your arrival. A fine family, the Fairadays. Michael Fairaday is an amiable young senator, and his wife Carissa is well known for her beauty and graciousness. I know you shall feel most welcome there."

For a brief moment, a look of doubt crossed Serenity's lovely face. She did not look forward to staying with strangers, even ones as amiable as Reynolds had claimed. "I shall be most grateful to the Fairadays, sir. But I have no intention of staying for long. As soon as I find employment, Joshua and I shall seek a place of our own. I wish not to be a burden to anyone."

"Oh, my dear, most certainly you would not be a burden. I do admire your spirit. Not many young women would take their lives in hand to fend for themselves as you have done. Obviously, that is why Captain Harrowe has made it a point to see you properly established. A woman with beauty and brains is a rare thing indeed. You have spunk. Spunk, my dear. Not like most women, who must rely upon men for their comfort."

A frown still creased Serenity's fine brow, and her blue eyes remained troubled, though she did not reply. She did not think of herself as having spunk. Yet, if that was true, she was certainly in need of it now. There was only herself on whom she could rely, that was for certain.

Still, a short time later, when their carriage pulled up in front of the Fairadays' manse, she was pleasantly surprised to find that everything John Reynolds had said about them was true.

"How delightful to have you stay with us, Serenity," Carissa Fairaday said, drawing her inside, with Joshua and Biscuit following close behind. "All of your rooms are in readiness. And

107

we shall be dining very soon. I'm certain you must be weary and hungry after such a long journey."

Carissa Fairaday was a lovely woman who possessed a certain ageless quality. Her upswept hair was tawny in color, as were her sparkling eyes, while her face was smooth and unlined. She wore a gown of deep gold velvet that emphasized her unusual coloring, and jewels twinkled at her ears and throat.

"Please feel you are welcome here," Carissa continued, her manner warm and genuine. "I have been so in need of company."

Gazing about her, Serenity could not help being impressed with the beauty and opulence of the room. Brocades and satins draped the windows and covered the furniture. A handsome writing desk and carved tables lined the walls; objets d'art sat about the room. An ornate clock rested on the mantel of the marble fireplace, while a painting of George Washington hung just above.

"Your home is very beautiful," Serenity observed.

"Why, thank you, Serenity. But wait until you see Colonel John Tayloe's Octagon House. Of course, it is actually hexagonal in form. But that is splitting hairs, I suppose. It is *truly* lovely. And everyone is always impressed. One day, I shall take you there to visit."

As Carissa led them into the drawing room, Serenity felt as though she had stumbled upon a different world. "Perhaps my dog should remain in the stables," Serenity said, feeling that she was already imposing far too much upon the woman's hospitality.

Carissa tilted back her head and laughed, her golden eyes dancing in merriment. "No, of course not, my dear. Gabriel has explained in his missive. I was expecting the dog. I have arranged a suite of rooms for Joshua and Biscuit, with easy access to the out of doors," she replied, using the dog's name as though they had known each other far longer than only a few brief minutes. It was obvious Gabriel had told her that as well.

"You are most kind, Madame Fairaday," Serenity replied.

"Oh, no, my dear. I am delighted to have you. I am certain if Gabriel wanted you . . . And please, will you call me Cat? A childhood name, I fear, but one which has remained with me my entire life. I must admit I do much prefer it to Carissa. We are going to be friends, I am certain of that. Friends must call each other by their dearest names. Now, don't you agree?"

Serenity could not help smiling. She had never known anyone quite so captivating as Carissa Fairaday. Obviously, the woman could have anyone under her spell in less than a few short moments. It was no wonder Gabriel had seen fit to send her here.

"Friends, Serenity?"

"Friends, Cat," Serenity replied in return.

Frowning slightly, Carissa Fairaday read again the missive she had received from Gabriel; then, folding it, she quickly put it once more in the drawer. What was her charming rake of a cousin up to anyway? Though Carissa was older than Gabriel, they had grown up together, and she knew him well. When they were children, he had always been up to some devilish trick or adventure, and she'd never been surprised by anything he'd done. Yet, this was somehow different. And she was not certain she approved of his latest escapade in the least.

Serenity was a Quaker. Gabriel had not said that in his letter. And beautiful. Very. What kind of a strange relationship did the two of them share? Gabriel had never lacked for women, though there were few of them of whom one could approve. But Serenity?

Stranger still was Gabriel's request that she not reveal that the two of them were cousins, that he had asked her as a personal favor to see to Serenity's welfare, and that he had even provided a generous stipend of money to be used on the girl's behalf. Well, it was that request which had made her know she must take matters into her own hands.

Her cousin Gabriel be hanged, she would see to it that Serenity was introduced to a nice young man. Someone quite suitable, of course. And she would have Serenity safely wed before Gabriel's return. It was the best thing for the girl. She refused to be a party to having an innocent like Serenity compromised by her cousin's vanity.

"Cat . . . " Serenity began as she stepped into the drawing room, "I hope I am not interrupting you."

"Why, no. Of course not, Serenity. I am delighted to have your company. Since my children are grown and away, it is a pleasure to have someone in the house once more."

Taking a seat on a high-backed chair, Serenity sat nervously facing Carissa. "I cannot thank you enough for your kindness, Cat. You have done so much. But, please, I must insist that you do no more. I cannot accept the gowns."

"I do not understand, Serenity," Carissa replied, feeling genuinely distressed when only a short time before she had been so elated, knowing the gowns seemed so perfect for the Quaker girl. "Perhaps I should have consulted you, but I was so anxious for you to have them. If they are not to your liking, we can consult the dressmaker and have her make more. You can select anything you like. You may choose the colors. The fabrics. The styles . . . "

"It is not the gowns," Serenity reassured her. "They are far lovelier than I could ever imagine."

"Perhaps it is in the way they fit?"

"Please, Cat. You must believe me. I would not change them in the least. But I am used to plainer fare." Serenity's blue gaze dropped to where one delicate hand smoothed the skirt of her one and only serviceable gown. "Those gowns are far too fine. And much too costly. I could not accept them as a gift. And I could never repay you the cost of what they are worth. Therefore I cannot accept them. Please understand," she concluded softly. "I do not wish to seem ungrateful."

Suddenly understanding, Carissa sighed. *Drat that cousin of mine,* she thought with irritation. Serenity must at least be told about the gowns.

"Serenity . . . " Carissa began. "So long as you are pleased with the gowns, you must keep them. Or choose others. It is you who do not understand. The gowns were a gift, but not from me. Gabriel arranged for them to be purchased for you, but he bade me not to tell. Perhaps he feared you would feel compromised. And perhaps you do. But it was his gift, and his alone. You have no choice but to accept them."

For a moment, Serenity was speechless. "Gabriel should not . . . "

"I know, my dear. It is a bit uncomfortable. But nothing that cannot be fixed. Trust me. I will see matters set right before you know it."

Serenity felt strange as she twirled before the mirror in one of the new outfits. All of the gowns were plain and simply cut, as though the dressmaker had known precisely what she would wear, yet this one was special. Where the rest of the gowns were in shades of plum and gray, this one was of deep blue velvet and matched precisely the color of her eyes. She had never thought to own a gown quite so lovely. Had Gabriel instructed Carissa on exactly what to buy?

Of course, Gabriel had been correct in assuming she would never accept the gowns from him directly. She would not deny that. However, there was little she could do about them now.

It is his sense of duty, Serenity reminded herself again as she fastened her long flame-colored hair securely upon her head. Nothing more. Still, she wondered.

A soft knock on the door interrupted her thoughts, and Serenity quickly spun away from the mirror in anticipation.

"Oh, my dear Serenity," Carissa said, as she hurried into the bedchamber. "You truly look lovely. Gabriel was right. Such a wonderful color for you . . . "

Shyly, Serenity smiled. Compliments were something new to her, and it was wrong for her to take much notice. Yet, she appreciated Carissa's enthusiasm just the same. She was extremely nervous about meeting Carissa and Senator Fairaday's friends.

Carissa motioned for her to follow. "Come, now. The dinner guests are arriving. It will be your introduction to Washington society. And I have someone in particular I am most anxious for you to meet. An attractive young senator from Pennsylvania. A Quaker, Nathaniel Bentley." Then, she added with a sly wink, "And he is wonderfully available too."

For a moment, Serenity was too stunned to reply. Did Carissa think she might take a personal interest in the young senator? Of course, Carissa did not know about her marriage to Gabriel.

"Cat," Serenity began, trying to stop her, "Cat . . ."

But it was too late. Carissa had already disappeared out of the room.

Chapter Twelve

The invitation requesting the presence of Senator and Carissa Fairaday to dine at the Octagon House on the next Tuesday also included Serenity. Still, though she had readily accepted the invitation, as Serenity climbed into the carriage on the night of the event and the driver set the matched bays on a brisk pace toward their destination, she could not help dreading the evening ahead.

Despite some self-recriminations, Serenity had decided against confiding in Carissa that she and Gabriel were wed. Obviously, the alliance between Gabriel and herself was not a marriage in the true sense of the word. And if Gabriel had wanted anyone to know, he would have revealed the fact himself. Consequently, Serenity felt she could not reveal it either. Still, it had left her with a dilemma which threatened the evening ahead. Whatever was she to do about the young senator from Pennsylvania, Nathaniel Bentley?

Upon their arrival, Serenity found Octagon House to be every bit as impressive as Carissa had described it. Built for Colonel John Tayloe on a plot of ground that was formed by an acute angle of two converging streets, it was unique in shape and design, and quite the most unusual structure Serenity had ever seen.

Hundreds of candles welcomed the guests as they walked through the door, while liveried servants served wine and attended to their every need. The tables were set with still more candles and fine china, while the sideboards were laden with an astounding assortment of food. Roast turkey, roast duck, whole rounds of roast beef, fried beef, a new foreign dish called macaroni, several kinds of ices, mounds of cakes and tarts. Never before had Serenity seen such fare.

The guests were equally as resplendent as the food. Dressed in her discreet plum gown with a white bonnet covering her hair, Serenity felt quite out of place amidst the array of turbans and colorful satin gowns that were all around her.

Serenity could think of neither the food nor the guests a short time later, when just as she had feared she found herself pointedly seated next to Nathaniel Bentley. And judging from the solicitous smiles all about her, Serenity was certain Carissa was not the only one in Washington intent on matchmaking.

"Our dear president's wife, Dolly Madison, was a Quaker too, my child. Though you would not detect it by her dress," a plump woman, seated just across from her, remarked conspiratorially. "So you are highly favored. It is quite the thing. And, of course, our gracious president, Jemmy Madison, fairly dotes on the woman. Perhaps they shall even make an appearance later on this evening."

Serenity tried to concentrate on the words the woman was saying, but her mind was intent on the man who was seated by her side.

Above average in height, Nathaniel Bentley possessed a lean, muscular build, as though he had spent much time in the fields before making his home in Washington. His hair was dark blond in color, worn slightly long and without powder or wig, and on the rare occasions when he smiled, Serenity had found him, both warm and pleasant.

Oh, what was she to do? She could not tell anyone she was wed to Gabriel, and she dared not encourage Nathaniel.

"It is said Dolly has dozens of pairs of evening slippers from Paris," the woman seated across from them, whose name Serenity had since learned was Mrs. Deerfield, continued undauntedly. "And she always carries a copy of *Don Quixote* to all of the events. Not to read, of course. But merely for conversation, so there will not be a lull. And a snuff box . . . "

Glancing over at Nathaniel, Serenity could tell he cared no more for the conversation than she. Impulsively, she took his hand for a brief moment, squeezing it lightly. Then, realizing she had made a mistake at Nathaniel's pleased grin, she immediately blushed and lowered her blue eyes.

"What was this I heard about Dolly entertaining a British spy?" a distinguished gentleman to Serenity's left interjected hastily. "They say he entered the President's House dressed as a woman."

"Why, Senator Williams," Mrs. Deerfield interjected defensively, "the President's wife would do no such thing. That rumor was started by the much too elegant French ambassador. The man fairly delights in running to the President with each and every tale he hears about British spies he thinks are invading the capitol. Dolly told everyone quite plainly that she knows personally every single woman who has been in the President's House for the past six months. But she declined to say which of them would pass for males, since that was hardly the point."

There was muffled laughter at Mrs. Deerfield's remark.

The conversation went on from there, with more tales of British spies, the progress of the war, and the possibility of Washington itself being invaded by the British. Though she tried to appear attentive, Serenity was anxious for the dinner to end.

It was a relief when the men in the group finally began to

drift away to other rooms for their brandy and tobacco. Still, Nathaniel remained by her side, and there was no avoiding a confrontation.

"Serenity. I had hoped to call on you. . . . "

"Nathaniel, I value your friendship. But there can be nothing more."

"You are so beautiful . . . "

A slight frown creased Serenity's delicate brow. "I cannot . . . "

"I'm not asking anything more," he said. "Not yet . . . "

Serenity searched for the right words to say, but none were forthcoming. Her only hope was that eventually Nathaniel would lose interest in her.

"Cat," Serenity began, "we have been through this before. I cannot accept such a gift."

Carissa smiled. "Of course you can, my dear. The other gowns were from Gabriel. This one, and this one alone, is from me. Surely you will not deny me this pleasure? You have never been to the President's House for a ball before. And you are an invited guest. That calls for something very special in the way of a gown. You will be meeting the President himself, and his wife."

Hesitantly, Serenity replied, "The gown is much too elaborate. . . . "

"That is the way it was meant to be. You are certain to look lovely in it. Now, run along and dress. Tonight will be a marvelous occasion."

Starting for the door, Serenity stopped and slowly turned back around. Suspiciously, she asked, "Will Nathaniel be there as well?"

An innocent expression on her lovely face, Carissa gazed back with wide-apart, golden eyes. "Why, silly goose, how would I know? I suppose he might be. But, then, everyone in Washington is invited to absolutely everything. Besides, you should look forward to seeing him. Nathaniel is quite taken with you, you know."

Should she tell Carissa the truth? She was finding it more and more difficult to keep it from her. Still, if Gabriel had not wanted anyone to know . . .

Turning away and slowly mounting the stairs to her bedchamber, Serenity resolved once more to keep her secret. With any good fortune, Nathaniel would not even be at the President's House.

Entering her bedchamber, Serenity sighed softly as she once again gazed at the gown Carissa had given her. It lay waiting upon the bed.

It was quite extraordinary. Never before in her life had she thought to own anything like it. The dress was fashioned of yellow satin, its skirt embroidered with dancing butterflies of black. Despite herself, she could not help wondering what it would be like to try it on. But how could she wear such an outfit?

Even now, she could imagine Obed Ramsdell's stern disapproval if he knew what she considered wearing. Peering down his long nose at her, he would state that to wear the gown was sheer vanity—it could only invite disaster. Quaker dress was to be plain. Still, she was going to the President's House and was to be introduced to the President himself—and Carissa had insisted she wear it.

Serenity's head was spinning.

A short time later, dressed in the gown Carissa had given her, Serenity slowly descended the stairs.

Unaware of the enchanting picture she made, Serenity tried to hide her trepidation. The dress rustled in her wake, like the whispering of leaves when the wind brushed through the trees. Her pale copper hair was caught upon her head with a comb, while a few stray wisps escaped about her face.

At the bottom of the stairs, Carissa awaited her. "Oh, Serenity," she murmured with a warm glow in her eyes. "It is exquisite on you. Truly, you shall capture the heart of every man in the room."

There was something almost sinful in wearing the gown, and

had she not been on her way to the President's House, Serenity would have refused to have worn it at all.

Dropping her gaze to the neckline of the gown, Serenity frowned slightly. "The gown is much too revealing."

"Nonsense, my dear. Trust me, your skin is like porcelain. And that gown is far more discreet than what you will be seeing on anyone else this evening."

"I could not manage the turban."

"The turban would have been an overstatement anyway, Serenity. You are better off without it. Your hair is like silk. And I often think the natural look, without wigs or turbans, is far superior. Why try to improve on something nature has already bestowed with great beauty? There will be many people surprised by you this night. Just wait and see. . . . "

The President's House was far grander than anything Serenity had yet seen in her life. There were candles everywhere, myriads of liveried servants, the sound of raucous music, enormous amounts of food, and people in elaborate dress wherever she looked.

As she entered the large reception hall, Serenity had the feeling all eyes were turned toward her. It left her distressed. Perhaps Carissa had thought it necessary that she dress in this manner, but to draw such attention to herself went sorely against her nature. She was tempted to flee.

Numbly, Serenity was led toward the receiving line by Senator and Carissa Fairaday. There she was introduced to President Madison, and to his dark-haired wife. Graciously, Dolly even smiled at her and took an extra moment to greet her before they quickly moved away.

After that, however, everything was a blur of unfamiliar faces. Serenity tried to remember the names of the people she met, but it seemed impossible. Just as she sought to remember one person, she was quickly diverted to someone else. Soon, Senator and Carissa Fairaday became occupied with old friends, and Serenity was left quite on her own. Feeling lost in the throng of talking, laughing people about her, Serenity longed for the evening to end.

After what seemed an interminable length of time, Serenity could not help feeling almost joyful when she saw Nathaniel approaching.

"Serenity . . . "

There was no mistaking the admiring glow in his eyes. "Nathaniel . . . "

"I had hoped to see you here. You look so lovely."

"Thank you, Nathaniel."

Serenity could not meet his eyes. Gazing downward at her satin gown, she brushed one hand across an embroidered butterfly. It was wrong to encourage him. It would have been better to remain alone than to have him think they shared a common interest in each other.

"There is someone I would like for you to meet, Serenity. I hope you will not mind. He is new to Washington. When I first saw you here, I could not help pointing you out, and he expressed a desire to greet you."

Grateful for the distraction of another person, Serenity smiled sweetly. "Of course, Nathaniel," she replied. "I shall be pleased to meet your friend."

With her hand on Nathaniel's arm, Serenity went dutifully along as he made a path through the crowd. Others greeted them on the way, and Nathaniel beamed proudly as they were noticed.

Momentarily, they approached a tall, well-dressed man whose back was turned toward them. There was something strangely familiar about him.

"Lance . . . " Nathaniel began.

Slowly, the man turned.

For one startling instant, Serenity felt as though she might faint. There was no mistaking the gentleman's face. It was Lieutenant Evan Lancaster. How many times had she relived the night when she had struggled with him? Over and over, she had blamed herself for Joshua killing him. Now, here he stood. It was like seeing a ghost.

"Lancaster Evans," Nathaniel said, introducing them, unaware of the play on the lieutenant's true name. "I would like you to meet Serenity Penn."

The lieutenant's face exhibited no trace of surprise. "Delighted, Miss Penn," he replied, his eyes sweeping over her in keen appraisal. "Please, call me Lance."

"Lance?"

"Why, Nathaniel, I do believe the lady looks slightly pale. Perhaps a cup of punch . . . "

Nathaniel was immediately concerned. "Certainly. Serenity, you *do* look pale. I shall be right back. It will only take me a moment."

Watching Nathaniel depart, Serenity was suddenly frightened. The lieutenant was deliberately sending Nathaniel away; he was intent on being alone with her. She wanted to run after Nathaniel. To stop him.

"No need to look so distressed, Serenity. I wish only a moment of your time. And I shall warn you, if you don't want there to be gossip, you would be advised to do your best not to swoon in my arms. Others might think you have come face-to-face with your lover."

Still trembling, Serenity allowed the lieutenant to guide her through the other guests and toward the doors that opened out into the gardens. She had no choice but to go with him. Still, she wished someone would come swiftly to her aid.

Once they were outside, the lieutenant drew her away from the door so they stood in the shadows.

"I do not understand . . . " Serenity began.

"How it is I came to be here, Serenity? Or why I'm still alive, when you and that overgrown child were so determined to see me dead and buried?"

"I thought you were dead. But it was not of my choosing. I am most grateful you are still alive."

A chuckle of laughter escaped him as he grasped her arm.

119

"Truly? Then why don't you show me how glad you are to see me?"

She struggled as he drew her toward him. "Let go of me," she protested. "Nathaniel will be looking for me."

"That dolt?" he countered caustically. "Nathaniel Bentley is hardly worth the bother it would take to dispose of him. A distinct departure from your erstwhile husband, I would venture to say. Harrowe would have been a worthier opponent. Pity it never came to that. However, it was obvious the man meant only to use you, since he seemed only too happy to deposit you here in Washington at the first opportunity, and to once more be on his way. Still, nothing was lost. For one as beautiful as you, there is always another man willing to take an interest."

"How did you find me here?"

"It was really quite simple," the lieutenant stated blandly. "After you and your foolish brother very nearly killed me and then conveniently disappeared, I began to make inquiries about the scarlet-masted vessel that had been sighted off the coast shortly before your untimely departure. It wasn't difficult to discover such a rare and intriguing vessel's name. The *Firefly*. Many of the British vessels had encountered it before. A short while later, I learned it hailed out of the Carolinas and its captain was none other than your husband, Gabriel Harrowe. It is a pity I didn't make such an investigation sooner. It would have saved us all a great deal of time and trouble." He grinned. "From there, I learned that your American captain was a frequent visitor to Washington and that he has the President's ear. I simply asked for a transfer of my duties."

Serenity's eyes flashed with anger. "I have to go. Release me . . ."

"Not until we understand each other, Serenity."

"What is it you want of me?" she demanded.

Briefly, a smile lit Lieutenant Lancaster's handsome, mustached face. "To begin with, my sweet, my name is currently Lancaster Evans. But call me Lance. That should be simple enough for the time being. If you have thoughts of revealing my

120

true identity, think better of it. You have protected Joshua well enough in the past, but I owe him for what he tried to do to me. If you'd like your brother to come to no harm, you will do exactly as I say."

Serenity gazed at the lieutenant in disbelief. For one horrified moment she pressed her fingertips to her mouth as though she were reluctant to utter the words she was about to say aloud. Then she burst out accusingly, "I do know what you are doing here. It is not because of me. Or Joshua. You are a British spy."

"Be careful what you say, Serenity. There are others who might overhear. And there is Joshua's safety to be considered, as well as your own. You would do well to heed my warning."

"You are spying upon the president . . . "

Gently, his hands stroked her bare shoulders. "What difference does it make? Quakers are to remain neutral. Remember? Do you now wish to take sides? Which side is good? Which side is evil?"

Serenity burned with indignation. "It is Joshua I care about. Joshua alone. You must promise not to harm him."

"Of course, Serenity. That is a simple enough matter. I hope to be seeing more of you. You will no longer see Nathaniel Bentley. I cannot abide him touching what was already rightfully mine. I will not allow it. You see, my Serenity, when I saw you again tonight, I realized you were the most beautiful woman in the entire ballroom. No one else could even compare. I find you infinitely more fascinating than I found you on Nantucket. There, you were merely a trinket, something to be toyed with at my leisure. Now, I can see you glow like the rarest of jewels. All you need is the proper setting. . . . "

Drawing her hard up against his chest, the lieutenant grasped the back of her neck so she could not escape him. Brutally, his mouth came down on hers, his teeth bruising her lips.

In desperation, Serenity shoved him away with all her might. Breaking free from his grasp, she dashed back into the safety of the ballroom, her cheeks flushed and her heart pounding.

The yellow satin gown had indeed brought disaster.

Chapter Thirteen

Serenity had not slept well. Indeed, she had not slept at all. Dismally, she gazed at the yellow satin gown that was draped over a nearby chair. It was a mistake to have worn it. How many times had she acted impulsively, only to regret it later? Perhaps, if she had never worn the gown in the first place, the lieutenant would not have noticed her. Now she was at a loss to know what to do.

Lieutenant Evan Lancaster was now Lance Evans, a British spy, and she dared not tell anyone. The lieutenant had threatened to harm Joshua if she did, and she did not doubt for a moment that he would be true to his word. But if she kept his secret, would it end there? What more would he expect of her in the future if she did as he said?

Sighing, Serenity sat down on the bed. So much was not working out as she had planned. She had hoped to find employment and provide for Joshua and herself on her own. But Carissa had filled Serenity's days with social calls and teas, dining, even the new ice-cream parlors and visiting the open-air arena where *Macbeth* was being performed. In this hectic activity she had almost forgotten her original intentions. She had even failed to notice how unhappy Joshua had seemed of late. While she had been so busy, he had been left alone much of the time in a place where he undoubtedly felt he did not belong.

Serenity had made a decision. Something had to be done, and she intended to see to it that very day. She and Joshua could not return to Nantucket, even though Lieutenant Lancaster was alive. The lieutenant might decide to follow, and Joshua would still be placed in danger. No, she must choose another plan entirely.

She dressed quickly, and a short while later hurried down the stairs and into the dining room, where Carissa sat buttering a warm muffin.

"Do sit down, Serenity," Carissa said, greeting her with a smile. "I was not certain if you would be up quite this early after your long evening, so we began without you. Michael— Senator Fairaday—had a meeting and has already left for the day."

"Thank you, Cat. However, I cannot stay for more than a moment. There is something I must do today."

Suddenly serious, a slight frown creased Carissa's brow, as though she had something disturbing on her mind. "There is something I must tell you. Two messengers were sent around this morning, Serenity. They both carried messages for you. One was from that very handsome gentleman, Lancaster Evans. He wanted to send his regards," she explained, as though Serenity should feel complimented. "I understand he is a financier, new to Washington. It seems he was quite taken with you at the ball last night. The other message, however, was of a more distressing nature. I hesitate even to mention the unfortunate event, as perchance the matter will upset you. But, alas, I fear I must. It seems Senator Nathaniel Bentley was set upon by ruffians late last night and beaten within an inch of his life."

Serenity gasped. "Nathaniel has been attacked?"

"Yes, my dear. I am afraid so."

Frowning, Serenity sat in stunned silence for a moment. How could it be? Was it a mere coincidence, or had Lieutenant Lancaster arranged for it to happen? Lancaster had said that he did not like the idea of Nathaniel touching her, and the lieutenant had purposely sent his card around that very morning, as though reminding her pointedly of his presence. Still, there was nothing to actually suggest that the lieutenant would do such a thing.

"Will Nathaniel be all right?"

"Yes. However, I do think he was hoping for a visit from a cheery face. He mentioned in his message that he was anxious to see you again. Men always crave sympathy when they are not feeling well. They are much like little boys in that respect."

"Of course . . . " Serenity replied, more distressed than Carissa could possibly know about the whole situation.

Serenity's first stop of the day was at Mrs. Deerfield's home. It was obvious by her welcome that the woman was very glad to see her.

"Why, Miss Penn, I am delighted you have come to visit. When you sent word you would be paying a call, I cannot tell you how surprised I was. To have a young woman such as you take the time . . . well, I have been very lonely since my husband's death. William and I were wed for many years, you know. And I still miss him dreadfully."

Feeling decidedly guilty because her reason for coming was not nearly so noble, Serenity smiled kindly at Mrs. Deerfield, then replied quite honestly, "I should have called before, Mrs. Deerfield. I had not realized you would be so anxious for visitors."

Taking her by the arm and leading Serenity from the entry to the drawing room, Mrs. Deerfield responded cheerily, "Do come and sit, Miss Penn. I shall ring for tea. Or perhaps you would care for a fruited punch?"

"The punch sounds refreshing. . . . "

A short while later, after they had been served and Serenity had listened to Mrs. Deerfield's complaints about her health, the latest gossip around Washington, and the state of the war with England, Serenity finally found a moment to approach the reason she had come. "I believe you mentioned, Mrs. Deerfield, that you knew people from the Quaker community of Brookeville in Maryland. I was hoping you might have some knowledge of a distant cousin of mine who lives there. Her name is Emmalina Green. I have not heard any word of her in years."

A frown creased Mrs. Deerfield's brow for a moment as the

woman gave the matter some contemplation. "Why, yes, my dear. I believe I do remember Emmalina. She is widowed now, of course, much like myself, and that is cause for loneliness. Yet, I believe she was in fine health the last time I heard her name mentioned. Spends much of her time making the most exquisite of quilts. . . . I wish *I* were so handy."

"I am pleased to hear she is doing well, Mrs. Deerfield. Thank you so much for informing me about her."

"If there is anything else you would care to know, I should be only too happy to tell you, Miss Penn. By the way, did you hear about poor Senator Nathaniel Bentley? Only this morning I heard he had been set upon by purse snatchers and is very near death's door. . . . "

Mrs. Deerfield's exaggeration of the event did nothing to lessen Serenity's concern for Nathaniel. She only hoped that she was not responsible in some indirect way for Nathaniel being harmed.

As quickly as it was polite to do so, Serenity excused herself. The woman obviously would have been delighted to keep her there all day with a steady stream of chatter, but Serenity had other matters to attend to. And one of those matters pertained to a certain young senator from Pennsylvania.

It was nearing midmorning when the carriage pulled up in front of Nathaniel Bentley's lodgings and Serenity knocked at his door.

As she was shown into the drawing room, Serenity was uncertain what she would find. Seeing Nathaniel reclining in a chair, she was cheered to note that he appeared much better than she had imagined.

"Nathaniel," Serenity said, her brow furrowed with concern and her blue eyes troubled, "how are you feeling? I was so distressed when I heard what had happened."

Nathaniel's face was bruised, and one eye was swollen shut and blackened. Still, he managed a warm smile. "I was set upon

125

by some rabble who were bent on robbery, I fear, though they escaped without my money purse. It happened quite suddenly, a short time after the ball."

"Will you be all right?"

"Of course," he assured her. "With just a few days' rest . . . "

Relieved, Serenity stayed only long enough to exchange pleasantries with Nathaniel. After wishing him well, she excused herself and left. She was comforted to see that Nathaniel had fared no worse, under the circumstances. Still, there was the mystery of why such a thing had happened in the first place.

Stepping out of Nathaniel's town house and starting toward the carriage, Serenity noticed a man waiting by its side. Though he was dressed in the newer style of men's clothing, which was fast becoming fashionable, with a tall beige hat, a tail coat with a high, rolling collar, and long pantaloons, Serenity recognized him instantly.

"Good day, sir," Serenity said, refusing to use Lieutenant Lancaster's new name as she attempted to brush past him.

"Good day, Miss Penn," the lieutenant replied. "I have asked that you address me as Lance. It is much less formal."

She had to be careful. The driver of the carriage sat waiting. She did not want the man to rush to Carissa with gossip about whatever he might overhear. "Why are you here? Have you come to pay a call on Senator Bentley? You must have heard of his dreadful accident."

"Most unfortunate," the lieutenant replied, though his expression was not in the least sympathetic. His eyes remained on her face. "But such things can happen. Perhaps Senator Bentley should be glad he was not killed. Surely that was a possibility."

Serenity bit back an angry retort. Any doubt that she had previously entertained about the lieutenant being behind what had happened to Nathaniel vanished in an instant. There was no question that the lieutenant was responsible for his injuries. What was more, now he was informing her that it could have been much worse.

Gabriel's Fire

"I see no reason for it to have happened at all," she shot back.

"Some men breed problems, Miss Penn. It is as though they ask for them by what they do. Perhaps you would be wise to avoid the senator in the future."

"Such a warning is not necessary," she countered icily.

"Just a word to the wise—or the innocent, as the case may be. Sometimes one such as you is not aware of the true dangers in the world. The senator's life might still be in jeopardy."

Trembling with anger, Serenity started to brush past him once more and climb into the carriage. She had no wish for any more games of cat and mouse. She had already taken note of what he implied. Was not having Nathaniel beaten dreadful enough? Now, the lieutenant felt it necessary to threaten Nathaniel's life as well, if she did not do what he desired.

The lieutenant grabbed her arm and held her there for a moment. Leaning close to her ear so only she would hear, he murmured, "You are mine, Serenity. Never forget that. Sooner or later, that is the way it will be."

Jerking away from him, Serenity climbed into the carriage. Her chin held high, she refused to look in Lancaster's direction again, even though she could feel his gaze upon her. "Please take me back to the Fairadays, Mr. Sloan," Serenity directed the carriage driver, as though the lieutenant was not there.

By the time she walked through the door of the Fairadays, Serenity had regained her composure. Her delicate chin was set with determination. Earlier that day, she had decided the course of action she must take, and Lieutenant Lancaster and his threats had only intensified her desire to follow it through as quickly as possible.

Stepping into the drawing room, Serenity hesitated. Carissa was seated at her cherry writing desk. "Cat? I am sorry to interrupt, if you are busy. Should I come back at another time?"

Carissa turned a bright smile in her direction. "I was just working on some correspondence, but I have finished. You may take all the time you would like, Serenity."

Gloria Pedersen

Rising from the writing desk, Carissa motioned Serenity over to the striped settee, where the two of them sat down together.

"Now, what is this all about, Serenity? Did you see Senator Bentley?"

"Yes," Serenity replied, turning her head slightly to avoid Carissa's inquisitive gaze. "The Senator shall soon recover, and I do not look for him to have any more problems in the future."

Carissa did not fail to note something was amiss. "Then why do you appear so troubled, Serenity? Has something else happened to disturb you?"

Serenity drew a deep breath. "There is something I must tell you. I have appreciated your kindness, Cat. More than I can possibly say. However, I have reached a decision. One to which I have given much thought. Today, I went to pay a call upon Mrs. Deerfield."

"Mrs. Deerfield!" Carissa exclaimed in surprise.

Nodding, Serenity continued, "When we had the opportunity to dine at the Octagon House, I heard Mrs. Deerfield mention that she was acquainted with a number of people from Brookeville. I wanted to inquire if she had any knowledge of a distant cousin of mine, who once lived there. Emmalina Green."

"And did Mrs. Deerfield have news of your cousin?"

"Yes. Mrs. Deerfield informed me that my cousin Emmalina is still there, and in good health."

"Were you hoping to correspond with your cousin?"

"No, Cat. Something more. I have truly enjoyed my stay here in Washington. It has been delightful. But I cannot make my home here. I hope you will understand. It would not be best for Joshua, nor for myself. Brookeville is a Quaker community. I can easily find employment there. The Quaker way of life would be much more in keeping with what Joshua is familiar, and I must think of his welfare. He is my first consideration. And there are others . . . "

Her voice trailed away as she thought once again of Lan-

Gabriel's Fire

caster's threats against both Joshua and Nathaniel. She could not tell Carissa, but they were both in very real danger as long as she remained in Washington.

"Oh, I see," Carissa replied without enthusiasm. "I will be saddened to see you go, Serenity."

"I shall miss you too, Cat. However, I have no choice."

Trying to accept Serenity's decision, Carissa offered more brightly, "Of course, if it is for the best, I do understand. Whenever you choose to go, I shall arrange for Mr. Sloan to take you to Brookeville and see you settled. But, certainly, there is no need for you to leave just yet. I have enjoyed having you here. Surely you could stay a few weeks longer?"

There was a troubled light in Serenity's blue eyes. She dared not delay. Except for Carissa, no one could know that she was leaving. There was no way to know what the lieutenant might do if he found out. "I should like to leave as soon as possible. I must write to Emmalina, first, of course. Then, when I receive word back from her, I will make plans to go. In the meantime, Cat, may I ask that you keep this our secret? I do not intend to tell anyone, including Joshua, until I am certain Emmalina will welcome us."

Carissa appeared puzzled. "Most certainly. You have my promise."

The month of August was already slipping away by the time Serenity received a missive from her cousin. Emmalina wrote that she would be delighted to have Serenity and Joshua come to stay with her in Brookeville, and even Biscuit would be most welcome. Serenity felt relieved. It had been a difficult wait. In the weeks since the ball, she had avoided attending any social functions where she might encounter Lieutenant Lancaster, and she had been forced to offer one excuse after another to Carissa. She was certain Carissa suspected something. Now, with the missive from Emmalina, Serenity hoped she would not have to make any more excuses and could leave as quickly as possible. First, however, she must explain to Joshua that they would be going.

129

Each Tuesday and Thursday for the past several weeks, Serenity had asked Mr. Sloan to take them to the park, where she and Joshua could spend time together. It seemed the perfect place. The boy had been through so many changes, and changes were difficult for Joshua. She did not want him to feel disturbed about going to Brookeville. They had left Nantucket so suddenly in the night, and their departure from the *Firefly* had been little better. This time she wanted to prepare him before it was time to leave.

The park was located in the midst of the city and was lovely. Tall trees seemed to catch the breeze, and there was a pond. Mr. Sloan remained with the carriage, while she and Joshua strolled. Joshua always looked forward excitedly to going there. He suffered under the confinement of the Fairaday manse. He was accustomed to much more freedom. Laughing out loud, Joshua watched as Biscuit raced on ahead to chase a squirrel up a tree.

The sound of Joshua's laughter pleased and troubled Serenity at the same time. He had laughed very little since leaving Nantucket. Would her brother ever be truly happy again?

It was obvious Joshua needed the freedom that he had enjoyed on Nantucket, along with the sense of accomplishment he had known while helping the crew aboard the *Firefly*. Gabriel and Kane had been so good, allowing Joshua to do just what he could manage, then praising him sincerely for each effort. There was no doubt that Joshua missed them. For a moment, Serenity felt an ache near her heart. It was better not to think about such things. All of that was behind them now. One had to accept what one cannot change.

Catching up with her brother and Biscuit, Serenity called Joshua over to her side. "There is something I must tell you, Joshua."

Joshua stopped what he was doing to gaze at her, his laughter at Biscuit's antics gone from his face. He was immediately suspicious. "Why?" he asked.

"You must not worry. It is pleasant news. Something you will like very much. A surprise. We will be leaving Washington soon."

"Why?" he asked again. "Are we going home?"

Serenity had not imagined that he would dart to the wrong conclusion. "No, Joshua. We are not going back to Nantucket." He began to stub the toe of his shoe into the grass at his feet, making a gouge in the earth. It was obvious he was disappointed. "I know you have not been very happy here. But we have a cousin who lives in Brookeville. Her name is Emmalina. I wrote to her some time ago to ask if we could visit her. Just this morning, I received a missive saying that she would be delighted to have us come to stay with her. It won't be like Washington. There will be much for you to do there."

He seemed to think about it for a moment. "Why can't we go back to Nantucket? I want to go home."

"I know, Joshua. Nantucket will always be our home. I miss it too. But we have each other. That is more important than anything else. One day, perhaps, we will go back to visit."

He thought it over for a moment. "Is Brookeville far?"

"Not far. It is in Maryland. The Fairadays have already arranged for Mr. Sloan to take us there, whenever we decide to go. First, though, I will send word ahead to Cousin Emmalina of our arrival."

Biscuit began to bark again and raced after another squirrel. Joshua laughed once more, their conversation already far from his mind. Racing after Biscuit, Joshua no longer had any interest in anything but being in the park.

Serenity breathed a sigh of relief. She would write back to Emmalina tomorrow. Soon, she thought. Soon . . .

As Serenity stood patiently waiting for Joshua to return to her side once more, she gazed around herself. She had been so intent on her conversation with Joshua that she had not noticed the three men conversing near the pond, a short distance away. She did not recognize two of the men. However, the third man she knew instantly. She gasped softly. It was Lancaster. Even from that distance, it was obvious their conversation was a serious one. The lieutenant had not even bothered to glance up and see her standing there.

Quickly, Serenity stepped back into the shadow of a tree. Despite the heat of the day, a chill ran through her and she shuddered. What was the villain up to now? She yearned to tell someone that the lieutenant had harmed Nathaniel, and that she believed he was a spy. But she dared not say a word. Still, Cat had assured her that the city was full of spies for both sides, and one side watched the other. At least *that* was a comfort. Surely Lancaster could do no more harm than any other spy in the city. Still, the man was not to be trusted on any level.

When Joshua returned to her side, Serenity quickly informed him that they must leave. He appeared disappointed. "I am sorry, Joshua. I do not feel well."

It was the truth. Serenity had felt ill the moment she'd seen the English spy. She did not want Joshua to see Lancaster as well. There was no way of knowing how Joshua would react to seeing a man whom he believed was dead.

Joshua nodded his dark head.

"Hurry, Joshua. You and Biscuit run back to the carriage. You can get in. I will be there in a moment."

Joshua wheeled about and ran to do as she had bid him. Pivoting, she started to follow. However, as she did so, she glanced back in the direction of the lieutenant. Unexpectedly, she realized that the lieutenant had seen them. Standing there, his gaze was fixed directly on her. For a moment, she felt panic; then she regained control. She would not give him the opportunity to speak to her. And he could not prevent her from leaving. Without acknowledging him, she spun around and hurriedly followed Joshua and Biscuit back to the carriage.

Serenity retired to her bedchamber early to write her final missive to Emmalina. A trunk, which Carissa had insisted she take along as a parting gift, sat on the floor. Most of Serenity's gowns, and what few belongings she had, were already packed inside. She and Joshua would leave in two days, allowing time for the message to Emmalina to precede them. After seeing Lieutenant Lancaster in the park, even that did not seem soon enough.

Lost in thought as she stood gazing out the window at a beautiful sunset in shades of pink and mauve, Serenity was startled by the sound of urgent knocking on the door.

"Serenity," Cat called anxiously.

Quickly crossing the bedchamber, Serenity opened the door for Carissa. It was obvious her friend was distressed. "What is it, Cat? What has happened?"

"You must leave this night, Serenity. There is no time for delay. Something dreadful has happened. The British are planning to invade the city and burn the Capitol, this very night."

Startled, Serenity replied, "Burn the Capitol?"

"Yes. No one will be able to stop them. Our sources have learned that the British marines will land tonight. We have little defense against it. Everyone is being told to evacuate the city— the President, his cabinet, all officials. Our spies have assured us it is true. You must leave now, Serenity. Mr. Sloan will take you and Joshua to Brookeville in the carriage. Once you are safely away, Senator Fairaday and I plan to leave, as well."

"But where will you go, Cat?"

"We will be quite all right. The Senator and I will travel to the countryside, where we will be safe at the home of his brother. We can only hope they do not burn our home in our absence. Senator Fairaday and I plan to return to Washington as soon as possible to assess the damage. We can only hope the British will settle for burning the Capitol and the public buildings. Hurry now, while there still is time. It would not do for you to be caught within the city limits when the British arrive."

Serenity started for the door. "I shall hurry and tell Joshua." Spinning back around as she reached the door, Serenity added, "Thank you, Cat. I hope everything will be all right." Then she fled.

Gloria Pedersen

* * *

Shortly before dusk, all was in readiness. Joshua and Biscuit were waiting in the carriage, along with what belongings she and her brother possessed. It was fortunate that she had spoken with Joshua earlier in the day about their departure. He did not realize that their leaving was taking place even more quickly than she had anticipated. His face had lit up the moment she had told him, and he had danced around with excitement until it was time to climb into the carriage. There was no doubt they were doing the right thing in leaving Washington behind them.

Anxious to be on her way, Serenity stood in the doorway of the Fairaday manse giving a final farewell to Carissa.

Holding her by the hand, Carissa managed a sweet smile despite the circumstances, her golden eyes misty with unshed tears. "For the first time in my life, I have felt I had a sister in these past weeks, Serenity. I hope we will not lose touch."

"My thoughts and prayers shall be with you, Cat. But I feel it unwise to try to correspond."

Carissa was immediately troubled. "I know there is more to this than meets the eye, Serenity. It is obvious your decision to leave was not simply for Joshua's welfare. Please, I wish you would tell me, while there still is time."

Giving Carissa one last heartfelt hug, Serenity replied, "All I can tell you is that I feel I have no choice in my decision. And I must ask you to tell no one where we have gone. No one."

"I can assure you, Serenity. Senator Fairaday and I will never tell a soul, if you do not want us to. And Mr. Sloan will keep your confidence, as well. You can trust us all. Still . . . "

From the carriage, Biscuit gave a loud bark, and Joshua poked his head out to call, "Serenity, hurry . . . "

Pulling away from Carissa and starting toward the carriage, Serenity called back once more, "Thank you again for everything."

Carissa's expression was still troubled. "You are certain about this, Serenity? I must not tell a soul? No one? No one at all? You shall not change your mind?"

Remembering the lieutenant and his dire threats, Serenity threw a glance in Carissa's direction.

"*He* must never know. . . . " Serenity said. Then, catching herself, she left the sentence unfinished as she climbed into the carriage.

Chapter Fourteen

Gabriel stood on the quarterdeck of the *Firefly* and watched as his men loaded supplies. He had taken yet another British vessel as a prize and had just delivered it into a secluded Carolina harbor. Now he was preparing to set sail again, but it was no longer something he looked forward to.

Privateers such as the *Firefly* were still able to outmaneuver British vessels and succeed in taking prizes, but no one could gain much from any of it.

This was a war that could not be won by either side. There had been many American naval victories in the north that had tremendously lightened the gloom that the military blunders along the frontier had cast over the American people. For centuries, British sea captains had been accustomed to winning against all odds. However, American vessels were designed to carry more guns and sails than British ones, and American warships and privateers had taken a heavy toll of British commerce. But in the spring of 1813, the British had established a tight blockade of the American coast, and American ships scarcely dared to leave port.

The whole business had left a bitter taste in Gabriel's mouth. He had never taken prizes simply for the reward. It had only been a means to an end. He had chosen to captain a privateer because the young United States Navy was ineffectual on the open seas. Now, England and the U.S. were at an impasse. Both American and British commerce were being damaged and nothing was being accomplished.

His long legs braced apart, Gabriel frowned as one of the crew hastily boarded the vessel and ran toward Kane. Stopping before him, the crewman spoke rapidly, while gesturing excitedly with his hands.

Gabriel could not hear what was being said, but whatever it was appeared to be serious. He waited impatiently.

Kane listened intently to the crewman, then wheeled about and headed straight for Gabriel. "Captain Harrowe," he said without preliminaries, "the British have burned the Capitol."

Gabriel was not surprised. In fact, he had almost expected something like this to happen. It was like two brothers fighting, each trying to blacken the other's eye. The attack had little strategic relevance. Suddenly, a stunned realization took over. "Serenity . . ."

Kane understood. "What are you going to do?"

"Get the supplies and crew on board without delay, Kane. We sail on the morning tide."

"Aye, Captain."

"Where is she?" Gabriel demanded, his dark brows drawn together in a frown and his anger barely held in check as he addressed his cousin, Carissa Harrowe Fairaday, who seemed not in the least interested in telling him what he wanted to know.

After receiving word that Washington had been invaded and burned by the British, Gabriel had journeyed to Washington as quickly as possible. He had believed Serenity would be safe in the nation's capital when he'd sent her to stay with Carissa. However, now he'd found by doing so, he had placed her in even graver danger than before. Castigating himself for his idiocy and fearing the worst, he had left Kane in charge of his vessel and taken a jolly boat to shore, then had secured a horse and ridden all night.

Entering Washington, Gabriel had gone directly to the Fairadays'. However, on the way he had grown even more anxious as he noted the devastation all around. In two hot August days the British had invaded and destroyed virtually the entire city. They had set fire to the city's major public buildings and left the Capitol and the President's House standing as gutted shells. Fortunately, however, the British troops were only a raiding party and not an occupying force, and they had quickly moved on toward Baltimore after the city was in ruins.

"Now, Gabriel," Carissa said, trying to do her best to soothe him, "please sit down. Let us discuss this rationally. Perhaps you would care to rest first, or have something to eat. . . . "

"Cat," he returned, his handsome face hard. "You have not seen the extent of my anger, if you think you can put me off. I want to know about Serenity. Now!"

Seeing she could not placate him, Carissa sighed softly. "Serenity is quite all right, Gabriel. Though that is no thanks to you."

"What do you mean by that?" he countered dryly.

"Only that you have done your utmost to compromise the girl from the very beginning. She is far better off without you."

Gabriel shot Carissa a dark glance. "In what way, precisely, have I compromised Serenity? I left her here with you. That was hardly forcing her to my bed."

Seating herself on the settee, Carissa folded her hands in her lap and smiled sweetly. "Gabriel, do sit. You are making me nervous. We are no longer children, and I have no more patience for your rages."

Mollified, Gabriel took a seat in a velvet-covered chair opposite his cousin and stretched out his long legs before him. "All right, Cat. I'm in control. Now, start at the beginning."

"Perhaps it was the yellow satin gown . . . " Carissa murmured distractedly. "Oh, I don't know. Perhaps I forced too much upon her that was new and different. . . . Well, never you mind. I shall ring for tea, and then I shall tell you all I can."

Forcing himself to relax, Gabriel waited until Carissa sent a house servant for refreshments, then he returned once more to the matter at hand. "Is Serenity all right?" he prompted. It would do Carissa no good to know that in a few short moments she had planted a myriad of disturbing thoughts inside his head. Compromised Serenity, indeed. What did that mean? He needed to know. Had their stolen moment aboard the vessel left her carrying his child?

"To begin at the beginning, I have always believed you to be a rake with women, Gabriel Harrowe," Carissa explained, her golden eyes quite solemn. "You are dear, and I love you. But you always were an imp, even as a child. Still, I would never have thought you would be so intent on bedding Serenity, you would forget completely how you might destroy her in the process. She is not of that kind. And so, I set about to get her wed to someone nice. Someone quite suitable. Someone who would make her happy . . . "

"You *what?*"

"I introduced her to Senator Nathaniel Bentley, and he was quite taken with her. Nathaniel is a Quaker, too. I saw to it they were together. At the President's ball, she looked incredibly lovely in her yellow satin gown. And I knew he could never resist."

A muscle tightened along Gabriel's jaw. He could not believe what he was hearing. Carissa had deliberately thrown his wife at another man.

"And what did Serenity think about all of this, Cat?"

Twisting her hankie idly in her hands, Carissa looked evasive. "I thought she liked the senator. They got on well."

Frowning darkly, Gabriel did not like the twinge of jealousy that suddenly twisted his gut. Had he misjudged Serenity after all? He had thought she was different. Or was he just a fool? Even aboard his own vessel, he had wondered about Serenity

138

and Kane. First, Kane—and now the senator. Innocent, his foot. The woman possessed as many feminine wiles as every other woman he had ever known.

Carissa sighed once more. "Serenity left the night of the British invasion. She had already made plans to leave. She felt it was for the best. She was never in the slightest danger, Gabriel. Never. She was gone before the British arrived." She paused. "But, even if she had not already been planning to leave, everyone of consequence left the city before the British came. Even the President himself and his cabinet, along with his resourceful wife. She even took it upon herself to rescue a fine portrait of George Washington! In the end, only the disgraceful street trollops remained to greet the British and ply their wares."

Pausing, Carissa met his gaze straight on, then returned to the subject at hand. "Perhaps Serenity could not bear to face you. After all, you did send her to my keeping and paid for her new gowns. She was grateful to you, but she probably knew what you would expect upon your return. She was too honest to encourage the senator, knowing she was indebted to you. Well, she is gone, and it is done. No one is the winner."

"*Damnnation!*" Gabriel fumed, rising from his chair and beginning to pace the floor. "I told you to take care of her. Nothing more . . ."

"She was not a woman you should use, Gabriel. This is for the best."

Wheeling about, Gabriel stopped to shoot Carissa a look of glowering condemnation. "I won't let her go."

"You have to, Gabriel. She is gone already."

Wasn't this what he had wanted all along, to be free of Serenity? He should be relieved. So why did he not feel any joy? *Let her go,* he told himself bleakly. *Let her go. . . .*

He eyed Carissa. "You know where she is, don't you, Cat?"

"Whatever do you mean?"

"You know exactly where she went."

"I shall not argue with you, Gabe."

He stood gazing at her, his eyes like shards of ice. "I want you to tell me."

"I cannot."

"You can't, or you won't? Which is it, Cat?"

She looked decidedly uncomfortable. "I became very close to Serenity while she was here. I promised to tell no one where she went. Her final words to me were, 'He must never know.' "

Gabriel felt the pain once more in his gut, like a knife that had found its mark. Carissa was right. Serenity had decided to have nothing more to do with him. It was exactly what he deserved.

Gabriel took a deep breath. "She is mine," he murmured softly.

"You cannot go after her," Carissa said firmly. "I refuse to tell you where she is. Can you not see you are wrong for her?"

"Wrong or right, you have to tell me, Cat," he said, his voice cold and deadly. "I should have told you in the first place. I can *never* let her go. Not now. Not ever. What's more, I have found in these past weeks that I have no desire to. She is mine, whether she wants to be or not." He paused for a moment, as though he had suddenly realized the truth himself for the very first time. "Serenity is my wife."

Gabriel stood on the deck of the *Firefly*, lost in thought. It had been several weeks since he had learned from Carissa that Serenity had gone to Brookeville, and that she wanted nothing more to do with him. Yet he had done nothing about it.

"Captain?" Kane said, approaching him. "You wanted to see me?"

Gabriel glanced over at Kane as he replied, "It is a matter of a personal nature, Kane. And I'm going to need your help."

"Is this about the Quaker?"

Gabriel nodded. "I told you when I reached Washington, Serenity was no longer there. She had gone to live in a little Quaker community called Brookeville. What I failed to mention was that from all appearances it would seem she wants nothing more to do with me. I can hardly blame her, considering what I have done—or failed to do, as the case may be. Still, I am not prepared to leave it at that. Serenity is still my wife."

"What do you propose to do?"

"The war will not continue much longer. Neither side can win. It is hurting normal trade relations on both sides. It's like fighting one's brother. Neither side can gain from it, because in the end one has to call a truce and get on with one's life."

"But what about the burning of Washington?"

"It was more of an embarrassment to the Americans than anything else, Kane. I doubt that damages will even be brought up. Representatives for the governments of both sides are already negotiating. They should reach a truce at anytime. They are said to be meeting at Ghent."

Kane nodded. "So what will you do now, Cap'n?"

"It is time I put my own house in order. I want Serenity in Carolina with me."

Kane looked doubtful. "But if she's decided she wants nothing more to do with you . . . "

"That is the problem. Believe it or not, I wasn't the unwilling bridegroom in this marriage. Serenity was the unwilling bride. I felt it was best for all concerned, since Serenity has an uncanny habit of placing herself in the most uncertain of circumstances. She is independent. She has never relied on a man for anything—and I doubt she would start now. But that doesn't mean I'm willing to let her go."

"What is it you plan to do?"

Taking several paces, Gabriel wheeled around and strode back toward Kane, his hands clasped behind his back. "I can't force her to my home, or to my bed. If I went to Brookeville and demanded she come with me, she would likely refuse. And since I have a commitment to the plantation I inherited from my grandfather, I need to know if Serenity could ever share it with me. It is not her way of life; we might have too much against us there. Still, if we're to have any hope of a future together, it must begin in Carolina."

Kane let out a deep sigh. "It won't be easy. Have you decided how you're going to get her there?"

Gloria Pedersen

"That is where you are going to come in, Kane. After we put
into port, I will contact my mother and have her write a missive
to Serenity, asking her to come for a visit. I'll already have passage booked for Serenity on a merchant vessel. What I want you
to do is this, Kane: look after her until she arrives in Carolina.
Too much can happen to her with only Joshua and the dog
along. And I don't want to risk not having her arrive safely. But,
understand, I don't want her to be aware of you being there
either. If she knew I was behind this, she would probably never
come. . . . "

A twinkle lit Kane's eyes as he answered. "You can count
on me, Gabriel. At least this is one thing we agree on. I
thought you were a fool to let the Quaker go in the first place."

"A fool," he replied. "And more . . . "

Emmalina's home was simple. It consisted of only a few rooms
and was dominated by a large combination kitchen-parlor with
a big fireplace. Attached to the house was a dairy stocked with
cheeses and crocks of milk whose sides glistened with fine
moisture.

It was pleasant here. Joshua helped Emmalina with the
chores, while Serenity had been substituting for a teacher at the
local school. The former teacher there, a woman, had recently
given birth to a fine, healthy boy, but she would soon be returning to her classroom. The following school year, Serenity
hoped to have classes of her own.

It was evening. Seated in the main room of Emmalina's
small house, Serenity unfolded the pages of the letter that had
arrived that morning, and she gazed down at the carefully written script. She had no idea who would be writing to her, especially from Carolina. She had been certain no one knew of her
whereabouts.

Her cousin thrice-removed, Emmalina, gazed at her curiously as she waited for Serenity to open the letter. "What is it,
Serenity? Who is it from?"

Glancing up, Serenity smiled at the woman. She was most grateful to Emmalina for taking her and Joshua in, and she felt truly at home in Brookeville. She had never thought to be quite so content again, after having left Nantucket. And Joshua had fairly thrived since their arrival.

Serenity quickly scanned the contents of the missive. It was in a woman's hand, and began familiarly, "Dearest Serenity." A frown creased her delicate brow, and Serenity read on. "We have never met. But, recently, I have been informed that you are my son's wife. I regard this fact with much delight. However, a certain matter has come to my attention. I must beg that you please come to Carolina for a visit, so we might discuss it. Your passage has been booked one week hence. We shall be looking forward to your arrival." The missive was simply signed, "Elissa Harrowe."

Surprised, Serenity gazed over at Emmalina as she sat sewing on a quilt. Thoughts raced through her mind. She had not allowed herself to think of Gabriel since the night she had left the *Firefly.* If the good Lord had willed that their union be blessed, it would have been. But they had gone their separate ways, and Gabriel was not to be a part of her future. How could she doubt the Lord's will in all things?

"Who is the letter from, Serenity?" Emmalina prompted.

Just as it had been a secret while she was still in Washington, Serenity had not mentioned her marriage to Emmalina either. It was a private matter, and she had seen no need. Now, she could delay no longer. "There is something I must tell you, Emmalina. I am wed to a man named Gabriel Harrowe. I had never thought to see my husband again. However, this missive is from his mother, and she asks that I come to visit her."

"Why, Serenity," Emmalina said with enthusiasm. "You are wed? How wonderful. Surely you must pay his mother a visit as she requests. One never knows if she is in failing health, and a visit might bring her such pleasure. It is the charitable thing to do. Remember the story of Ruth and Naomi in the Lord's word? She honored her mother-in-law, though she too had no husband present."

Serenity was far more doubtful. Whatever would she say to Gabriel's mother? How could she make her understand that theirs had never been a marriage in the true sense of the word? There would be too many questions. She wished Elissa Harrowe had not learned where she was.

Hours later and into the night, Serenity was still seated beside the fireplace, contemplating the matter. Should she go to Carolina? Of course, she could not leave Joshua or Biscuit behind. They would have to go with her. Yet, the idea of even such an indirect contact with Gabriel frightened her a little. She was aware of the dangerous feelings she had felt for Gabriel at one time. Would this give rise to even more of those feelings? There had been no mention of Gabriel in his mother's missive. He must still be away on the *Firefly*. And Emmalina had encouraged her to go . . .

Serenity tried to reach a decision. Emmalina had already retired for the night, and Joshua had sought his bed as well, while Biscuit slept at her feet.

If she were to go, now would be a good time. Once school began in the fall, it would be impossible if she had a teaching position. At the present, there was only her own reluctance to become involved with Gabriel's family that caused concern about leaving for a time.

Closing her blue eyes and leaning her head back in the chair, Serenity's thoughts turned to Gabriel. The memory of him holding her and kissing her was still vividly etched in her mind. He had taught her what it was to be a woman, to feel complete. The sweet mystery of his body entwined with hers came back to her in a bittersweet rush. She could never forget.

And there were other moments as well. Their wedding. When she had thrown the egg at him; the way he had scooped her up into his strong arms. Suddenly, she realized how very much she missed him. He had swept into her life like a summer storm, and ever since he was gone it had seemed like something was missing.

Perhaps she should go to Carolina after all. How could there be any danger in confronting something from the past?

As they stood on the deck of the merchant vessel, Joshua and Biscuit appeared eager for a new adventure, while Serenity felt only a sense of inevitability. Her long plum gown was whipped by the breeze, and Serenity drew her gray cape more securely around her. The late October weather was starting to chill, and she would be glad at least of the warmer clime of the Carolinas for a short time.

Since their arrival on board, the captain had been most kind to them. He had treated them as though they were honored guests, deserving of great respect, and he had not even questioned Biscuit's presence. Serenity had appreciated how kind he had been, but it was also puzzling.

There did not appear to be other passengers on board, only them. Obviously, this was not a passenger vessel. However, as they boarded the ship, she had caught a glimpse of one man. But he had disappeared so quickly that afterward she wondered if he had been there at all. Further, the man had not come to the captain's cabin for the evening meal. Still, there were times when she could almost sense his presence, and she wondered if he was watching them. Why else would the man choose to remain hidden?

Joshua enjoyed being on the ship, and she had to admit that she liked it as well. Gazing out over the water from the rail in the late afternoon, she marveled at the sun as it started to dip low on the horizon. Soon it would be sunset.

Biscuit barked joyfully.

What was it the dog saw? Then Serenity saw the man again. Wearing a hat and a heavy cloak, he was just down the deck, and she wondered if he'd been watching them as they stood there.

Eagerly, Biscuit bounded up the deck toward him, but immediately the man disappeared once more. She hoped that the man had not been frightened by Biscuit. Perhaps the dog was why he was avoiding them.

The wolfhound came back with a whimper. Giving the dog a pat, she asked, "What is it, Biscuit? Did you think it was someone you knew?" There were very few people the dog liked, yet Biscuit had appeared almost eager to see the man.

Joshua drew closer. "When will we be there, Serenity?"

"In a few days, Josh," she replied, feeling all the more uncertain now that the moment for meeting Gabriel's family was drawing near. Did they know she was a Quaker? Would she meet with their approval?

"How long will we stay?"

Serenity could see the man was back out on the deck again, standing in the shadow of a mast. A troubled frown creased her brow as she tried to see him more clearly. There was something almost familiar about him.

Sighing softly, Serenity forced herself to dismiss the man from her mind and give her attention to Joshua once more.

"We shall remain in Carolina no longer than is absolutely necessary, Joshua. No longer . . . "

Chapter Fifteen

As though someone had known precisely the moment they would arrive, Serenity found a driver and coach awaiting them when they disembarked at the port of Charleston.

"Mistress Harrowe," an exceedingly tall man said when he approached them, "my name is Lot. You're to come with me."

Serenity smiled. The man was very impressive. Although not the liveried servant she had grown accustomed to in Washington, his skin gleamed like black marble and he must have stood nearly seven feet tall. What was more, he possessed a good biblical name.

"Lot," she replied, her manner friendly. "Please meet my brother, Joshua, and my dog Biscuit. They have come with me on my journey."

Biscuit growled.

Uncertainly, Lot frowned at the big wolfhound. Then he nodded in Joshua's direction.

"Please forgive my dog, Lot. He shall warm to you after a time."

A suspicious eye on the animal and a doubtful expression on his face, Lot moved to pick up the portmanteau that contained her clothing, but Serenity put out her hand to stop him. "I can manage for myself, Lot. You need not trouble yourself." Serenity had no wish to be an added burden to anyone while visiting Gabriel's family.

Lot appeared perplexed, but indicating for her to follow, he said simply, "The coach is over here, Mistress Harrowe."

Serenity, Joshua, and Biscuit followed dutifully as Lot led the way to the waiting coach. Once he had helped them all inside, Lot closed the door behind them and took his place on the driver's seat.

Leaning back against the velvet-covered seat cushions as the coach set off, Serenity was suddenly filled with misgivings. She felt distressed, knowing she would arrive at the home of Gabriel's mother in a travel-weary, disheveled state. What would Elissa Harrowe think of her? As it was, she already felt at a definite disadvantage. It was obvious from the luxury of the coach that Gabriel's family had much in the way of material things, and it was equally obvious that Serenity herself had come from a much simpler beginning. There might be many questions as to why Gabriel had even chosen to wed her in the first place. What would she reply? That the two of them had been forced into a marriage neither of them wanted?

Joshua looked uncertain as well. "Do you think we'll have friends where we're going, Serenity?"

Giving him an encouraging smile, Serenity replied, "I am certain there will be, Joshua. And, in any case, you have me and Biscuit."

For a moment, Joshua appeared more troubled than before. A glint of moisture in his eyes, he wiped his nose on the back of his sleeve and kicked his boot against the floor of the coach. "I miss them . . . "

Immediately concerned, Serenity sat up straighter in her seat and inquired softly, "Who, Joshua? Who do you miss?"

"Friends . . . " he said. "On the *Firefly*. I liked Gabriel and Kane. They were nice. They let me help . . . showed me how to do things."

"Yes, I know," Serenity murmured, drawing him closer and smoothing his dark hair back from his face. Sometimes, she forgot how important it was for Joshua to feel accepted by others, and certainly Gabriel and Kane had shared the rare ability to do just that. "They did understand you, Joshua."

"Do you think we will ever see them again, Serenity?"

Sighing softly, Serenity gazed at Joshua with a touch of sadness. She wished she could say yes, but it was doubtful they would ever see Gabriel or Kane again. Once they had visited Gabriel's mother, they would soon return to Brookeville. "Perhaps . . . " she said, feeling it better not to rob Joshua of all hope. "Rest, now, Joshua. This journey shall likely take some time."

Serenity was not aware of the two riders who fell into pace with the horse-drawn coach a short time later. It was Joshua who first noticed them, when he restlessly poked his head out of the coach window to gaze around. Spying them following at a short distance, he insisted Serenity take a look.

Clad in hats and rugged-looking clothing, it was impossible to distinguish their faces. Still, Lot seemed unperturbed by their presence, and thinking they might well be fellow travelers, Serenity thought no more about it.

Serenity was much more concerned about reaching their destination. It had been a long day, and the swaying and jouncing of the coach made her wish fervently for a brief respite. Mercifully, after they had traveled some distance more, she felt the coach start to slow as Lot drew the horses to a halt. Had they arrived?

Peering from the coach, Serenity did not see the mansion she had anticipated. Instead, the coach had drawn up before a small cottage that sat nestled in a grove of trees. "Mistress Harrowe," Lot said as he opened the coach door, "I thought you might need a short rest. We've still got some way to go. It'll be nightfall before we get to Marihaven. There's a cottage here where you can wash up. The boy and your dog can stay here with me."

Grateful for his thoughtfulness, Serenity allowed Lot to help her down from the coach. Briefly, she observed that the two riders were no longer there; they must have gone on their way sometime before.

The door to the cottage was unlocked. Gingerly drawing it open, Serenity could see a warm fire glowing inside. As though someone had been expecting her, on the table there was a pitcher filled with water and a bowl with which to wash, as well as fresh cloths. Yet, no one was there. She had the cottage entirely to herself.

She felt guilty about keeping everyone waiting. Still, as Serenity prepared to leave she could not help taking a moment to gaze longingly at the bed. Spread with a downy comforter, it appeared soft and inviting. If only there was time to lie down upon it. . . .

But they had to be on their way. Even now, it was nearing dusk.

Reluctantly going to the cottage door, Serenity started to open it. But there was something about the cottage that made her turn back around once more. Strangely, the cottage reminded Serenity of her home on Nantucket. Perhaps it was its simplicity. It brought back sweet memories. Seahawks flying, sandy beaches, and ribbons of silver across a purple moor . . . She had not forgotten. And Gabriel . . .

Suddenly, the door was thrust aside and a tall man loomed in the doorway. Startled, Serenity caught her breath. For a moment, she did not recognize the man who stood there. Then, as he drew his hat from his head, there was no mistaking his handsome face. It was achingly familiar.

"Gabriel . . . "

There was no time for rationalization, nor for questions as to why he had appeared to her in such a way.

Slamming the door behind him with a booted foot, Gabriel pulled her into his arms. A moment later, his mouth found hers.

Breathlessly, she pulled away. "The driver . . . Joshua . . . they are waiting for me—"

Scooping her up into his strong arms, Gabriel halted her protests. "I sent them on ahead to Marihaven. Joshua will be all right. Kane will look after him." He nibbled at her lower lip.

Serenity shook her head. "But your mother will be expecting me."

"She is expecting you tomorrow."

His mouth on hers was making her frightfully dizzy. Unable to stop herself, her arms twined about his neck. "You planned all this," she said in mild accusation. "When you knew I would be coming."

"Yes . . . "

He strode over to the bed and seated her upon it, following her down to place more kisses along her neck and to the tender spot just below her earlobe.

"What makes you think—"

"What, Serenity?" he asked, not bothering to raise his head.

She tried to catch her breath, but she tilted her head back involuntarily as his mouth found her throat. "I did not agree . . . "

Stopping for a moment, he removed her cap and loosened her hair. Then, gently, he brushed a kiss across her mouth. Sliding his hand down to one breast, he teased at the tip through the cloth of her gown. "This is no time to be independent, Serenity."

"Please stop," she said.

But even as she said the words, his hand had moved beneath her gown. Finding its way through the tangle of her petticoats, he slipped it inside her pantaloons. Gently exploring, his hand found her most sensitive place. "Stop this?" he said in a husky voice. "Or this . . ."

Serenity gasped and struggled to get away. "We cannot . . ."

"We are husband and wife, Serenity. Before God . . ."

Her breathing was quick. If he was bent on seducing her, he was certainly doing a remarkable job of it. Rapidly she was dispensing with every reason she could think of to deny him.

Neither of them could wait to be free of their clothing. Stripping it off as quickly as they could, together they rolled over on the bed, with Gabriel ending up on top. His mouth was close, stealing her breath away, though their lips did not quite touch. Parting her mouth with his tongue, slowly he let it penetrate inside.

Never before had she been so ready for him. Never before . . .

They both glistened with a fine sheen of moisture, as the firelight cast golden shadows on their skin. Moving away from her rose-dusted mouth, he found first one breast and then the other, making her tingle and yearn for him all the more. Then he raised his head.

His eyes dark with desire, his voice gentle, he said, "I want you, Madame Harrowe."

Tears misted her blue eyes. Had she been mistaken, or was he finally claiming her as his wife?

As he drew her to him, Serenity could feel him tremble as her body yielded completely to his. Undeniably, it was what they both wanted. Kissing his cheek and then his mouth, she moved beneath him. Rising and falling. Faster and faster. Instinctively, she knew she was taking him over the threshold. Then she felt it as well. For a single moment, her spirits soared and hung as though suspended; then when she thought she could bear it no longer she cried out as she felt the sudden quaking deep within. At precisely the same moment, he shuddered in a primal response.

Afterwards, her heart still beating rapidly, she lay in his arms. It was too soon for questions, though there were many. Nuzzling up against him, she only vaguely felt him draw the covers over them. Then, tired and replete, his body next to hers, they slept.

"Good morning," she said, tickling him with a feather that she had found in the pillow just beneath his nose. "You must wake and tell me if I am dreaming, for only yesterday I thought I would never see you again."

Stretching out his long arms to draw her closer, Gabriel grinned sleepily. Then he tousled her hair. "Do you always have dreams of men in your bed?"

With a shove, she pushed him away and rolled onto her back, as though to ignore him. "Just what are you implying, sir?"

Gabriel chuckled and drew her closer to place a kiss on her nose. "I've missed you, Serenity."

"Am I to assume you were the one who wanted me to come to the Carolinas? It was not your mother's desire at all?"

He sighed and drew away slightly. "Would you have come if you knew I was behind it?"

A frown creased her delicate brow for a moment. "No . . . "

"Well, then, I guessed correctly."

She could feel Gabriel withdraw from her, as his handsome face grew hard once more, making the scar across his cheek more pronounced.

"I am not your concern. We agreed . . . "

"You are still my wife," he countered irritably. "Like it or not."

"A wife sees to her husband. A wife cares for him. They share a life one with another. Are you asking that of me?"

Rolling onto his side, he faced her. "I haven't yet decided what I'm asking, Serenity." He traced a finger along her cheek. "I have no more idea than you do if this can work out. Would it be so painful to simply give it a try?" His mouth grazed hers.

It was difficult arguing with him, when the two of them were lying in bed, divested of all their clothing, and he was starting to make her head spin once more with the way his silvery eyes were perusing her. Taking her small hand in his, he drew it beneath the covers and down much lower to touch him.

"Parts of me want it to work out very much," he said pointedly.

Serenity blushed. He was utterly impossible. But did she not know that already?

"You are a rogue," she countered. "I have no doubt you have a woman lurking in every corner, eager to warm your bed."

"There is only one to whom I would care to give that honor at the moment, Serenity." He rolled over on top of her.

Serenity allowed him to kiss her as he parted her thighs. She wanted to think about what he had just asked her. Was she willing to remain in the Carolinas and be his wife? As he slipped gently inside her all other thoughts fled. "Gabriel . . . "

He was making it very difficult for her to refuse.

As the coach drew up in front of the mansion at Marihaven, Serenity gazed at it in awe. Lot had returned for them late that afternoon, and it was now evening. Torches lit the exterior of the mansion, while candles glowed brightly from within. Strains of music could be heard even as Gabriel helped her down from the coach.

Was this the home of Gabriel's mother? Or his? She had never expected anything as magnificent as this. She had known that Gabriel came from wealth, but she had never before comprehended to what extent that affluency might be.

"This way, Serenity," Gabriel said, noting the stunned look on her face as she drew back slightly. "This is to be your new home. Marihaven. It once belonged to my grandfather. Now it belongs to me. I intended for your arrival to be much quieter. But, apparently, someone in the family has decided to welcome you in a grand style."

As the heavy front door swung wide, a maid in a white apron and mob cap gasped in surprise, then immediately dashed away, calling out in an excited voice, "Mistress Raven. Mistress Raven. They're here. . . . "

At Serenity's puzzlement, Gabriel took her hand in his. "My sister Raven must be the guilty party. She delights in any excuse for a ball. You'll find she is well known for acting on impulse."

"Gabriel . . . " Serenity began; then she quickly stopped herself. This was his way of life. There was no use telling him that she would have much preferred remaining in the little cottage in the trees to all this, or that it was one thing to visit Carissa in Washington for a time, with all her finery, and quite another to find she might actually have to call a place like this her home. Was that why Gabriel had put off having her see it until today?

Gabriel pulled her close. "Is something troubling you, Serenity?"

At that moment, a beautiful dark-haired young woman of about nineteen in a stunning pink ball gown burst into view. Her eyes were silvery gray, just like Gabriel's. She smiled in delight. "Gabriel . . . Gabriel . . . do bring her in. Mother and Father are here. And everyone wants to meet your new bride."

Placing her hand on his arm, she let Gabriel lead her inside.

Clad in her white cap and her simple gown, Serenity felt even more out of place here than she had in Washington. As they stepped into the flower-bedecked ballroom, the music stopped abruptly and all eyes turned toward them. For a moment there was a stunned silence. Then a lovely woman with golden hair and blue-green eyes moved forward to greet them with a smile.

"Gabriel," the woman said, "would you care to introduce us?"

"Yes, Mother. This is my wife, Serenity," Gabriel returned warmly. "Serenity, I would like you to meet my mother."

At that moment, a tall dark-haired man with a hint of gray at his temples stepped forward as well. There was no mistaking who he was. He had to be Gabriel's father. The two of them were so similar, the height, the appearance, even the reserved manner and slightly dangerous aura. The elder Harrowe's eyes were a startling silver-gray as well. "Serenity," he said, taking her hand for a brief moment. "I'm Gabriel's father, Nicholas Harrowe."

After greeting her, there was an exchange of glances between Gabriel and his father. Though there was clearly affection in the way they gazed at each other, there was also a certain amount of reservation. For a moment, there was silence.

"Father . . . "

"A lovely bride, Gabriel."

The music had begun again. Serenity felt a sudden surge of desperation deep inside for the slightest familiar thing. Catching Gabriel's eyes, she murmured, "Joshua?"

"Don't worry, Serenity. I am certain he is all right."

The dancers swirled around the floor. Excusing themselves discreetly as though they suspected how overwhelming the situation was for her, Gabriel's parents joined the dancers as well. For a moment, Serenity watched the two of them. It was strange, but in a ballroom filled with other people, Nicholas and Elissa Harrowe appeared to dance alone. Even now, they had eyes only for each other. She could almost envision the way they had looked when they were young.

"Would you care to dance, Serenity? It is customary for the groom to dance the first dance with his bride."

"You know I don't dance."

"I thought perhaps in Washington . . . "

Serenity thought she detected something in his face for a moment as he said the words; it was decidedly unpleasant. Then it was gone.

Would this be one of the many ways she would inevitably disappoint him? They were possessed of so little in common. She felt like a sparrow, seeking to invade a hawk's territory.

Sighing softly with weariness, Serenity gazed up at him. "Would it be unforgivably rude for you to take me to my room now, Gabriel?"

Gabriel nodded silently. There was a closed expression upon his tanned, harshly handsome face. "Whatever you wish, Serenity."

Chapter Sixteen

The soft knock on the bedchamber door alerted Serenity that someone was outside. Pushing herself up in the spacious bed, she gazed around herself for a moment uncertainly. Upon the bed was her grandmother's quilt, yet she had no recollection of the room. Then it came back to her. She was at Gabriel's plantation, Marihaven. Her new home . . .

Drawing the covers up tightly beneath her chin, Serenity called out, "You may enter."

Gabriel peered around the door. "Still in bed, Serenity?" He bore a tray with a tempting array of food.

Smiling, Serenity waited for him to come in. It seemed she had slept an inordinate length of time. Certainly, it must be midmorning, or even later, and this her first day at Marihaven.

Serenity watched as Gabriel sat the tray on a nearby table. "I must have been more weary than I thought. I am sorry if I have kept you waiting."

"I wanted you to sleep," he said. "You are not a guest here, Serenity. This is your home. You may do exactly as you please."

Guiltily, Serenity thought of the many things she should be doing. "But I have not yet checked on Joshua or Biscuit to see if they are content. And I should like to see more of Marihaven."

He buttered a hot muffin, then came over to sit on the edge of the bed to hand it to her. "I thought once you were dressed we might look around together. I have to admit, it will refresh my mind as well. Despite the fact that Marihaven is my inheritance, I have never spent any time here. Perhaps you can make me see it through unprejudiced eyes."

Considering his words, Serenity took a bite of the muffin. It was obvious he had less than a fond regard for Marihaven. Swallowing, she said the only thing she could think of, "The ballroom was quite grand."

"A recent touch," he replied. "The entire place was gutted by fire during the War for Independence, and the ballroom was added to what was left of the original structure when Marihaven was restored. Last night's ball was the first the estate has ever boasted. It was my grandfather who originally built the place for my grandmother, and he was not inclined to balls. He was an English sea captain who cherished the sea until the day he died."

Teasingly, she returned, "Is that your feeling, too?"

Gabriel frowned slightly. "I love the sea, but I have no interest in spending the rest of my life there, Serenity. Still," he added thoughtfully, "to remain here at Marihaven will present certain problems."

Serenity wanted to ask exactly what those problems might be, but she was uncertain if she should. He seemed to have no desire to go on. "I shall dress quickly. Will you wait?"

For a moment, Gabriel's silvery gaze met hers. There was something unfathomable in his expression. Then he arose from where he was seated beside her on the bed. "I shall wait for you downstairs, Serenity. Come down when you are dressed."

Frowning darkly, Gabriel gazed out the window at the grounds of the plantation, his thoughts still on Serenity and the delightful vision she had made as she sat up in bed, her long, copper hair framing her lovely face and her cheeks still rose-dusted from sleep.

Most of the night before, he had lain awake and restless, wanting to go to her bedchamber and feel again the warmth of her body next to his. Yet it would not have been right. He had seen her reaction at the ball. Serenity looked as though she might bolt from the room at any moment.

He had been wrong in assuming that Serenity's stay in Washington would have changed her, prepared her to some extent for what life would be like here at Marihaven. He had even experienced a sharp twinge of jealousy, remembering that she had spent a good deal of her time in the capital in the company of Senator Nathaniel Bentley. Obviously, the two of them had shared some sort of relationship there. But precisely what that relationship had been, or whether Serenity entertained any fondness for the man, he could not venture to guess.

Still, judging from the way she had reacted when he'd asked her to dance, Serenity had learned very little of the ways of the world during her stay there—even if Carissa had dressed her in a fancy ball gown and waved her before the senator's eyes like a red flag before a bull. It bothered him more than he cared to admit. No doubt, Serenity must have been the most beautiful woman at the President's ball.

"Gabriel . . . "

He turned to gaze at her. Wearing her white cap and a mauve gown, she was incredibly lovely just as she was. "Are you ready?"

"Yes," she replied, lowering her blue eyes for a moment. "I am sorry to have kept you waiting.

For a moment, his hands clenched into fists and a muscle tightened along his jaw. Put first things first, he reminded himself firmly. Serenity must get used to her new surroundings. It did not matter that he was aching to hold her, to pull off her cap and set her hair free, to kiss that soft pink mouth, then take her back up the stairs and press her down upon the bed and spend the rest of the day exploring every inch of her silken body.

Gabriel had sworn to himself that he would not force Serenity to his bed if she came to the Carolinas. He would give her time. Then, unthinkingly, he had done precisely that at the cottage. He had seduced her in every way he knew how. He had known she would find the cottage appealing; he had purposefully seen to it that it was as much like her home on Nantucket as he could. Then he had given her no opportunity to resist him physically. He had even reminded her they were husband and wife, knowing all the while that it would force her to his bed as nothing else would. Well, he refused to do so again.

"I thought perhaps I would take you to see Joshua first," Gabriel said carefully, "so you can see that he is happy and thriving. Between Lot and Kane, they have kept him busy. Biscuit, however, is another matter. Undoubtedly, that cantankerous wolfhound won't stop his growling until he sees you are here, safe and sound." Pausing for a moment, he gave her a wry grin as he caught the twinkle in her blue eyes. "Once we've seen Joshua and Biscuit, we shall tour the mansion. Then, later, if you would like, I'll have the carriage brought around so we can take a ride and I can show you some of the land."

Was it so important to please her? If he did not know better, he might think he was actually starting to fall in love with Serenity.

From the first night of her arrival, Serenity had found everything about Marihaven to be awe-inspiring. She had never imagined living in such luxurious surroundings, let alone that she would be expected to help oversee what went on there.

The mansion itself was exquisite. The wood-paneled front entry was large and boasted a wide staircase, while to one side was the great hall, in which the ball had been held, with its walls of white, its ceiling sculpted of intricately decorated plaster, its spacious interior echoing each footstep when it was not filled with people.

There were two drawing rooms, the larger of which was downstairs and decorated in cream with gold damask draperies. The smaller one was upstairs and done in pale green with drapes of rich green velvet and touches of rose. There was a library lined with an impressive array of books, a sunshiny morning room with a pianoforte, and several bedchambers, each tastefully decorated in a different hue. Her own was of pristine white with touches of blue, as though it awaited only the addition of her grandma's quilt to complete its decor.

Gloria Pedersen

And that was not all. In order to maintain the mansion, there were servants in livery to take care of every chore. Outside there was a stable, and farther on there were more buildings that housed the many people who worked the plantation. Serenity wondered if she would ever feel she belonged, or that she was capable of performing the duties that had been thrust upon her as the new mistress of the manor. And it was precisely this last thought that concerned Serenity as she heard the sound of a commotion outside.

Quickly, Serenity hurried to the door. Gabriel had left some hours earlier for a meeting in Charleston, and although she'd been at Marihaven one full week, this was the first time she had been faced with any sort of crisis requiring her attention when he was not there.

Swinging the door wide, Serenity was shocked to see a kicking and screaming Raven, Gabriel's younger sister, held in Kane's arms.

"Let me go, you oaf!" Raven ordered angrily. "You blackguard! You . . . you reprobate. Let me go, I say. You have no right . . ."

Promptly obliging, Kane immediately let her go, dropping her in a furious heap on the ground. "I should think twice, Miss Harrowe, before you try that again. I have no patience with spoiled young ladies."

Raven glared at him, then shot a glance at Serenity. "Reprimand your servant," she demanded. "Have him beaten within an inch of his life. He has no right to treat a Harrowe this way."

Serenity could not help herself. She smiled. Kane was hardly a servant. And telling Kane what to do was a little like trying to capture the wind. "Here, Raven. Let me help you up," she said, quickly going over to where the girl sat on the ground. "We shall discuss this matter in the drawing room. Come, now."

Once inside, Serenity saw to it that Raven was comfortably seated, then sent a young serving girl named Daisy for refreshments. That done, she sat down beside her new sister-in-law and sought to make sense of what had transpired. Obviously,

160

Raven's dignity was more bruised than anything else. Serenity was also certain that Kane had been reacting only to the girl's provocation.

"You must start at the beginning, Raven."

Gazing at her with silvery-gray eyes, Gabriel's sister relaxed slightly. There was a hint of a pout about her pink mouth. "When I rode in, that man was standing there. He accused me of abusing my horse. He said I had ridden the horse too hard, and I should be ashamed. I knew he was right, but I detested his impudence. I could not help myself. I struck him with my quirt. It was then that he dragged me down from my horse and would not release me."

"I am sorry Kane handled you so roughly, Raven. But, knowing the man, I suspect you were quite fortunate that was all he did. Kane is not a servant, as you had supposed. He is Gabriel's friend, and mine. And I am certain he can be very dangerous upon occasion." .

Raven considered her words for a moment. Then, she smiled haughtily. "Well, I have no intention of seeing the ruffian again, in any event. And I shall not let him ruin my day. I have come from Twin Oaks to visit you, Serenity. I was hoping we could get better acquainted. I feel I owe you an apology for surprising you with a ball on your first night here. Perhaps it would have been better to have waited and given you more time to adjust."

"You need not apologize," Serenity replied, though she agreed that the ball should have waited. "Your kindness in planning it was sincerely appreciated."

Sighing softly, Raven gazed at her in wonder. "It's easy to see why Gabriel fell in love with you, Serenity. You are so very beautiful and gracious. It would take someone precisely like you to make my brother finally settle down. No one else ever came close to succeeding at such a feat before."

For a brief moment a frown flitted across Serenity's lovely features. Love had never been a factor in the relationship between herself and Gabriel. What was more, since their arrival at Marihaven, Gabriel had chosen not to even share her bed. For days, it had troubled her. She had thought everything was so

Gloria Pedersen

wonderful at the cottage. So perfect. When he had held her, touched her, made her tremble with desire.

After that night, she had thought they would truly be husband and wife. What had she done to make him turn away in the time since? Every night, Gabriel would see her to her bedchamber door, and then he would promptly say good night and go on his way. Each time when he left her, Serenity had hoped he would return later to hold her in his arms, but he never did.

Choosing to change the subject, Serenity remarked honestly, "You are by far the loveliest person I have ever seen, Raven. Far more beautiful than me. And you are endowed with great spirit."

"If that is your polite way of saying I invite trouble," Raven murmured with a smile, "then perhaps you are right. I am afraid Gabriel and I share that in common, as well as the dark hair and gray eyes. Our brother, Brandon, of course, was far different in every respect than either of us. You see," she explained, "each of us was given a family name. Gabriel was named for a cousin who was a war hero who died during the War for Independence. I am named for my mother's family, the Ravenels. Brandon was named after my grandfather, Brand Harrowe. But Brandon never favored the Harrowe side of the family in the slightest, with their dark looks and wild dispositions. Brandon took after my mother's side. He was fair-haired and charming. Ask anyone; Brandon was perfection."

"I have never heard Gabriel mention a brother before."

Startled, Raven looked away for a moment, as though suddenly distressed that she had mentioned it. "Perhaps that's one subject Gabriel still finds painful to discuss. And if I had been aware that you did not already know, I would have held my tongue as well."

"You were not wrong to have mentioned it," Serenity prompted hurriedly. She was curious as to why Gabriel had never spoken of Brandon. "Gabriel's reluctance does not mean I should not know, Raven. Sometimes the most painful of

162

things are the very ones a person must know to understand another."

"Yes, of course, you are right, Serenity. It's just that the way Gabriel feels about Brandon is something he's never discussed with any of us. However, I thought he might have made an exception with you."

"That makes it all the more important . . . "

Turning slightly, Raven gazed at her intently. "Brandon is dead, Serenity, and Gabriel feels responsible. You see, as children, Brandon always admired Gabriel and looked up to him because he was the older brother. It did not matter that Brandon was so special in his own way. Gabriel was an adventurer; everything he did was on the edge of danger. And Brandon always wanted to follow in his footsteps."

For a moment, Raven paused, as though remembering, then she continued on. "Brandon joined the navy to be exactly like Gabriel. Sometime during the Barbary War, Brandon even managed to get himself assigned to the same area that Gabriel was in. Then, as fate would have it, after a time both Gabriel and Brandon were chosen as a part of a select band that was to sneak into the harbor of Tripoli. Under cover of darkness, they were assigned to burn a vessel named the *Philadelphia* right under the Barbary pirates' noses. It was then that Brandon was fatally wounded. Of course, my parents were notified of Brandon's death. But it was not until much later that everyone learned Brandon had died in Gabriel's arms. A virtual stranger told them." Raven sniffled and leaned back in her chair. "I believe that's why Gabriel refused to come back here for so long to settle down. There were too many reminders."

Her blue eyes troubled, Serenity had remained silent while Raven was speaking. She had never imagined Gabriel harbored such a painful secret. Was this the reason for his reticence to return to Marihaven? And now, at a time when he needed comfort the most, he had chosen to turn away from her.

"Thank you for telling me, Raven. Perhaps I can help Gabriel in some way, now that I am aware. And I hope you will come to visit me often. I think I can learn much from you. . . . "

Laughing delightedly, her eyes bright once more, Raven interjected, "Why, Serenity, I came here hoping to learn from you. I fear I shall never capture a man's heart if I don't start behaving with more restraint. The finishing school has failed. My mother has thrown up her hands in utter despair. My only hope is that some of your graciousness will be catching, sort of like the pox or yellow fever, or else my tongue will see me an old maid. But I can assure you, if there is the slightest thing I can possibly teach you in return, I shall be more than happy to do so."

Gabriel saw Serenity to her bedchamber door, then continued down the hallway to his own bedchamber at the end. Though the two rooms were only a few doors apart, it might as well have been miles.

Entering his room, Gabriel went over to turn up the lantern. He dreaded the night ahead. He had thought being here at Marihaven with Serenity would banish the ghosts from his past. It had not. He had known there would be problems for him in coming back to Marihaven, and he was certain there would be more problems in the future. However, it was thoughts of Brandon that he was finding the most difficult to live with at the moment. Time had not healed the wound.

He did not know what he had expected. Acceptance of what could not be changed? Wisdom to keep him from thinking about Brandon at all? But how could he expect Serenity to help him when she did not even know what devils pursued him?

Restlessly, Gabriel went to the window and stood gazing out at the moonlight. He ran the fingers of one hand through his hair, his thoughts brooding.

His father had requested that Gabriel come for a visit tomorrow, and Gabriel knew precisely what the elder Harrowe was going to say. It would not be about Brandon. It never was. Both of them carried their own guilt where Brandon was concerned. His father had been a notable adventurer during the War of Independence, commanding a privateer as well as taunting other forms of danger. And Gabriel had followed his example. The real pity was that Brandon had chosen to follow in their footsteps, as well. However, Gabriel's guilt went far deeper than his father's, for he'd been there when his brother died. Still, it was something they never discussed. Most certainly, it would not be discussed now. No, his father clearly had something else on his mind.

Lost in thought, Gabriel did not hear Serenity enter the room. "Gabriel . . . "

Spinning quickly, Gabriel saw her standing there.

A vision of loveliness, his wife was already dressed for bed in a white gown. Her silky hair fell like a curtain about her slender shoulders, and her cheeks were dusted with pink.

"Is there something wrong, Serenity?"

"Your sister came to visit me today."

Gabriel sighed. He had almost forgotten the incident between his sister and Kane. And since Serenity had not brought up the subject at dinner, he had wrongfully assumed she had chosen not to discuss it.

"I already know," he replied. "Kane mentioned that Raven had been here—in less than flattering terms. I think he felt the need to explain before I heard what happened from someone else. I should have guessed, when you did not mention it earlier, that you were concerned that I would be angry with Kane. Well, you need not worry, Serenity. I know how Raven can be at times."

"I am grateful to you for your understanding," she replied. "But that is not the only reason I have come. . . . "

His eyes were silver in the lantern light. "There was something else, Serenity?"

Moving closer, Serenity replied, "Raven told me about Brandon."

A muscle tensed along his jaw. He had not counted on that; he did not want to burden Serenity with his past. "What did she tell you precisely?"

"Raven told me that he died in your arms," she murmured softly. "I am so sorry, Gabriel. I want you to know I understand."

"I try not to think about it, Serenity."

"But you do . . ."

His eyes on her enchanting face, Gabriel realized that he had not even kissed her since the cottage. If he did so now, he would never be able to stop there. "You should go back to your bed."

Serenity made no effort to leave. Instead, she stepped closer and slid her arms up around his neck, then brushed a kiss across his mouth with honeyed sweetness.

For a moment, he closed his eyes and did not move. Then, opening them again, he gazed down into her blue velvet eyes. There was the unmistakable scent of lavender in her silky hair, and her mouth was soft and inviting. Still, he wanted there to be no mistake about why she was there. "Why, Serenity?" he asked huskily. "If this is pity because of my brother, I can do without it. I have been forced to do so, thus far."

Beneath her gown, he knew she wore nothing at all, and her skin was as soft and silky as a cat's. Unbidden, he felt the heat rise within him. Already she was making him ache with desire.

Dark lights of emotion danced in her eyes, and Serenity murmured softly in return. "Don't you know? I need the touch of your skin to help me warm the night, Gabriel. I need you."

Chapter Seventeen

Leaving Serenity curled in his bed, Gabriel had reluctantly risen early, then taken a shortened route through the swamp to reach his parents' mansion at Twin Oaks. Although his parents still maintained their stately home in Charleston and resided there a part of each year, Nicholas and Elissa Harrowe now divided their time between it and Twin Oaks, the beautiful plantation that had been his mother's home while she was growing up and which she'd inherited upon the death of her father. It was there Gabriel knew he would find them.

"I would not like to see you hurt your new bride, Gabriel," Nicholas Harrowe reprimanded his son quietly, after his arrival. "Nor for you to be hurt yourself. You have made enemies here, and they will soon know of your return. The matter must be carefully considered. I know you were not entirely to blame for what happened with Veronique. I have never attempted to counsel you on affairs of the heart. Certainly, I have suffered enough with mistakes of my own in the past. But the gossip could hurt Serenity deeply. It is something as a Quaker she might never understand. And Veronique's father may well call you out the moment he sets eyes on you."

"I'll admit I behaved rashly where Veronique was concerned, Father. But I cannot go back and change the situation."

Nicholas Harrowe frowned. "You don't seem to realize the seriousness of this, Gabriel. This matter is not of minor importance. Not only did you leave Veronique in the hotel lobby, but you left her there without a stitch of clothing on. The talk did not die down for months. The Beaumarchais were the laughing-stocks of the entire city, and it even went so far as to cost Veronique her betrothal to the senator. Such a scandal is not easily forgotten or forgiven."

Gabriel countered, "I was told Veronique did wed soon after."

Heaving a weary sigh, Nicholas replied, "Yes, almost immediately after, to be exact. But it was not to the senator. The man's name was Durand. By all accounts, he was respectable enough, and he did own some property. But he was in financial straits at the time. It was obvious he was bought by Charles Beaumarchais in hopes of salvaging his daughter's tarnished reputation. Not longer after, the man died of yellow fever."

"I see."

"You can then understand the cause for alarm, Gabriel. Don't assume for one moment you can ignore this."

A soft voice interjected. "Nicholas . . . "

His manner immediately softening, his father glanced at the door. "Come in, Lissa. Gabriel and I have finished."

"Gabriel, dear," his mother said, coming to his side. "Did your father speak to you about our plans? We have something we must ask of you."

Gabriel gazed down at his mother fondly. It was no wonder she had captured his father's heart years before; her beauty was ageless. "I don't know anything about your plans, as of yet. Perhaps you should tell me."

Throwing a warm glance in her husband's direction, Lissa responded, "We are going to Paris again. It has been far too long."

"And I suppose this was entirely your idea, Mother? You're certain Father is not simply using this trip as an excuse to set foot on the deck of a ship again? So much for saying he has retired."

Her musical laughter warmed the room as Lissa replied, "It does not matter the reason, Gabriel. We are both excited to go."

"Admit it, Father. The sea is still in your blood."

Nicholas grinned. "And will be, undoubtedly, until the day I die. But I must be getting old. I only enjoy going if your mother is by my side."

His parents were a remarkable pair. Whatever was between them had not faded over the years. "You said there was something you wanted to ask of me?"

Nicholas grew suddenly serious once again. "For some time we have wanted to return to France, but with the blockade it has been impossible. Now I understand negotiations between England and our country have been going on in Ghent since August. And I've learned from private sources that an agreement will soon be reached."

Gabriel nodded. "Yes, I have heard that as well. The time for it is favorable. With Napoleon's defeat in Europe, and Great Britain sending more troops to Canada, our hopes for conquest of that country have failed, which is to the British advantage. Meanwhile, during this spring and fall, we have had some notable victories on other fronts against the British, which puts both sides in good bargaining positions for a treaty to be signed."

"Personally, I feel it is long overdue," Nicholas said. "With things finally more favorable, we should like to travel to France without delay. And that leaves us with the problem of what to do about Raven, since she has no desire to go along. As with most of the Harrowes," he continued, throwing a pointed glance in Gabriel's direction, "she is slightly incorrigible. And since Raven has not chosen to wed, we cannot let her remain in Carolina alone and to her own devices. First of all, it would not be proper, and secondly she would take outrageous advantage of the situation. So now we have come to you . . . "

"Yes, Gabriel," his mother chimed in. "It seems Raven is quite taken with your Serenity, and I am simply delighted by it. Raven has ridden over to Marihaven this morning to spend time with your new bride. I know Serenity will be a marvelous influence on Raven. We were hoping, Gabriel, that you might consider having Raven as a guest for the months we are gone. Of course, you must discuss it with Serenity first. But it would be such a relief to know Raven would be so well in hand."

Gabriel was always happy to oblige his parents in any way he could, but he had a feeling this was one time when things were bound to end up more complicated than it seemed. But he could not refuse. "I shall indeed ask Serenity. But I am certain she will have no objections. And I promise to keep an eye on Raven myself while you are gone."

"Oh, thank you, Gabriel. You have always been so good with your sister. Now I know when we leave I shall truly enjoy myself."

"And when will that be, precisely?"

Nicholas exchanged a glance with Gabriel. "Provided there

Gloria Pedersen

are no problems, the sooner the better. It is best if we leave before the weather turns."

"But we must at least wait until after the Pierponts' ball," Lissa reminded her husband quickly. "They would never forgive us if we did not attend. And it will be Serenity's first opportunity to be truly out in society. We should be there."

Nicholas nodded. "Then it is done. The Pierponts' ball is two weeks hence, and we shall leave for Paris immediately after." Then he added in an aside to Gabriel, "Unless you see a need for me to remain . . . "

"Teach you to dance?" Raven said in amazement. "Why, Serenity, whatever for? I thought you did not believe in dancing. Or it was prohibited, or some such thing. Surely you cannot be serious?"

Refusing to acknowledge her uncertainty, Serenity smiled at her dark-haired sister-in-law, then replied, "There are many things I would not do, Raven. But I am wed to your brother now. I can see no true harm in dancing, if it is with one's own husband. And it is a part of your culture. I can hardly ignore the fact that it is done, nor will I deny Gabriel the pleasure of it. Marriage is made up of compromise. And I should like to please Gabriel."

"Then why not tell him, Serenity? I am certain Gabriel would be delighted to teach you."

Rising from her chair, Serenity took several paces, then nervously spun back around. "The Pierponts are having a ball two weeks from today. Gabriel has said there will be many people there. I wanted to surprise him. And there is one thing more . . . "

"Something else you do not want Gabriel to know?"

"I am afraid so. I should like for you to help me choose a gown. A real gown . . . "

Raven's lovely face lit up and her gray eyes sparkled. "A gown?"

170

For a moment, Serenity hesitated. Was she doing the right thing? She could not help remembering the night she had worn the yellow satin gown with such disastrous results. But this was not the same, and she wanted Gabriel to be proud of her. "I want to appear . . . different," she said, using her hand to indicate the area from the top of her head down to the tips of her toes. "At least for one night."

As though she suddenly understood, Raven said gently, "Never for one moment think that Gabriel is not content with you as you are, Serenity. I have seen the way he looks at you. He is a man in love."

Serenity sighed. How could she tell Raven that the girl was merely imagining things when she believed Gabriel was looking at her in any special way? There was nothing to bind Gabriel to her but a marriage of convenience. Yet, last night, when she'd lain in his arms, she had suddenly realized she yearned with all her heart to make it more.

"You will help me, then?" she asked.

"Certainly, Serenity," Raven replied. "My brother shall have eyes only for you, the night of the Pierpont ball."

As Raven gazed on, Serenity stood in the dressmaker's shop being pinned and poked and measured. Gabriel was to be occupied for the entire day with the purchase of some blooded horses, and after she had made Kane faithfully promise not to tell, Serenity had asked him to drive them into town so that she could select fabric for a gown.

Turning slowly, she frowned at herself in the floor-length mirror. It was strange giving thought to the way one looked. Never before had she cared a whit; to do so would have acknowledged vanity. Yet, now, she knew that she did. It was not for vanity's sake in the least. She was doing it for Gabriel.

"Oh, yes, Madame Caron," Raven remarked. "I do believe the azure watered silk enhances the color of her eyes. It will be perfect for her. And the simplicity of the gown will make it look

171

all the more elegant. There were too many ruffles on the other
design you showed us. This one will be far more stunning on
her. And there must be ribbons the exact same shade of blue to
tie in her hair, and all of the accessories." Then, frowning
slightly, Raven reminded the little dressmaker, whose shop was
the most exclusive in all of Charleston, "But there are less than
two weeks until the Pierponts' ball. Will there be any problem
finishing the gown in time?"

"No, *ma chere*," the woman returned, as she continued with
her pinning. "No problem at all. I shall set Michelle and
Claudette upon it immediately. I will see to it that they do their
finest work, just as they always do on your own beautiful
gowns. Madame Harrowe's introduction to society will be an
astounding success, rest assured."

"Thank you, Madame Caron," Raven said with a smile.

"It shall be quite an evening," the dressmaker went on,
delighted at the opportunity to chat. "Many others have ordered
gowns from me as well." She paused for emphasis. "Including
Madame Durand. How that woman dares to go out in public
after the scandal of a few years past, I shall never know. Of
course, she was not a Durand then. She was a Beaumarchais."
Then, seeing that they knew nothing of the tale, she continued.
"It seems one night the woman was left—as bare as the day she
was born—in the lobby of the nicest hotel in Charleston by
some wickedly handsome gentleman. Apparently, the matter
was provoked, however—she had slashed the gentleman across
the face with a knife. But, oh, the stir it caused . . . They still
talk about it even now."

Feeling uncomfortable listening to such idle gossip, Serenity
turned to Raven. "We should be hurrying, Raven. Kane is waiting for us in the carriage, and I have imposed upon him quite
enough by making him bring us into town. I would not like to
take advantage of his friendship further by keeping him waiting
too long."

"How you can abide that man I shall never know," Raven

replied in exasperation, her hands on her hips and her eyes raised to the ceiling. "I declare, he sets out to irritate me at every turn."

Serenity smiled. "It is true that you and Kane have gotten off to a poor start. But he is truly a fine man. And, given time, I am certain the two of you will begin to like each other."

"Somehow I doubt that," Raven countered. "He is by far the most arrogant man I have ever met. In fact, if I had my way, I would see him set down a measure or two. It is precisely what he deserves."

Serenity held her tongue. There was no use recounting all of Kane's virtues to Raven. Obviously, she had already made up her mind to dislike Kane and appeared to have no desire to change it.

Stepping out of the shop a short while later with Raven by her side, Serenity gazed around her at the puddles that had been left by a heavy rain earlier in the day. "We shall have to step carefully to get to the coach. Perhaps we should let Kane give us a hand. . . . "

"You may call for Kane if you like, Serenity. As for me, I would rather fall in a mud puddle than allow that man to help me."

A frown creasing her brow, Serenity gazed for a moment at her sister-in-law. It occurred to her that Raven was protesting far too much. Was she really attracted to Kane, and afraid to admit it even to herself?

Climbing down from the carriage, Kane approached the two of them where they stood. "Perhaps I should give you a hand."

"No, thank you," Raven replied haughtily. "I shall manage for myself."

Serenity threw her a glance. Raven truly did need a lesson in graciousness. Turning to Kane with a smile, Serenity replied, "I should be most grateful for your help, Kane." Then she added, "I have no wish to land in a puddle."

173

Kane did not hesitate. Effortlessly scooping her up into his arms, he took several long strides toward the waiting carriage and deposited Serenity carefully on the seat. Then he stood waiting to see what Raven would do.

Raven started toward them. Carefully she maneuvered around first one puddle and then another.

"You should let me help you," Kane said, a frown on his face.

There was a stubborn lift to Raven's delicate chin. "Never . . ."

At that precise moment Raven slipped. Before she could catch herself, she fell with a splat in a rain-filled puddle. There was a shocked look on her face.

Serenity stared at her, aghast. It was of no use to think that Raven's impudence had gotten her precisely what she deserved; Serenity's only thought was how to remedy the situation.

Tears welled up in Raven's eyes in utter humiliation.

Immediately, Serenity thought of how she had felt when she had landed in the broken eggs and Gabriel had laughed at her. Somehow she had a feeling Raven would never be so forgiving. If Kane laughed at Raven now, there would never be any hope for their relationship. She must get to Raven quickly.

Leaning forward, Serenity started to climb down from the carriage.

"Stay there," Kane ordered. "I'll get her."

As though it was something he did every day, Kane scooped Raven up as if she weighed no more than a feather.

If Raven had hoped to bring Kane down a degree, the tables had certainly turned. However, Kane did not laugh. He did not even smile. Without word, he bore Raven back over to the carriage and set her inside with a slight thump. Then, not even looking in the girl's direction, he climbed in himself and immediately flicked the horse's reins to set them on their way.

Aware of the embarrassment Raven must be feeling, Serenity squeezed her sister-in-law's muddy hand. Raven needed no chastising. What had happened had been enough. Now they could only pretend it had never occurred.

Riding along in silence for a short way, Serenity finally ventured, "I hope we arrive at Marihaven before Gabriel does. The hour is growing late."

Eager to talk of anything but Raven's recent disaster, Kane threw Serenity a grin. "There should be no problem," he replied, his hands gripping the horse's reins. "Gabriel was arranging for the purchase of some horses. That should take him most of the day."

Serenity felt strangely elated. Her surprise for Gabriel was working out precisely as she had planned.

However, as the carriage rounded a corner, Raven reacted in startled surprise. "Gabriel . . . "

Instantly alert, Serenity peered up the street. Could it be? She had not wanted him to find out about her surprise.

In the middle of the block ahead a tall, dark-haired man stood talking to a strikingly beautiful woman with pale gold hair, his head bent close to hers.

Serenity looked closer. There was no mistake. It was Gabriel.

Shooting a worried glance in her direction, Kane said hastily, "Don't entertain any rash judgments, Quaker."

"Of course," Raven chimed in, anxious to set Serenity's mind at ease. "Gabriel knows many people in Charleston."

Still, as the carriage drove past the two of them, Gabriel did not even bother to glance up, and Serenity felt a sudden dull ache begin inside her. She need not have feared her surprise would be spoiled; Gabriel had not even so much as noticed they were there. The stunning woman had held all his attention.

Feeling foolish and naive, Serenity leaned back against the seat with a troubled sigh. She should be relieved that Gabriel had not seen them. Yet, the thought brought no joy. No joy at all.

Suddenly, her hope that she and Gabriel could have something more than a marriage of convenience teetered precariously over a yawning abyss.

175

Chapter Eighteen

"You are looking well, Gabriel," Veronique Durand commented as she stood gazing up at him with innocent green eyes. If there was venom in her words, she was hiding it remarkably well.

"And you, Veronique."

"The years have been kind. You are still just as handsome as ever."

A muscle tightened along Gabriel's strong jaw, and he held himself in control with an effort. He was in no mood to waste his time in conversing with Veronique, now or ever. She was a part of his unpleasant past. He had come into Charleston to finalize the purchase of some horses for his stable, and to make certain he obtained one horse in particular that he had chosen for Serenity—a little gray roan called Blue Lady that was gentle enough for her to ride. It was just his misfortune to run into Veronique while he was here.

Veronique smiled sweetly.

His skin prickled along his scar.

Why did he have the strange feeling that she was like a card player, already certain she held the winning hand?

"I have to be going," he said abruptly. "Good day, Veronique."

"Oh, Gabriel," Veronique replied, putting a hand on his arm to stop him before he could walk away, "do say hello to your new bride for me. I understand her name is Serenity, and that she is a Quaker. I would not like her to think I was unfriendly, since we share so much in common."

Frowning darkly, Gabriel threw her a glance. "That's where

you are wrong, Veronique. I think the two of you share very little in common. And for that I'm eternally grateful."

His words did not seem to bother Veronique in the least. Reaching out, she brushed her fingertips pointedly across the scar on his cheek, then drew them away. "There are some things you can never deny, Gabriel. And this is one of them. Everyone in Charleston knows the truth. You see, that is one advantage of gossip. Some things are never forgotten. There was a time when I hated that fact, but now I find it quite delightful, since you will not be able to escape it either. You shall always be bound to me in word and thought, whether you want to be or not. Will your new bride find that to her liking?"

Gabriel did not reply. Wheeling around, he started to stride away. He wanted to put as much distance between himself and Veronique as possible, in the shortest amount of time. Still, as he did so she called after him.

"I understand simply everyone will be at the Pierpont ball. I hope to see you there."

He prayed he would not.

Gabriel was up early. As soon as he was dressed, he had gone out to the stables to check on the little gray roan; then he had come back inside to wake Serenity. The night before, when he had gotten back to Marihaven, it was so late that Serenity had already been in her bedchamber, fast asleep. Not wanting to disturb her, he had retired to his own bed alone, though it left him feeling slightly frustrated. For the last several nights he'd enjoyed the warmth of her beside him. This morning, he was anxious to see her without delay.

"Serenity," he said, sitting on the edge of the bed and toying with a strand of her silky hair, "wake up. I have a surprise for you."

Rousing, Serenity opened her blue velvet eyes and smiled sweetly at him for a moment. Then suddenly she grew serious. "You wanted something, Gabriel?"

177

"Yes," he replied, watching her snuggle back beneath her grandmother's quilt once more, as though she wished to ignore him. Having noticed the shadows beneath her eyes, he wondered if she had slept well. Still, he persisted.

"I would like to join you in that bed. But since I have already dressed, I shall let that particular pleasure wait until later. For now, I would like you to put on these clothes," he continued, indicating a new deep green riding habit and other items he had purchased for her from Madame Caron. He had ordered them some time before and had picked them up in Charleston the previous day. "When you are dressed, I will show you the surprise I brought home for you last night."

Sitting up in bed, Serenity stretched for a moment, then looked at the velvet riding habit curiously. "You bought this for me?"

"Of course," he replied. "Who else?"

"You did not have to do this."

"Put it on," he ordered softly. Perhaps she would hurry faster if he went back downstairs and she knew he was waiting. He was anxious to have her see Blue Lady. And he planned to teach her how to ride.

Slipping from the bed, Serenity gazed at him slightly askance for a moment, as though something was bothering her, but finally she replied, "I'll be down as quickly as I can."

"Good," he said, starting for the door. "I'll have Daisy fetch you something to eat. Hot chocolate, biscuits, and eggs. You'll need something hardy. It will be waiting."

Frowning slightly, Serenity washed herself and dressed her hair, then slipped on her cotton petticoat. Next, she put on her new lace-trimmed white blouse and the velvet riding habit. There was a matching hat with a flat crown and brim, which perched upon her head and sported a long sash of pale green silk. She stood gazing into the mirror without really seeing herself.

178

Oh, what was she to do? She had been unable to sleep most of the night for thinking about it. One part of her wanted to believe nothing was amiss, while another questioned Gabriel's relationship with the woman with whom she had seen him in Charleston. He was behaving as though there was absolutely nothing wrong. In fact, he had even brought her a surprise. Those were hardly the actions of a man who had found an interest in someone else. Still . . .

After she had dressed, Serenity hurried downstairs to find Gabriel seated at the table and her breakfast ready. Gazing at all the food, her stomach suddenly rebelled. "I cannot eat all of this."

"A bit out of sorts this morning, Serenity?" he countered, giving her a roguish grin as she stood by the table. "I suppose one must accept the bad with the good. Or should that be the other way around? At least there are no raw eggs handy for you to throw."

His good humor was infectious. Try as she might, she was having a difficult time doubting him.

Once she had eaten what she could manage, Gabriel took her by the hand and drew her outside and toward the stables. Lot nodded at her as they went inside, and she saw Kane standing by one of the stalls after they had entered. Serenity smiled at him.

Stepping aside, Kane indicated the horse in the stall, then strode away, leaving them alone.

Its coat as shiny as satin, the horse was gray in color and bespeckled with ebony. Gabriel gave her a pleased grin. "She's yours, Serenity. Her name is Blue Lady. What do you think of her?"

Drawing a deep breath, Serenity gazed awkwardly at the animal. It was utterly beautiful, yet she had never ridden a horse before. The thought of actually riding so large an animal frightened her. Still, she did not want to disappoint him. "You are so kind, Gabriel. But I have never ridden—"

"I know," he assured her, a twinkle in his eyes. "I thought I

179

would teach you. That's why I picked this particular horse. Not only is she a beautiful creature with a goodly measure of intelligence, she is also incredibly tame. You'll see. You don't have to be frightened of her in the least. In fact, that was why I waited to have Blue Lady saddled. I thought you should get to know her a little first, feed her a carrot or two from your hand." As he spoke, he reached out to stroke the horse's soft nose. "Then, if you would care to give it a try, we'll have Kane saddle her and you can begin your riding lessons."

Serenity's eyes were doubtful. It was certain he had given this much thought. But she had no inclination to ride the animal.

He handed her a carrot. "You have to relax, Serenity. A horse—or any animal for that matter—can sense if you are uncertain with it. Of course, that's with the exception of Biscuit. I don't think that wolfhound has ever totally accepted anyone but you and Joshua."

Taking the carrot from him, Serenity gingerly offered it to the horse. She watched as it snapped it away from her with big, square teeth.

"Once you have learned to ride well," Gabriel explained further, "I'll show you the swamp not far from here. When we were not living in Charleston so my father could be near his shipping interests, we spent much of our time at Twin Oaks—where my parents and Raven are residing now. The swamp lies between Marihaven and Twin Oaks, with my uncle Thorne's plantation of Pleasantridge on the other side. When I was growing up, I would always take the trails through the swamp to visit my uncle and aunt and my cousin Cat, and sometimes I would ride over to Marihaven to plan how I would restore it once I was grown."

Continuing to eye the horse suspiciously, Serenity chided softly, "I still cannot forgive you, Gabriel, for failing to tell me that Cat was your cousin. What must she think of both of us for keeping our marriage a secret from her while I was visiting in her home?"

For a moment, Gabriel's ruggedly handsome face became

serious. "You're right," he admitted. "It was not wise to have placed you in such an awkward circumstance. Cat has a way of taking things into her own hands when left to her own devices."

There was no doubt Gabriel was speaking of Carissa's matchmaking, and what had happened with Nathanniel Bentley. Serenity was uncertain how Gabriel had learned about it, but she was convinced that he knew. Still, now as before, whenever the subject came up, Gabriel never mentioned the matter directly, nor did he ask her for any explanations. She had been grateful for that, since everything had been completely innocent between her and the young senator.

A slight frown furrowing her delicate brow, Serenity was suddenly reminded of her thoughts about the woman she had seen Gabriel with in Charleston. The two of them had merely been conversing. Nothing more. Was that completely innocent as well?

Gabriel handed her another carrot for the horse. "Here," he directed with a grin. "Get better acquainted with Blue Lady. I want to begin your riding lessons."

Kane brushed Blue Lady's back with long, sweeping strokes. Gabriel stood to one side.

His head turned to the task, Kane observed, "This is a beautiful horse."

"Yes," Gabriel replied. "A worthy choice. Still, I think Serenity was more frightened of Blue Lady than she was letting on. I'll have to go slow in teaching her to ride."

"This morning's lesson did not go well?"

"It went well enough," Gabriel said. "It's just a feeling I had. I thought something might be bothering Serenity."

Kane fell silent. He knew precisely what that something might be. Should he tell Gabriel that Serenity had seen him with a woman in Charleston? It was none of his business, and obviously the Quaker had chosen not to mention anything about it to Gabriel. Perhaps he should just stay out of it, unless he saw that Serenity was about to get hurt.

181

Gabriel continued to watch him as though he had something else on his mind. "Did you decide to go to the Pierponts' ball?"

"I'm not certain," Kane answered, throwing a suspicious glance in Gabriel's direction. "I haven't been to a formal affair for some time. And I still have no idea why they decided to invite me. I was meaning to ask you about that."

Gabriel grinned. "Trust me, I had nothing at all to do with it. I'm perfectly content with things the way they are. Why should I want anyone to know that the best man who ever worked for me is indecently wealthy in his own right, and well connected to boot? People would think we both had gone daft. Besides, I think this way there may be a chance my sister Raven will take a liking to you, given enough time. But if she found out you were just as jaded as the rest of us, she might turn her fancy little tail and run."

"Then, you would approve of Raven and me?"

Chuckling, Gabriel returned, "Is there any doubt of it? Even if you had been as poor as a proverbial church mouse, I still would have thought you suitable for my sister. I know what kind of a man you are. It's Raven who needs work."

"We didn't get off to the best start . . . "

"That only makes it all the more interesting," Gabriel interjected. Then, pausing for a moment, he grew more serious. "I would rather have you for a brother-in-law, Kane, than as a rival."

There was a sudden tension between them. "The Quaker?"

"No need to act surprised," Gabriel countered. "I've known it for quite awhile. I see it every time you look at her."

Kane met his gaze squarely. "I know she's yours, Gabriel. I've no quarrel with that. Just be careful not to hurt her."

A muscle tensed along Gabriel's jaw. "Do you believe I might?"

Starting to brush the horse once more, Kane replied succinctly, "Yes."

* * *

Hurriedly drawing Raven inside her bedchamber, Serenity closed the door behind them. Serenity's new gown lay upon the bed. She went over to it and held it up.

"Oh, Serenity," Raven murmured, "it is simply lovely. I can hardly wait to see you in it at the Pierponts' ball. Do you think my brother suspects anything?"

Serenity smiled. "I hope not. Although he did inquire if I would like something new to wear to the ball. I simply told him I had a gown that was quite suitable. I am certain he thinks I am content to wear something I already have."

"Then he truly will be surprised when he sees you in this gown, Serenity. However, I suspect he thinks you look beautiful in anything you wear, and a new gown is not very important."

Once again, Serenity felt a twinge of insecurity. Raven did not understand. She and Gabriel were committed to one another, and they even shared the pleasures of the marriage bed. But Serenity had never been assured of what Gabriel wanted. He had wed her on Nantucket merely to spare her from the British. There had never been one word of love spoken between the two of them.

Deciding to change the subject, Serenity observed lightly, "Though the gown may be a success, I fear my dancing will leave something to be desired."

Laughing, Raven grasped Serenity by the hands and whirled her around the room. "Just let him spin you around. In dancing, as in life, men are delighted to take the lead."

For a moment, Serenity felt incredibly dizzy. Stopping in a turn, she disengaged herself from Raven's hands and went to sit on her bed. "I'm sorry, Raven. It seems my head is spinning as well. I think it is all of the excitement. I have not felt like eating these past few days, and perhaps I am feeling the effects."

Immediately concerned, Raven went to sit by her side. "You are certain that is all it is, Serenity?"

"Yes, of course," she replied. "Too much excitement. Please do not mention it to Gabriel. I am much better already."

"It would not hurt for you to rest, Serenity. And I must be going anyway. I took the short way through the swamp, and it will soon be dark. That is one place I would not care to be at night."

"I think you are brave even to venture there by day. Gabriel has shown me a small part of it."

"Not a place for the faint of heart, that's true. But I manage it well enough. Now, do take care, Serenity. No need to see me to the door. And I shall be looking for you the day after tomorrow, at the Pierponts' ball."

As Raven slipped from the room, closing the door behind her, Serenity quickly put the new gown back in the place she had been keeping it hidden, then climbed up on the bed and leaned back against the plump pillows.

The bout of dizziness had fled, but she had not felt well for days. She had merely suspected it before. Now she was quite certain. While on Nantucket, she had been around Anna Hussey enough through the woman's childbearing years to know all of the signs were there. She was going to have Gabriel's baby.

She was debating when she should tell him. Would he be happy? Would he wish for a child?

Sighing softly, Serenity closed her eyes. Perhaps she should tell him after the Pierponts' ball. It would be a night for surprises. First, the gown. Then, the dancing.

Falling into a deep slumber, Serenity dreamed of the ball. *Dancers whirled around the floor as the music played. Raven was there. And Kane. And she was in Gabriel's strong arms. Smiling down at her, he held her close. Then, abruptly, he was snatched away to dance with another. The woman she had seen him with in Charleston.*

"Serenity . . ." Gabriel said, trying to rouse her. "Serenity . . ."

Serenity sat bolt upright. It had only been a dream.

"What is it? I came to wake you for dinner, and you seemed to be having a bad dream." He reached out his hand to brush unmistakable tears from her cheeks.

She gazed up at him. Would she care so very much if Gabriel wanted another woman? Somehow she knew that she would. She only hoped this particular dream was not a portent of the future.

"Was I dreaming?" she replied. "I have forgotten it already."

Chapter Nineteen

Her eyes aglow, Serenity slowly descended the stairs on the night of the Pierpont ball. Gabriel stood waiting for her at the bottom. She wore the new gown of azure silk, with its tightly fitted bodice and ruching at the low neckline that emphasized the slight curve of her breasts. Her flame-colored hair had been curled softly about her lovely face, then twined with ribbons of a matching hue. "Gabriel . . ."

For a moment he seemed at a loss for words. "When you told me to wait downstairs until you were ready, I never suspected you had such a surprise in store for me, Serenity. Without a doubt, you are the most beautiful woman I have ever beheld in my life."

Serenity blushed. She felt as lighthearted as a schoolgirl. "I wanted you to be proud of me."

There was an unfathomable light in his silver gray eyes. "I'm always proud of you, Serenity. Even without the gown."

She had never seen Gabriel look quite so wonderful himself. His beautifully tailored velvet jacket was blue as well, of a very dark shade, and it fit his broad shoulders superbly. His white linen shirt contrasted with his tanned, harshly handsome features. Black satin breeches and knee boots encased his long, muscular legs.

Sighing, she replied, "But there will be many others at the ball. Most of them I have never met. I did not want to appear so . . . so different."

He grinned in wry amusement. "You *are* different, Serenity. You are more beautiful than all of the rest." Then, as though he could read her very thoughts, he added softly, "Are there any more surprises in store for me, this night?"

Her blue eyes glowing, Serenity thought again of their baby as she slipped her hand around his proffered arm. "Perhaps."

At that moment, a firm knock on the door interrupted them. Suddenly, Kane swung it wide. For a moment, he just stood there, gazing at Serenity in undisguised admiration. Clothed impeccably as well in a coat of dark green, he looked as though he too was going someplace special.

Grinning, Kane said, "Is everyone ready for the ball?"

Once again reliving the same feelings she had experienced in Washington, Serenity felt distinctly out of place after arriving at the Pierponts' mansion. Still, she was determined not to let it show. Madelaine Pierpont was most kind, greeting them politely the moment they came through the door. Then, as the woman's eyes lit on Kane, the gray-haired dowager eagerly introduced her daughter, Deborah Rose.

As they moved on into the ballroom, others gathered around them. Gabriel's parents were there and greeted them fondly, and there was Raven of course, looking ravishing in cream satin and lace. Other guests not of the family also stopped to exchange a few words.

"You look so wonderful," Raven whispered to Serenity, when they had a brief moment to speak to each other without the others overhearing. "Was Gabriel surprised?"

Smiling, Serenity nodded.

Raven appeared pleased. "Just wait. This is only the beginning."

The music began a lilting waltz. It filled the ballroom with its joyous sound.

Kane stood to one side. Stepping forward, he faced Raven. "Would you care to dance, Miss Harrowe?"

Serenity and Gabriel exchanged glances. Would Raven accept?

It was obvious Raven had seen the hint of a challenge in Kane's compelling gaze as she gave her reply. "If you are not afraid of having your toes stepped upon."

Curling Raven's arm around his, Kane drew her toward the dance floor. "I think I'm man enough to stand it, Miss Harrowe."

Once the two of them had departed, Gabriel gave Serenity a pleased grin. "Unless he was merely trying to escape the Pierponts' daughter," he said, keeping his voice low, "it appears Kane has decided to take an interest in my sister."

Suspiciously, Serenity's eyes rested on his chiseled features. "And was that your idea, Gabriel? Did you put him up to it?"

"It would not hurt for Kane to have someone of his own," he countered softly. "Maybe then he would stop gazing at you like a cat crouched before a delectable mouse."

Serenity threw him a glance. Was he jesting? "You are totally mistaken. Kane has never looked at me in such a way. He has been a good friend."

"I don't deny that, Serenity. He's the best friend I'll probably ever have. But the fact remains, if it were not for that friendship, he would undoubtedly be the first in line to seek your favor."

Serenity was shocked at Gabriel's attitude. "You certainly do not think I would encourage him?"

The teasing light had left Gabriel's gray eyes. "Kane is a bit your champion, you know. He's warned me not to hurt you."

"And is there a danger?"

Gabriel drew her toward him, until it seemed the two of them were alone in the midst of the crowd; his broad shoulders and lean, hard body seemed to dominate the room. She could feel the charged atmosphere between them. "I don't know,

Gloria Pedersen

Serenity. I hope not. But there are some things over which I have no control."

What a strange conversation, Serenity thought to herself. It was as though he was more worried than Kane that he might hurt her. But, in what way? She dared not ask. Perhaps, things would be better between them once he knew about the child she was carrying. But that she was saving until later, after they returned home to Marihaven.

"You have not asked me to dance, Gabriel. Did you not say it was the custom to have the first dance with your wife?"

Again, there was a surprised expression on his handsome face. "You would like to dance?"

"Not with anyone but you . . . "

He pulled her toward where the dancers twirled and spun, the men so distinguished, the women so lovely in colorful gowns that were reminiscent of hollyhocks; then he took her in his arms. He held her much too closely, yet she did not care as they danced together for the very first time. It was better than her dream.

Bending down, his mouth close to her ear, Gabriel murmured, "I don't deserve you."

As the evening wore on, Serenity grew weary. She longed for a moment to rest. Finally, when she and Gabriel stopped to talk to Kane and Raven, it was Gabriel's animated younger sister who suggested that the two girls retire upstairs for a few minutes.

Gratefully, Serenity let Raven lead the way.

As Raven drew her into one of the upper rooms, the two of them found a place to sit down. "You are looking quite pale again, Serenity. As you were the other day. At least one of us must see that you take better care of yourself."

"Thank you, Raven. I believe it was the heat of the ballroom."

"Nonsense, Serenity. I believe you've had a touch of malaise this past week, and you have simply not recovered."

"Perhaps," Serenity replied with a secretive smile, wishing she could tell Raven about the child she and Gabriel would soon share. "I am enjoying the ball, however. And dancing with Gabriel. I had never realized dancing was such an enjoyable activity. Before, I considered it a form of decadence, a mating ritual of sorts. But, of course, I was brought up to believe that way. Now I must confess, I see no true harm in it. Tell me, did you like dancing with Kane?"

Her eyes evasive, Raven actually blushed. "I should hate him."

"Whatever for?" Serenity asked, immediately concerned.

"Because," Raven explained breathlessly, "he is impossible. We shall never get along. Never. And I'm afraid I'm falling in love with him."

Serenity could not help herself. She laughed. "I think it is delightful."

"But Kane may never love me in return," Raven protested.

Suddenly subdued, Serenity replied, "I know. It can be very painful if you are not loved in return. I think that is why most of us fear love so much. We are more vulnerable with the one we love than with anyone else in the world. More capable of being hurt."

Raven nodded. "It is a wonder people ever take the chance at all."

"Yes," Serenity said softly, knowing in her heart that she had been speaking of her own fears about loving Gabriel as well as counseling Raven. Suddenly anxious to be with Gabriel again, she added, "I am much refreshed now, Raven. I believe we should return to the ballroom before Gabriel and Kane grow impatient."

Hoping to catch a glimpse of Gabriel and Kane once they had returned to the ballroom, Serenity and Raven stopped for a moment behind a group of women who stood conversing near the swirling dancers. Though neither Serenity nor Raven had any desire to listen, one woman spoke loudly enough that it was impossible for them not to hear.

"That Veronique Durand," the woman said, gazing in the direction of the dance floor. "She knows nothing of propriety.

Gloria Pedersen

As if she had not set everyone to talking for ages past, now she must flaunt her affairs before our very eyes. After all, the gentleman dumped her in the lobby of the hotel like a common trollop, without so much as a stitch of clothing on, and now she must dance with him right in our midst. One would think they would use more discretion. Everyone knows he is the one—he wears the scar across his cheek."

Another woman's voice chimed in, "And they say his wife is here, as well. Poor woman. What she must be feeling at this moment, to see him dancing with that brazen Veronique."

"It's an outright disgrace," a third woman said.

Although she had taken no interest at the time, as the women gossiped, Serenity could not help recalling that the dressmaker, Madame Caron, had talked of the same scandal. Now, apparently, the two were dancing together here at the Pierponts' ball, without the least degree of shame.

As the speakers parted, Serenity peered past their shoulders. Raven grasped her arm. Quickly drawing her away, Raven spun toward her. There was a distressed look on her heart-shaped face.

It was too late. Before Raven pulled her away, Serenity saw them. They were there on the dance floor. Gabriel and the woman that Serenity had seen him speaking to that day in Charleston. With golden hair and wearing a stunning gown of emerald green, the woman smiling up at Gabriel appeared even lovelier than she had the first time Serenity had seen her.

There was no longer any need for someone to tell her the woman's name. Suddenly, Serenity knew. The woman was Veronique Durand, the object of everyone's gossip.

And the gentleman with the scar—the man who had left her in the hotel—was none other than her own husband.

Gabriel had known it would be a mistake to dance with Veronique. Still, he had thought it better at the time than allowing her to create a scene, which she was threatening to do. At

190

least for the moment, Serenity was safely upstairs. Even so, he could feel all eyes upon them, and knew that everyone was whispering.

"You need not look so sullen, Gabriel," Veronique teased. "One would think you are not used to gossip. Certainly in the past two years I have grown quite used to the whispers, the turned heads. I thought you should have the chance to experience it as well."

A muscle tightening along his jaw, Gabriel gripped Veronique's arm so tightly that she let out a little gasp. "You said that you wanted to speak to me, Veronique. I would advise you to get straight to the point. This dance will soon be over, as will your chance. I've no intention of giving you another."

Veronique gave him a coy smile. "I did indeed wish to speak to you, Gabriel. But now I find it difficult. Perhaps, at another time."

Frowning darkly, Gabriel knew Veronique was hoping to arrange some sort of a meeting between them. She had merely gotten him to dance to let him know it. "I won't have the time."

"I was afraid you might find yourself too busy, Gabriel. But I thought there was one little item you would care to discuss. It is something that should interest you very much. A surprise, one might say, of sorts."

As usual, Veronique was set on playing games. She wanted him to wonder, to wonder enough, in fact, that he would give in and meet her as she wished. It was like a carrot dangled before a horse's nose, meant to lead him where it was she wanted him to go.

"Let's get to whatever it is you want of me," he countered impatiently. "You already know I have no desire to meet with you."

Veronique smiled, and there it was again—that feeling Veronique held all of the cards. It made him angry as hell to admit it even to himself, but he had a healthy enough respect for Veronique to be slightly frightened of her.

As though not bothered in the least by his attitude, Veronique tilted her head back and laughed softly. Then, her innocent green eyes on his face, she murmured, "I have a son. Did you know that, Gabriel? He is a charming little fellow. Handsome. Dark-haired. His name is Alexandre. However, I am not certain who it is he favors. Perhaps you might have an opinion, should you ever see him . . ."

Stunned, Gabriel stopped dancing in the center of the ballroom. Lithe and dangerous, he stared hard at Veronique. Was she implying that there was a child, and that the child could possibly be his? Or was this merely another one of her games?

For a moment Gabriel gazed at her with a murderous gleam in his eyes. He would like to force the truth from her right there and then. Still, before he could do or say anything, Gabriel was distracted by the sight of Raven, who was pushing her way anxiously through the swirling dancers. It was obvious something was wrong.

"Do come, Gabriel," Raven pleaded softly, pulling at his arm. "And quickly. Serenity has collapsed. . . ."

Serenity sat in her cozy bedchamber at Marihaven, gazing absently into her dressing mirror as she brushed her hair in long strokes. Her face was pale and drawn. What had started out to be a special evening had turned into a night of disaster.

Undoubtedly, Raven had told Gabriel what they had accidentally overheard, and he must have assumed her fainting spell had been the result of distress. Consequently, except for assuring him that she was quite all right and protesting the need of a doctor, she and Gabriel had spoken not one word to each other on the long ride home.

Serenity could not deny that she had been shocked to learn of the scandal between Gabriel and Veronique Durand. Obviously, there was much he had not told her. Further, Serenity had seen Gabriel dancing with the woman, and she could not help wondering what had been between them at one time. Had Gabriel been in love with Veronique? Was he *still* in love with her?

A soft knock on the bedchamber door interrupted her thoughts. Pushing it open, Gabriel stepped inside.

Even now, Serenity could not help thinking he looked achingly handsome. Although he had removed the velvet jacket he had worn to the ball, he still wore the white linen dress shirt, which contrasted with his night-dark hair and was left carelessly open to the waist, as well as his black satin breeches and boots.

Striding farther into the room, he stood with his legs braced apart. Although he exuded an aura of raw masculinity, his words were surprisingly gentle. "I think we should talk."

Having turned on the bench when he entered the room, Serenity twisted away from him once more to face the dressing mirror and continue brushing her hair. "Perhaps you should wait until the morning."

"No, Serenity," he countered. "I'm not content to let this wait. I owe you an explanation. And we'll speak of it now, before any more harm is done."

Sighing, Serenity circled slowly back toward him. "I know what you are about to say."

"I should have told you about Veronique before. I had no right to keep it from you. But it was a thing of the past."

"And you thought I would not understand?"

His silvery eyes resting on her face, he nodded and repeated simply, "I thought you would not understand."

Serenity did not trust her own emotions. It would be so simple to rise and go into his arms, feel his mouth on hers.

"Will you see her again?"

Gabriel hesitated for a moment. Carefully, he said, "Only if I must."

Once more, a frown creased Serenity's features. She was not certain that what he had given her was enough. It frightened her to think she might lose him to another, and somehow she had the feeling Veronique was still a threat. Now, more than ever, she wanted to win Gabriel's love. There was already passion between them; in time there could be much more.

Rising slowly, Serenity went over to him. They were almost touching. For a moment, she just stood there; then she softly inquired, "Would you care to take me to bed?"

Without any hesitation, he asked huskily, "Mine, or yours?"

"Whichever you choose," she murmured softly in reply. "But from this time on I would prefer we claim only one bed."

He grinned. Then, bending low, his mouth found hers with a fiery intensity. When he raised his dark head once again, he said, "We'll burn the rest of them."

With one swift movement, he swept her nightrail up over her head and let it drop to the floor, leaving her completely naked before him. Momentarily, his darkened gaze lingered over her body, as though memorizing its every detail. Then, reaching out, the palms of his hands brushed across the tips of her breasts and slowly slid down to the curve of her small waist. Drawing her to him, he raised her slightly to mold her against his hard body. She could feel the assurance of his desire.

Should she tell him now that she carried his child? At least that was one thing Veronique could never possess—his child.

She began, "I wanted to tell you . . . " But the sentence was left unfinished as Gabriel scooped her up into his strong arms, then carried her to bed.

Chapter Twenty

In the following days, life at Marihaven became much too busy for Serenity to give more than passing thoughts to what had transpired at the Pierpont ball. Gabriel's parents set sail for Paris as planned, and Raven moved in with her vast quantities of gowns and other items she thought necessary for her stay with them. Even so, though it made life more frantic, Serenity enjoyed having Gabriel's sibling there. Her young sister-in-law was marvelous company, and Raven went out of her way to be kind to Joshua. Only Kane seemed indifferent to the whole affair.

Puzzled by Kane's new attitude, one sunny morning Serenity decided to go to the stable and ask Kane to saddle her horse, as an excuse to talk to him about Raven. "I thought I would take a ride on my own today, if you would be so kind as to saddle Blue Lady for me."

A frown furrowing his brow, Kane asked suspiciously, "Does Gabriel know you're planning on riding alone, Quaker?"

"He has gone into Charleston on business and I saw no need to tell him before he left. I have mastered the sidesaddle well enough. However, I had thought to get more practice."

Still concerned, Kane hesitated. "Admit it, Quaker; there are many things you do well, but riding a horse is not one of them. Nor do you enjoy it. You are doing it merely to please Gabriel."

This was not going as she had planned. They had not even gotten to the subject of himself and Raven. "I like the animal," she protested. "It is merely being upon Blue Lady's back that I do not enjoy. Perhaps if I ride more often, I shall master it."

"Very well, then. But you'll have to let me go along with you. Gabriel would not take kindly to me letting you break your neck."

Serenity smiled at him. Perhaps this would work out as she had planned after all. Now she could speak to him about the girl.

Following him as he went to saddle Blue Lady, as well as a horse for himself, she inquired innocently, "Why have you not come up to the mansion since Raven has arrived, Kane? Do you wish to avoid her?"

Shooting her a glance, Kane replied, "I have no reason to come."

"But you always came before. What is the difference now?"

Kane went back to saddling Blue Lady. Bluntly, he replied, "Raven and I have nothing in common."

Not to be put off, Serenity countered, "And you think Gabriel and I do?"

For a moment, he simply stood there, his compelling gaze intent on her face, as though he was thinking over what she had just asked. "No, Quaker, I don't. But I think the two of you are giving it a devil of a try. I admire you both for that, and I only hope you succeed. Gabriel has seen your world, lived in it for a time. Now you are starting to find out what his world is truly like. Until the Pierponts' ball, Gabriel was able to protect you to a certain extent. But, as you discovered, that won't always be possible. Whether it works out in the end will be up to both of you."

Serenity's blue eyes were troubled. She had not intended to speak to Kane about Gabriel, but now she could not help herself. Though she had tried to forget it, she still could not put from her mind the memory of Gabriel dancing with Veronique at the Pierpont ball. In fact, if it were not such a sinful emotion, she would suspect she was even slightly jealous. "You know about Veronique?"

Although she had not voiced it aloud, Kane seemed to sense what she was feeling. His look held a touch of sympathy. "Yes," he replied. "Just remember, Quaker, love is the best bridge between two worlds.

Rewarding him with an uncertain smile, Serenity offered some advice of her own. "Perhaps you should remember that as well, Kane."

Stepping out of the office building where he had just arranged for the shipping of some rice and indigo from the plantation, Gabriel's mind was on Serenity and their relationship.

Already, Serenity had lent her special charm to the running of Marihaven. Taking it upon herself, she had made certain the black men and women who worked the plantation would be given a more than adequate amount of medicine and cloth, salt, sugar, and tools, besides their normal supplies, and was constantly seeing to their welfare. Then, each morning, she would take time to teach the younger ones to read.

In a few short weeks, everyone on the plantation had become enchanted by her, and it was no wonder. She was like a breath of springtime all year 'round. Loving. Open. Admittedly, he was in danger of losing his heart to her. Yet, even now, though he had no desire for any other woman in his life or in his bed, he was afraid to care too deeply. Too much still stood between them. Not the least of which was Veronique and her insinuation about a child.

Earlier that day, Gabriel had contacted a lawyer to discreetly look into the matter for him. He had to know whether Veronique had spoken the truth. He would not have Serenity hurt if he could help it.

His thoughts still on Serenity and Veronique's child, Gabriel scarcely noticed the three gentlemen who stood conversing a short distance down the street, but strode directly toward them. Admittedly, he would have done well to avoid them. However, had he not chanced upon the men this particular day, sooner or later a meeting would have been inevitable. At least with one of them—Veronique's father.

Charles Beaumarchais was a stately gentleman of medium height, with slightly graying hair, glowering brows, and a harsh, unyielding face. He had not changed to any degree in the years since Gabriel had been away.

"Good day, sir," Beaumarchais said, moving forward directly into his path. "I believe we have a matter of business."

Gabriel did not reply. There was little he could say, and he had a fair idea what would soon be forthcoming.

Drawing a glove from his pocket, Beaumarchais struck Gabriel across the cheek with it. It was a formal ritual; one which had been enacted many times before. The harsh gesture was a call to arms on the dueling field, to avenge Veronique's tarnished honor.

197

It would do no good to remind Beaumarchais that Veronique had been responsible in the first place for what had happened to her. Despite everything, Veronique was still the man's daughter. Beaumarchais had every right to demand satisfaction, and there was nothing Gabriel could do but oblige him.

With cool dignity, Gabriel responded, "To your pleasure, sir. Name the time and the place."

"Tomorrow morning," Beaumarchais declared. "At the edge of Hunter swamp. There should be no danger of the authorities disturbing us there. It is your right to name the weapons, Harrowe."

Gabriel did not hesitate. "Pistols at ten paces."

"Very well, then," Beaumarchais replied. "It is done."

After his return to Marihaven a short time later, Gabriel approached Kane near the stables so they could speak in private. "I'm to meet Charles Beaumarchais on the dueling field at dawn. I would like you to be my second."

"Your what?" Kane shot back. "Dueling is practically suicide for both parties. The authorities have outlawed it."

A dark frown gracing his handsome features, Gabriel responded, "The man has demanded satisfaction for what I did to his daughter's reputation. I have no other choice but to oblige him."

"Then you're a fool," Kane observed without humor.

Gabriel appeared unmoved. "This won't be the first time . . . "

"And the Quaker? What about her? Do you think she will sit still while you go on your merry way to the dueling field?"

For a moment, Gabriel felt a knot in his gut. He was not certain what to do about Serenity. He knew well how she abhorred violence. It was foreign to her in every way. And dueling was a violence of the worst sort, since it was not performed in the heat of anger, but was an act designed to cold-bloodedly kill one or both of two men.

"I haven't as yet decided what to do about Serenity."

"Well, you'd be wise to give it some thought," Kane retorted hotly. "And, if I were you, I would not wait until after it's done—provided you even live through it. I don't think she takes too well to surprises."

Gabriel shot Kane a questioning glance. Had Serenity said something? "Will you or won't you act as my second, Kane?"

Kane's hard face softened slightly. "Yes. But I don't like it. You are my friend, and you have the Quaker to think of. Why get yourself killed over something that happened a long time ago?"

Gabriel felt suddenly weary. "Granted it happened a long time ago, Kane, but others haven't forgotten. Much as I wish they had."

It had been a lovely evening. Serenity had planned it well. First, she and Gabriel had sat down to a sumptuous meal, with everyone in attendance, even Biscuit. She had even managed to have Kane and Raven sit by each other's side, though both of them had known precisely what she was doing. There had been roast duckling in orange sauce with rice, and sweet cakes for dessert, which she had insisted on helping to prepare. Then, after dinner, when she had encouraged Kane and Raven to go for a stroll, and Joshua had retired to his room with some books full of drawings she had given him, Serenity had asked Gabriel to take her for a walk as well.

Though she had worn one of her simple plum gowns for the evening, she had left her hair loose in the manner she knew Gabriel preferred, and it brushed against her cheeks in the gentle breeze.

She had already decided. This was the night she would tell Gabriel about their baby. The days were slipping away, and she was eager to share the news with him. There could not be a better time.

Overhead, there was a full autumn moon to light their way.

Strolling beneath the moss-draped live oaks, Serenity and Gabriel soon found themselves at a little gazebo that was hidden in the trees. Stepping inside, she took Gabriel's hand and drew him into the small structure with her.

"I do love this little gazebo," she said, turning her head upward to gaze through the lattice openings at the stars that twinkled in the black velvet sky overhead. "Was it always here?"

"My grandfather originally built it for my grandmother," Gabriel replied quietly. "But it had nearly fallen to ruin over the years. When I planned to bring you here to Marihaven, I thought you might find it pleasant on sunny days, so I had it restored."

Serenity smiled up at him as they stood in its center. "I like being here with you," she said, truly meaning it. More and more each day, she cared for Gabriel. He was becoming her life. Her love.

"You look particularly enchanting this evening, Serenity."

A mischievous glint suddenly lighting her eyes, though Gabriel could not see it in the moonlight, Serenity murmured, "I will soon be in need of new gowns."

Gabriel was silent for a brief moment, as though slightly surprised by her remark. Then, he replied, "You know you may have anything you desire, Serenity. There is no need even to ask. I would gladly have paid for your gown for the Pierpont ball, if you would had given me the opportunity. In the future, I will settle all accounts with Madame Caron."

Were men always so practical? She could not resist teasing him a few moments more. "It is just that I am not certain how much longer these gowns will fit."

Gabriel hesitated. "I don't understand. Why would they not fit?"

Serenity smiled at him in the darkness.

"Serenity . . . "

"Do you care to become a father, Gabriel?"

Damnation! Gabriel thought bleakly to himself as he gazed out the window of his bedchamber. He had meant to tell Serenity about the duel when they walked to the gazebo. It was wrong to keep it from her. Yet, when she had told him about the baby, all else had fled from his mind. He could think only of the marvelous gift she was about to give him, and he had not wanted to spoil the evening in any way. Still, it was a matter that he could not simply ignore.

Having already removed his shirt, his broad chest was bare and the muscles rippled slightly as he clenched his fists in frustration. What was he to do, tell her about the duel or not?

Gabriel gazed at Serenity with lowered eyes as she finished brushing her fiery hair. He ached with wanting her, and he'd done so ever since he had kissed her thoroughly in the gazebo a short time before. Yet, the gazebo was no place to claim her in anything but the most perfunctory of ways, and tonight he wanted to savor every moment between them.

Noticing him gazing at her, Serenity went over to sit on the edge of the bed. In her prim white nightgown, she appeared almost angelic as she smiled up at him. He had never seen anything quite so lovely as the way she looked to him tonight.

Waiting for a moment, she held out her arms, then murmured softly, "Make love to me, Gabriel."

For a moment he held back, savoring the idea. Yes, it was true. He did make *love* to her, even if his mind refused to let his heart take heed. He loved her with every ounce of his being. It was just his fears that made him continue to deny it.

Dimming the lantern, he strode slowly over to her. Somewhere before the dawn he would have to leave her. He felt no fear of the duel ahead. He had faced worse than that, many times before. But he was aware of the senselessness of it. Violence gained nothing. It was merely an end to a conflict that could be resolved no other way. It was no wonder Serenity found the whole idea reprehensible. Even he could not condone it.

More and more their two worlds seemed to collide. If he told her about the duel, she would undoubtedly try to stop him. And if she learned of it after it was over, she might never forgive him. Yet, he knew he had to go through with it. As strange as it seemed, he felt he owed it to Charles Beaumarchais.

Sitting down beside her, Gabriel softly caressed Serenity's cheek with his long fingertips and felt the fragile bone structure beneath her satin skin. She was like a work of art, a sculpture of flesh and blood that could rival Michelangelo's Virgin Mary. He smoothed her silky hair and lifted it back from her neck to view the exquisite delicacy of her throat, the barely visible veins. He let his fingers discover her rapidly beating pulse as he brushed a single kiss across its base.

With tender patience, he slipped off her gown, then he gently eased her back upon the bed and rolled her onto her stomach. Taking a place beside her, with tantalizing slowness he stroked her satin flesh. First, the shoulders. Then, her back. Next, her delightfully curved derriere and on down the backs of her legs to place a kiss just behind each knee. Not protesting, she was languid beneath his touch, sensitized to each tender nuance of his skill.

Once more, his hands explored, and he could feel her tremble with desire and her breath catch in a funny little gasp. Well and good, he told himself. Prolong the agony. The only problem seemed to be that he was in agony himself. The longer he took to tease and arouse her, the harder it was for him to hold back. Soon. Very soon . . .

Shifting her over onto her back, his eyes never leaving her beautiful face, he quickly divested himself of his pants and slipped up over her willing body. Like the petals of a flower, she opened beneath him, and their bodies were joined as one.

On a tide of desire, they rose and fell as they strained to reach a peaceful shore.

Hours later, he held her in his arms as though she were as fragile as a Dresden figurine. She had made him happier than he could ever imagine. Tomorrow, she might hate him for all he represented. Things might never again be the same. But for tonight, he held the world in his arms. He had Serenity, and the child that grew within her. What more could he ask?

Chapter Twenty-one

In the gloomy dawn mists, several men gathered at the edge of Hunter's swamp. Gabriel Harrowe and Charles Beaumarchais were more easily identifiable than the rest, since only moments before they had shrugged off their coats and waited in white shirts. Along with each of them, there was a surgeon and another man to act as a second.

Standing off to one side, Gabriel and Kane waited for Beaumarchais to take his choice of the weapons, as was his privilege, since Gabriel was the one who had provided them. The dueling pistols had once belonged to Gabriel's grandfather, a man to whom dueling was a way of life, and it was no secret that Gabriel's own father had been forced to use them on at least one occasion. Gabriel had always taken a secret delight in the tale when he was still a lad. The hard edge of danger did not seem nearly so romantic when he was the one who was involved.

Throwing him a questioning glance, Kane asked quietly, "What do you intend to do, Gabriel?"

"Beaumarchais gave no indication that he would be satisfied with the drawing of first blood," Gabriel replied succinctly. "That leaves me little choice."

"Yes, I know," Kane agreed. "And it would be wise for you to see the man dead before he gets a chance to fire. Though I have the strange feeling you're not about to do that. So let me warn you, my friend. If you've taken some foolhardy notion that violence doesn't pay now that you're trying to impress the Quaker, you're the one who'll wind up dead. Beaumarchais will have no such qualms. And this is no time for an attack of self-righteousness."

Gabriel tensed slightly. "Beaumarchais had every right to call me out. Others would think him a fool and a coward if he'd let the matter pass. But that doesn't mean he deserves to die for it. Certainly, Veronique is not worthy of any man's life. Not his or mine. She has always been trouble, and I think her father knows it."

"So why don't you walk away? Let him be the victor by default?"

A muscle tightened along Gabriel's jaw, and his eyes were like cold gray steel. "Because I know it wouldn't end there. Beaumarchais doesn't want to be the victor. He wants to see me dead."

Kane sighed heavily. "I see no solution."

"There is none." Then, giving his friend a hard look, he added, "I suppose it goes without saying, Kane, if anything happens to me, I want you to take care of Serenity. Stand by her."

Kane's eyes swept over his friend's ruggedly handsome face, as if realizing something for the first time. "I can tell there's more to this than you're letting on. You love her, don't you? And you're afraid she won't forgive you if you go through with this."

Not bothering to deny it, Gabriel gave Kane a nod of farewell, then strode to take his place on the dueling field. This whole affair could not be over soon enough to suit him—whatever the outcome.

Pivoting around, Gabriel and Beaumarchais took their positions back-to-back. Neither man had a final word for the other. The gray mists rose around them as they stepped off their paces. Then, turning, there came the directive, "Present. Aim. Fire."

Because he was the younger of the two men and his reflexes more keen, Gabriel's shot rang out before the other man could fire. The sound pierced the air, and it was followed instantly by Beaumarchais's cry of pain as he was hit in the right shoulder. The man let his gun slip uselessly from his hand.

Stunned, Beaumarchais slumped to the ground and sat there for a moment.

Gabriel waited. Each man had been given two shots at the outset, yet Gabriel made no move to take advantage of his opportunity to fire again. Despite Kane's advice, he had no desire to kill his opponent.

As the man's surgeon rushed to tend to his wound, Beaumarchais directed his second to pick up the dueling pistol. A thin-faced gentleman of about fourty years named Preston, the man raised the weapon and pointed it directly at Gabriel.

Hesitating, a frown creased Gabriel's dark brows as he too took aim. Must he kill or maim another man before this was through?

"Present. Aim . . . "

Beaumarchais's second was a nervous man. Preston's hand was shaking, and he appeared terrified. Even before they were given the command, his weapon discharged. In surprise, Gabriel felt the ball as it whizzed past his head—so near it ruffled his dark hair.

The shot had come close to ending his life. Though it was still quite cool, Gabriel's brow was beaded with sweat as he realized exactly how close. Would Beaumarchais be satisfied?

The surgeon helped Beaumarchais to his feet. The wounded man stood there for a moment reeling uncertainly as he gazed in Gabriel's direction. "Justice is served, Harrowe," he finally ground out. "But one day we may meet again. . . . "

Where had Gabriel gone? Serenity asked herself as she stood gazing out of the bedchamber window. He had not been there when she awoke, and she had found the missive he had left her on the little table near the bed, saying he would be gone for some time.

She had never felt so close to Gabriel as she had the night

before, when she had told him about their baby. It had been almost magical. Never had she dreamed that first being with him, and then having him make love to her a short time later, could be quite so wonderful. Something had been different this time. Yet, she was afraid to admit what that something might be. In her effort to make Gabriel fall in love with her, had she simply fallen deeper in love with him instead?

Gabriel's coach finally returned at midmorning.

Busy with the tasks of the day, Serenity had been on the grounds in front of the plantation for some time, helping Joshua draw pictures and throwing a wooden stick for Biscuit to fetch, when she caught a glimpse of a horse-drawn vehicle.

Rushing over to greet Gabriel as the coach pulled up, Serenity was surprised to see that Kane was inside as well. "Why, Kane," she chided playfully, "I did not know you were with Gabriel. What have the two of you been up to? I do hope it was proper."

Exchanging a glance with Gabriel, Kane replied carefully. "A matter of importance, Quaker. But your husband will have to do the explaining, if he chooses to. I have other matters to attend to." He seemed anxious to leave.

"We shall see you later, then, Kane," she called after him as he strode quickly away. Had she been wrong, or was her husband's friend acting strangely?

Gabriel's face appeared hard, and once again the scar was pronounced on his cheek. It was always more noticeable when he was upset or weary. "You must be tired," she said, hoping it was the latter. She had expected him to be as jubilant as she was today, and she was slightly disappointed that he was not.

Gently taking her by the shoulders, Gabriel gazed at her with searching, silvery eyes. "I need to talk to you, Serenity. Let's go inside."

Once inside the drawing room and perched upon a striped satin settee that sat near the window, Serenity peered at Gabriel suspiciously. She had a feeling that whatever he was about to say she would not like it, yet she chastised herself for anticipating the worst. Surely nothing could threaten their happiness—today of all days.

Pacing the floor, Gabriel stopped to gaze down at her. "I dread telling you this, Serenity. More than you can possibly know. But I will not be dishonest with you, and keeping this from you is precisely that." He drew a deep breath. "This morning, I was involved in a duel with Charles Beaumarchais. I failed to tell you about it ahead of time because I did not want you to try to stop me. The man had every right to call me out for what I did to his daughter, even though the matter is in the past. I found it impossible to back away."

Serenity gasped softly. What did Gabriel mean, he had been involved in a duel? Was that not where two men each held a weapon and shot directly at the other? Had Gabriel killed Charles Beaumarchais?

Gabriel waited for a moment, then he continued, "I know violence is something you've never condoned. But here in Carolina, everything is different. A gentleman has a certain code he must live by."

Serenity was silent for a very long time. Finally, she asked, "Did you kill the man?"

Gabriel shook his head. "No, Serenity, I didn't kill Beaumarchais. I merely wounded him in the shoulder."

A frown creased her delicate brow. Suddenly, she was aware of all the implications. Not only could Gabriel have killed the man he dueled, but he might have been killed as well. Then, their life together would have been over. Her child would never have known a father. The thought of it terrified as well as appalled her. How could he risk such a thing? Did he care so very little for her and their unborn child?

Rising from the settee, Serenity stood facing Gabriel, hurt and angry. The night before he had seemed so happy about the baby. He had held her in his arms and made love to her as never before. Yet, all the while he had kept a terrible secret, knowing he was to face Charles Beaumarchais and perhaps kill him or be killed only a few short hours later. What she might think about it had mattered not at all. She felt utterly betrayed. And she had very nearly given him her heart.

Her face ashen, Serenity observed, "Until this moment, Gabriel, I never realized how very different we are." Then, spinning around, tears sparkling in her eyes, she dashed from the room.

•

Serenity had barred Gabriel from her bedchamber. It had been more with silence than with anger. Serenity had spoken to him very little since their conversation in the drawing room, and she had retired early that night and the next, without so much as bidding him a good morrow. Yet, she suffered more for it than Gabriel could know. She longed to have him hold her once again. Now, more than ever, she needed to know everything would be all right. That somehow they could still share a life together with their child.

Marihaven was their baby's home and birthright. The child deserved to have a father. Yet, it was so painful being near Gabriel after what had taken place, she was uncertain she could endure it.

Finally, however, Serenity decided to take the matter into her own hands. If ever she was to have a life with Gabriel, she must face their problems squarely and not run from the unpleasantness of the way things were. That was the first step. Once decided, she explained politely to Gabriel that she needed Lot to drive her into Charleston to visit Madame Caron, the dressmaker.

Since she had already mentioned the need for new gowns to him the night in the gazebo, Gabriel had seemed not at all surprised. He even smiled when she said that was what she was going to do. But what he did not know was that the visit to Madame Caron's small shop was only to be a minor part of her day. She had something much more important in mind. Something of which Gabriel might not approve.

Once in Charleston, Serenity's stopped first at Madame Caron's shop. The woman reminded her somewhat of the gossipy Mrs. Deerfield, whom she had met in Washington, and

Serenity was quite certain with a few careful questions she could find out precisely what she wanted to know. Of course, in order not to arouse the woman's suspicion, Serenity ordered a new gown with a waistline that could disguise her soon-to-be-expanding body.

When Serenity left the woman's shop she directed Lot to drive her a short distance farther. Then, taking with her a basket filled with sweet cakes that she had brought along, Serenity directed Lot to remain there and continued the rest of the way on foot. She must avoid having Lot see the exact place where she was going, or she would run the risk of having Gabriel find out as well.

Knocking on the door of a regal mansion, Serenity waited patiently. She would not be put off. The man must see her, whether he chose to or not. That was the only way it could be.

Once she had stated who she was to a stern-looking black servant in liveried clothing, who had promptly informed his master, Serenity was quickly ushered into the drawing room. Immediately, her gaze was drawn to Charles Beaumarchais reclining in a chair, his face unwelcoming and distant.

"What do you want, Madame Harrowe?" he inquired testily, not bothering to rise from his chair. "As you can see, your husband has done quite enough damage without your help."

Serenity was not frightened by his manner. She was used to cantankerous older men. Her father's disposition had often been just that way. What was it she had heard? Often their bark was much worse than their bite? And at least he was well enough to growl.

"Sir," Serenity began, "I was very distressed to learn of your injury. That is why I have chosen to come. Inside this basket there are sweet cakes that I baked myself. I am hopeful you will accept them."

"You need not have bothered, Madame Harrowe. I expect nothing from you, nor do I want it."

Serenity smiled. "No?" she inquired. "Well, I shall want something from you, in that case. Everyone has need of something from someone else. A kind word. Friendship. A gentle touch. Oh, I believe there is much we can give one another."

"Nonsense, young lady. I know you're a Quaker, and you mean no harm. But you are still Harrowe's wife. I want nothing at all to do with you. Leave now, before I have my servant throw you out."

Drawing closer, Serenity set down her basket and knelt on the floor near his chair. Gazing up at him, she said, "Truly? Have you so many friends, you have no need of another? That is all I want. I answer to the name of Serenity. If you would be so kind—"

Beaumarchais frowned.

Grasping the basket she had brought once more, Serenity held it up for him to see inside and removed the cloth that covered the sweet cakes. "I promise you, they are delicious. And I would appreciate something cool to drink."

"My dear young woman . . . " he began.

"Serenity. Please."

"Well, then . . . " he said, clearing his throat with a harumph. "Serenity. What makes you think you can be my friend, after everything your husband has done?"

"Do I judge you by another?" she countered. "I see only your face before me."

He sighed. Then he picked up a little bell, which sat on the table to one side, and rang it as loudly as it would ring.

For a moment, Serenity was certain she had failed in her attempt to befriend him as the servant rushed into the room. Was he going to have her thrown out onto the doorstep?

"Bring tea," he ordered briskly. Then, he added, "And a cool drink. I have a guest." Then, turning to gaze down at her as she knelt by his side, he gave her an order as well. "And Serenity, or whatever your name is, find yourself a proper seat. You'll develop arthritis in your knees in your old age, sitting like that. If you choose, you may call me Charles."

On the way back to Marihaven, Serenity felt happier than she had been since learning of the duel. At least some good would come from the evil doings if she had her way about it. Obviously, Charles Beaumarchais was a lonely man, despite having his daughter Veronique. With determination and persistence, she might even melt the gentleman's cold heart and truly be his friend.

A night breeze ruffled Gabriel's dark hair as he stood just outside the tiny gazebo. In the moonlight, it appeared a ghostlike structure. Empty. Still. The only sound was the whisper of the wind through its lattice sides.

He could not help remembering the night Serenity had told him about the baby at the gazebo. It had seemed a special place then. He had held her and kissed her. He'd wanted to make love.

Now, it was as lifeless as the way he felt inside.

Tonight, Serenity had retired to her bedchamber early once again, just as she had for the two nights before. And, once again, he knew he'd lay awake wanting to go to her, simply to be near her, to have her curl warmly in his arms as she slept. But it could never be. He knew she would not forgive him for what he had done.

Slowly, he strode back toward the mansion. Entering, he made his way up the stairs and to Serenity's bedchamber door. For a moment, he hesitated just outside. He knew she lay sleeping, her fiery hair like a curtain framing her delicate face. He wanted to shove the door open. But it would be of no use.

A muscle twitched along his jaw. He was a fool ever to have given his heart to someone so different.

Chapter Twenty-two

"What we need is another ball," Raven said enthusiastically. "It will bring you and Gabriel closer together. It is so dreary having the two of you barely speaking. And do not deny it is true. I have noticed something is wrong."

Serenity was in no mood for another ball. Not in the least. She had seen the disastrous results before. Washington. Her first night at Marihaven. The Pierpont ball. They were fast becoming too numerous to mention.

"Please be reasonable, Raven," she replied. "No one is in a festive mood."

"Fiddlesticks, and horse feathers besides," Raven interrupted impatiently. "That is precisely the time when you need a ball. Trust me. I shall do all of the planning. All of the work. There shall be candles and music. You can dance with Gabriel. I promise it will be a wonderful evening."

Serenity sighed, wishing fervently that Raven would give up on the idea, but knowing that her lovely sister-in-law would not. "Is it possible you are simply looking for an opportunity to dress in your fanciest gown, Raven, and dance with Kane once more?"

Lowering her eyes, Raven actually blushed. "Well, of course, that is another reason. I can think of no one else but Kane. I lean out my bedchamber window . . . I dangle from the banister . . . simply to catch a glimpse of him. I think of any excuse I can to go to the stables. If I get any more forward, Kane will think me a shameless hussy and begin to run each time he sees me. Oh, please, Serenity. Let us have this ball. Perhaps something very special will happen for both you and I. Have you never heard of playing cupid?"

"A mythical character with terrible aim," Serenity retorted, unable to resist the temptation to tease the younger woman. "I shall talk to Gabriel. If he is agreeable—"

"He will be, Serenity. I'm certain of it."

Despite Raven's assurance, Serenity still felt doubtful. Gabriel seemed even less in the mood for a ball than she did. Even so, she did not want to disappoint Raven and was determined to try.

After dinner that evening, as soon as Raven had discreetly excused herself from the table, throwing a pointed glance in her direction as she did so, Serenity approached her husband on the subject at hand. "Do you have a moment, Gabriel? I have a matter I would like to discuss.

"Yes. Of course, Serenity." Leaning back in his chair, he stretched his long legs before him. His silvery gaze rested intently on her face, and there was a certain wariness in it.

Suddenly, Serenity realized how much she had missed conversing with him in the past few days. Obviously, there were still many problems—problems that could not be easily resolved. However, she did not like the coldness between them either, and she would hate for it to continue. Perhaps if they did have the ball . . .

Hesitantly, Serenity began, "I should like to give a ball at Marihaven. If it meets with your approval."

For a moment, Gabriel appeared startled by her request. Then, a moment later, his expression changed to one of suspicion. "Why?"

"Because it would be a welcome diversion," Serenity explained. There was no need to tell him that his sister had suggested the idea, or that in the past few moments Serenity had begun to harbor a secret hope of her own, that a ball might bring her and Gabriel closer together again.

"Somehow that does not seem an adequate argument to me, Serenity," Gabriel countered blandly.

He was being even more disagreeable than she had anticipated. Did he truly hate such things as formal balls, or was he being deliberately stubborn? Leaning forward, she said, "There is another reason."

"Is it better than the last one?"

Feeling the hot color rise to her cheeks, Serenity gazed at him in sudden annoyance. She had never known him to be so unbending. "Raven hoped she and Kane—"

"Raven and Kane," he interjected. "I guessed that much already. Anything else?"

He was making this as difficult for her as possible. Were they to be at cross-purposes with each other from now on? Could he not see that she was trying to make things better between them?

Her eyes flashing blue fire, Serenity quickly rose to her feet. She would not stay to argue with him a moment longer. Spinning on her heels, she marched to the door. Then she stopped to shoot him a parting glance.

With icy candor, she remarked, "You are insufferable."

Her words did not seem to bother him in the least.

Troubled, Serenity sat in Charles Beaumarchais's drawing room, devoid of her usual good spirits. She could not put the thought of Gabriel from her mind. Although he had finally agreed to the ball, she was certain Gabriel had done it more for Raven's sake than out of consideration for her. The distance between them was growing ever larger.

"What is it, Serenity, my dear?" Beaumarchais asked when he noted her silence. In the time since she had begun visiting him, the two of them had gradually grown closer and were more at ease with one another.

Serenity sighed. "We are giving a ball at Marihaven, I am afraid."

"Oh, I see," he replied. "You don't care for things of that nature?"

"It is not that, Charles. I can hardly look forward to it when Gabriel and I are at such odds. We have barely spoken for many days."

A frown creased Beaumarchais's aging brow. "Is this because of the duel? I know it met with your disapproval, Serenity. I have already deduced that much by your visits here without your husband's knowledge."

Serenity nodded. "I was most sincere about becoming your friend, Charles. I truly mean that. I wanted some good to come from what had occurred. But, in gaining your friendship, I hoped for something else as well. I was hoping to find a way to forgive Gabriel."

Beaumarchais gazed at her with understanding. "Far be it from me to champion your husband's cause, Serenity. No one could accuse me of that. Harrowe has hardly endeared himself to me. Yet, you must understand, my dear—I was the one who called him out. To refuse would have denied me a right to a justice that I deserved. It set a matter to rest, which could be resolved no other way. Your husband did what he had to do. Now that I know you, I realize how difficult that decision must have been for him. Do not judge him too harshly."

"I am trying," Serenity replied. "However, now it seems things between us may never improve."

"What makes you believe that, Serenity?"

Serenity could not tell Beaumarchais that Gabriel had not come once to her bed, nor mentioned their child, nor given her the slightest indication that he cared for her at all since the night at the gazebo. He had even been positively hateful when she had approached him about the ball. It had been as if Gabriel was determined to drive her away.

At a loss for any response, Serenity rose from her chair as though she had suddenly remembered the lateness of the hour. "I must be going now. Gabriel believes I am at the dress-maker's. He will wonder why I am taking so long."

Beaumarchais nodded. "Thank you for your visit, Serenity. You brighten the day considerably whenever you come. But there is no need for you to bother any further with an old repro-bate like me. I'm certain you have better things to do."

"You will not dissuade me," she chided with a parting smile as she started for the door. "I promise I shall return, Charles. On Thursday next, at this same time."

A slight grin appeared. "I shall be looking forward to it. And you might bring some more of those sweet cakes."

Frowning darkly, Gabriel realized that he should never have agreed to the ball in the first place. He was certain it was all Raven's doing. He had no desire to act the doting husband before guests when all the while he knew Serenity could

215

hardly bear the sight of him. If he were wise he would send Serenity away, back to Brookeville or wherever else she wanted to go. That would be far easier on him than the way things were now. Why continue to hope for something that could never be?

Standing before the mirror, Gabriel straightened the silk stock at his throat. Tonight, except for his white shirt, he had worn all black. It gave him a slightly dangerous appearance, which matched precisely the way he was feeling at the moment. He could hardly refuse to go to his own ball, yet he longed to slip out of the mansion and go to the stables for his horse, and then ride until the dawn. He was not certain he could get through the long evening ahead.

Still, albeit reluctantly, a short time later Gabriel found himself downstairs, standing in the ballroom at Serenity's side, greeting guests as though the ball was something he had looked forward to and had not dreaded in the least, even smiling pleasantly upon occasion. With cool deliberation, he had kept his eyes trained straight ahead, trying to ignore the intoxicating effect Serenity was having upon him—and had since the moment she had walked down the stairs.

Tonight, Serenity was enchantingly beautiful. Her gown was of creamy white silk trimmed in satin and lace, with a flowing skirt enhanced by the palest of pink satin roses. In her dusky hair, more pale pink roses entwined as well.

Once the guests had finished arriving, Gabriel spun toward her. Whether she chose to or not, it was only proper for them to dance the first waltz together. "Would you care to dance, Serenity?"

Silently, Serenity nodded her head and took his arm.

Leading her to the dance floor, Gabriel drew her into his arms. It felt so right, he almost had to catch his breath. But he was careful not to hold her too closely. He knew that she found him detestable. Like characters on a stage, they spun and turned, going through the motions all the while knowing they were merely acting out parts. When the dance was finally over, he once more returned her to the side of the ballroom.

"Thank you, Gabriel."

"Others would talk if we hadn't danced," he replied tersely.

For a moment, there was something in Serenity's expression he could not quite define. Had he hurt her by acting as though he was merely doing his duty? That could not be. Undoubtedly, she was relieved to have the dance come swiftly to an end. If she could not bear the sight of him, how could she endure his touch?

He started to turn away, but Serenity halted him, her delicate hand touching his arm. "Kane has not yet danced with Raven."

"I see that, Serenity," he retorted with icy indifference. "And of course, that was the reason for this whole charade. Was it not? It would be a pity if the effort was to no avail. Would you care to have me order Kane to dance with her? Is that what you were hoping for?"

She gazed at him with something akin to frustration. "This is not a contest between you and me, Gabriel. I want Raven to be happy. But that was not the only reason I agreed to this ball. I was hoping—"

"You were hoping what?"

"Never mind," she said. "You would not listen."

Gabriel felt the prick of his conscience. Yet, he was not about to heed it. He did not want any false hopes. It was better to arm himself against her by being indifferent.

Approaching the two of them, Kane interrupted with a grin and a slight bow. "Would you grant me the privilege of dancing with your beautiful wife, Gabriel?"

Glancing quickly at Serenity, Gabriel hesitated for a moment. At the Pierpont ball, Serenity had told him such an intimacy should be reserved for one's husband. Yet, now, perhaps she might feel differently. She might even welcome another man's arms about her, since there was nothing more between the two of them.

"Do as you like, Serenity," he directed. "Far be it from me to interfere."

Then, wheeling around, Gabriel left Serenity and Kane standing there.

Watching him go, Serenity felt like stamping her foot in anger and frustration. Nothing was working out as she had planned. Gabriel was being cold and obstinate, and she was at a loss for what to do. What was worse, now he had put her in the position of dancing with Kane when he knew how she felt about such things. If not a sin, it would seem an uncomfortable breach for her to dance with another man. Yet, Gabriel had acted like it mattered not at all to him.

"Quaker?" Kane asked.

Impulsively, Serenity grasped his arm. If Gabriel truly cared so very little about what she did . . .

However, once they were upon the dance floor, Serenity whispered softly to Kane, "You should be dancing with someone else, Kane."

Kane threw her a grin. "I know. But it won't hurt Raven to simmer awhile. The little minx has already won my heart. I will not have it going to her head. Otherwise, the moment she crooks her little finger, she'll expect me to come running. I intend to keep my pants on, at least part of the time, or she'll wear them as well."

Despite her own trials with Gabriel, Serenity could not help smiling at Kane's crudity. At least some things were working out for the best. "I am so happy for you, Kane. You and Raven shall make a fine couple."

"Hold on now, Quaker. I'm not ready to recite any vows. Raven has not proven she can control her temper. And I have no wish to wed a shrew, whether I'm in love with one or not."

"She will learn, Kane. I am certain of it. Just give her time."

"And what of you and Gabriel?" he asked, changing the subject, his expression suddenly serious.

For a moment, Serenity's blue eyes darkened with pain. "I do not know what the future holds for us, Kane. We are having great difficulties. But I cannot give up. I carry his child."

218

Kane stopped dancing on the spot to gaze in amazement at Serenity. Then, laughing out loud, he spun her around in jubilation before he came to a stop once again. "That is wonderful."

"I know," she replied. "It *is* wonderful. But Gabriel and I—"

"Don't worry, Quaker. This will take care of everything. Wait and see. A child . . . his child can only bring you closer together."

Leaning against the carved archway into the ballroom, Gabriel watched Serenity and Kane together, his mood darkening by the moment. It gnawed away at him even to see her in another man's arms. Friend or not, he felt like taking a swing at Kane.

A glower on his handsome face, Gabriel could not help remembering what it was like to hold Serenity in his arms . . . to kiss her . . . to have her beneath him, her eyes aglow with passion, her silken body responding to his. He wanted her in every way. Yet, he could not go to her so long as he knew the way she felt about him. Like a festering wound, it seemed to grow inside him.

Momentarily, Raven came to stand nearby. She, too, was watching Serenity and Kane, and her heart shone in her gray eyes. "I could almost be jealous of them," she murmured softly, "if I did not know Serenity so well."

Glancing down at her, Gabriel only grunted. His feelings were too close to the surface to discuss with Raven, and he felt too disheartened himself to lend her any comfort.

"Why does Kane not care for me, Gabriel? I have done everything I can think of. And I love him so pitifully."

Raven seemed to require some response. Yet, there was no answer Gabriel could give her. A man could not control whom he fell in love with. Even on Nantucket, he had known it was a mistake for him to ever fall in love with Serenity. Yet, here he stood, like some lovestruck youth, waiting for Serenity to take notice of him. Was he any different than his sister?

I have to get out of here, Gabriel told himself fiercely, unable

219

to bear it a moment longer. Without even bothering to bid her farewell, he wheeled around sharply and left.

When Gabriel returned, Marihaven was already dark. The guests had long since gone, and everyone else had retired to their chambers. Unsaddling his horse and leaving it with a sleepy stableboy, Gabriel entered by the rear entrance, knowing he still had to pass Serenity's door.

Soon it would be dawn, yet he still chafed from the sight of Serenity in Kane's arms. Even if she never loved him, he could not bear to lose her to another man. She was still his wife.

Striding past her door, Gabriel was angry and resentful. The anger was for himself, for falling in love with Serenity in the first place, and his resentment was because she did not love him return.

Reaching the end of the hallway, Gabriel slowly opened the door. He had been fooling himself, thinking she might be there. Damnation! When was he going to learn? His handsome face hard and ruthless, he entered the bedchamber and began to pace the floor. How could he sleep? Like a caged animal, he counted the steps that marked the confines of the room.

Yanking off his black jacket and then his shirt, he threw them on the bed, glancing at the bitter reminder of their past shared passion with clear disdain. He should have burned the rest of the beds in the mansion when he'd had the chance. That was what he had told her he would do, the night she had made him promise they would share one bed from then on. And not long after it had proven to be a lie.

He had ridden almost the entire way to Charleston before he had decided to turn back. Now, he was sorry he had not continued the rest of the way and gotten himself a room for the night. It would have been no problem to have a woman sent around. Yet, fool that he was, he wanted no one but Serenity. He could not even imagine wanting anyone else again.

"Fool!" he said aloud. He detested the power she had over him.

His hard-muscled chest bared, he strode with determination to the door and, swinging it wide, went back down the hallway to Serenity's bedchamber. Jerking her door open, he took two steps inside.

In the moonlight that streamed in through the window, he could see Serenity stir. Rousing slightly, she sat up in bed. Her tangled mass of copper-colored hair streamed about her shoulders and her face was hidden in shadows. Striding over to her, he yanked the covers back.

Leaning down, he scooped her up into his arms and headed back toward the door; then he kept on going down the hallway until he reached his own bedchamber once more. Entering, he kicked the door shut behind him.

For a moment, he stood there with Serenity cradled in his arms. If he had expected her to protest or resist in some way, he had been wrong. It was not forthcoming. Instead, she snuggled closer to his chest and sighed softly.

Slowly, the anger and frustration drained from him. What was he to do, now? Crossing to the bed, he gently placed Serenity upon it.

Stretching like a sleepy kitten, her blue eyes fluttering open for a moment, she smiled up at him. Then, she rolled over and went back to sleep without a word.

He drew the covers up around her. "You can despise me all you want tomorrow, Serenity, " he murmured. "But, if nothing more, tonight you will at least sleep in my bed."

Chapter Twenty-three

Joshua raced from the stable and ran as fast as his legs could carry him, to the place beneath the huge oak tree where Serenity sat giving the plantation's servants' children their morning reading lessons.

"Serenity!" Joshua called anxiously. "Come quick. Kane is hurt. There's lots of blood."

Not taking time to ask what had occurred, Serenity hurriedly told her students that their lesson was over for the day. Then she and her brother sped back toward the stable.

Once inside, Serenity rushed over to where Kane lay on the floor. He struggled to get up, his head bloody.

"Kane! Are you all right?" she asked, dropping to her knees beside him. She quickly examined his head. As with all head wounds, there was much blood, yet the gash she saw did not appear to be large.

"That new black stallion of Gabriel's got spooked," Kane grumbled. "I should have been more careful. The foul-tempered beast caught me on the side of the head, but I managed to crawl out of the stall before he could do worse damage. Afterward, I must have blacked out for a few minutes. But now I'm fine."

"You do not look fine to me, Kane. Quickly, come into the house. You will need stitches to close that wound—it is bleeding badly."

Kane frowned. Blood trickled down his forehead, and he wiped it away with one hand. Taking a look at his sticky palm, he finally nodded in agreement. Shakily, he let Serenity help him to his feet.

Once inside the mansion, Serenity sent Joshua to fetch a pan of clean water and a cloth. Then, seating Kane in a chair near the window where there was good light, she went in search of a needle and thread. When she had everything she needed assembled, she sent Joshua back outside with the assurance that Kane would be quite all right.

Once Joshua was gone, she began to clean the area around the wound. "I am sorry, Kane, but I have nothing to give you to ease the pain of the stitches."

"If you are saying there is not one drop of whisky in the house, Quaker," he said, with a slight grin, "I never expected there would be. I will do my best to be brave without it."

Drawing a breath, Serenity took the needle and thread in her hand and made the first stitch. She felt Kane wince. "I have great practice in doing this, Kane," she said, trying to distract him. "All of the little girls and even some of the small boys on Nantucket learn to stitch on quilts by the time they reach the age of five."

"Do you miss Nantucket, Quaker?"

She gave him a quick smile. "Sometimes."

Kane winced again as she put in another stitch. "How are things between you and Gabriel?"

Serenity sighed. "Not much better, I am afraid. I had hoped the ball would ease some of the tension between us, but it seems it has not. It is no longer just the duel. I do not condone violence, but I have finally come to understand why Gabriel could not back away. However, there is still a wall of sorts between us. It is as though I am starting to see the other side of him that I failed to see on Nantucket. He is convinced I will never accept him as he is."

"And will you, Quaker?" Kane asked quietly. "I think he is justified in his fear to some degree. His life has always been far different than yours. The duel was merely one episode. There are bound to be more incidents in the future. I warned you of that before. If Gabriel has to question whether each one might drive you away, then he may be afraid to care too deeply for you."

"There. I'm finished," she said, setting her needle down. She picked up a damp cloth once more and cleaned the area around the wound again. Then, she stood back to gaze at Kane. There was a slight frown on her delicate face. "I know what you are saying, Kane. But even I do not know the answer yet. In these past few weeks, I have discovered that I love Gabriel with all my heart and being, in a way I shall never love again. As for accepting the differences between us . . . "

Unshed tears shone in her fathomless blue eyes.

Rising, Kane drew her against his broad chest. "I feel confident the two of you will find a way, Quaker. You and Gabriel were meant for each other."

Gloria Pedersen

Serenity stood for a moment wrapped in Kane's strong arms, letting him comfort her. Kane had always been such a good friend to both her and Gabriel. It was good to have him there.

A slight noise from behind alerted Serenity and Kane that someone else was there as well. Kane was the first one to move. A look of startled horror appeared on his face when he glanced up to gaze over her head. He released Serenity immediately.

Quickly turning, Serenity saw who it was as well. Raven stood there, her lovely face as pale as a ghost. It was clear the younger woman had misunderstood what she had seen.

In shock and anger, Raven cried out in an accusing voice, "How could you, Serenity? How could you? I trusted you! Gabriel trusted you. When all the while it was Kane you wanted—Kane you desired. Was it not enough for you to possess my brother's heart? Must you steal Kane's as well?"

With that, Raven spun away from the two of them and raced for the stairs as Serenity and Kane stood helplessly gazing on.

Striding into Percival Benjamin's law office, Gabriel took a seat and stretched out his long legs before him.

The little man on the other side of the desk peered back at him from over a stack of papers and books, a slight grin on his face. Pushing his wire-framed glasses up higher on his long nose, he grasped a paper in his hand. "I have it here, Gabriel. What you've been waiting for. But I'm not sure you're going to like it."

A frown creasing his dark brow, Gabriel drew a deep breath. "Give it to me without the embellishments, Percy. Even as a lad, you were inclined to milk a tale for all it was worth. It is a wonder the two of us ever stayed friends. This time I want the simple facts. Does Veronique have a child? And could it possibly be mine?"

Percy tossed him another grin. "I can only give you dates, Gabriel, nothing more. You will have to determine for yourself if those particular dates coincide with any involvement you may . . . ahem . . . or may not have had with the lady in question."

"Percy," he prompted dryly, "I'm waiting."

"The facts are that Veronique Beaumarchais Durand was delivered of a baby boy not six months after she was wed to Jean-Paul Durand. The child's name is Alexandre, and he has black hair—much like yours, I might add—and green eyes. A precocious lad, according to his gossipy nurse, an indentured young Frenchwoman who goes by the name of Ninette. But whether or not the child could be yours, I have absolutely no idea."

Gabriel felt a moment of icy frustration. He had been afraid of this. There was no definite proof either way that the child was his. There was only just enough evidence of the possibility to wreak havoc with his life. He could not claim his son, and he could very well lose Serenity.

"Thank you, Percy. For all you have done."

"Legally," Percy retorted, "you have no rights. None at all. Perhaps your only recourse is to talk to Madame Durand. Ask her about the child. If she is willing to talk to you . . ."

A muscle tightened along Gabriel's jaw. "Veronique's willing," he stated bluntly, even now anticipating the smug smile that would be on her face when he asked to see her. "But whether she will tell me the truth about the child is something else."

Serenity and Kane stared at each other aghast as Raven dashed up the stairs. What were they to do? Raven had completely misunderstood the reason Serenity had been in Kane's arms.

"I'll go after her," Kane said, starting from the room.

"No," Serenity countered quickly, catching his arm. "I am the one who should go to her, Kane. I am the one whom she blames, not you. Somehow I must explain. At this point, Raven would only turn you away. Go now," she continued, pushing him toward the front door. "You should rest for awhile because of your injury. I will make certain Raven understands that there is nothing between us."

His face ashen, Kane nodded slowly. "I will be in my quarters, if you need me."

A frown creasing her delicate brow, Serenity watched as Kane went out the door. He still seemed shaken from his accident, and she waited several moments until she was certain he could manage on his own. Then, whirling around, she hurried up the stairs and to Raven's bedchamber door.

Knocking softly, Serenity called, "Please, Raven, may I come in? You must let me explain. It is not as you think."

There was no reply.

Serenity tried again. "You must hear me, Raven. Kane and I are only friends. It is your brother I love. No other. Kane thinks of me only as his friend. Please let me come in."

There was still no reply. Tentatively, Serenity tried the door. Slowly, she pushed it wide and peered inside. The bedchamber was empty.

Serenity gazed about in confusion. Where had Raven gone? She had seen her run up the stairs.

Was it possible she had left by another way?

Racing down the rear stairs and out the back door, Serenity nearly ran into their young serving girl, Daisy, as she was coming back in from the cookhouse. "Daisy," she cried. "Have you seen Raven? Did she come this way?"

Daisy looked uneasy. She gazed down at her feet evasively.

"Daisy, if you know something, this is no time to keep it to yourself," she said. She took the young black girl by the shoulders and forced her to gaze into her eyes. "Raven has need of me. I must know where she is. Hurry."

"Miss Raven says, 'Tell only Master Gabriel where I'm goin'.'"

Impatiently, Serenity responded, "Gabriel will be gone for some time, Daisy. What if something happens to Raven in the meantime? You would be to blame. Gabriel would be angry."

"Oh, lawsy, ma'am. I don't want to be blamed for nothin' by Master Gabriel. He's been mighty awful kind." Daisy sighed in resignation. "Miss Raven says to me, she ain't stayin' here no more. She's goin' back to Twin Oaks. An' she went to get her horse."

Serenity glanced up, hoping to catch sight of Raven in the distance. It had only been a few minutes. Raven could not have gotten far. "Did you see in which direction she went, Daisy?"

"No, ma'am."

"That's all right, Daisy," Serenity said kindly, releasing the girl's shoulders. "I think I already know. Raven always takes the short way through the swamp. If I hurry, maybe I can catch her before she gets too far. I must have her back at Marihaven before Gabriel gets home."

With that, Serenity made a dash for the stables. Seeing her run by, Joshua and Biscuit were fast on her heels.

Once in the stables, Serenity raced to the tack room. "Help me, Joshua," she directed anxiously. "I must saddle Blue Lady."

"Can't!" Joshua replied as he stood back, his dark eyes troubled. "Never saddled Blue Lady before." Then, he added more brightly, "I can put on her bridle. Kane showed me how."

Serenity had never saddled Blue Lady either, but she had no wish to tell Joshua that. Surely, it could not be that difficult. She had watched both Gabriel and Kane do it a number of times before, and it appeared quite simple. There was no time to find another stableboy. "Don't worry, Joshua. I shall saddle Blue Lady myself. You may help with the bridle."

A short time later, after much effort, Blue Lady was ready to go. Leading the horse from the stable, Serenity instructed Joshua to boost her up into the sidesaddle. "I will be back as soon as I can, Joshua." Then, quickly nudging the horse's sides, she set off at a brisk pace.

It had never been Serenity's intention to follow Raven into the swamp. She had hoped to catch up with her sister-in-law long before it would be necessary. Yet she had not, and she dared not turn back without Raven. Gabriel would never forgive her for

Gloria Pedersen

driving his sister away. Nor could Serenity allow Raven to believe the falsehood that she did. Still, the swamp seemed more frightening than she had ever anticipated.

Even Biscuit whimpered as he trotted along by her side. The big wolfhound had followed her when she'd left the stables, and Serenity had not bothered to send the animal back. Now, she was more than a little grateful for the dog's presence.

The late afternoon sun filtered softly through the branches of the live oak and moss-draped cypress, and the musky smell of the swamp assailed her senses. Slowing the horse's pace, she attempted to follow the pathway. But which way? Should she go to the right or to the left? There was no indication that Raven had chosen either one.

Behind each tree, shadows played—dancing, disquieting shadows—that made her think of wild beasts lurking in the darkness. Oh, the darkness. Soon, it would be dark. She had not thought of that. She must be out of the swamp before nightfall.

"Raven! Where are you?" Serenity called. The sound of her voice had an eerie quality to it, as though it were an intruder in the swamp, in and of itself. She was wrong to have ventured this far. She should have turned back to Marihaven long before now. But how could she face Gabriel? Traveling on, Serenity turned left and then right.

Ahead, there lay a confusing maze of pathways, each as unfamiliar as the last, one leading here, one leading there. Serenity drew Blue Lady up sharply. There was no longer any choice. She must turn back. Turning in the saddle, she suddenly realized she was no longer certain which path would lead her back to Marihaven either.

In desperation, Serenity started up another pathway. Kicking the horse's sides gently, she urged Blue Lady on. Suddenly, a snake hissed up from the brush, startling the animal and making her rear back slightly, then setting her off on a gallop. Unable to do anything but hold on, Serenity tried to keep her seat in the saddle as the terrified horse charged through the trees. Branches stung Serenity's face and hands and tore at her gown

228

as she clung blindly to the saddle strapped to the horse's back. Then, she felt herself falling, falling, as the saddle broke free and gave way beneath her.

Serenity felt the impact of her body striking the ground as the horse sped on without her. For a moment, she just lay there, uncertain what had happened, her body still aching from the fall. Then, cruelly, Serenity felt another more severe pain start from within. It made her catch her breath in fear. Something was dreadfully wrong.

"My baby," she whispered. "My baby . . . "

Gabriel saw Kane waiting for him by the stables as the carriage drew to a halt. It was growing late. The dinner hour was already well past. Had Serenity been waiting for him?

Hurrying to the carriage, Kane impatiently watched as he climbed down. "I've been anxious for your return, Gabriel. Something has happened."

Alarmed, Gabriel shot him a glance. "What do you mean?" he demanded. "Is Serenity all right? Raven?"

"It's the Quaker."

Turning toward the mansion, Gabriel took several long strides before Kane could halt him.

"Wait, Gabriel!" Kane called. "She's not in there."

Wheeling around, Gabriel's face was hard and his eyes were like cold gray steel. "What happened?" he demanded.

"The Quaker is missing," Kane began. "She must have gone riding. But Blue Lady came back alone, the saddle torn from her back."

For a moment, disbelief registered on Gabriel's face. His voice was accusing. "You let her go alone?"

"I swear, Gabriel, I had no idea what Serenity intended to do. Joshua was the one who told me. But that was not until sometime later. Otherwise, I would have stopped her. Serenity was never very good on a horse. I hate to think what happened to her."

"Where were you?"

Kane winced. "Earlier today, that big black brute you just

purchased, El Capítan, took a notion to kick me in the side of the head. The Quaker was good enough to stitch me up. Afterwards, I went back to my quarters to rest for awhile. I'm sorry, Gabriel. I never imagined—"

"Have El Capítan saddled and ready for me," Gabriel ordered tersely. "Then find Joshua. I want to talk to him myself. Also, bring anyone else to me who might have knowledge of the direction in which Serenity rode. Have all of them wait in the drawing room. I'm going to see if I can find any clues myself."

Starting to wheel away, Gabriel stopped for a moment to gaze quickly at the dying rays of the sun. A hard knot of fear suddenly twisted his insides. "It will be dark soon," he added, more to himself than to Kane. "I've got to find her quickly."

Chapter Twenty-four

As soon as he had looked about, Gabriel hurried back down to the drawing room, where Kane had everyone assembled. Joshua was there, as well as Lot, several stableboys, and a number of household servants. Only Raven was noticeably absent. Yet, at present, Gabriel decided that was for the best. There was no need to upset his sister unduly. With any luck, he would find Serenity before Raven even knew she was missing.

"Joshua," Gabriel said, trying to restrain his own anxiety. He would gain nothing by upsetting Joshua. "I know you are as worried about Serenity as I am. Would you tell me everything that happened?"

Gazing down at his feet, Joshua scuffed a toe of one boot against the floor. "Serenity wanted to go for a ride. She wanted me to saddle Blue Lady. I told Serenity"—he paused, as though trying to think of the exact words— "Kane didn't show me how to saddle Blue Lady . . . "

"I see," Gabriel replied patiently. "Did someone else saddle the horse for her?"

"No," Joshua replied slowly. "Serenity saddled Blue Lady."

"Serenity?" Gabriel repeated in exasperation. "She had no business . . . "

"Master Gabriel," Daisy interrupted. "Master Gabriel . . . "

Ignoring Daisy, Gabriel continued to question Joshua, "Is there anything more you can tell me, Joshua? Anything at all?"

"Master Gabriel," Daisy interrupted again.

Gabriel shot the girl a dark glance, which effectively stilled her tongue.

Joshua thought for a moment. "Biscuit went with her."

Thank heavens for that mangy brute, Gabriel thought wryly. He took comfort in the fact Serenity had the dog with her. At least Biscuit could offer her some small measure of protection.

"Master Gabriel," Daisy interjected again.

Sighing, Gabriel turned his eyes in the serving maid's direction. "Now you may have your turn, Daisy. What is it you want to say?"

"I been tryin' to tell you, Master Gabriel. I know where Madame Harrowe has gone."

Immediately alert to what the girl was saying, Gabriel gave her his full attention. "Where is she?"

Daisy sighed. "Well, Master Gabriel, I'll have to start at the beginnin'. First, Miss Raven, she comes down the back stairs and says to me, 'Tell Master Gabriel I ain't gonna live at Marihaven no more. I'm goin' back to Twin Oaks.' Then, Madame Harrowe, she comes down an' she says, 'Daisy, tell me where Miss Raven is.' I told Madame Harrowe, Miss Raven don't want no one but you to know. But Madame Harrowe said something terrible might happen to Miss Raven if I didn't tell. So I told her. Madame Harrowe says to me, 'I know the way Miss

Raven is goin'. She always takes the short way through the swamp.' Then, she runs to get her horse."

His face dark with anger, Gabriel shot a glance at Kane. "So Raven is gone as well?"

Kane appeared stricken. "I didn't know . . . "

A muscle tightening along his jaw, Gabriel ordered, "The rest of you can return to your duties for the time being. Kane, I want you to remain here."

Once the two of them were alone, Gabriel said harshly, "I'm not certain what happened, Kane. And right now I don't want to hear it. Have Lot ready the carriage. Then, the two of you ride to Twin Oaks to see if Raven is there. Inform my impetuous sister that if she knows what is good for her, she will be back at Marihaven before my return, and I'll brook no arguments to the contrary. There's going to be a full moon out tonight. I'll ride to the swamp. And everyone concerned had better pray I find Serenity. . . . "

Filtering down through the branches of oak and cypress, the moonlight illuminated the trail ahead. The horse's hooves drummed a cadence against the moist earth, and the night sounds were all around.

It had been a long time since Gabriel had ridden the swamps by night. Still, his memory served him well as he followed the twisting, winding trails. He was desperate to find his wife. Was she injured? Was she afraid?

Gabriel could not help thinking of the tales he had heard about the swamp as a child, of the "ha'nts" and "plat-eyes" that the slaves claimed were there. They were only tales. Yet, he could readily imagine the terror Serenity might be experiencing at that very moment by being in the swamp at night. He had taken her from a place where she was safe, and with people of her own kind, to live where it seemed impossible to protect her at all. Now, here she was, lost in this forsaken bog. How could he ever forgive himself if something happened to her?

Turning up first one trail and down another, Gabriel methodically covered them one by one. But there was an endless maze. What if Serenity had gotten off the trail even slightly? He might never be able to find her.

For endless hours, he kept on searching. Though weary, he would not give up. If she was there, he had to find her. Somehow.

Then, he heard something. It sounded like a dog's bark in the distance. He drew El Capítan to a halt and listened intently. For a moment, there was only silence. Then he heard it again.

Kicking his horse, he turned up a trail that headed in the direction of the sound. It had to be Biscuit. Stopping every so often, he waited for the sound again. Each time it would come, drawing him ever closer.

"Biscuit!" he called when he knew he was almost there.

The dog barked anxiously again.

"Biscuit."

Suddenly, the dog burst out from the brush, into the trail ahead of him. The animal stopped dead still. Not wanting the dog to dart away from him, Gabriel dropped down from the horse's back and tied El Capítan to the dead branch of a tree. Slowly, he walked toward the wolfhound. "Biscuit," he said again. "Find Serenity . . ."

Reacting to the sound of his voice and his scent, for a moment the wolfhound seemed almost jubilant to see him, nudging up against him. Then, leaping sideways, it crashed back through the trees and brush. Gabriel was close behind. He could not lose the dog now.

Sweat beaded his brow as he ran, while the brush whipped at his face and hampered his progress. He was breathing heavily from exertion and fatigue, yet he had to keep going. Then, abruptly, the dog stopped just ahead and began barking once again.

Almost hidden by some brush, Serenity lay in a glimmer of moonlight, her lovely face seemingly carved of alabaster and

233

her flame-colored hair a mere shadow on the ground. Racing toward her, Gabriel dropped to her side. Was she alive?

Serenity stirred, as though awakening from a dream. "Gabriel."

"Thank God in Heaven," he murmured, a catch in his throat as he gathered her into his arms. Unseen in the darkness, tears glistened in his eyes.

Softly, she whispered, "I lost our child."

Holding her against his hard chest, he replied, "As long as I still have you, Serenity, nothing else matters."

But Serenity did not hear him. Her blue eyes had already closed once more.

Standing near the bedchamber door, Gabriel and the physician conversed as Serenity slept. It had been dawn before Gabriel had gotten Serenity home, and it was going on late afternoon now. It had taken Gabriel some time to check Serenity for broken bones and carry her to where he had tied his horse, and much more time than that to ride back out of the swamp and finally reach Marihaven. Immediately after, he had sent Lot for the physician. Now, his handsome face was tired and drawn as stood by Serenity's bedside facing the physician.

"Will she be all right?" Gabriel demanded.

Outside the bedchamber door, Biscuit growled softly. After their return, the dog had not appreciated being banished from Serenity's side for even a moment. But the physician refused to examine Serenity until Gabriel had put the animal from the room. Now, Biscuit waited by the door impatiently.

The physician gazed at Gabriel solemnly. "Your wife has been through quite an ordeal, sir. And, of course, you are aware of the loss of the child. But she is strong, and I am certain she will recover quickly. I would, however, allow her a short time before attempting . . . " He cleared his throat slightly. "Well, six to eight weeks should do it. Just stay away from her for that period of time. Should the need arise for any diversion, it might be better for you to ride into Charleston—there are plenty of accommodating ladies there. Madame Harrowe needs a chance to recover physically before attempting a family again."

A glower on his harshly handsome face, Gabriel resisted the impulse to take a swing at the man. However, it was not because the physician had implied that Gabriel should not go near Serenity for a period of time. More, it was because the man had so blithely suggested he could simply take a trip into Charleston to slake his baser needs, as though what was between he and Serenity was so easily replaced.

Gabriel had come to some hard conclusions as he had searched for Serenity in the swamp. One of them was how very much he loved her. It was much more now than when he had first made the discovery. In fact, in his heart and his life, there was room for only Serenity. He would do anything to keep her. Yet, because of his love for her, he would also be willing to let her go if that was what she wanted.

"Good day, sir," Gabriel said. "One of my servants shall see you to the door, and Lot shall take you back to your home in the carriage. Thank you for coming."

As the physician started out the door, Biscuit immediately rushed back in. Gabriel gave the dog a brisk pat. It seemed he and the wolfhound had also reached an understanding in the swamp. If not for Biscuit, Gabriel would never have found Serenity and, for the first time, the dog seemed finally to have accepted him.

Walking back to the bed, Gabriel gazed down at Serenity. Though she stirred beneath the covers, she did not awaken. Even with the angry scratches on her cheeks caused by the bushes, she was incredibly beautiful. Her cheekbones were high, and her features the sweetest perfection. She was as beautiful on the inside as she was without. He ached for what he had lost. Yesterday, she had carried his child. Today, there was nothing left to bind them.

Raven and Kane awaited Gabriel in the drawing room. Slowly, he stepped inside.

"How is she?" Raven asked, rushing toward him. "Will she be all right?"

"Yes," he replied wearily. "Soon. But there will be no child."

Raven gasped. Then she said, "Oh, Gabriel, I am so sorry. This is all my fault. If I had not gone to Twin Oaks as I did—"

"Raven," Kane interjected, giving her a look that quickly stilled her tongue, "may I have a moment with your brother alone?"

Raven nodded slowly. "I shall go to sit with Serenity, in case she awakens."

Once Raven had slipped from the room, Gabriel waited for Kane to speak.

"Something happened yesterday that I would like to explain," Kane began. "I didn't want the Quaker to have to tell you about it."

"Does this concern the reason for Raven's leaving?"

"Yes," Kane replied. "After Serenity stitched up my head, Raven walked in on something between the two of us that she misunderstood. Like a fool, I let Serenity talk me into leaving and letting her handle the matter alone. Serenity said she would explain to Raven. Apparently, Raven had already slipped out the back way before she could do so."

"And Serenity followed."

"It was a completely innocent thing, Gabriel. The Quaker and I have never been more than friends. You must believe that. I thought, considering the circumstances, it might be uncomfortable for Serenity to be questioned about it."

"Then, how do matters stand between you and Raven?"

For a moment, Kane hesitated. Then, rather sheepishly, he replied, "Last night, when I went to get Raven at Twin Oaks, I asked her to marry me."

Gabriel managed a grin despite himself. "How did *that* come about?"

"I convinced Raven there was nothing between me and Serenity, and that she was the one I've loved all along."

"At least some good has come from all this."

Kane heaved a sigh. "I only wish it could have come about differently, Gabriel. Please believe that. I don't want this to drive you and Serenity farther apart."

Gabriel remained silent.

After a moment, Kane continued. "I'll be leaving soon. I plan to travel to Virginia and use my inheritance to buy some land there. Raven has agreed to wait for me. Then, as soon as your parents return from France, I'll come back and Raven and I will be wed. I only hope you and Serenity . . . "

For an instant, a look of undisguised longing crossed Gabriel's handsome face, then as quickly disappeared. "Some things were never meant to be."

Awakening, Serenity found Raven by her side. Smiling kindly, she said, "You have returned, Raven. I am so glad. I was worried."

Tears glistened in Raven's gray eyes. "Oh, Serenity, can you ever forgive me? I thought the worst of things about you and Kane. Now I know I was so wrong. If I had not run away—"

Serenity sighed. "We must accept what we cannot change, Raven. I do not hold you responsible for what happened. My only sorrow is that I lost Gabriel's child."

Raven took her hand and gave it a comforting squeeze.

Quietly, Gabriel stepped inside the bedchamber and stood near the door.

Glancing up and seeing him there, Raven rose from her chair. "I must be going now, Serenity. Kane is waiting for me. And you and Gabriel must have many things to talk about. I'll return at another time."

After Raven left them alone, Serenity felt suddenly at a loss for words. Would Gabriel blame her for the loss of their child?

"I am sorry . . . "

"There's nothing to be sorry for," he replied. "I came to make certain you are all right."

"But if I had not acted so impulsively—"

237

Gabriel sighed heavily. "You did what you felt you had to do, Serenity. Kane explained everything to me."

Serenity gazed up at him. He appeared so tired, so drawn. "I don't know how you ever managed to find me. But I am grateful."

"We can both thank Biscuit for that."

Serenity felt suddenly shy with him. What was he thinking? Why was he looking at her in that way? If only he would come closer, bend down, take her hand, something.

He seemed ill at ease. "Perhaps I should go now. You need your rest."

They had both suffered a loss. Was this not the time they should draw closer and comfort each other?

Heaving a sigh, Gabriel turned about and strode from the room.

A mist of tears clouded Serenity's blue eyes. She ached to call him back, but she let him go.

Chapter Twenty-five

The day was brisk. Clad in a long scarlet cloak, Serenity quickly stepped from the dressmaker's shop with a small bundle in her hand. She had purchased another ribbon for her hair. She detested wasting Gabriel's money needlessly on frivolous things, yet there was no other way to explain her trips to Charleston without having at least one small item to occasionally show for them.

Even now, Serenity still felt an emptiness inside for the loss of their child. Still, she had forced herself to set it aside for the day. It had been several weeks since she had visited Charles Beaumarchais, and there had been no way to send him any word about the reason for her delay. She did not want him to think she had forgotten him completely, or that her offer of friendship had been given lightly.

Today, however, Serenity had been plagued by a certain uneasiness when she had gone into the dressmaker's tiny shop, and now it returned as she stepped outside again. Undoubtedly, it was her imagination playing tricks on her. Still, she had the distinct feeling someone was watching her.

Allowing Lot to help her up into the carriage, Serenity gazed about herself for a moment before they set off. Seeing no one, she finally dismissed the thought from her mind as the carriage pulled away.

A short time later, Serenity knocked at Charles Beamarchais's door. Immediately, a servant took her cloak and showed her into the drawing room. Once inside, Serenity discovered the man was not alone.

"Serenity," Beaumarchais said, greeting her fondly, "I was not expecting you. I thought when you didn't come for some time that you had changed your mind about visiting me. Or perhaps your husband had discovered where you were going and put a stop to it."

Smiling sweetly, Serenity replied, "No, Charles. It was nothing of that nature. I was merely indisposed for a time, and there was no way of sending word. But I did miss you."

"I missed you as well, Serenity," he countered. "Now, come and meet my other guest." Then, noting the basket she carried over her arm, he added, "Perhaps, with one of your special smiles and a sweet cake, you could manage to charm him as well."

Her blue eyes dancing, Serenity gazed at the dark-haired child being held in his nurse's arms just across the room. He looked to be nearing two years of age, and his little face was quizzical. Setting down her basket on a nearby table, Serenity took out a sweet cake and slowly approached him. "Would you care for a sweet cake, little one?"

The child drew back shyly. Then, unable to resist, he took the tempting treat from her hand.

"His name is Alexandre," Beaumarchais explained. "He is my grandson."

There was something about the child that Serenity found immediately appealing. Holding out her arms to him, she said, "Would you come to me, Alexandre? I am especially fond of little boys."

The child reached out his arms for her, and Serenity took him from the nurse. Solemnly, Alexandre looked directly into her face, studying her for a moment. Then, wrapping his little arms around her neck, he hugged her tightly.

Beaumarchais chuckled. "Well, the lad is certainly taken with you. And much more quickly than I thought, I might add. He rarely goes to anyone but his nurse. Not even his own . . . " Suddenly, he stopped in mid-sentence, a troubled look upon his face. "Come, Serenity," he went on, immediately changing the subject. "Let us sit down. The boy might be too heavy for you."

"Not at all," Serenity replied, though she did as Beaumarchais directed. There was a glimmer of unshed tears in her eyes. Holding the child bore a special magic all its own, and she wished she would never have to put him down. It reminded her poignantly of her own loss. She had wanted Gabriel's child with all her heart. Now, the child in her arms seemed to fill an aching need.

The time passed quickly, and though she stayed longer than usual, Serenity was sorry when her visit had come to an end. Promising to return the following week, she raced from the Beaumarchais mansion to where Lot awaited her with the carriage, knowing it would be nearly dark before they got home. Still, smiling to herself, she felt happier than she had been for some time. It had been a wonderful afternoon.

Striding into the secluded restaurant, Gabriel frowned darkly as he gazed around himself. He was not pleased to be forced into confronting Veronique in such a public place, yet he refused to meet her in a hotel room, as she had suggested in her note. He had no wish to let her compromise him any more than she already had. It was bad enough he must meet with her at all. And if it were not for the boy . . .

Taking a seat at a small corner table, Gabriel stretched out his long legs before him and forced himself to relax. Veronique would be fashionably late, of course. Make him sweat a little, no doubt. That was the way she had always played things. Why should he expect her to be any different now?

He had come very close to telling Serenity about the child before she had lost their own. The night he had come home to find she was lost in the swamp, he had planned to do precisely that. Now, he feared the knowledge might hurt his wife all the more.

He had been there some time before Veronique finally arrived. Approaching him with a smile, she murmured, "Oh, did I keep you waiting, Gabriel? I must have forgotten the time."

Impatiently, Gabriel rose and held out a chair for her. "Sit down, Veronique. Let's get on with this. I have no intention of being here all day."

Slipping into the chair, Veronique gave him a coy smile. "I remember a time when you sought out my company, Gabriel. Please remember that."

"I was a fool," he stated bluntly, refusing to allow her even the slightest delusion.

"Must you have chosen this place?" she returned, gazing around her in disapproval. "Certainly, as heir to Marihaven, you could have purchased some discreet place for us to meet in, if you had been so inclined."

Gabriel was growing more impatient with her by the moment. "Spare me your discussion of my financial status, Veronique. I would like to get to the reason for our meeting. I want to know if the child is mine."

Wearing a secretive smile, Veronique twisted her lace-edged handkerchief with her hands. "The matter is most delicate."

241

"In other words, you are not certain who the father is," he returned coldly.

She gazed up at him with innocent green eyes. "Alexandre does look like you, Gabriel. I am almost certain . . . "

Damnation! Gabriel cursed silently to himself. Veronique was determined to see him claim the child, whether the boy was his or not. She knew he would not turn his back on Alexandre if the slightest possibility existed that he was the father.

Glowering, Gabriel shot back, "I want to see him."

"Certainly," she replied in a honeyed voice. "You may visit us as often as you like."

"I want to see the boy without you being there, Veronique."

Pouting prettily, she countered, "I suppose that could be arranged. Perhaps the first time you might visit Alexandre with only his nurse present. But, after that, Gabriel, my sweet, if ever you choose to see him again, you must plan to see me as well. I shall expect certain arrangements. I was wrong to have turned my back on you before."

Gabriel tightened his fists. "What is it you want?"

"Don't you know?" she inquired, stopping to moisten her mouth with her small pink tongue. "I want you."

Dimly lit, the hotel could not boast the slightest elegance. It was a place for clandestine meetings, quick assignations. Not a place one would care to stay for any period of time. It was also a place that Veronique would never have dreamed of going under ordinary circumstances. But, this time, it could not be avoided.

Veronique quickly stepped inside the hotel room when the door was opened for her. "I detest this place," she said pointedly to the handsome man with the mustache who had been waiting for her for some time.

Slipping around behind her, the man brushed stray curls of pale flaxen hair from her neck, then placed several kisses below her nape and behind one ear. "What kept you, Veronique? Didn't things go as we had planned with Harrowe?"

Tilting her head back, Veronique reveled in the sensation of his mouth upon her neck. "It went well enough," she returned. "I let Gabriel know that if he wants to see the child, it will be on my terms."

His hands moved from around behind her to cradle her breasts. He teased at the tips. "Does Harrowe believe the child is his?"

Veronique laughed softly. "Enough to want to find out."

"And is the child really his?" he inquired, turning her around in his arms to gaze down into her beautiful face.

"That is my secret. And mine alone."

"Then you don't intend to tell Harrowe either?" the man prompted.

"Never."

"Why are you going along with this plan?"

Unbuttoning her gown, Veronique watched as his gaze became more intense. Slowly, she let the gown slide to the floor, her petticoats following soon after, and lastly her lace-trimmed chemise. "I want revenge against Gabriel for what he has done to me. And, this, I have discovered, is the perfect way."

Crossing to the bed, Veronique lay provocatively upon it.

His gaze became more heated. "Our mutual concern is that he leaves his wife. Can you guarantee me of that?"

"Never fear, my pet," she replied, watching as he began to slip off his clothing. "You shall have the insipid Quaker—though why you would want her I will never know. Gabriel will never stay with her, once he believes the child is his."

The man dropped down beside her and pulled her roughly up against his hard chest. "But you said you wanted revenge."

"True, I *do* want revenge," she agreed with a sigh. "I have thought of nothing else for more than two long years. But I want Gabriel as well. I will let no one else have him—especially not that Quaker." Closing her eyes, she felt his first thrust, hard and swift, inside her. But her mind still lingered on

243

Gabriel. It was easy to detach herself and pretend it was him instead, *his* heated body next to hers. It had been such a long time.

Admittedly, there had never been anyone to compare with Gabriel in bed. Not even this arrogant British lieutenant.

Serenity waited anxiously for Gabriel to return home. Where had he gone? Though she had no right to question him—not when she was unable to explain her own whereabouts for the afternoon.

Smiling to herself, Serenity thought once more of Charles Beaumarchais's grandchild. How she had loved holding him. And his little face; it was so dear. She hoped Beaumarchais would have him there again when she went for another visit. She had been afraid to ask, but she was certain Beaumarchais had seen it in her face.

As she sat stitching on several small quilt pieces, Serenity glanced up as Raven entered the room and flopped down in frustration on a chair across from her.

"I hate it," Raven complained. "I truly do. Just when Kane finally declares himself to me, he must leave. And I am left here like an ugly spinster with nothing at all to do." Noticing that Serenity was stitching on a tiny quilt, Raven was suddenly mollified. "Oh, Serenity, please forgive me. I know I have so little to complain about, while you are dealing with a much bigger loss. How can you bear to sew on that baby quilt when there is no longer any need for it? Is that not rubbing salt into the wound?"

Serenity smiled patiently as she went on sewing. "At first, I had no desire even to look at the quilt. But, today, I felt a need to see it completed."

"You do seem much happier," Raven commented, gazing at her curiously. "Of course, I am delighted. Has something occurred?"

Shaking her head slightly, Serenity returned, "No, Raven. Nothing of importance." She wished she could tell Raven about the child. For some reason, seeing the boy had given her hope for the future.

At that moment, Serenity heard the door open in the front entry. Quickly setting her sewing aside, she excused herself and hurried to see if it was Gabriel.

Already shrugging off his cloak by the time she got there, her husband's face brightened when he saw her. Then, as suddenly, it darkened once again as he handed his cloak to Daisy.

Peering at him, Serenity decided he seemed very tired. He must have had a long day. "Would you care to dine, Gabriel? I have saved your supper."

"No, thank you, Serenity. Not right now. I'm tired and I think I will go on up to my bedchamber. Perhaps, later, one of the servants could bring something up."

A slight frown arched Serenity's brow. Gabriel had not bothered to visit her in her bedchamber since the loss of their child, and she missed the feel of him beside her. Did he not miss her too? Since they had wed, it seemed they waged a battle between bedchambers. What could not be resolved by day could not be resolved by night either.

With a sigh, Serenity watched as Gabriel ascended the stairs. Then, seized by a sudden idea, she smiled to herself and a moment later quickly disappeared into the library. Crossing to the desk, she hurriedly penned a note requesting that Gabriel meet her in the gazebo. Seeking out Daisy, she told the girl to take a tray of food to Gabriel, and to place the note on the tray.

Soon after, Serenity donned her cloak, then left the mansion. She was not certain what she would say to Gabriel, but she refused to allow the gap to continue widening between them.

Once at the gazebo, Serenity stepped inside. The moonlight barely glimmered overhead, and there was a chill wind blowing. It whipped at her long cloak and blew her fiery hair. Still, she did not mind. For one brief moment, she and Gabriel had been happy here. Perhaps more than the memory lingered on.

After what seemed an interminable wait, Gabriel finally

arrived. "Serenity . . . " he said briskly as he drew near the building. "What are you doing here? You will catch a chill."

Reaching out, Serenity took his hand and drew him inside with her. "There are memories hiding in this place," she said. "Quickly, Gabriel. Close your eyes. Are they closed?" With her fingertips, she gently touched his eyelids to make certain. "Now, imagine we are on Nantucket and there is a norther blowing in. Hear the wind?"

"Serenity—"

"Hush, Gabriel," she murmured softly. "Now, feel the wind blow on the deck of the *Firefly*. Is it not marvelous? The salt mist. The men calling watch . . . "

"Why are you doing this, Serenity?" he asked impatiently, starting to draw away.

"No, Gabriel. You must not open your eyes. Not yet." She took his hands once more to keep him there. "Now, remember the night we came here together, and I told you about our child. The wind blew through the gazebo that night too. A gentle, warm wind."

Relaxing slightly, Gabriel replied, "I remember."

"The wind comes and it goes. It can surprise you when it is least expected. Now it is here. Now it is there. But when it is gone, the remembrance of it remains. We know at any time it may return again. Happiness is much like the wind."

Gabriel sighed deeply. "You see everything through enchanted eyes, Serenity. A realist would say, if happiness is like the wind, it is also incredibly illusive and only fleeting at best."

"I believe it still awaits us, Gabriel."

His dark hair tousled by the night wind, Gabriel's handsome profile was silvered by the moonlight. His face hardened slightly as he replied. "I wish that was true. But our worlds seem destined to remain separate, Serenity. I can't promise I won't hurt you."

For a moment, Serenity was certain he meant to go on; then he seemed to think better of it. Drawing her to him instead, Gabriel peered at her through the darkness, then brushed her hair from her delicate face and placed a gentle kiss upon her parted mouth. It held a tantalizing sweetness, but it did not deepen.

"Now, I think we'd better go back inside," he said gently as he pulled away from her. "While I can still recall what the physician told me about restraint."

Chapter Twenty-six

Arriving at the Durand mansion, Gabriel announced his name to the aging black manservant who answered the door and was promptly led up the stairs. There had been no need for preliminaries. The servant had known precisely what he was there for the moment he had given his name. Following him down the hallway to the nursery, Gabriel felt a momentary hesitation. Would he know if the child was his own?

"*Monsieur*," the French nurse said in greeting as he entered the room. "The child is asleep. He was fretful today."

"And your name?" Gabriel asked of the woman.

"Ninette," she replied with a slight curtsey.

Gabriel nodded, remembering that Percival Benjamin had told him the nurse's name when they had met in his office. Striding quietly toward the small bed with the sleeping child, he paused at its side. The boy was innocent in sleep, his handsome little face slightly flushed. Gabriel gently touched his smooth forehead. Immediately concerned, he glanced back at the nurse. "Is the boy unwell?"

"Only a slight fever, *monsieur*. I've been watching him."

Gabriel frowned. It was ridiculous to feel such concern for a child he was not even certain was his. Still . . .

"Has his mother looked in on him today?"

247

Gloria Pedersen

Ninette shook her head.

Suddenly suspicious, Gabriel pressed further. "And yesterday?"

The girl shook her head once again.

"I will arrange for a physician to examine the boy," he said quietly, his anger at Veronique dangerously close to the surface. "See to it that he is admitted, Ninette. I'll explain to his mother."

"There is no need for me to concern myself with Alexandre," Veronique stated defensively, a short while later. "He has a nurse."

They were seated once more in the small restaurant where they had met before to discuss the child. This time, however, Gabriel's anger at Veronique had reached new proportions. "Your behavior where the boy is concerned borders on neglect, Veronique."

Veronique seemed nonplussed. "Have you decided to take a personal interest in Alexandre's welfare?"

"I have arranged for a physician to see him, if that is what you mean."

Smiling, Veronique responded, "Be careful, Gabriel. One would think you were his father."

Grasping her arm brutally, Gabriel ground out, "What is it you want, Veronique? Name it."

Others in the restaurant were staring at them in curiosity.

Rising quickly, Veronique pried his hand from her arm in disdain. Her cool green eyes held a challenge. "I shall let you know."

Evan Lancaster waited in the hotel room, impatiently pacing the floor. Everything was going precisely as he had planned. Without realizing it, Veronique was playing right into his hands. Today, Harrowe would meet her in the restaurant again. Others would see them, notice their tryst. Then, when she was found dead, with Harrowe nearby . . .

It had not been an easy matter for him to find Serenity. If

not for a casual comment of Mrs. Deerfield's while still in Washington, he would never have known Serenity's destination after leaving the city. But, even with that piece of luck, by the time he could conveniently reach Brookeville, Serenity had already gone. Once he arrived in Charleston, matters had become much simpler. Everyone was only too happy to oblige him with discussions about Harrowe marrying a Quaker, and the scandal from the past with Veronique Durand. It was then that he had come up with his brilliant idea for disposing of Harrowe once and for all. All he needed to do was to meet Veronique and set his plan into motion.

Lancaster grinned to himself as he thought of it. Harrowe should never have taken what was his. Why could he have not been content to have Veronique? Serenity was Lancaster's, and always would be. He was even more obsessed by her now than he had been before. The ice princess, cold and aloof, yet just waiting for him to claim her. And he would.

Still, it was not enough simply to have Harrowe out of the way and to take Serenity. Harrowe must pay for what he had done, and even Harrowe's death—though a pleasurable idea in itself—would not satisfy him. Harrowe must be made to suffer. If everything went as planned, he would. Harrowe would be left to rot away in a prison cell, or better yet, sent to the gallows, knowing that Serenity was lost to him forever.

A soft knock on the door alerted him that Veronique had arrived. Drawing it open, he pulled her toward him with one arm and slammed the door shut with the other. "Tell me, Veronique. Did it go well today?"

She slipped her arms up around his neck, her mouth very nearly touching his. "Yes," she whispered, then smiled with satisfaction.

He could feel her firm breasts pressed against him. One day, he would hold Serenity. But, for now, Veronique would have to do. Spinning her around, he violently shoved her down on the bed and jerked up her gown. Why bother being gentle? Veronique was not like Serenity. With Serenity he might be patient.

"Don't, Evan! You are hurting me," Veronique protested.

"Not nearly enough," he replied. "Not nearly enough . . . "

Several days later, as she stepped from the dressmaker's shop, Serenity once again had the strange feeling that eyes were upon her. Quickly gazing about her, she saw no one was about. But this time she could not dismiss the feeling so lightly. There was a sense of malevolence in the air.

Allowing Lot to help her into the carriage, Serenity could not put the disturbing thought from her mind until sometime later, when she was safely inside Charles Beamarchais's drawing room. There, it was soon forgotten, as Alexandre played with a wooden horse on the floor at her feet.

"The boy was a mite under the weather this past week, according to his nurse," Beaumarchais said. "But he is over it now."

"He is such a lovely child," she said, gazing fondly at the dark-haired boy. "His mother must certainly cherish him."

Beaumarchais frowned for a moment, then softly replied, "Perhaps not enough, my dear. But it is obvious that Alexandre relishes his time with you. It never hurts for a lad to receive extra love and attention. That is why I arranged to have him here today. I am pleased you have taken such a fond interest in him. He is my only grandchild, and it is doubtful there will be another."

Gazing over at the man, Serenity noticed some reticence in his expression. "Is there something that troubles you?"

"You obviously know the child's mother is my daughter, Veronique," he replied. "Considering the circumstances, does that change the way you feel about him, Serenity?"

Serenity smiled as she slipped onto her knees on the floor beside Alexandre. "Of course not, Charles. I know of the relationship your daughter shared with my husband. But if I feel anything, it is a touch of envy for Veronique for bearing such a precious child. I only hope one day . . . "

As her voice trailed away, Beaumarchais countered, "You will, Serenity. Someday soon. And the child will be extremely lucky, indeed, that has you for a mother."

Once more, Serenity thought of her relationship with Gabriel. How could there be a child, when he would still not share her bed? The weeks were passing, and she felt fully recovered. Still, he stayed away from her. It was as though he had deliberately chosen not to risk having her conceive another child.

Alexandre stood on his little legs and toddled over to her, throwing himself into her arms. He giggled in delight as she caught him. Snuggling close, his arms went around her neck as he rested his head on her shoulder. It felt so right having him in her arms. "I think he is sleepy," she said, and she gave Beaumarchais a misty-eyed smile.

As he entered the room, Gabriel saw Veronique reclining on a rose satin settee. With her hair loose about her shoulders and clad in a sheer silver dressing gown, she smiled warmly at him. The robe parted, leaving her shapely legs bare to his view, and she made no attempt to cover them.

"I was not dressed to greet you downstairs," Veronique murmured, tossing her champagne-colored hair so that it swirled a moment about her face. "I hope you didn't mind being brought to my bedchamber."

"Where is the boy?" Gabriel demanded. He could tell Veronique was up to her old games once again. She had purposefully told him to come today. Yet, when he'd arrived, one of the servants had told him the child was not there and Veronique wished to speak to him in her bedchamber. Like a fool he had gone.

"I am sorry, Gabriel. This is one of the afternoons Alexandre spends with his grandfather. Somehow it must have slipped my mind. But his nurse should be returning with Alexandre shortly.

In the meantime, perhaps you would care for refreshment of some sort?"

Gabriel stood with his long legs braced apart, his face livid. "If you think I intend to go through this each time I come to visit the boy, you are sadly mistaken, Veronique."

She looked as though she had expected him to protest and was already prepared. "What other choice do you have?"

"I am still not convinced Alexandre is my son. Why don't you enlighten me as to why I should believe he is. Dark hair? Many children have the same. Features? They say his eyes are green, while mine are Harrowe gray. Perhaps you are afraid to have me around the boy for fear I will discover the truth. It only benefits you so long as I believe . . . "

Veronique merely smiled. Stretching her arms before her and gazing at the backs of her hands as though to inspect her fingernails, she observed, "Why are you here then, if you do not believe Alexandre is your son? I make no pretense of what I want, Gabriel. If you want to see Alexandre, you must first see me, each and every time you come. Otherwise, I shall bar you from ever seeing him again."

"I have asked you before what you want, Veronique. For me to claim Alexandre as my son and heir? Money? Property?"

Rising from the settee, Veronique came to stand before him. He could see the curve of her bare breasts beneath the dressing gown. "Once before, as I recall, you rejected me. This time, your rejection could cost you a son. I know you will think of the right thing to do."

"I still have no proof."

A knock on the door interrupted Gabriel before he could finish. "Madame Durand," the liveried servant said as he entered, "Master Alexandre and his nurse have returned."

"Yes, of course," Veronique returned. "Will you please show our guest to the nursery."

* * *

Gabriel entered the nursery. This time the child was awake and seated on his nurse's lap gazing solemnly at a book of pictures. His hair night-dark and his eyes a deep green, he was a handsome lad. Yet, there was nothing in his sculpted features that proved to Gabriel that the boy was actually his son.

"Alexandre," Gabriel said softly.

The child peeked up at him quizzically, then seemed to draw away. Ninette smiled. "He is shy with strangers, Monsieur Harrowe. Perhaps if you sit down for a few moments."

Gabriel did as she instructed.

After a moment, Alexandre wiggled down from his nurse's lap and picked up a blue ball. Examining it, he threw it across the room, then gazed back at Gabriel to see if he was suitably impressed. When Gabriel smiled, Alexandre ran to pick up the ball again. Contemplating what he should do with it next, the boy finally sat down and rolled it across the floor toward him.

Gabriel caught it. He rolled it back.

For some time, they continued their child's game of thrust and parry, as though each was gauging the other—the boy deciding if Gabriel was friend or foe, and Gabriel looking for something that would indicate whether Alexandre was his son.

Rising once more on sturdy little legs, the boy approached him. Drawing as close as he dared, he held out the ball.

Gabriel took it, then said, "Would you care to sit on my lap, Alex?"

The child thought it over for a moment, then inched closer. Setting the ball aside, Gabriel reached for the small boy and picked him up. Awkwardly, Gabriel held him. Perhaps learning to be a father was a little like learning to ride a horse—one just kept trying until one mastered the skill—but it did not always come naturally. Still, he had no sense that Alexandre was his own.

Abruptly sliding from his lap, Alexandre made a quick dash for his nurse and the safety of her arms. Then, gazing back over his shoulder, he threw Gabriel an impish grin.

With a soft laugh, his nurse remarked, "I am afraid he has a little of the devil in him, *monsieur.*"

All of the Harrowes do, Gabriel thought wryly to himself. *All of the Harrowes do.*

Serenity had never been to the theater in Charleston before. But, since Raven was very restless with Kane off in Virginia, and after much pleading from her young sister-in-law, Serenity had finally agreed to go.

Only one time before had Serenity been to the theater, and that had been the open-air theater in Washington, where she had watched *Macbeth.* She had not found it suited to her taste at all, with its witches and violence. Yet, Raven had promised that she would like this play much more, since it was about two lovers, Romeo and Juliet.

Wrapped in a black velvet cloak that Gabriel had surprised her with only the week before, and clad in a simple gown of rose watered silk, Serenity stepped down from the coach after it had drawn up before the theater. Her flame-colored hair was piled upon her head. Smiling at Gabriel as she stepped down, she caught the admiring glance he gave her.

"You look very beautiful tonight, Serenity," he whispered close to her ear. "I shall have difficulty keeping my eyes on the play."

Blushing becomingly, Serenity felt suddenly light of heart. Was Gabriel paying court to her? It had been so long since there had been anything more than polite conversations between them. Even the night in the gazebo had been of no benefit. Gabriel had still not seen fit to share her bed.

Tonight, he looked rakishly handsome in a well-tailored coat of black superfine with a white silk cravat at his throat, and Serenity trembled as he took her hand to curl her arm around his. Then, with Raven on his other arm, the three entered the theater.

Shown to a box, Serenity could feel eyes on them as they sat down. It felt rather unnerving being on public display, yet once the play began Serenity completely forgot about the rest of the audience and thought only of what was before her. Serenity found the play very sad. It was about two lovers who came from families opposed to one another. And, when the final curtain rang down, it saddened Serenity to know that the two of them could never be together, except in death.

"Did you care for the play, Serenity?" Gabriel inquired, as he helped her into her cloak.

Serenity sighed. "I thought it was very sad."

"They were star-crossed lovers," he replied. "Their relationship was doomed from the start."

"But, if there is love—"

"Life is never simple," he countered softly. "Sometimes love is not enough." His gaze was suddenly intent upon her face.

Taking his arm once more, Serenity walked with Gabriel out into the hallway, then descended the stairs to the entry. Others were leaving the theater as well. All around them, there was talking and laughter. Seeing someone she knew, Raven bid them to wait for her a moment and flitted away through the crowd.

"Raven seems happy enough," Gabriel commented as his sister disappeared behind a portly gentleman and three dowagers in satin gowns.

"She misses Kane," Serenity murmured.

"I know. But Kane will be back soon."

A striking woman with light golden hair moved through the crowd toward them. For a moment, Serenity did not recognize her. Then, as the woman drew closer, Serenity realized that she had seen her before, once on a Charleston street and another time at the Pierpont ball. And both times the woman had been with Gabriel.

Gabriel's handsome face hardened slightly as she come to stand before them. "Veronique."

The woman was even more beautiful than Serenity had realized when she had seen her at a distance.

"Gabriel, my pet," Veronique replied in a honeyed voice. "I don't believe I've met your new bride. I thought perhaps you would like to introduce me."

Gabriel hesitated for a moment. Then, as though he knew he could not avoid it, he said, "This is my wife, Serenity."

"Serenity," Veronique interjected quickly, "I am Veronique Durand. Your husband and I are old friends. I did not realize you were so lovely. I always thought of Quakers as being quite . . . plain."

Serenity did not know what she should reply. It was obvious the woman was being falsely friendly toward her, and her last comment was meant to be a barb.

Still, Serenity smiled sweetly. "I have met very few people since I have been in the Carolinas, Madame Durand. I shall not forget your name."

"Veronique, my dear," she responded. "You really must call me Veronique."

Veronique appeared to look Serenity over quite thoroughly, then she pointedly turned her attentions to Gabriel. "My carriage is waiting, so I must be going," she said, her gaze resting upon his face. "I hope to see you again very soon."

Serenity watched as Veronique disappeared into the crowd. The woman had left a disturbed feeling deep inside her. Veronique was so very beautiful. It was not difficult to understand why Gabriel had become involved with her. Did he still find her attractive? Was he ever regretful?

Raven appeared by Gabriel's side.

With a dark, unfathomable expression on his harshly handsome features, Gabriel took them both by the arm. A few moments later, they were outside and he was helping them into the waiting coach.

Serenity could feel his tension. Was it seeing Veronique in the theater? With a sigh, she settled back against the coach seat.

It was difficult for her to imagine that Veronique was Alexandre's mother. Alexandre, she thought to herself; precious

Alexandre. Beaumarchais had seen to it that the child was there each time she had called of late. She was growing so attached to the child. Still, she had been right from the start—right from the very first moment she had laid eyes upon him. And after having met Veronique and seen her vindictiveness, Serenity could not wait to see Alexandre and hold him once again. There was nothing about the child even slightly reminiscent of his mother.

In the darkness of the coach, Serenity glanced at Gabriel. He had not spoken a word since Veronique had approached them in the theater. She had seen the brooding look on his face as they had climbed into the coach.

Serenity could not help smiling to herself. Recently, she had seen that same expression on someone else. Only the face had been much younger. It had belonged to a dear little boy. Alexandre.

Chapter Twenty-seven

Stepping from the dressmaker's shops, Serenity was startled by the sound of a masculine voice directly behind her.

"You are far too predictable, Serenity."

Quickly jerking around, Serenity was too stunned to reply.

"Each and every Thursday, as regular as the workings of a clock," Lieutenant Evan Lancaster continued. "And each time with so little to show for your efforts. What is it this time, Serenity? Another ribbon or piece of lace? Nothing in excess. Only just enough to keep Harrowe from guessing why it is you come into Charleston with such frequency. I wonder how he would feel if he knew you visited with his enemy, Charles Beaumarchais, on such a regular basis."

Serenity gasped softly. "How do you know—"

Lancaster smiled as he interjected, "How do I know precisely every place you go, every move you make? Because, sweet Serenity, I shall always make it my business to know. Mrs. Deerfield was most obliging in telling me that you had gone to Brookeville. Then your cousin Emmalina dutifully supplied the rest. It just took me a bit longer to catch up with you than I had expected. But I would have figured it out, sooner or later. I should have known Harrowe would never let you go so easily. The man may be dangerous, but he is not a fool. Few woman can compare with you, Serenity."

Leveling her delicate chin, Serenity replied, "What is it you want of me?"

"I have been watching you for weeks, Serenity. Did you know that? Watching every move you make. Not only have I watched you here in Charleston, but I have also seen you at Marihaven. I know Joshua is still with you, and that you teach the black servants' children to read. While you and your husband keep secrets from each other, neither of you have managed to keep any secrets from me."

Serenity trembled slightly. He frightened her. Not because she feared that his behavior was irrational, but because she was certain it was not. With cold, calculated deliberation, he had invaded her life without her even knowing it.

"Lieutenant Lancaster," Serenity countered in an icy tone, "you should not waste your time in foolishly following me. I can offer you nothing. Nothing at all. You should return to England."

Reaching out, Lancaster grasped her cloak firmly but gently and drew her up against him. His handsome face bent close to hers. "Both of us know that your marriage was a mistake, Serenity. Harrowe married you for one purpose only, and that was to keep himself from being captured by my men. He cares nothing for you. You should remember that. I can offer you so much more. I would adorn you in satin and jewels. There would be nothing I wouldn't give you."

"Madame Harrowe," Lot said in a deep voice as he stepped

forward, "is there some problem? The carriage is waiting."

Immediately, Lancaster released her and took a step backward as he saw the towering black man. Relieved that Lot had come precisely when he did, Serenity spun around and started for the carriage without a backward glance. She did not even bother to say farewell.

She hoped never to see Lieutenant Lancaster again.

Seated in Percival Benjamin's office, Gabriel's face was hard. "Veronique has made no secret of the fact that she cares little for being a mother. And she deliberately plays upon my concern for the boy's welfare."

Leaning back in his chair, Benjamin peered at Gabriel through his wire-framed glasses. "I am sorry, Gabriel. I told you at the outset that there is nothing I can do, legally or otherwise. You have absolutely no claim to the boy. Veronique has not even admitted that he is your son. And should something unforeseen happen to the mother—heaven forbid at this point—custody of the child would go to the grandfather."

A muscle tensed along Gabriel's jaw. "You know that I dueled with Beamarchais?"

"I heard—"

"Then you know how the man feels about me. If Beaumarchais ever gained custody of Alexandre, I would never see the boy again."

"What of Veronique? Have you determined what she wants as of yet?"

"I have a fair idea," he replied, his gray eyes stormy. He ran a hand through his dark hair, then rose from the chair to pace the room. After a moment, he stopped and twisted back around. "Unless I miss my guess, Veronique wants the Harrowe name"

There was a moment of shock on Benjamin's face. "Your name? But you are already wed."

"Veronique knows that. But this is just another game to her, one in which she holds the majority of the cards. She wants me to choose between my wife and my son and his welfare."

Gloria Pedersen

Benjamin's breath escaped in a slow hiss. "What will you do?"

"Believe me, Percy, if I knew that, I wouldn't be here right now. But, for what it's worth, I have no intention of giving up either Serenity or the boy without a fight."

Entering the drawing room at the Beaumarchais mansion, Serenity was greeted by a bundle of energy who spread his arms and came racing toward her. Scooping Alexandre up into her arms, she gave him a hug.

"Mama . . . " the child said, with his arms about her neck.

Glancing at the aging gentleman who stood to one side, Serenity saw his grin. "What have you been saying to him, Charles?"

"I am not to blame, Serenity. I think the lad has some confusion as to who you are. That is all."

A frown creasing her brow, Serenity inquired, "You do not mind?"

Beamarchais sighed deeply. "I love Veronique dearly, as any father would. But I have come to realize that she knows nothing of being a mother. With you, it comes quite naturally."

Unable to understand how Veronique could not simply dote on the child, Serenity countered, "You judge Veronique too harshly, I fear, Charles. I am certain she must love Alexandre with all her heart. How can one love the father and not love the son?"

For a moment, Beamarchais gazed back at her in silence. Then, he said, "Some people pick roses and see only the thorns. Others, such as you, Serenity, see only their beauty. That is a remarkable quality."

Setting the child down on the floor, Serenity curled her legs beneath her and sat down beside him. "I have brought you a gift, Alexandre," she said, producing a little carved wooden dog from her pocket. "My brother, Joshua, made it for me. He says it looks like our dog. I wanted you to have it."

Beamarchais's face softened as he sat down in a chair to watch Serenity and Alexandre together. Softly, he said,

260

"Sometimes I wonder if the good Lord knows what he is doing."

The morning sun streaming in through his bedchamber window, Gabriel stood dressed in boots and breeches, his muscular chest bare, as he reread the missive in his hand. It had been delivered to Marihaven before he awoke and had been brought up a short time later. What was Veronique up to now? She wanted him to meet her that afternoon at one of the most disreputable hotels in Charleston.

It puzzled and annoyed him. Why meet Veronique there? He had frequently been to the Durand mansion. Whatever she had to say could be said there. But, to ensure he would come, Veronique had added that she must speak to him about a matter of mutual concern. That could only mean Alexandre. It left him with no choice. Heaving a resigned sigh, Gabriel knew he would have to meet her.

Knocking softly on the door, Serenity stepped inside. "I am sorry to intrude—"

"You never intrude, Serenity. You know that."

She smiled sweetly. Clad in a morning gown of pale pink, her fiery hair cascading down around her shoulders and her eyes bright, she came toward him. "I was hoping you might spend the day with me, Gabriel. We have had little time together of late. I thought perhaps we could ride. I have not been on Blue Lady since—"

He felt the heat rise uncomfortably within him. It had been so long since he had taken Serenity to his bed. He had not wanted to risk the possibility of another child, not until the matter with Alexandre had been settled. She must be under no obligation to remain with him, once she found out the boy was his. Still he delayed, knowing Serenity might leave him as soon as she knew the truth.

"Are you certain you want to ride again?"

"I miss our rides together."

Gazing into her sapphire eyes, he wanted to pull her against him and kiss her soft pink mouth. Tonight, he would tell her. He had to know one way or another whether she would turn away from him. It twisted his gut to remain in this limbo. He would meet with Veronique. Then, regardless of what the woman had to say, he would tell Serenity everything and discover once and for all whether she was prepared to share his world completely.

Suddenly desperate to have her know, he said, "I love you, Serenity."

For a moment, she simply gazed at him. Then a mischievous smile lit her lovely face. "You think I did not know?"

"No," he replied. "I know you didn't know."

There was a twinkle in her eyes. "You have loved me since Nantucket. I already guessed."

This was supposed to be a serious moment. He had declared his love for her and she was deliberately making light of it. "You are impossible, Serenity."

"Am I?" she teased. "I knew you loved me after I threw the egg at at your forehead."

"Why then?"

"Because you did not murder me shortly after."

He could not help himself. He laughed. "That does not prove anything. Maybe I was just fascinated by what you might do next."

She moved closer to him. Her cheeks were flushed. Gabriel could not help thinking that she had never looked more entrancing.

Softly, she said, "I love you."

She had never told him before. Neither of them had ever admitted it aloud, although they both knew.

"I knew that too," he murmured.

"When did you know?"

Gabriel frowned in contemplation. "I am not certain. But I did know I wasn't deserving of it."

They stood gazing at each other, their hearts beating as one.

There was a sudden mist in Serenity's blue velvet eyes. "What do you think we should do about it now, Gabriel?"

Fiercely, Gabriel caught her to him. He could feel her breath against his mouth. "I know what we should do. We should walk away while there still is time. But neither of us has ever chosen the wisest course, where the other is concerned . . . "and I doubt we shall now."

Opening the door, Evan Lancaster watched as Veronique stepped inside. He was filled with anticipation. Everything was working precisely as he had planned.

"Good day, Evan."

Veronique was dressed becomingly in a green striped gown that emphasized her ripe curves and small waist and a wide straw hat adorned with green satin flowers. By any man's standards, she was a most attractive woman. He would almost miss her. But she was not Serenity.

"Did you make certain Harrowe would come, Veronique?"

"Yes," she assured him. "Gabriel will be here, just as I said he would be, in one hour's time. But I still cannot understand why it was necessary for me to meet him here, at this horrible place. It would have been much simpler for me to have Gabriel come to the mansion."

Lancaster smiled. "Only if you had something important to tell Harrowe about the boy, Veronique. Such as whether or not Alexandre is truly his son. But you do not. And since that is the case, it will be much more compromising for him to meet you here. To others, it will appear as a liaison between the two of you, not merely that he has come for a visit. Then, when his wife finds out . . . "

"And you intend to make certain she does. Is that correct, Evan?"

"We will both have what we want," he countered icily. "You want Harrowe. And I want Serenity."

Laughing lightly, Veronique threw him a haughty glance. "You are a fool to want the Quaker, Evan. Do you know that? A woman raised in such a manner is much too proper to be any good in bed. She will bore you completely. You'll be in need of a mistress before even a month is through. But I suppose that is your choice."

Pivoting, Lancaster went to gaze out the window, his teeth gritted in annoyance. Veronique just might push him too far before—

"I have wanted Serenity for a very long time," he said, more to himself than to her. "When I first met her on Nantucket, I had never known anyone so beautiful or so pure. Then I wanted to snatch from her the very thing that made her so attractive to me, and Harrowe stole her from right beneath my nose. Now she is his wife. His lover. When she should have been mine all along."

Veronique laughed again. "Why, Evan," she taunted, "I do believe you are in love with the woman, more's the pity. She will never return your affections. Quakers hold fast to their principles, I have been told. I predict that not only will she be as cold as the arctic in bed, she will fight you every step of the way in getting her there."

Wheeling around, Lancaster shot Veronique a venomous glance. "Your prediction will not come true. Serenity will be willing enough when the time arrives. All she needs is to be convinced that Harrowe has betrayed her. That he wants you and his son instead of her. The rest will take care of itself."

"Well, it will not be long now, Evan. You will have your chance to find out."

"Yes," he agreed smoothly. "There is little time left."

Approaching her, Lancaster began unfastening the buttons on her gown. He undid them slowly one by one, until the soft curve of one, breast was exposed at the neckline of her gown. Bending down, he nipped at her breast with his teeth.

Starting to push him away, Veronique protested, "There is not enough time, Evan. Gabriel will be here in less than an hour."

"That is precisely enough time."

He pushed her backward toward the bed. Then, shoving her down, he fell down upon her. Brutally, his hand gouged at her bare breast. Letting out a cry of protest, she tried to shove him away once more.

"I do not care to be hurt, Evan. Save your barbaric ways for the street whores."

Quickly, his mouth covered hers and his touch gentled slightly. Then, raising his head, he murmured, "Do you still want me to stop?" His tongue slipped inside her mouth, to still her reply. After a moment, he pushed up her gown and unfastened his trousers. Her eyes were glazed. She lay sprawled before him, ready for the taking.

"Let's make this one a good one, Veronique. Since it will be the last."

She smiled up at him. "Yes, Evan. Yes."

Chapter Twenty-eight

Striding into the dingy hotel, Charles Beaumarchais quickly slipped up the stairs. Only a short time before, Fitzgerald, a man he had hired to follow Veronique, had brought him word that his daughter had met someone at the hotel, and Beaumarchais was determined to go there himself and put a stop to it. He would not allow Veronique to become involved in yet another scandal. Not with Alexandre to consider.

Beaumarchais knew which room Veronique was in. According to Fitzgerald, it was the one at the end of the hall. In horror, he gazed about him. The place was ill kept, and there was the cloying odor of stale cigars. *Why here, Veronique? Have you so little pride?*

Reaching the end of the hall, Beaumarchais halted before the door. To his surprise, the door stood slightly ajar. Had Fitzgerald made a mistake about Veronique being there?

Hesitantly, he started to push it open. The room was bathed in shadows, yet he felt compelled to step inside. For a moment, he stood there, uncertain what it was that he felt. Dread? Fear? His breath caught in his throat.

Veronique lay sprawled ignominiously on the bed. He drew closer, gazing at her still form.

Beaumarchais could not think what to do. He was too shocked. Too numb. His daughter was . . .

With tender care, he straightened her gown and smoothed her hair. Then, slowly forcing himself to turn around, he walked back out the door.

Gabriel strode down the hallway and to the room at the end. He knocked firmly on the door. He did not know what Veronique had to say, but he wanted this whole matter over with as quickly as possible. Tonight he was determined to tell Serenity about Alexandre.

Impatiently, he waited.

There was no answering response. No one called out to him. No one came to the door. Was this another of Veronique's games? He would step inside, and she would be . . .

Dead! Gazing down at her, he could see there were bruises on her throat. Who would have done this to her? Despite everything, he had never wished her dead. He bent down to examine her more closely.

"Hold!" a harsh voice ordered from behind.

A short while later, Gabriel found himself in the Provost dungeon, locked in a tiny cell. Pacing the floor, he waited for Percy, a grimace on his face. He could not believe what had happened. It was as though someone had deliberately wanted him blamed for Veronique's death. He had walked right into a trap.

Glancing over at the door as the jailer swung it wide, Gabriel was relieved to see his lawyer finally arrive. Benjamin greeted him unceremoniously. "You are charged with the murder of Veronique Durand."

"That is hardly a surprise, Percy. What I want to know is how you are going to get me out of here."

"It is unfortunate that the courts will not accept the claim of an episode of insanity."

Gabriel threw him a dangerous glance. "I didn't do it, Percy."

"You had enough reasons—"

"Yes," Gabriel snapped. "I had enough reasons. But Veronique was dead when I got to the hotel."

"This is a sticky situation," Benjamin said, shaking his head.

Gabriel sighed. "I need you to do something for me, Percy. Make certain Serenity receives a message before the day is out. Give her none of the details. Just say I have been detained in Charleston on business for a day or two, and that I will be home as soon as I'm able."

"Nothing short of a miracle will get you out of here, Gabriel. You must know that. There were no physical signs of abuse except the bruises on her throat. It is obvious Veronique and some man met for a liaison; then, in the throes of passion, he murdered her. With the past history between you and Veronique, combined with the fact that you were in the hotel room with her when the authorities arrived, you will be readily assumed the guilty party. And that is even without the further damaging evidence that Veronique had implied you were Alexandre's father just a short time before her death."

A headache was starting behind Gabriel's stormy eyes. "What makes you think that's the way it happened?"

"Trust me. It is."

"I will trust you to get me out of here, Percy," he responded angrily. "At this very moment, there is a man somewhere out there with a reason great enough to want Veronique dead and me arrested for her murder. I want to know what that reason is."

Serenity stood facing Evan Lancaster in the drawing room at Marihaven. "What are you implying, Lieutenant?"

"Serenity," Lancaster said with a smile, "how many times

must I encourage you to call me Evan? My name on your sweet lips would give me great pleasure."

Impatiently, Serenity gazed up at him. It was obvious the man had come with a purpose. But what could the reason be? Stiffening slightly, she replied, "If I promise to use your given name in the future, may we get on to the reason for your visit?"

Lancaster was suddenly serious. "Much as I dread doing so, I am afraid I must bear ill tidings, Serenity. At this very moment, in a hotel of the lowest regard, your husband is meeting with Veronique Durand."

Serenity did not believe him. Only that morning Gabriel had told her he loved her. Certainly, her husband would not meet Veronique in some disreputable hotel mere hours later.

"Why should I believe you?"

"I told you in Charleston, Serenity, I have made it a point to watch both you and your husband for the past several weeks. Neither of you have any secrets from me. I am concerned for your welfare, and I will not stand by and see you hurt."

Trying to hide the dismay that she felt inside, Serenity drew a sharp breath. "Perhaps the meeting is entirely innocent."

Lancaster gazed at her with great sympathy as he replied, "I think not, Serenity. I care a great deal for you. You must know that. I want to take you away with me to England. I will take care of you. You may have anything your heart desires. And, most especially, you need not remain here to be subjected to your husband's cruelty."

Serenity's head was spinning. What did Lancaster mean, her husband's cruelty? "I do not understand."

He drew closer to her. This time, he was not at all as he had been before. He was gentle. His eyes were kind. Taking her by the hand, he murmured, "I had hoped not to tell you this, Serenity. I had planned to plead with you simply to go away with me. Yet, I can see you will never do so, as long as you do not know the truth. Your husband is the father of Veronique's child,

Alexandre. It is you who stands in the way of him ever gaining his son. Sooner or later, he will set you aside. Now he simply conspires behind your back."

Her lovely face ashen, Serenity felt as though she might faint. She wanted to rail at Lancaster that he was mistaken. Gabriel could not be the father of Veronique's son. Yet, deep in her heart, at the very core of her being, she knew it was true. She had known it from the first moment she had set eyes on Alexandre. Perhaps that was the reason she had been immediately drawn to the boy. Something about him. His expressions. His mere essence. If one loves the father, one must also love the son.

Tears started in her blue eyes. She was the one who stood between Gabriel claiming Alexandre.

"You see, Serenity. You know it is true. Now, do you not think it would be better for everyone concerned if you simply came with me to England? I would put no demands upon you. I would be your friend and companion. When we arrive there, I would arrange for a simple divorce. After it is done, your former husband would then feel free to claim his son and heir. If you care for him at all, you would not deny him that privilege."

"Divorce is a sin." she murmured.

"Perhaps to some degree," he returned patiently. "But is it not a greater sin to deny a child his father? That is what you are doing, Serenity. Imagine the boy's need. I know how you care for Joshua and protect him. You must certainly be aware of how much children need someone to love them. And I have it on very good authority that Veronique Durand is not the best of mothers."

Helplessly, Serenity wheeled around and tried to regain her composure. Though she found it difficult to admit, the lieutenant was right. Even Charles Beaumarchais had implied that his daughter was not a good mother. Alexandre needed Gabriel, as much as Gabriel needed Alexandre. There was nothing else she could do. She must be brave.

Turning back around to face Lancaster, Serenity said softly, "I will go with you to England."

He grinned. "There is no time to delay, Serenity. We must leave before your husband has a chance to stop us. He would most certainly protest. But this is for the best. You must know that. I have already booked passage for the two of us on a vessel, the *Regal Princess* leaving at dawn. We will board and await its departure."

"What about Joshua? I cannot leave him here."

"It would be too difficult for him to come along. At least at this time, Serenity. We must go quickly. It would only frighten and confuse him. Wait until you are settled and have a place for him. Then you can send for him."

Serenity's head was spinning. It was true; it would be far too upsetting for Joshua. She could not take Joshua with her if she left with the lieutenant, not after everything that had happened in the past. Joshua would be better off here, in familiar surroundings. She was certain that Gabriel would take care of him. Despite everything. And she could return for Joshua, after . . .

Serenity sighed. "I must gather a few things."

"No need to take much, Serenity. I shall see to it you have everything you need from now on."

"That is most kind, Evan," she replied. "However, I must beg for your indulgence in allowing me a moment alone with Joshua before I go. He would not understand otherwise."

"Of course, Serenity. Quickly, now."

After she had gathered a few articles of clothing into her portmanteau, Serenity took a moment to write two short messages—one to Raven, who had asked Lot to drive her to a neighboring plantation for the day, and the other to Gabriel, to say farewell and ask him to watch after Joshua.

When she was ready, Serenity quickly went back down the stairs to where Lancaster waited in the entry by the door. "I believe I am ready," she said, glancing around one final time. It was so difficult for her to leave. Marihaven had begun to seem like home. It would be no more.

Noticing the folded paper she held in one hand, Lancaster inquired, "What have you there, Serenity?"

Serenity had left Raven's missive in her bedchamber. The missive she held was meant for Gabriel, and she had thought to ask Joshua to give it to him upon his return. "It is a missive for Gabriel," she replied. "I have told him I am leaving, and asked that he see to Joshua's welfare."

For a moment, a troubled expression flitted across the lieutenant's face. "May I see it, my dear?"

Seeing no point in not letting him, Serenity handed Lancaster the folded paper, as she explained, "It is very brief. But I could not leave without asking him to see to Joshua for me."

Unfolding it carefully, Lancaster read aloud, "'Dear Gabriel, I am leaving, and I shall not return. I know you are the father of Veronique Durand's child. I will not stand in the way of your claiming him. However, I must beg your compassion in seeing to it that Joshua and Biscuit are returned safely to my cousin Emmalina's home in Brookeville. That is all I ask. Serenity.'"

After he had finished reading, Lancaster glanced up at her as though she was waiting for his approval and said, "I see no reason for you not to give the missive to Joshua. I shall wait for you near the coach."

Once they were outside, Serenity hurried to the stables to find Joshua. Lancaster had seemed so anxious to be on their way, she was afraid he would not allow her much time in finding him. Fortunately, however, she quickly found both Joshua and Biscuit inside the stable. Joshua was putting clean hay in one of the horses's stalls. "I must speak to you for a moment, Joshua. I have little time."

A smile lighting his face, Joshua stopped what he was doing and came out of the stall to stand beside her. "What is it, Serenity?"

271

"I am sorry, Joshua, but I must go away, and I cannot take you with me right now."

The smile faded from his face. "When are you coming back?"

Serenity remembered her resolve to be brave. It did not matter that she was leaving all she loved—but it was the only way. She must do so for Gabriel and little Alexandre. Their need was much greater than hers. Fighting back the tears that threatened to spill from her blue eyes, she said, "I can never come back here, Joshua. But I will send for you. I have asked Gabriel to take you back to Brookeville to stay with Cousin Emmalina for awhile. I will come for you there. Will you give Gabriel this missive for me?"

"I can't go to Brookeville without you."

"You must, Joshua." Then, bending down to give the dog a pat, she added, "Please be brave. I need you to take care of Biscuit. Biscuit cannot come along, and we cannot leave him here, all alone. Will you take care of Biscuit for me?"

Instantly, a smile was restored to Joshua's face, as he replied, "I will take care of Biscuit, Serenity."

Joshua was so eager to please, it broke her heart to leave him. Rising from her knees, Serenity murmured, "Thank you, Joshua."

"I will take good care of Biscuit," he repeated.

"Now, Joshua, you must keep Biscuit in the stables until after I have gone. He must not follow. And I want you to stay with him." She gave Joshua a warm hug in farewell. "I shall miss you terribly, Joshua. But it will only be for a little while. I will come for you and Biscuit at Brookeville. I promise." Then, afraid of dissolving into tears, she quickly spun around and dashed back out of the stables and hurried to where Lancaster awaited her by the coach.

Allowing Lancaster to help her inside, his hands on her waist, Serenity glanced back to see Joshua racing from the stables, intent on watching her depart. She felt a moment of panic.

No! She had told Joshua to stay inside the stables until after she was gone. She had not wanted Joshua to see her go, or for him to see the lieutenant.

Raising his hand, Joshua began to wave a vigorous farewell. Then, quite suddenly, he stopped, and his mouth fell open as he quite obviously recognized the man who was helping her into the coach. Joshua knew it was Lieutenant Lancaster.

Desperately, Serenity started to climb back down from the coach and go to him, but Lancaster barred her way before she could do so.

"There is no more time, Serenity. We will miss our ship."

In defeat, Serenity sat back down on the coach seat. Lancaster climbed in beside her, then ordered the driver to hasten on.

A frown on his weathered face, Charles Beaumarchais paced the floor of his drawing room. He warred within himself. Earlier, when he was leaving the hotel after finding Veronique, he had heard someone approaching down the hall and had slipped into a doorway. Recognizing who it was, he had watched as Gabriel Harrowe entered the room where Veronique's body lay. It was only a few moments later that the authorities arrived. He had continued to remain out of sight until, unnoticed, he had slipped from the hotel.

Veronique was dead. Soon the authorities would come to apprise him of that fact, unaware that he already knew. Perhaps it was better that way. Why admit he had followed his daughter to the hotel? It would only add to the scandal. Let Harrowe explain to the authorities.

"Charles Beaumarchais," a man said as he stood in the open doorway, "your servant admitted me. I'm sorry to trouble you, sir. But I'm afraid I bear distressing news of your daughter."

Gabriel had been unable to sleep. The hours until dawn had been spent in pacing the tiny confines of his cell, wondering what trick of fate had placed him there. Now it was nearing midday, and still there was no word from Percival Benjamin as to when he would be released. Perhaps Benjamin had been unable to do anything in his behalf. Perhaps everyone believed him guilty of Veronique's murder.

If only he had some idea who might have killed her. Certainly, she was not above making enemies. Yet, he had heard of no one Veronique was presently involved with. And there was still the gnawing feeling that in some perverse way he was connected to what had happened to her.

Lines of weariness etching his face, Gabriel spun around as he heard the door to his cell start to open. Expecting to see his lawyer, Percival Benjamin, Gabriel was shocked to see it was Charles Beaumarchais instead. Immediately, Gabriel tensed. No doubt the man wanted to face his daughter's murderer in person. There would be no use denying that he had killed Veronique. Beaumarchais was bound to believe the worst after what had happened in the past.

"I asked for this moment alone with you, Harrowe," Beaumarchais began. His eyes were red-rimmed, and he appeared shaken. "I have come in regard to my daughter's murder."

"I'm not responsible for taking Veronique's life."

Beaumarchais nodded slowly. "At first I wanted to believe you were," he replied. "It was much simpler that way. From the time the authorities arrived at my door, I tried to convince myself it was true. However, all the while I knew it was not. Despite what happened between you and Veronique, I know you are a man of honor. You saw fit to face me on the dueling field. And when I lost my advantage and you were given the opportunity to see me dead, you merely wounded me. The man who murdered Veronique knew of no such honor. With his two bare hands, he squeezed the very life from her fragile body without a second thought."

Gabriel listened in silence. He could not believe Beaumarchais was actually defending him.

Beaumarchais went on. "I had followed Veronique to the

hotel and found her there shortly before your arrival. When I saw you coming up the hall, I stepped into an open doorway. I left immediately after, when the authorities arrived. I should have come forward more quickly to tell them what I knew of my daughter's death, but at first I had to struggle with my own human frailties." He paused long enough to draw a deep breath. "I must admit, Harrowe, a part of me wanted to see you punished for leaving Veronique in the midst of a scandal that night several years ago. I tried to convince myself that you were guilty. It took me until this morning to finally realize I could not stand by and see you condemned for a crime that I am certain you did not commit."

"I appreciate your stepping forward, Beaumarchais," Gabriel returned. "I know this could not have been easy for you. If it is of any comfort, I intend to find the man who murdered Veronique myself. The man who killed her did it with deliberation, making certain I would be blamed for her death. Obviously, he wanted both Veronique and myself out of the way. He must have had his reasons—although I have yet to discover what those reasons might be. I'm determined to track him down, and once I do, I will make certain he answers for what he has done."

Chapter Twenty-nine

Leaning against the rail of the *Regal Princess,* Serenity gazed at the vast expanse of ocean that extended as far as her eyes could see. The freshening wind filled the white sails above her and loosened tendrils of her silky hair. She was leaving those she loved farther and farther behind. Gabriel. Joshua. Little Alexandre. Would they miss her? Certainly she missed them already. Yet, she knew there had been no other choice. She could never be happy, knowing she had denied Gabriel the ability to claim his son.

"Serenity . . . " Lancaster said, coming up behind her.

Turning, she gazed up into his intent face. "Yes, Evan? Did you want something?"

Lancaster smiled, his white teeth flashing beneath his brown mustache. As usual he was impeccably dressed. "Only you," he replied. "I went to your cabin, and when you were not there . . . "

"I merely thought to take a walk. The cabin had grown quite confining." There was no need to tell him that she had been dangerously close to tears as she sat in the cabin thinking of Gabriel, and had hoped to find some solace in going out on deck. At least with the sunlight on her face she could force herself to think more positively about the reasons for her leaving.

Placing his hands gently on her shoulders, Lancaster said, "I know you must find the thought of traveling to England difficult. In these past months, you have been forced to live in so many different places. But, I promise, Serenity, you will love it there. And I shall remain by your side."

Bravely, she gave him a smile. "Is it very beautiful in England?"

"Most certainly," he replied. "And once you are my bride : . . "

A frown creasing her brow, Serenity interjected, "I have not agreed . . . "

He gazed at her solemnly. "We have already discussed this many times, Serenity. Divorce is the only answer. Your husband will not be free to claim his son unless he can also claim the child's mother. You know how willful Veronique is. You must release him from all ties to you. Once that is done, you will be free to wed me."

To divorce Gabriel was one thing. To wed Evan Lancaster was yet another. "Were I to divorce Gabriel," she stated bluntly, "I would not choose to marry again."

For a moment, there was a flicker of something that appeared to be anger on Lancaster's handsome face. "You are under my protection, Serenity. Others would not think it proper if we did not wed. Surely you must see that."

Sighing softly, Serenity turned away. Even though the lieutenant had been most kind, she did not like the feeling that her life was beyond her control, with someone else deciding her future for her. Still, there was no use in arguing with him. At least, not at the moment. But, sometime soon, she must let him know it could never be. Then, if he grew angry or upset with her, she would simply have to bear the consequences. Whatever they might be.

Alone in his study at Marihaven, Gabriel sat at his desk, gazing once again at the letter he held in his hand. Joshua had brought it to him shortly after his return to Marihaven on the previous day. He was still trying to accept its contents.

Serenity was gone. She had found out about the child and had left, just as he had feared one day she would. At first he had wanted to go after her and bring her back. But of what use would it be? Nothing would repair the damage that had already been done. Sooner or later, it had been destined to happen. If not over this, it would have been something else. The only irony was that he had lost her over Alexandre. And, now, with Veronique's death, he had lost his chance of ever claiming his son as well. It left a gnawing emptiness deep inside him.

"Gabe," a soft voice said, interrupting his thoughts. It was Raven. "I know you said not to disturb you, but there is someone here I am certain you will want to see."

Glancing up, Gabriel saw Kane standing in the doorway. Rising quickly, he strode over to him. Clasping his hand he said warmly, "I didn't expect you back so soon. Were you able to acquire suitable land for you and Raven to settle in Virginia?"

"Yes," Kane replied. "I was fortunate enough to find exactly what I was looking for without any delay. And, knowing what a penchant your sister has for trouble, I chose to return as quickly as I could. But all that can wait until later. What is this I hear about the Quaker leaving?"

Frowning darkly, Gabriel tore away from him.

Gloria Pedersen

Not to be put off so easily, Kane closed the door behind him to give them some privacy, then strode over to sit down in a chair. Patiently, his eyes followed Gabriel as the latter paced the room. "Raven said she didn't know any of the details, Gabriel. Only that Serenity has left—and you refuse to go after her."

"I have no idea where she went," he stated acidly.

"Is that her fault, Gabriel? Or yours?"

Throwing a black glance at Kane, he stopped his pacing. "She had every right to leave me."

"Fine," Kane retorted with a touch of wry humor. "No doubt the Quaker is better off without you."

"She is."

"And you don't wish to have her back?"

"This was no lovers' quarrel, Kane."

Kane frowned slightly. "What was it, then? Did her leaving have anything to do with Veronique Durand?"

With a slight edge to his voice, Gabriel replied, "A fortunate guess."

Kane sighed. "This is one time I'd listen to your heart and not your fool head, Gabriel. If you let the Quaker get away, you know you'll regret it to your dying day."

There was no use in explaining to Kane all that stood between him and his wife. Before he'd gone to meet Veronique in Charleston, even Gabriel himself had started to believe his and Serenity's love could survive anything. Why was he so willing to give up on it now?

Late that evening, after everyone else had retired to their beds, Gabriel found himself alone once more in his study, the note from Serenity again in his hand, his thoughts dark. From the beginning, he had vowed he would not stop Serenity if she ever decided to leave him. Yet, now he knew he had been wrong. He loved her more than his very life. He would not let her go without a fight.

His brow furrowed in concentration, Gabriel gazed at the carefully penned words. Where had Serenity gone? At first, he had only been aware of the reason for her leaving; he had seen nothing more. But now there was something about the brief contents of the missive that disturbed him.

Why had Serenity not taken Joshua and Biscuit with her? The three of them had never been separated since leaving Nantucket. She had gone to great trouble to secret them away on the *Firefly*, and under far more difficult circumstances. Why leave them behind now? What was more, Serenity had asked that he see to it that Joshua was returned to Brookeville. Why had she not gone there herself?

Something was not right.

Despite the rocking motion of the vessel, Serenity could not sleep, and it was of no use to remind herself of the lateness of the hour. She sat on the narrow built-in bunk, her hand lingering on the coarse blanket that covered it. She had left her grandma's quilt at Marihaven. Was it true a person left something behind when they subconsciously hoped to return one day?

Slipping from the bed, Serenity crossed to her portmanteau and knelt down beside it. Searching quickly through its contents, she drew out her small book of poetry by Wordsworth. She had barely looked at the book since fleeing Nantucket. For some unknown reason, it was one of the few things she had thought to bring along when she had left Marihaven behind.

Returning to her bed, Serenity chose a page at random and began to read in the dim lantern light. " 'But how could I forget thee? Through what power . . . even for the least division of an hour . . . ' "

The words on the page seemed to mock her. Tears glistened in her blue eyes as once more she thought of Gabriel, and she was forced to set the book aside. From the very beginning, theirs had been a star-crossed love. It was never meant to be. Yet, even so, she could never forget him, though an ocean and eternity stretched between them.

With a sigh, Serenity dimmed the lantern and lay back down upon her pillow. Loving someone meant you must give up your aloneness. Now, that aloneness came back to haunt her, and it was all the worse because she knew what she had lost.

Shortly after dawn, Gabriel hurried to the stables to seek out Joshua. He found the young man pitching clean hay into a stall. Without preliminaries, he demanded, "Do you have any idea where Serenity has gone, Joshua?" Then, aware that impatience would gain him nothing, he added more gently, "I am concerned for her welfare."

After a strained glance in Gabriel's direction, Joshua returned to the task at hand as he replied, "Serenity just said she was going away."

"Nothing more?"

Slowly, Joshua replied, "No."

Aware of the pensive look on his face, Gabriel was suddenly suspicious. "Is there something else you want to tell me, Joshua?"

Pausing in his work, a frown creased Joshua's brow, and his dark eyes were uncertain. His response came slowly, "The bad man was here."

Gabriel gazed hard at Joshua. "What bad man?"

Hesitating for a moment, Joshua finally said, "The soldier. He didn't have on his uniform anymore, but I knew it was him."

A muscle tensing along his jaw, Gabriel was aware of a feeling of apprehension. For Joshua's sake, he forced himself to remain calm as he prompted, "Which soldier, Joshua?"

"The one who hurt Serenity," he explained, as though Gabriel should already know. "I pushed him real hard, and he hit his head. But Serenity told me not to worry. We dragged him out of the house and hid him in the bushes. She promised he wouldn't bother us again. Not ever. But I saw him. He took her away."

With sudden shock, Gabriel realized the man Joshua was referring to could only be Lieutenant Lancaster. But how was it possible? Serenity had told him about the lieutenant's death. She had seemed certain of it at the time. Now, it would seem the man was still very much alive and had been here at Marihaven. What was more, he had taken Serenity away with him.

"Are you positive this was the same man, Joshua?"

Joshua nodded. "I locked Biscuit in the stables so he wouldn't follow—like Serenity told me—then I went outside. I saw him standing by the coach. He looked right at me. His face was mean."

There was no use chiding Joshua for not telling him sooner; Gabriel knew he had not given the young man any opportunity. Gabriel was well aware what an error he had made.

"Don't worry, Joshua," he ground out, spinning on his heels and starting from the stable. "I will arrange for Kane to look after things here at Marihaven. Then I intend to find out precisely where the lieutenant has taken her."

Evan Lancaster stood in his cabin, carefully smoothing the wrinkles from his officer's coat as it lay on the bed. It was unfortunate that he could not wear it. He never felt quite right unless he was attired in his full uniform. He looked forward to the day when he could return to the regiment. Once he had Serenity settled in England. And she bore his name . . .

He had surprised even himself by asking her to marry him. But there was no other way. She was not a common trollop, and he would not treat her that way. He would dress her in fine gowns and jewels, and he would be the envy of every man they met. He had always known one day Serenity would be his. It was just a matter of time.

Picking up his saber, Lancaster slipped it from its sheath. With cool deliberation, he placed his thumb against the blade's razor-sharp edge; then, drawing it away, he gazed at the blood that sprang from his flesh. It was an admirable weapon. Pity he did not get to use it more often. It was a man's weapon. It took skill and daring to handle it, unlike a pistol, which one merely aimed and fired.

He had not cared for acting as a British spy while in Washington. There was something cowardly in not facing one's enemy head on. However, if not for that assignment, he would never have been fortunate enough to happen onto Serenity once again. Perhaps it had been fated from the start.

Replacing the saber in its sheath, Lancaster turned toward the door. It would be time to escort Serenity to the captain's cabin. Captain Winthrop had asked that they join him to dine, and Lancaster found himself looking forward to the evening ahead. Let everyone see that Serenity was his.

Serenity had worn her blue velvet gown, the one Gabriel had asked that Carissa obtain for her in Washington. It was the only thing she had brought along that was not simply serviceable. She wanted to appear as presentable as she could since they were to dine with the captain.

Hearing Lancaster's soft knock on her cabin door, Serenity quickly went to open it.

Lancaster frowned slightly as he inspected her gown. "You are looking lovely as always this evening, Serenity. But as soon as we reach England, you will be wearing only the finest of satins and silks. I'll see to it myself."

"You need not trouble—"

Presenting his arm for her to take, Lancaster threw her a pointed glance. "For you, it would be no trouble."

Sighing softly, Serenity slipped her delicate hand around his arm, then replied, "You have done quite enough for me already."

"When you are my bride there will be no more need for gratitude, Serenity."

Seated in the captain's cabin, Serenity struggled to put the lieutenant's words from her mind. Though she must release Gabriel from his worldly vows to her in order for him to claim his son, in her heart she would always be Gabriel's wife. That would never change. She could not wed Lieutenant Lancaster, now or ever, and it was wrong for him to believe such a thing. Still, this was not the time or the place to settle the matter.

Leaning over in her direction, Captain Winthrop gave her a broad grin. "Is the food not to your liking, Madame Harrowe?" he asked. The captain was a rotund man in his early fifties, with silvering hair and a jovial disposition. "I notice you have not tasted a bite. Perhaps we could arrange for something else."

Glancing up, Serenity realized that everyone in the room was gazing directly at her, and the color rose to her fair cheeks. "I find the food most delightful, Captain Winthrop. My mind was merely elsewhere for a moment."

The captain laughed. "Somehow, I believe your thoughts were on someone other than those seated at this humble table. I notice the flush to your cheeks. Your husband, perhaps?"

The captain's presumption was more astute than he knew. Serenity could not help noticing the expression that appeared on Lancaster's face at the question. Carefully, she replied, "I am afraid, Captain Winthrop, my mind was taken with concern for our voyage. Now the blockade has been lifted, are we at any risk on the open seas?"

The diversion had been a good one. Immediately, all the gentlemen at the table began to discuss the war, which was now for all intents and purposes over. However, one of the younger gentleman, a ship's officer named McCauley, continued to gaze longingly in her direction with complete disregard for the conversation at hand. Serenity tried not to take notice.

"You must find it difficult traveling alone, Madame Harrowe," the young officer observed a short time later, when there was a lull in the conversation. "Perhaps you would care to accompany me on a stroll around the deck?"

Serenity hesitated, at a loss for what to say.

"*I* am Madame Harrowe's companion on this voyage, sir,"

Lancaster interjected hastily, throwing the young officer a quelling glance. "And I shall see to it, myself, that the lady is taken for a stroll on the deck." With that, the subject was closed.

Once dinner was over, Serenity and Lancaster did indeed stroll on the deck. As soon as they had gone a short distance, Serenity stopped and twisted around to face him, her chin set with determination. Like a moth caught in a silken spider's web, she was becoming more and more entangled in his plans for her. She had to put a stop to it.

"I must speak with you, Evan," she began.

His gaze was suddenly intent. "Of course, my dear. We are quite alone here."

Serenity chose her words carefully. "Perhaps I made a mistake in coming with you aboard this vessel."

"A mistake?" Lancaster countered softly. "You cannot possibly wish to go back?"

They stood at the end of the deck. The moon was hidden behind a cloud, and there were only the ship's lanterns to lend their faint glow.

"No," she replied. "I have no wish to return to Marihaven. You know full well that I would not deny Gabriel his child. But neither must I allow you to believe I shall be your bride. I fear that is precisely what I have done by accompanying you to England."

Lancaster relaxed slightly. "We have been over this before, Serenity. Soon you will be free of Harrowe. I will handle everything. There will not be the slightest difficulty."

Serenity slowly shook her head. "You do not understand, Evan. I have tried to explain to you before. I value your friendship, but I have no wish to ever wed again. Not you. Not anyone."

He seemed taken back by her words. "You cannot mean what you are saying."

When she did not reply, Lancaster suddenly grasped her by

the upper arms and forcibly drew her to him. "I am not Nathaniel Bentley to be brushed away at your whim, Serenity," he shot back angrily. "Since Nantucket, I have meant to possess you. I am not given to changing my mind. You should feel honored that I would offer you my name. There are other ways of dealing with you that you would not find so pleasant."

"You are making this more difficult—"

"It would be so easy to have done with you right here and now, Serenity. Do you know that? Everyone would believe you merely slipped on the deck . . . fell overboard. Such accidents occur frequently at sea."

Serenity gasped as his grip tightened on her slim arms. "Please, Evan . . . "

"You will belong to me or no one, Serenity. It is that simple. Choose which it will be."

Chapter Thirty

Standing impatiently in Percival Benjamin's office, Gabriel stated succinctly. "The *Firefly* is in readiness. I intend to sail with the tide."

Benjamin nodded. "How many days does the *Regal Princess* have on you, Gabriel? Do you think you will be able to catch her?"

"They have a five-day lead," Gabriel replied. "But I know their course is bound for England, and the *Firefly* is one of the swiftest vessels to weigh anchor. However, finding them will be a little like searching for a gold coin in a haystack. Success may well depend on good luck."

"If anyone can accomplish it, I know you can."

"Thank you for your confidence, Percy," he replied. "Now, for the matter at hand. Have your inquiries about Lancaster turned up anything? I know you had little time, but I was hoping you might at least discover why the man was in Charleston."

Benjamin frowned slightly, then drew a deep breath before replying, "As it happens, I was indeed able to find out something, Gabriel. But much of it is pure speculation. Still, if the matter is as it seems, you may have even greater concern for your wife."

"What do you mean?"

Distractedly, Benjamin drummed his fingertips against the hard surface of his desk for a moment before he replied. "Apparently, Lancaster was in Washington for a time before coming here to Charleston. And, after his arrival, he kept a very discreet profile. It was difficult to find anyone who knew even the slightest thing about him. Even so, while I was checking places where he might have resided during his stay, I made a disturbing discovery. A gentleman of his description was seen on numerous occasions meeting a beautiful woman in a certain hotel of less than noble stature. Of course, there is still some doubt as to whether this particular man was indeed Lancaster."

Gabriel was growing impatient with Benjamin's penchant for dallying around the proverbial bush. "Get to it, Percy."

Pausing for effect, Benjamin trained his eyes on Gabriel, then concluded dramatically, "It would seem, the man in question was meeting Veronique Durand. And the hotel in which they were carrying on their tryst was the very one where the authorities found her body."

Stunned, for a moment Gabriel stood there in silence, his mind racing over what Benjamin had just revealed. Why was Lancaster meeting Veronique, and why in that shoddy hotel? He tried to make sense of the startling implications. Did the two of them have an alliance of some sort? Why avoid being seen together in public? Unless . . .

Deliberating aloud, Gabriel said slowly, "Someone wanted

286

Veronique dead, and that same someone wanted me blamed for her murder. There was something he had to gain. Something . . ." With aching clarity, it came to him. Lancaster's frequent visits on Nantucket, the fact that he had been in Washington, his far-too-coincidental arrival in Charleston, Veronique's death—there was only one thing that could possibly link those disparate events together. A single word formed on his hard mouth. "Serenity."

Perplexed, Benjamin shot back, "Do you believe your wife had something to do with Veronique's death?"

Disregarding the lawyer's question, he replied, "It was right there before me, all the time, Percy."

"What was right there before you, Gabriel? I don't understand."

A bitter certainty inside him, Gabriel murmured, "Lancaster was interested in Serenity from the very start. On Nantucket, I gave it little thought. But the man was intolerably persistent. He came to our wedding. I thought it was a test of sorts, that he wanted to make certain we would actually wed. That he hoped to arrest me for being on the island. Now I realize it was all because of Serenity. I had seen it before me, yet I was completely blind to what it meant."

Benjamin wore an expression of astonishment. "You mean your wife and Lancaster plotted against you?"

In exasperation, Gabriel threw him a black glance. "No, Percy. I mean the man was obsessed with Serenity, that he would do anything to have her. Anything. And, now, he does."

Benjamin appeared mollified. "Do you believe he would harm her?"

Cold apprehension swept through Gabriel. Suddenly he felt a moment of raw fear, just as he had the night he had learned Serenity was lost in the swamp. Joshua had told him that Lancaster had hurt Serenity once before, and there was ample evidence to connect the man to Veronique's murder. Lancaster had already proven he would stop at nothing to gain what he wanted. And if Serenity chose to resist him . . .

His face grim, Gabriel replied, "For whatever it's worth, I know Serenity loves me, Percy. Unfortunately, that fact alone could place her in even graver danger with Lancaster, since I am convinced he wants her for himself. In the past, Serenity has never given thought to the consequences when there is something she believes in. I doubt she would think of them now. And this time I am certain she is dealing with a murderer."

Her delicate chin held high in defiance, Serenity threw an accusing glance at Lancaster as he opened the door. "What did you hope to gain by keeping me locked in the cabin the entire day, Evan? Am I now to be your prisoner?"

Lancaster grinned amiably. "Of course not, Serenity. Whatever gave you that idea? I was only taking the necessary precaution of ensuring your safety. I would not want you to behave rashly and force me into doing something we might both regret—when I know it is only a matter of time until you come around to my way of thinking."

"There is nothing to be gained from this."

Lancaster stopped abruptly. "Don't believe for one moment that someone will come to your rescue, Serenity. Your husband was the only man who could have been of any real help to you, and you have turned your back on him to come with me. Granted, with good cause. But, now you must accept our relationship. It would be far easier on both of us if you would try to be pleasant about it. Now, if you are ready, we shall go to the captain's cabin to dine. You would be well advised to watch very carefully what you say to anyone."

Without resisting, Serenity allowed Lancaster to place her hand over his arm. But she shuddered inside. The man was utterly ruthless; he would stop at nothing to gain what he wanted. Even so, she could not bring herself to involve Captain Winthrop or anyone else in her difficulty. She could never forget how Lancaster had hurt Nathaniel Bentley and threatened to take his life. She refused to see anyone else hurt because of her.

During dinner, Serenity did her best to act in her usual

manner. Still, she felt ill at ease and kept silent for most of the time. It was not until Captain Winthrop remarked on the absence of his young ship's officer, McCauley, that she could contain herself no longer. "Has Officer McCauley been taken ill?"

"If only that were the case, my dear," the captain replied, gazing fondly in her direction. "We are not quite certain what happened. But it appears young McCauley slipped on the deck and struck his head. At any rate, when he awoke some hours later, he had no recollection of what had occurred. It was fortunate it was not worse."

Where was it she had heard those words before? Lancaster had said very nearly the same thing in regard to Nathaniel Bentley. Suddenly, Serenity was filled with a dark suspicion. Had the lieutenant been behind this as well? Had Officer McCauley been deliberately harmed?

Throwing a glance at Lancaster, Serenity murmured softly, "Please give my wishes for a speedy recovery to your officer, Captain Winthrop."

For the rest of the evening, Serenity paid little attention to the conversation that went on around her. She could not stop thinking of the young officer, and wondering how much involvement the lieutenant had had in his accident. It was not until they had left the captain's cabin behind that Serenity saw her opportunity to confront Lancaster.

As though there were nothing at all amiss, Lancaster said, "I thought we would take a little stroll on the deck again, Serenity. I know you are probably in need of one, after being confined to the cabin for the entire day. This one, I trust, will be much more pleasant than that of last night."

Though she was still angry with him for locking her in the cabin, Serenity chose not to argue with him. She was far more eager to learn about McCauley. Twisting toward him, she demanded, "Did you have anything to do with what happened to that officer? Must I feel responsible for that as well?"

"You give me far too much credit, Serenity," he countered.

"What makes you think I would bother with a mere ship's mate?"

"Then, you deny having any knowledge of his accident?"

"Of a certainty."

Serenity still felt unconvinced. She had come to the conclusion that Lancaster was a man who delighted in evil doings.

In silence, the two of them continued farther down the deck.

Walking slowly, Serenity demanded of him once more, "Do you intend to keep me locked in the cabin again tomorrow?"

Coming to a halt near a mast, Lancaster intentionally backed her up against it, his arms to each side of her, pinning her there as he smoothly replied, "Would you care to give me some sort of a bribe, Serenity? Show me how grateful you would be for such a consideration?"

Stiffening her spine, Serenity retorted with icy indifference, "I would prefer to stay in the cabin."

One hand jerking her toward him, Lancaster's other hand grasped her delicate chin as his mouth ground down on hers. Once he had finished, he shoved her back against the mast once more. "The problem seems to be, Serenity, that you do not know how to treat a man. Harrowe did not train you well enough, I see. Like a good horse, a woman must be broken to a man's touch or she will keep on resisting. It is my intention to see you receive the proper instruction in the future. That will make the inevitable ride more pleasant."

"You are crude," she remarked in disgust.

Lancaster chuckled in amusement, then responded, "Crude, you say? What do you know of crudeness, Serenity? Crudeness would be taking you to the cabin this very moment and throwing you down on the bed and pushing up your skirts. But I have decided to wait until the time is right. I have always known you were made of ice. Crystal cold. Virginal—whether you are virgin or not. It is that which intrigues me most. What kind of fire does it take to melt an ice princess? I intend to find out once we are wed. And I am certain, when that time comes, I shall find it well worth my wait." Then, toying with a lock of her fiery hair, he added, "But, Serenity, my sweet, don't push me."

Tearing away from him, Serenity made a dash back toward the cabin. It was better to be locked inside than to have his hands upon her. Before she could get far, Lancaster grabbed Serenity and spun her back around once more. Just then, Captain Winthrop approached them on the deck.

"Good evening," the captain said briskly. "Is there some problem?"

"Nothing of concern, Captain," Lancaster retorted hastily. "I was just seeing Madame Harrowe back to her cabin when she suddenly felt a slight indisposition. It is the walk on the deck, I believe. Perhaps it would be better if she remained in her cabin again tomorrow. I will see to it myself that the lady receives the best of care. Her welfare is of the utmost importance to me."

Serenity started to say something to the captain; then she stopped herself. How could she explain the precarious position she was in? Of her own free will, she had fled her husband to run away with Lancaster; any claim that he now held her virtually prisoner would seem completely ridiculous.

Once they had returned to her cabin, Lancaster was only too eager to point out that fact to her as well. "You were wise not to tell the captain anything while we were on deck, Serenity. A married woman who leaves her husband to be with another man would hardly gain his sympathy. You cannot expect him to help you in any way."

Twisting away from him, Serenity gazed out the porthole at the moon-kissed waters in silence. Where was Gabriel now? Did he think of her? She prayed that he and little Alexandre would be happy. At least that thought would give her courage for whatever she must endure in the future at Lancaster's hands. She had made a grievous error.

"You have won," Serenity said softly, unwilling to face

him. "But your victory shall be a hollow one. I promise you that."

Lancaster came to stand behind her, placing his hands on her slim shoulders. "I have won? I had no doubt of that, Serenity. No doubt at all."

Shrugging away from his hands, Serenity twisted around. His touch made her feel soiled. "Only a fool would believe I could ever belong to you completely. I love my husband. I left him for one reason, and one reason alone. I wanted him to claim his son, and I chose to leave the pathway clear. Gabriel will always possess every part of me . . . every part . . . whether or not I ever see him again. Before the Lord, I am pledged to him. Only he can claim my heart. When you hold me, I will be as an empty shell upon the seashore."

Suddenly angry, Lancaster raised his hand and struck her viciously across the face, knocking her onto the bed before she could utter another word. Standing menacingly over her, he shot her a venomous glance. "I'm losing patience with you, Serenity, my sweet. This time I shall simply give you a warning. You will never speak of your husband again. He is dead to you. Do you understand? More's the pity I did not see to it myself. I can see now that was an unfortunate mistake. But you shall forget him, just as if he were dead. And if you choose not to—if you continue to defy me—I shall make certain you regret each day for the rest of your life."

Her face still stinging, Serenity sat up with tears of defiance sparkling in her eyes. "Your threats are of no consequence."

For a moment, Lancaster looked as though he would strike her again. Then he drew back slightly. "Take heed, Serenity, before it is too late," he said, his voice low and deadly. "I will share you with no one."

Standing on the deck of the *Firefly*, gazing up at the star-filled night sky, Gabriel shuddered unaccountably. Why did he have this sudden feeling of horrible disquiet connected to Serenity?

Each day as they drew closer, there was no denying his apprehension had increased. He did not like to consider the possibilities, yet they were there. One moment he was frightened Lancaster would force himself upon Serenity, and the thought galled and tortured him. Then, the next moment, to his horror he was actually wishing that Serenity would not resist Lancaster if he did, so that the man would not kill her as he had done Veronique.

Gabriel had never been a religious man. When he and Serenity were wed, it had been before Serenity's God. It had seemed quite simple. Gabriel had pledged his love and devotion, and Serenity had pledged to love and cherish him in return. Until now, he had not realized what those words had truly meant. Before Serenity's God, they were one, belonging only to each other. That knowledge held a mystical quality. Now he prayed to that same God to protect her for him.

"Evenin', Captain," young Thomas Brady said as he approached him. "It's a beautiful night. Don't you think so, sir?"

"Yes," he replied.

"You think we'll have the *Regal Princess* in our sights tomorrow?"

Gabriel thought it over for a moment. "I believe so, Brady."

"What do you intend to do then, sir?"

"I will board alone."

"Alone, sir?" Brady countered. "But they'll see the *Firefly* comin'. And I thought the man who had your wife—"

"We're in international waters now, Brady. Lancaster is a British citizen. He can't be arrested for murder when there is no tangible proof. It's better if I keep this between him and me. Unless I miss my guess, Lancaster won't give Serenity up without a fight. And I don't want to do anything to jeopardize my wife's safety. If others are with me, he might behave irrationally. But, should I appear alone, he will believe the odds are in his favor."

Brady nodded in the darkness. "I never thought when me and Kane left you on that island . . ."

Gabriel felt an intense ache inside. "I know, Brady," he returned softly. "Sometimes fate deals us a winning hand, and we don't realize our good fortune until it is nearly too late."

Chapter Thirty-one

Serenity stood on the deck of the *Regal Princess*, gazing off into the distance at the sleek scarlet-masted vessel that had appeared on the horizon a short time earlier. Lancaster stood by her side.

"Well, my dear," he said, "it appears your husband was not quite so eager to give you up as I had thought. How unfortunate that I didn't dispose of him properly when I had the opportunity. Now, my error has come back to haunt me."

"Whatever do you mean?"

Lancaster threw her a disbelieving glance. "I thought even you would recognize his vessel, Serenity. There is none other like it. The *Firefly,* if I recall her name. And seaworthy enough to catch up with this lumbering merchant ship without the least trouble."

"Was this why you brought me out on deck?" she demanded.

"Let us not play games," he replied. "Within a short time your husband will be boarding the *Regal Princess*. And I am certain he has every intention of claiming what he considers his."

Serenity felt a sudden ache in the region near her heart. "Other vessels could look like the *Firefly*. You do not know for a certainty—"

"I know, Serenity. Perhaps this was even what I wanted all along. You see, some part of me has always anticipated one day facing Harrowe. There was a certain inevitability to it."

Her blue eyes remaining on the other vessel, Serenity could see it looked to be all sail and rode low in the wave troughs, approaching at an alarming speed. Was Lancaster right? Was it the *Firefly*? Tendrils of hair whipped before her eyes, and she brushed them away with one hand, frowning slightly. "I will not go with him," she said quietly.

Lancaster's handsome mustached face showed no apparent surprise. "I could almost take delight in your words, if I thought you desired to remain with me instead. But we both know that is not the case. It is touching, the concern you have for the man. You would give up your own happiness simply so he could claim his son, yet deny me the least of your favors. It seems, Serenity, the only way to rid you of him is to leave him dead at your feet. Then you will have no recourse but to accept what I have to offer."

Serenity had gone pale. "You would not kill him?"

Lancaster laughed softly, a cold gleam in his eyes. "With much enjoyment."

"Please . . . "

"You have nothing more to bargain with, Serenity, my sweet. You are already mine, whether you want to be or not. All that is needed is the final coup de gráce. Then the captain can wed the two of us right here aboard the vessel, without further delay. I could not have planned it better myself. This very night, you may well be my bride."

A tremor swept through Serenity. If Gabriel were to die, she could not bear to live herself. In desperation, she countered, "There is no need for his death. If I promise we shall be wed in England as you desire, will you spare him?"

"How did I know you would say that, Serenity?"

"It could be as you wish . . . "

His face suddenly suffused with anger, Lancaster interjected, "You would be wise to end your pleading now, Serenity. Your devotion to Harrowe only sickens me and makes his death the more imminent." Grabbing her roughly by one arm, he jerked her around. "Come, my dear. We have just enough time to prepare a special welcome for your soon-to-be departed husband."

Her hair already loose and falling heavy and long about her slim shoulders, Serenity trembled as Lancaster watched her undress. They stood in his cabin, and he held his saber in his hand. He stroked the blade lovingly as he watched her unfasten her gown.

"I cannot . . . " she began.

"No need to fret, Serenity. I have no time to indulge in your charms at the moment. That will have to wait until later. This is merely for your husband's benefit . . . though I doubt he will have time to appreciate it. Now, hurry, my dear. Or else I will be forced to help you myself. And I am afraid that would sorely test my restraint."

Serenity's gown dropped to the floor. She bit her lip as he watched her begin to remove her petticoats. It was humiliating to have to disrobe before him, yet Serenity told herself she was buying more time for Gabriel to take Lancaster by surprise while he was thus distracted. "If you would but turn around . . . "

"Come, now, Serenity. I am growing impatient," he said, stroking the saber's shiny blade once more. A drop of blood sprang from his thumb. Without even glancing at it, he reached up his hand to lick the blood away with his tongue.

Serenity felt ill. He would kill Gabriel as surely as she was standing there. If only there was some way she could warn Gabriel. . . .

Breaking away from him, she fumbled with her chemise.

"That is far enough, my dear," Lancaster instructed. "Now, you may lay down upon the bed."

Doing as he requested, Serenity knew a moment's panic as Lancaster came over to her and bent down. What did he intend to do now? Rolling her over, he quickly pulled her hands behind her back and bound them with a cord. Then he tied her ankles as well.

Heaving a sigh once he was done, Lancaster leaned down to stroke her shoulder. "Such an enticing picture you make, my sweet Serenity. I am truly enjoying this so much, perhaps we will do it again. When there is more time, of course."

Thrusting a twisted piece of linen into her mouth, Lancaster gagged her so she could not speak. Then, turning her to face the wall, he covered her partially with the bed linens and stepped back to admire his work. "Perfect, in every respect. Actually, Serenity, you are aiding me more than you know. Your husband will be so distracted, he will never even feel my blade."

The moment Lancaster left her, Serenity worked to free her hands. Somehow she must warn Gabriel before the lieutenant took him by surprise and ended his life.

After demanding the vessel heave to, Gabriel had Brady paddle him over to the *Regal Princess* in the small boat and climbed aboard alone, looking more the part of a fearsome pirate than a man come to retrieve his wife. Dressed in a white linen shirt, with breeches and boots encasing his long muscular legs, he wore his saber sheathed at his side. His tanned, harshly handsome face was hard, and though a slight beard shadowed his rugged jaw, it did not conceal the scar slashed across his cheek.

Hastily greeting Captain Winthrop, Gabriel explained in the briefest of terms the situation regarding Serenity, while at the same time withholding all details concerning Lancaster's involvement in Veronique's death. Gabriel still felt it was the wisest course. He did not want to force Lancaster's hand.

"I will show you to your wife's cabin immediately, Captain Harrowe," the captain offered. "It is right this way."

His outward appearance calm, Gabriel followed. Even before he knocked at the door, Gabriel was certain Serenity would not be there. It only confirmed his earlier suspicions. Somewhere aboard the vessel, Lancaster was waiting for him. And the man had Serenity.

"Lancaster's cabin, perhaps?" Captain Winthrop asked, his discomfort apparent on his face. Now that her husband had appeared, the captain seemed convinced that Serenity was involved in an indiscreet liaison. "Would you care to wait here, Captain Harrowe? I will see to it myself."

"No need, Captain Winthrop," Gabriel countered. "I think it advisable that I handle the matter on my own. You understand, I'm sure."

The captain looked as though he did indeed understand, and giving Gabriel directions to Lancaster's cabin, he beat a hasty retreat. It was precisely what Gabriel had wanted.

The hallway was deserted as Gabriel approached the cabin. Drawing his saber from the sheath at his side, he cautiously pushed the door open. Before him, the berth stood rumpled and empty, as though someone had been there only a moment before. His long, lean body tensed, he took one step inside. A slight movement from behind the door alerted him, and he spun around with his saber in his hand, prepared to strike. If Lancaster was in wait for him, it was to be a fatal mistake. But a slight gasp and the sight of terrified blue eyes froze his hand in midair.

"Serenity." he cried, as though the word had been torn from him.

He dropped his saber and she was in his arms instantly. Clad only in her chemise, she felt slim and fragile, her hair in tangled disarray. What had Lancaster done to her?

But Serenity was shaking her head and pushing him away wildly. "Watch out, Gabriel . . . "

With the swiftness of a striking snake, Lancaster appeared in the open doorway behind him, and the man's saber came slicing through the air toward him. Dropping to the floor with Serenity still in his arms, Gabriel rolled away from the blow. A

298

moment later, he was on his feet again, but Lancaster had already disappeared.

"Wait here, Serenity. I have to go after him."

Tears were streaming down her cheeks. "He will kill you," she murmured, clinging to him desperately.

"Never."

Setting her firmly aside, Gabriel strode out the door, already certain Lancaster would be waiting on deck for him. As he burst through the opening, Lancaster was there. Deflecting a blow from Lancaster's saber with his own, Gabriel thrust and then parried to gain himself more distance.

"Ah, at last a worthy opponent," Lancaster said in a pleased tone. "I have been waiting for you." The thrust of his saber missed Gabriel by scant inches.

"I am amazed, Lancaster. I thought killing women was more your sport."

Gabriel's blade sliced Lancaster's forearm. Undaunted, Lancaster thrust back, slashing Gabriel across the chest. A thin line of blood welled there. Spinning, Gabriel caught Lancaster's other arm.

Breathlessly, his eyes bright with anticipation, Lancaster countered, "I'm glad you are making this worth my while, Harrowe. I hate an easy kill."

Parrying once again, his eyes on his opponent's face, Gabriel asked, "Since you cannot be charged with her murder, would you care to tell me whether you were the one who killed Veronique and made it look as though I were to blame?"

Lancaster smiled. "Extremely clever of me, don't you think, Harrowe? The woman played right into my hands. Marvelous in bed. But, of course, she was not Serenity."

"It was Serenity you wanted, even on Nantucket. . . . "

Lancaster thrust, then drew back once more, slightly breathless. "She was always mine, Harrowe. Long before you appeared to steal her away."

Gabriel felt a slash of Lancaster's saber and then another. He

299

could feel the sting of the wounds, though none of them did more than draw blood. Lancaster was still playing the game. The man was trying to tire him before moving in for the kill.

Gabriel thrust and missed. "You will never have her."

"No?" Lancaster queried with false wonder. "You have handed her to me, Harrowe. Attacked by a wronged husband, I have no recourse but to defend myself. And when you are dead, Serenity will become my bride. No one aboard this vessel will even deign to raise an eyebrow. Captain Winthrop will even marry us. Isn't it said, to the victor belongs the . . . spoils?"

An icy glare in his eyes, Gabriel thrust again. Lancaster jumped aside.

Nearby, Gabriel could see that the captain and crew were gathering to watch them. No one made a move to interfere. Lancaster was right. If the man was to kill him, nothing would stop Lancaster from claiming Serenity. Rivalry between two men over a woman was not an uncommon thing, and—if honor served—the victor would indeed retain the spoils; with no one the wiser that Lancaster just happened to be a murderer.

Now they both fought in earnest.

Viciously, Gabriel thrust and thrust again, barely missing Lancaster each time. Sweat beaded his brow, and his face was hard with strain. He could not let Lancaster win. Putting all else from his mind, Gabriel fought to gain the advantage. All his strength and skill went into every movement.

There was the thrill of unleashed violence about him. Backing his opponent up against a mast, Gabriel kept him there, each time his blade thrusting closer. He *would* kill Lancaster.

Knocking the saber from the man's hand, Gabriel saw Lancaster's eyes widen in fear as he awaited the final thrust. Even before the act, the feeling of victory was sweetly intoxicating. He had won. The tip of his saber rested against Lancaster's heaving chest.

Then, as though in a dream, Serenity was there beside him, begging him to stop. Time seemed suspended as he glanced over at her. Though her feet were still bare, Serenity had hastily donned her gown; her wealth of flame-colored hair blew softly in the breeze. She looked an ethereal vision, yet her serene angel's face was masked with horror.

He had never seen her look like that before. If he killed Lancaster before her very eyes, she would never forgive him. Yet, she had no idea what the man had done, what he still might do, or that in the end Gabriel must protect her in the only way he knew how.

"Stop, Gabriel," she pleaded. "You must not kill—"

"Go away, Serenity. Let me do what I must."

Though she stood at a distance, he could almost taste her sweet breath on his mouth, feel her gentle hands as they slid up his chest. Had he come after her, only to lose her again?

"Please, Gabriel."

"Leave!" he ground out fiercely.

Everyone stood silently watching, yet it seemed there was no one present but the two of them.

"I won't leave. You must kill him before me, or not at all."

If he killed Lancaster, all hope of a future with Serenity would be denied him forever. Yet, the man did not deserve to live.

An eternity seemed to pass. Then, slowly, very slowly, Gabriel's arm dropped to his side, his hand still holding the saber.

Lancaster grinned in satisfaction.

Without a word, Gabriel turned around to face Serenity. Right or wrong, he had done it for her, because he could not lose her. His dark hair was damp with sweat, and his shirt was torn and covered with blood from the slashes Lancaster had inflicted. Yet his eyes held a certain triumph in their shadowy silver depths as he gazed at her.

Behind him, he did not see Lancaster snatch up his saber, or

301

move to thrust it into his back. It was only Serenity's terrified expression and her cry of alarm that warned him of what was to come.

Instinctively, Gabriel spun around with his saber raised.

As though in pantomime, Lancaster lunged desperately toward him, and in that precise moment was impaled on Gabriel's lethal blade. The Englishman's sword clattered to the deck from nerveless fingers. There was a frozen expression of shocked surprise on the man's face. Then, slowly, like a doll made of cloth, he crumpled to the ground. Lieutenant Evan Lancaster was dead.

As she stood on the deck of the *Firefly* watching the *Regal Princess* disappear into the distance, Serenity trembled slightly. The sun was starting to set; a hallo of fire sat on the horizon, changing to vibrant pink, then fading to a delicate lavender.

So much had happened to her this day. Once, long before, her life had been well ordered and she had known precisely what it was she believed in. Always, there had been a right and wrong of things. Yet, today, she had watched a man die and could only rejoice that Gabriel had lived. Whatever was to become of her?

Gabriel came to stand beside her. "Are you cold, Serenity?"

Silently, Serenity shook her head. A short time earlier, she had bandaged his wounds. There had been a strained politeness between them, and neither of them had spoken about the things that were truly on their minds. It was as though they had been strangers.

"Would you care to go back to the cabin?" he persisted.

"Soon," she said. Could he not feel the erratic beating of her heart at just having him so near? When he had burst into Lancaster's cabin aboard the *Regal Princess* she had wanted only to be in his arms and never to leave them again. Never before had she seen him look so fierce, or so utterly ruthless. With his darkly handsome features, he had appeared as dangerous as a dragon. Yet, nothing else had mattered except how very much she loved him. Until now.

Gabriel continued to stand beside her. "What is it you were thinking of, Serenity?"

"Joshua," she replied, unwilling to let him see how vulnerable she suddenly felt. Though Gabriel had come after her, still she could not deny him the opportunity to claim his son. Nothing had changed. Somehow, she must find the strength to leave him once again.

"Joshua?" he inquired.

"Joshua," she repeated. "One day soon, if you are agreeable, I should like to travel with him back to Nantucket. We left there out of fear that Joshua would be arrested for the lieutenant's murder. Now that the danger is gone, there is no need for us to stay away any longer."

"Of course I am agreeable, Serenity. You need not even ask." Then, he heaved a weary sigh. "I know it is impossible for you to forgive me for killing Lancaster."

A frown creased Serenity's delicate brow. "You misunderstand, Gabriel," she said quickly. "I do not blame you for the lieutenant's death. In good faith, you spared his life. The lieutenant forced your hand to turn against him. Though I still believe violence is not the Lord's will, I know you had no other choice."

For a long moment, Serenity and Gabriel continued to gaze at the dying rays of the sun in silence, each lost in their own thoughts.

Finally, Gabriel spoke once again. "I have to know, Serenity. Did you go with Lancaster willingly?"

Turning to gaze at him, she replied softly. "Yes."

With resignation, he asked, "Because of the child?"

Serenity knew he deserved her honesty. She should never have left Marihaven in the first place without telling him the precise reason why. "I wanted you to be able to claim your son, Gabriel. With me out of the way . . ."

He gazed at her incredulously. "With you out of the way?" he shot back. "Whatever made you think . . . " Then he continued more calmly, "I should have known it was something like that. You have always disregarded your own welfare whenever you were concerned for someone else. But, Serenity, you could not have been more wrong."

Serenity was still uncertain. "But if I set you free, Gabriel, you could wed Veronique and claim Alexandre. And I lost your child . . ."

Gabriel shook his head. "Sometimes you think too much. It was a sad thing when we lost our child. But I have no doubt in the least that, one day soon, you and I will have another. My only regret is that you were not Alexandre's mother as well." He paused for a moment, then continued. "I want you to know, what there was between Veronique and myself was nothing compared to the way I feel about you. Even had she lived, there could not have been any future for us—with or without you there."

"Had she lived?" Serenity asked in surprise. "I don't understand."

"Veronique is dead, Serenity. Murdered by Lancaster. And he tried to place the blame on me."

"But, why? Why would Lancaster do such a vile thing?"

"That is the simplest part of all to understand," Gabriel replied slowly. "Lancaster wanted *you*."

"But what of the child? What of Alexandre?"

For a moment, it seemed as though a cloud had suddenly passed before the sun. A muscle tightened along Gabriel's jaw; then he replied with an efforts. "Custody of Alexandre will revert to his grandfather, Charles Beaumarchais. I have no claim upon the child in any way. There is no proof Alexandre is even my son."

Everything she had done had been in vain. "Oh, Gabriel," Serenity murmured, tears stinging her blue eyes. "I am so sorry. I had wanted you to have your son. Now, all I can give you is me."

Drawing her close, Gabriel cradled her face gently with his two strong hands. "Don't you know, Serenity? I would be willing to go through eternity with just you by my side. I told myself when you came to South Carolina that if you ever wanted to leave me, I would let you go. But I was wrong. I can never let you go again. I love you more than my life."

"And I love you, Gabriel," she said, just before he pulled her tightly into his embrace and his mouth claimed hers so fiercely that she was certain he meant never to let her go. And she did not want him to. Not ever again. She was wrong ever to have left him. From this time on, whatever they must face, she promised herself it would always be together.

Chapter Thirty-two

Long before the handsome coach had pulled up in front of Marihaven and their visitor rapped at the door, Gabriel and Serenity had been alerted to his arrival. It was their first guest since arriving back at Marihaven the week before, and one of the servants had come running to tell them that the coach had been sighted. It was not until the man was shown into the drawing room that Gabriel and Serenity realized that their unexpected visitor was Charles Beaumarchais.

Declining the offer of a seat, Beaumarchais remained standing in the middle of the room. His manner was formal. It was obvious he had something of grave importance on his mind. "I have come to give you my regards in person, Harrowe, for seeing to it that the man responsible for my daughter's death was brought to justice. I know since your wife is a Quaker, she carries different views on the necessity of violence. But, myself, I could not have felt the matter was put to rest and behind me unless it had turned out precisely as it did. I wanted you to know that."

"I am sorry Veronique lost her life, Beaumarchais," Gabriel replied with complete sincerity. "I hope you will believe that."

"You have my sympathy as well, sir," Serenity added gently as she stood to one side.

Clearing his throat with a harrumph, Beaumarchais nodded in Serenity's direction.

For a moment, they all stood there uncertainly. With difficulty, Gabriel restrained himself from asking about Alexandre. Beaumarchais was certain to question his interest, and nothing could be gained by it. There was no need to belabor something that could never be.

Beaumarchais turned toward Gabriel. "There is also another matter of importance I would like to discuss with you as well, Harrowe." He paused for a moment. Then, his expression giving nothing away, Beaumarchais added with dignity, "That is the matter of your son."

The words were spoken so simply, it was as though they held little significance. Yet they were almost shattering in their impact. Gabriel could not believe what he had just heard. Was Beaumarchais actually admitting that he was Alexandre's father?

After a long moment, Gabriel managed uncertainly, "My son?"

Beaumarchais's face remained unchanged. "Of course, Harrowe." The man threw a glance in Serenity's direction. "I hope all of this will not come as a shock to your wife. But unless I miss my guess, she is woman enough to handle it." Then, his gaze returning to Gabriel once more, Beaumarchais continued, "I have known all along you were Alexandre's father—even before my daughter's betrothal to the senator or that unfortunate incident in the hotel. Veronique told me quite bluntly that she carried your child. She refused to inform you about it, since you were not a part of her plans. Instead, she agreed to wed the senator with the utmost of haste. It was his political career that intrigued her." Beaumarchais sighed deeply. "All her life, Veronique was indulged. She wanted her own way in everything. And this was no exception. However, after the scandal at the hotel, the senator would have nothing more to do with her. Veronique never forgave you for that. I know she kept the knowledge about Alexandre from you out of vindictiveness after your return. But I did not argue. Certainly, I had no fondness for you myself, and I thought I was protecting the boy. But now I know everything must be brought out into the open. I am an old man. If anything should happen to me, well . . . Alexandre belongs with you."

Stunned, Gabriel ran his long fingers through his hair. Not only had the man admitted that Alexandre was his son, but Beaumarchais was prepared to give him up as well. It was impossible to believe. "I don't know what to say, Beaumarchais. I thought I had lost all hope of ever claiming Alexandre. I had no proof he was even my son."

"I am not noble enough to say I am doing this for you, Harrowe. Nor is it because you brought Veronique's murderer to justice. I am doing it for my grandson. Because I want him to grow up in a home filled with love. And for someone I've come to hold very dear."

As Gabriel looked on, Beaumarchais looked back toward Serenity. "You are very much a part of this, Serenity."

Utterly perplexed, Gabriel countered, "How is Serenity involved?"

Not bothering to reply to his question, Beaumarchais grinned at Serenity, and she reciprocated with a dazzling smile.

"Charles and I are friends," she said.

Seeing his astonishment, Beaumarchais was less succinct in his explanation. "Your wife never approved of our duel, and she decided to set things right on her own. She can be very persistent at times, as undoubtedly you have discovered. She visited me regularly, and plied me with sweet cakes. Then, in my weakened condition, she won my heart."

Gloria Pedersen

Gabriel wore an incredulous look on his face. "Serenity?"

Her smile entrancing, Serenity moved toward him. "It's true, Gabriel. Charles and I have been friends for some time. I hope you do not mind. I could not let things stand as they were."

"Whyever should he mind, my dear?" Beaumarchais interjected hastily. "He is more fortunate than he knows to have you." Suddenly Beaumarchais became serious once again, and there was a troubled look on his face as he continued. "I only hope once Alexandre is in your home, I will not lose touch with him."

Serenity did not hesitate a moment. Tears sparkling in her eyes, she rushed toward Beaumarchais and gave him an unexpected hug that spoke volumes. "You will always be his grandfather, Charles. Always. I promise you that. And we want you to be a part of all of our lives in the future as well. I have no intention of letting you ever get away."

Beaumarchais's eyes held a suspicious sparkle of moisture in them when he pulled away. Regaining his composure, the gentleman cleared his throat and said, "Now, with that settled to everyone's satisfaction, there is someone outside in the coach who is very eager to come in and see you. And I think he has waited long enough."

Gabriel and Serenity watched as Beaumarchais swiftly spun around and left the room. Neither of them spoke, yet their eyes were filled with happiness and wonder as they gazed at each other. When Beaumarchais returned Alexandre was in his arms.

Setting the dark-haired child down on his sturdy little legs, Beaumarchais stepped back. For a moment, Alexandre just stood there, solemnly gazing first at Gabriel and then at Serenity. A grin of recognition suddenly lighting his small face, with a squeal of delight, he spread out his tiny arms and went racing pell mell across the room and straight into Serenity's waiting embrace.

Laughing, Serenity scooped Alexandre up and spun him around.

"Mama!" he cried, his arms clasped tightly about her neck.

Gabriel could not believe what was happening. Alexandre had run to Serenity as though that was precisely where he belonged. What was more, the child had called her Mama. How had this all come about? If this was some sort of a dream, he hoped never to awaken.

Gabriel chuckled as he watched the two of them together, Serenity and Alexandre, his happiness at last complete. Then, noting the way the dark-haired child was clinging to his new mother, he said, "It would seem my son has lost his heart to Serenity as well."

Once again it was night. Gazing down at their sleeping son, Gabriel's arms held Serenity close, his scarred cheek nuzzling against her silky hair. "Alex Harrowe," he said softly. "It sounds good, doesn't it, Serenity?"

Serenity sighed. "Yes. Very good."

"Beaumarchais said he would see my lawyer tomorrow, to take care of all of the details. Soon he will officially be ours."

"I am glad," she replied. "I love Alexandre so dearly. I would have it no other way."

Silver eyes met dark blue with love shining in their shadowy depths. "It's hard to imagine your kindness could bring about such a miracle, Serenity. If not for you—"

Blushing slightly, Serenity brushed a kiss across his mouth to silence him before he could complete the sentence. Then, she said in all modesty, "It is wrong of me to take credit where none is due. I think this was the way the Lord meant everything to be, right from the very beginning."

For a moment, Gabriel grinned, as though he was giving it some consideration. Did the Lord have a hand in this? Then, finally, he returned, "I have no doubt He did."

Serenity smiled. She had never dreamed such happiness was possible. Using the familiar Quaker language, which she and Gabriel had used when they were wed, she murmured, "I take thee, Gabriel . . ."

"And I take thee, my sweet Serenity." Almost with reverence, Gabriel kissed her. Then, releasing her, he said, "I think it is time we both admit that we no longer live in two separate worlds."

"Yes," she agreed, eager to surrender that last bastion.

Then, a frown creasing his dark brow, Gabriel added thoughtfully, "You do know that this means you will never be able to return home to Nantucket, except for an occasional visit?"

"I am already home, Gabriel. As long as I am by your side."

He kissed her once again, this time with a fiery passion that left her breathless in his embrace and promised so much more. Yes, as he'd said so long ago, she'd saddled a dragon. And he had taken her where he had wanted to go. But it had been the best thing she'd ever done.

What does it take to melt an ice princess? Lancaster had once asked her. The answer was quite simple. *Gabriel's fire . . .*

DECEPTIONS & DREAMS

DEBRA DIER

Sarah Van Horne can outwit any scoundrel who tries to cheat her in business. But she is no match for the dangerously handsome burglar she catches in her New York City town house. Although she knows she ought to send the suave rogue to the rock pile for life, she can't help being disappointed that his is after a golden trinket—and not her virtue. Confident, crafty, and devilishly charming, Lord Austin Sinclair always gets what he wants. He won't let a locked door prevent him from obtaining the medallion he has long sought, nor the pistol Sarah aims at his head. But the master seducer never expects to be tempted by an untouched beauty. If he isn't careful, he'll lose a lot more than his heart before Sarah is done with him.

___4582-6 $5.99 US/$6.99 CAN

Flames of Rapture

Lark Eden

"Great reading!"—*Romantic Times*

When Lyric Solei flees the bustling city for her summer retreat in Salem, Massachusetts, it is a chance for the lovely young psychic to escape the pain so often associated with her special sight. Investigating a mysterious seaside house whose ancient secrets have long beckoned to her, Lyric stumbles upon David Langston, the house's virile new owner, whose strong arms offer her an irresistible temptation. And it is there that Lyric discovers a dusty red coat, which from the time she first lays her gifted hands on it unravels to her its tragic history—and lets her relive the timeless passion that brought it into being.

_52078-8 $4.99 US/$6.99 CAN

SEVEN BRIDES
LEIGH GREENWOOD
VIOLET

Broken and bitter, Jefferson Randolph can never forget all he lost in the War Between the States—or forgive those he has fought. Long after most of his six brothers have found wedded bliss, the former Rebel soldier keeps himself buried in work, until a run-in with Yankee schoolteacher Violet Goodwin teaches him that he has a lot to learn about passion. But Jeff fears that love alone isn't enough to help him put his past behind him—or convince a proper lady that she can find happiness as the newest bride in the rowdy Randolph clan.

___4494-3 $5.99 US/$6.99 CAN

Dorchester Publishing Co., Inc.
P.O. Box 6640
Wayne, PA 19087-8640

Please add $1.75 for shipping and handling for the first book and $.50 for each book thereafter. NY, NYC, and PA residents, please add appropriate sales tax. No cash, stamps, or C.O.D.s. All orders shipped within 6 weeks via postal service book rate. Canadian orders require $2.00 extra postage and must be paid in U.S. dollars through a U.S. banking facility.

Name_____

Address_____

City_____ State_____ Zip_____

I have enclosed $_____ in payment for the checked book(s).

Payment <u>must</u> accompany all orders. ☐ Please send a free catalog.

        CHECK OUT OUR WEBSITE! www.dorchesterpub.com

SWEET FURY

CATHERINE HART

She is exasperating, infuriating, unbelievably tantalizing; a little hellcat with flashing eyes and red-gold tangles, and if anyone is to make a lady of the girl, it will have to be Marshal Travis Kincaid. She may fight him tooth and nail, but Travis swears he will coax her into his strong arms and unleash all her wild, sweet fury.

___4428-5 $5.99 US/$6.99 CAN

MIDNIGHT SUN

AMANDA HARTE

Amelia Sheldon has traveled from Philadelphia to Gold Landing, Alaska, to practice medicine, not defend herself and her gender to an arrogant man like William Gunning. While her position as doctor's assistant provides her ample opportunity to prove the stubborn mine owner wrong, the sparks between them aren't due to anger. William Gunning knows that women are too weak to stand up to the turmoil of disease. But when he meets the beautiful, willful Amelia Sheldon, she proves anything but weak; in fact, she gives him the tongue lashing of his life. When the barbs escalate to kisses, William knows he has found his true love in the land of the midnight sun.

___4503-6 $5.50 US/$6.50 CAN

Dorchester Publishing Co., Inc.
P.O. Box 6640
Wayne, PA 19087-8640

Please add $1.75 for shipping and handling for the first book and $.50 for each book thereafter. NY, NYC, and PA residents, please add appropriate sales tax. No cash, stamps, or C.O.D.s. All orders shipped within 6 weeks via postal service book rate. Canadian orders require $2.00 extra postage and must be paid in U.S. dollars through a U.S. banking facility.

Name_____
Address_____
City_____ State_____ Zip_____
I have enclosed $_____ in payment for the checked book(s).
Payment <u>must</u> accompany all orders. ❏ Please send a free catalog.
      CHECK OUT OUR WEBSITE! www.dorchesterpub.com

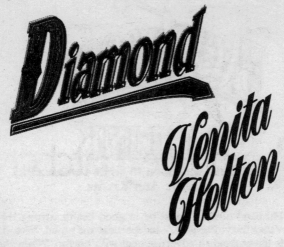

Diamond

Venita Helton

When the handsome Confederate soldier collapses at her feet, Lizzie's first thought is to let him die. But against her better judgement, the headstrong beauty helps him escape from her Yankee-occupied town. As they soar toward freedom in a hot-air balloon, Rafe shows her the heights of ecstasy, and Lizzie learns that this ride will yield the adventure—and the love—of a lifetime.

___4427-7 $5.50 US/$6.50 CAN

Dorchester Publishing Co., Inc.
P.O. Box 6640
Wayne, PA 19087-8640

Please add $1.75 for shipping and handling for the first book and $.50 for each book thereafter. NY, NYC, and PA residents, please add appropriate sales tax. No cash, stamps, or C.O.D.s. All orders shipped within 6 weeks via postal service book rate. Canadian orders require $2.00 extra postage and must be paid in U.S. dollars through a U.S. banking facility.

Name_____
Address_____
City_____State_____Zip_____
I have enclosed $_____ in payment for the checked book(s).
Payment <u>must</u> accompany all orders. ☐ Please send a free catalog.
    CHECK OUT OUR WEBSITE! www.dorchesterpub.com

ENCANTADORA

GAIL LINK

"Gail Link was born to write romance!"
—Jayne Ann Krentz

SUPERSTITIONS

ANNIE McKNIGHT

Beautiful young Billie Bahill is determined. Despite what her father says, she knows her fiancé won't just leave her. So come hell or high water, she is going to go find him. So what if she rides off into the deadly Superstition Mountains? Billie is as good on a horse as any of the men on her father's ranch, and she won't let anybody stop her—especially not the Arizona Ranger with eyes that make her heart skip a beat.

___4405-6 $5.50 US/$6.50 CAN